A Respectable Trade

PHILIPPA GREGORY

LONDON NEW YORK SYDNEY TORONTO

This edition published 1995
by BCA
by arrangement with HarperCollins*Publishers*

Second reprint 1998

CN 5110

Printed in England by Clays Ltd, St Ives plc

This book is dedicated to the children of Sika village,
in The Gambia, and to all the peoples of Africa,
wherever they are today.

Chapter One

Mehuru woke at dawn with the air cool on his outstretched body. He opened his eyes in the half-darkness and sniffed the air as if the light wind might bring him some strange scent. His dream, an uneasy vision of a ship slipping her anchor in shadows and sailing quietly down a deep rocky gorge, was with him still.

He got up from his sleeping platform, wrapped a sheet around him and went quietly to the door. The city of Oyo was silent. He looked down his street; no lights showed. Only in the massive palace wall could he see a moving light as a servant walked from room to room, the torch shining from each window he passed.

There was nothing to fear, there was nothing to make him uneasy, yet still he stood wakeful and listening as if the coop-coop-coop of the hunting owls or the little squeaks from the bats which clung around the stone towers of the palace might bring him a warning.

He gave a little shiver and turned from the doorway. The dream had been very clear – just one image of a looped rope dropping from a stone quayside and snaking through the water to the prow of a ship, whipping its way up the side as it was hauled in, and then the ship moving silently away from the land. There should be nothing to fear in such a sight but the dream had been darkened by a brooding sense of threat which lived with him still.

He called quietly for his slave boy, Siko, who slept at the foot of his bed. 'Make tea,' he said shortly as the boy appeared, rubbing his eyes.

'It's the middle of the night,' the boy protested and then stopped when he saw Mehuru's look. 'Yes, master.'

Mehuru waited in the doorway until the boy put the little brass cup of mint tea into his hand. The sharp aromatic scent of it comforted him. There had been a stink in his dream, a stink of death and sickness. The ship which had left the land in darkness, trailing no wake in the oily water, had smelled as if it carried carrion.

The dream must mean something. Mehuru had trained as an obalawa – a priest – one of the highest priests in the land. He should be able to divine his own dreams.

Over the roofs of the city the sky was growing paler, shining like a pearl, striped with thin bands of clouds as fine as muslin. As he watched they melted away and the sky's colour slowly deepened to grey and then a pale misty blue. On the eastern horizon the sun came up, a white disc burning.

Mehuru shook the dream from his head. He had a busy day before him: a meeting at the palace and an opportunity for him to show himself as a man of decision and ambition. He put the dream away from him. If it came back he would consider it then. It was a brilliant cream and white dawn, full of promise. Mehuru did not want such a day shadowed by the dark silhouette of a dreamed ship. He turned inside and called Siko to heat water for his wash and lay out his best clothes.

In the Bristol roads – where salt water meets fresh in the Bristol channel – the slaving ship *Daisy* paid off the pilot who had guided her down the treacherously narrow Avon gorge and cast off the barges which had towed her safely out to sea. She put on sail as the sun rose and a light wind got up, blowing from the west. Captain Lisle drew his charts towards him and set his course for the Guinea coast of Africa. The cabin boy had laid out a clean shirt for him and poured water for him to wash. He poured it back into the jug, holding the china ewer carefully in grubby callused hands. It would be two months at least before they made landfall in Africa and Captain Lisle was not a man to waste clean water.

Cole and Sons,
Redclift Dock,
Bristol.

Monday 15th September 1787

Dear Miss Scott,

I write to you Direct on a delicate matter which Perhaps should best be addressed to his lordship. However since I have not Yet his lordship's Acquaintance, and since you indicated to me that you have to make your Own Way in the World, perhaps I May be forgiven for my Presumption.

I was Delighted to meet you at my Warehouse when you applied for the Post of Governess, but your Family Connexions and own Demeanour convinced me that I could Never think of You as an Employee of mine. It was that Realisation which prompted me to draw the interview to a Close.

I had an idea Then which I now Communicate to you: Namely that I wish that I might think of you as a Wife.

Some might say that as a Bristol Merchant I am overly Ambitious in wishing to Ally myself with your Family. But you say Yourself that your circumstances do not permit the Luxury of Choice. And tho' I am in business – 'in Trade' as I daresay his lordship might say – it is a Respectable Trade with Good prospects.

You will be Concerned as to the House you would occupy as my wife. You saw Only my Warehouse apartment and I assure you that I am moving Shortly, with my Sister who will remain living with Me, to a Commodious and Elegant house in the best Part of town, namely Queens Square, which his lordship may know.

As to Settlements and Dowry – these certainly should be Arranged between his lordship and myself – but may I Assure you that you will find me Generous if you are Kind enough to look on my Proposal with favour.

9

*I am Sensible of the Honour you would do me, Madam, and
Conscious of the Advantage your connexion would bring me. But
may I also hope that this Proposal of mine will Preserve you from a
lifetime of employment to which your Delicate talents and Aristocratic
Connexions must render you unfit?*

I remain, your most obedient servant,

Josiah Cole.

Josiah sprinkled sand on the letter with a steady hand and
blew it gently away. He rose from his chair and went to the
high window and looked down. Below him were the wharves
and dark water of the Redclift dock. The tide was in and the
ships were bobbing comfortably at the dockside; a steady patter of sound came from their rigging, rattling in the light
freezing wind. There was a heap of litter and discarded bales
on the Coles' empty wharf, and mooring ropes were still
coiled on the cobbles. Josiah had seen his ship *Daisy* set
sail on the dawn tide. She should be at sea by now, with his
hopes riding on her voyage. There was nothing that he
could do but wait. Wait for news of *Daisy*, and wait for the
arrival of his second ship, the *Lily*, labouring slowly
through the seas from the West Indies, heavy with a cargo
of sugar and rum. His third ship, the *Rose*, should be loading
off Africa.

Josiah was not by nature a patient man, but the job of a
merchant in the Trade with only three little ships to his name
had taught him steadiness of purpose and endless patience.
Each voyage took more than a year, and once a ship had
sailed from his dock he might hear nothing from her until
she returned. He could do nothing to speed her, nothing to
enrich himself. Having provisioned and ordered *Daisy* and
watched her set sail, there was nothing to do but wait, gazing
down at the rubbish slopping on the greasy water of the port.
The distinctive smell of his ships – fearful sweat and sickness
overlaid with heady alcohol and sugar – hung around the
dockside like an infected mist.

Josiah's own clothes were lightly scented; the hair of his wig and his hands were impregnated. He did not know that throughout Friday's interview with Miss Scott she had been pressing her handkerchief to her face to overcome the acrid smell of the Trade, overbearing in his little room above the warehouse and never stronger than when a ship was in dock.

He glanced at the letter in his hand. It was written very fair and plain, as a man of business writes when his orders must be understood and obediently followed. Josiah had never learned an aristocratic scrawl. He looked at it critically. If she showed it to Lord Scott, would he despise the script for its plain-fisted clarity? Was the tone too humble, or was the mention of the Queens Square house, which he had not in any case yet bought, too boastful?

He shrugged. The stubborn ambition that had brought him so far would carry him farther – into social acceptance by the greater men of the city. Without their friendship he could not make money, without money he could not buy friendship. It was a treadmill – no future for a man. The greater men ran the port and the city of Bristol. Without them Josiah would forever cling to the side of the dock, to the side of the Trade, like a rat on a hemp rope. Miss Scott and her uncle Lord Scott would open doors for him that even his determination could not unlock . . . if she so desired.

Frances opened Josiah's letter and re-read it for the tenth, the twentieth time. She tucked it into the pocket of her plain gown and went down the vaulted marble-floored hall to his lordship's study. She tapped on the door and stepped inside.

Lord Scott looked up from his newspaper. 'Frances?'

'I have had a reply,' she said baldly. 'From the Bristol merchant.'

'Has he offered you the post?'

She shook her head, pulling the letter from her pocket. 'He makes no mention of post or pupils. He has offered me marriage.'

'Good God!' Lord Scott took the letter and scanned it. 'And what do you think?'

'I hardly know what to think,' she said hesitantly. 'I can't stay with Mrs Snelling. I dislike her, and I cannot manage her children.'

'You could stay here . . .'

She gave him a quick rueful smile, her pinched face suddenly softening with a gleam of mischief. 'Don't be silly, Uncle.'

He grinned in reply. 'Lady Scott will follow my wishes. If I say that you are our guest then that should be an end of it.'

'I do not think that I would add to her ladyship's comfort, nor she to mine.' Her ladyship and her three high-bred daughters would not welcome a poor relation into their house, and Frances knew that before long she would be fetching and carrying for them, an unpaid, unwanted, unwaged retainer. 'I would rather work for my keep.'

His lordship nodded. 'You're not bred to it,' he observed. 'My brother should have set aside money for you, or provided you with a training.'

Frances turned her head away, blinking. 'I suppose he did not die on purpose.'

'I am sorry, I did not mean to criticise him.'

She nodded, and rubbed her eyes with the back of her hand. Her ladyship would have fluttered an embroidered handkerchief. Lord Scott rather liked his niece's lack of wiles.

'This may be the best offer I ever get,' Frances said abruptly.

He nodded. She had never been a beauty, but now she was thirty-four and the gloss of youth had been worn off her face by grief and disappointment. She had not been brought up to be a governess and her employers did not treat her with any particular consideration. Lord Scott had found her first post, but had seen her grow paler and doggedly unhappy in recent months. She had replied to an advertisement from Cole and Sons thinking that in a prosperous city merchant's house she might be treated a little better than in a country house of a woman who delighted to snub her.

'What did you think of him as a man?' he asked.

She shrugged. 'He was polite and pleasant,' she said. 'I think he would treat me well enough. He is a trader – he understands about making agreements and keeping them.'

'I cannot write a contract to provide for your happiness.'

She gave him her half-sad rueful smile. 'I don't expect to be happy,' she said. 'I am not a silly girl. I hope for a comfortable position, and a husband who can provide for me. I am escaping drudgery, I am not falling in love.'

He nodded. 'You sound as if you have made up your mind.'

She thought for a moment. 'Would you advise me against it?'

'No. I can offer you nothing better, and you could fare a lot worse.'

Frances stood up and straightened her shoulders as if she were accepting a challenge. Her uncle had never thought of courage as being a woman's virtue but it struck him that she was being very brave, that she was taking her life into her own hands and trying to make something of it.

'I'll do it then,' she said. She glanced at him. 'You will support me?'

'I will write to him and supervise the contract; but if he mistreats you or if you dislike his life I will not be able to help you. You will be a married woman, Frances, you will be his property as much as his ships or his stock.'

'It cannot be worse slavery than working for Mrs Snelling,' she said. 'I'll do it.'

Mehuru, dressed very fine in a long embroidered gown of indigo silk and with a staff in his hand carved with Snake, his personal guardian deity, strolled up the hill to the palace of Old Oyo with Siko walking behind him.

It was yet another full meeting of the council in two long months of meetings. The Alafin – the king – was on his

13

throne, his mother seated behind him. The head of the military was there, his scarred face turning everywhere, always suspicious. The council, whose responsibility was for law and enforcement throughout the wide federation of the Yoruba Empire, was all there; and Mehuru's immediate superior, the high priest, was on his stool.

Mehuru slipped in and stood at the priest's shoulder. The debate had been going on for months; it was of such importance that no-one wanted to hurry the decision. But a consensus was slowly emerging.

'We need the guns,' the old soldier said briefly. 'We have to trade with the white men to buy the guns we need. Without guns and cannon I cannot guarantee the security of the kingdom. The kingdom of Dahomey, which has traded slaves for guns, is fast becoming the greatest of all. I warn you: they will come against us one day, and without guns of our own we cannot survive. That is my final word. We have to trade with the white men for their armaments, and they will take nothing from us but slaves. They will no longer buy gold nor ivory nor pepper. They will take nothing but men.'

There was a long thoughtful silence. The Alafin, an elected monarch, turned to the head of the council. 'And your view?'

The man rose to his feet and bowed. 'If we capture our own people, or kidnap men from other nations, we will be ruined within a generation,' he said. 'The strength of the kingdom depends on its peace. A nation which trades in slaves is in continual uproar, making war on individuals, on other nations. And we will never satisfy the white men's need for slaves. They will gobble us up along with our victims.'

He paused. 'Think of our history,' he continued persuasively. 'This great nation started as just one town. All the other cities and nations have chosen to join with us because we guarantee peace and fair trading. We *have* to keep the peace within our borders.'

The king nodded, and the queen, his mother, leaned forward and said something quietly to him. Finally he turned to the chief priest, Mehuru's superior. 'And your final word?'

The man rose. His broad shoulders, thickened by a cape of rich feathers, obscured Mehuru's view of the court and their serious faces. 'It is a sin against the fathers to take a man from his home,' he began. Mehuru knew that his vote was the result of months of meditation and prayer. This was the single most important meeting that had ever been held. On it hung the future of the whole Yoruba nation, perhaps the future of the whole continent of Africa. 'A man should be left free with his people unless he is a criminal. A citizen should be free.'

Mehuru glanced around. The faces were grave, but people were nodding.

'It is a sin against the Earth,' the chief priest pronounced. 'In the end it all comes back to the Earth, the fathers, the ancestors, and the gods. It is a sin to take a man from his field. I say we should not take slaves and sell them. I say we should protect the people within our borders. They should be safe in their fields.'

There was a long silence. Then the king rose to his feet. 'Hear this,' he said. The old women who had the responsibility for recording decisions of the council leaned forward to hear his words. 'This is the decision of the council of the Yoruba kingdom and my command. Slave trading with white men of any nation shall cease at once. Kidnap of slaves within our borders is forbidden. There shall be no safe passage for white men or their agents when they are on slaving hunts. Other trade with the nations of white men such as gold, ivory, leather goods, brassware and spices is allowed.'

There was a murmur of approval and the king seated himself again. 'Now,' he said with a rueful smile, 'we have the policy – all we have to do is to enforce it while black slavers hammer at our western borders and white men's ships cruise up and down our coastline in the south.'

Mehuru leaned forward and whispered to the high priest. The man nodded and rose to his feet. 'The Obalawa Mehuru

15

has made a suggestion,' he said. 'That we of the priesthood should send out envoys to the country and the towns to explain to the people why it is that we are turning away from this profitable trade. Already some cities are making hand-some fortunes in this business. We will have to persuade them that it is against their interests. It is not enough simply to make it illegal.'

The king nodded. 'The priests will do this,' he said. 'And we will pass the orders down to the local councillors, from our council down to the smallest village.' He shot a little smile at Mehuru. 'You can organise it,' he said.

Mehuru bowed low and hid the look of triumph. He would travel to the far north of the Yoruba kingdom, he would speak in the border towns and convince people that slaving was to be banned. He would serve his country in a most important way, and if his mission was successful he would make his name and his fortune.

'I am honoured,' he said respectfully.

Chapter Two

Whiteleaze,
nr Bath,
Somerset.

Thursday 25th September 1787

Dear Mr Cole,

I am Honoured and deeply conscious of the Compliment you pay me in your kind letter and your Proposal.

I was indeed Surprised at the Abrupt termination of our interview before you had explained my Duties or introduced my Pupils; but now I understand.

It gives me great Pleasure to accept your Offer. I will be your wife.

My Uncle, Lord Scott, will Write to you under a separate cover. He tells me he will Visit Bristol shortly to give himself the Pleasure of your Acquaintance, and to Determine the Marriage Contract, and date of the ceremony.

Please convey my Compliments to your Sister Miss Cole.
Your obdt servant,

Frances Scott.

Josiah tapped on the door of the parlour and entered. His sister was seated at the table, the company books spread before her. A small coal fire was unlit in the grate, the room was damp and chill. Her face was pale. Only the tip of her nose showed any colour, reddened by a cold in the head. She was wearing a brown gown with a black jacket and little black mittens. She looked up, pen in hand, as he came in.

'I have a reply from Miss Scott.'

'She has assented?'

'Yes. His lordship himself is coming to Bristol to draw up the marriage contract.'

'I hope it serves its purpose,' Sarah Cole observed coldly. 'It will cost a great deal of money to keep a wife such as her.'

'She will have a dowry,' Josiah pointed out. 'If nothing from her father then her uncle, Lord Scott, is likely to dower her with something.'

'She will need a larger house, and a carriage and a lady's maid.'

Josiah nodded, refusing to argue.

'Her tastes will be aristocratic,' Sarah said disapprovingly.

'It is a venture,' Josiah replied with a small smile. 'Like our others.'

'In the Trade we know the risks. Miss Scott is a new kind of goods altogether.'

Josiah's quick frown warned her that she had gone too far. As his older sister, responsible for him throughout their motherless childhoods, she still retained great power over him; but Josiah could always call on the prestige of being a man. 'We must take care not to offend her,' he said. 'She will find our business very strange at first.'

'She was prepared to come here as an employee,' Sarah reminded him.

'Even so.'

There was a brief irritated silence. Brother and sister waited for the other to speak.

'I'm going to the coffee house,' Josiah said. 'I shall see if anyone is interested in coming into partnership with us for the *Lily*. She is due home at the end of November; we need to buy in trade goods and refit her.'

Sarah glanced at the diary on her desk. 'She set sail from Jamaica this month, God willing.'

Josiah tapped his large foot on the wooden floorboards for luck. The modest buckle on his shoe winked in the light.

'You have the accounts for the *Lily*'s last voyage to hand?'

'You had better seek a partner without showing them. We barely broke even.'

Josiah smiled. His large front teeth were stained with tobacco. 'Very well,' he said. 'But she is a good ship and Captain Merrick is usually reliable.'

Sarah rose from her desk, crossed over to the window and looked down. 'If you see Mr Peters in the coffee house we are still waiting for his money for the equipping of the *Daisy*,' she said. 'The ship sailed two weeks ago and he has not yet paid for his share. We cannot extend credit like this.'

'I'll tell him,' Josiah said. 'I will be home for dinner.' He paused at the door. 'You do not congratulate me on my engagement to be married?'

She did not turn from the window, and her face was hidden from him. He did not see her look of sour resentment. Sarah's marriageable years had slipped away while she worked for her father and then for his heir, her brother, screwing tiny profits out of a risky business. 'Of course,' she said. 'I congratulate you. I hope that it will bring you what you desire.'

Siko was unwilling to leave the city of Oyo. He was a city boy who had sold himself into slavery with Mehuru when his parents died. He had thought that with a young man whose career was centred on the court he would be safe from the discomfort of farming work and rural life. He was deeply reluctant to venture out into the countryside, which he regarded as a dangerous place inhabited by wild animals and surly peasants.

'For the last time,' Mehuru said abruptly. 'Finish packing and fetch the horses or I shall sell you to a brothel.'

Siko bowed his head at the empty threat and moved only slightly faster. He was confident that Mehuru would never ill-treat him, and indeed he was saving money to buy his freedom from his young master as they had agreed.

'Should we not take porters and guards?' he asked. 'My brother said he would be willing to come with us.'

'We will be travelling along trading routes,' Mehuru said patiently. 'We will be meeting porters and guards on the trading caravans all along the way. If there is any danger on the roads we can travel with them. I am on an urgent mission, we are travelling at speed. You would have us dawdling along the road and stopping at every village.'

'I would have us stay snug in the city,' Siko muttered into a saddlebag. Aloud he said: 'We are packed, sir, and ready to leave.'

Mehuru nodded to him to load the bags and went into his room. In the corner were his priestly things, laid out for meditation. The divining tray made out of beautifully polished wood indented with circular cups filled with cowrie shells, the little purse filled with ash, a cube of chalk, a flask of oil. Mehuru picked them up one by one and put them into a soft leather satchel, letting his mind linger on them and calling for vision.

Nothing came. Instead he saw once more the prow of a ship, rocking gently on clear tropical waters. He could see a shoal of small fish nibbling at the copper casing of the wooden hull, something he had never seen in waking life. Again he smelled the heavy sickly smell of sugar and sepsis.

'What does it mean?' he whispered softly. 'What does it mean?'

He shuddered as if the day were not pulsing with heat, as if he could feel a coldness like death. 'What does it mean, this ship?' He waited for an answer but he could hear nothing but Siko complaining to the cook about the prospect of a journey and the chattering of a flock of glossy starlings, gathering on the rooftop, their deep blue feathers iridescent in the morning sun.

He shrugged. No ship could endanger him; his journey lay northwards, inland. To the north were the long rolling plains of savannah country, an inland river or two, easily forded or

20

crossed by boat, and then even further north – at the limits of the mighty Yoruba kingdom – the great desert of the Sahel. No ship could be a threat to him, he was far from the coast. Perhaps he should see the ship as a good omen, perhaps it was a vision of a slaving ship which would no longer be able to cruise casually off the coast of his country and gather in his country's children as greedily as a marauding hyena.

Mehuru picked up his satchel of goods and slung it over his shoulders. Whatever the meaning of the vision, he had a job to do and nothing would prevent him. He bundled his travelling cape into a neat roll and went out into the brilliant midday sunshine. The horses were waiting, and the great city gates set deep into the mighty walls of the famous city of Oyo had been open since dawn.

'So!' he said cheerfully to Siko. 'Off we go!'

The quayside coffee shop was on the opposite side of the river from Josiah's dock, and so he took the little ferryboat across and tossed the lad who rowed him a ha'penny. The coffee shop was the regular meeting place for all the merchants of Bristol from the finest men to the smallest traders. When Josiah pushed open the small door his eyes smarted at the strong aromatic smell. The place was thick with tobacco smoke and the hot familiar scent of coffee, rum, and molasses. Josiah, with his hat under his arm, went slowly from table to table, seeing who was there. All of the merchants were known to him, but only a few did business with him regularly. At the best table, farthest from the damp draughts from the swinging door, were the great merchants of Bristol, in fine coats and crisp laundered linen. They did not even glance up when Josiah said 'Good day' to them. Josiah was not worth their attention.

He nodded politely in their direction, accepting the snub. When he was nephew by marriage to Lord Scott they would return his greeting, and he would be bidden to sit with them.

Then he would see the cargo manifests which were spread on their table. Then he would have a chance at the big partnerships and the big trading ventures. Then he would command their friendship, and have access to their capital for his own ventures. They would invite him to join their association – the Merchant Venturers of Bristol – and all the profits and opportunities of the second-greatest provincial city in Britain would fall open to him.

'Josiah!' a voice called. 'Over here!'

Josiah turned and saw a table crowded with men of his own class, small traders who shared and shared again the risks of a voyage, men who scrambled over each other for the great prizes of the Trade and yet who would be wiped out by the loss of one ship. Josiah could not reject their company. His own father had been an even lesser man – trading with a fleet of flat-bottomed trows up and down the Severn: coal from Wales, wheat from Somerset, cattle from Cornwall. Only at the very end of his life had George Cole owned an ocean-going ship and she had been a broken-down privateer which had managed one voyage for him before she sank. But on that one voyage she had taken a French trading ship, and claimed all her cargo. She had shown a profit of thousands of pounds and the Cole fortune had been made, and the Cole shipping line founded. George Cole had put up his sign 'Cole and Sons', and bequeathed the business to his son and daughter. They had made it their life's work to expand yet further.

Two men seated on a bench moved closer to make space for Josiah. Their damp clothes steamed slightly in the warmth and there was a prevailing smell of stale sweat and wet wool.

'Good day,' Josiah said. He nodded at the waiter for coffee and the boy brought him a pot with a cup and a big bowl of moist brown lump sugar.

'You did well on the *Daisy* then,' the man who had called him commented. 'Prices are holding up for sugar. But you get no tobacco worth the shipping.'

Josiah nodded. 'It was a good voyage,' he said. 'I won't buy tobacco out of season. I'll only take sugar. I did well on the *Daisy* and we turned her around quickly.'

'Do you have a partner for your next voyage?' the man opposite him asked. He spoke with a thick Somerset accent.

'I am seeking a partner for the *Lily*. She will be in port within two months.'

'And who commands her?'

'Captain Merrick. There is no more experienced master in Bristol,' Josiah said.

The man nodded. 'D'you have the accounts for her last voyage?'

Josiah shook his head, lying with easy fluency. 'They are with the Excise men,' he explained. 'Some trouble over the bond last time. But the *Daisy* is a better example in any case. She was fresh into port and showed a profit of three hundred pounds for each shareholder. You won't find a better breeding-ground for your money than that!'

The man nodded. 'Could be,' he said uncertainly.

Josiah dropped two crumbling lumps of thick brown sugar into his coffee, savouring the sweetness, the very scent of the Trade, and signalled for a glass of rich dark rum. 'As you wish,' he said casually. 'I have other men that should have the offer first, perhaps. I only mentioned it because of your interest. Think no more about it.'

'Oh no,' the man said quickly. 'What share would you be looking for?'

'A quarter,' Josiah replied coolly. He looked away from the table and nodded a greeting at another man.

'And how much would that be?'

Josiah seemed to be barely listening. 'Oh, I couldn't say . . .' He shrugged his shoulders. 'Perhaps a thousand pounds each, perhaps nine hundred. Say no more than nine hundred.'

The man looked rather dashed. 'I had not thought it would be so much . . .'

Josiah turned his brown-stained smile on him. 'You will not regret it being so much when it shows a profit of twenty or thirty per cent. Eh?'

'And who will be the ship's husband? You? You will do all the fitting and the orders?'

'Myself,' Josiah said. 'I always do. I would trust it to no other man. But I should not have troubled you with this. There is Mr Wheeler now, I promised him a share in the *Lily*.'

'No, stay,' the man protested. 'I will take a share, Josiah. I will have my share in her.'

Josiah nodded easily. 'As you wish, Samuel.' He held out his hand and the other grasped it quickly. 'Come to my warehouse this afternoon, and bring your bond. I will have the contract for you.'

The man nodded, half-excited and half-fearful. He rose from the table and went out. He would be busy from now until the afternoon scouring the city for credit to raise his share.

'I had not thought he had nine hundred pounds to outlay,' one of the others remarked. 'You had best see your money before you sign, Josiah.'

Josiah shrugged. Despite himself, his eyes strayed to the table at the top of the room. The men had called for a pie, a ham and some bread and cheese for their breakfasts. They were drinking port. They were joking loudly, and their faces were flushed. They did not have to haggle over some small man's life savings to finance a voyage. They carved up the profitable voyages among themselves, they shared the profits from the docks – even the barges that plied up and down the Avon paid them a fee, the little ferryboat and even the lighthouses paid them rent.

'I have some news,' Josiah said abruptly. 'I am to be married.'

There was a stunned silence at the little table.

'To the niece of Lord Scott of Whiteleaze,' Josiah went

on. 'His lordship will be calling on me soon and we will settle the marriage contract.'

'My God! Josiah!' one exclaimed.

'Wherever did you meet the lady?' one of the others asked. The rest simply gaped.

'She called on us,' Josiah lied convincingly. 'She knows a friend of my sister's. They were at school together.'

The men could hardly find words. 'I had thought you would be a bachelor forever!' one of them said.

'And with Sarah to keep house for you! I never thought you would marry.'

'I was waiting for the right lady,' Josiah said precisely. 'And for my fortunes to be on such a rise that I could offer her a proper position in life.'

The men nodded. The news was too staggering to be taken in all at once. 'I had not thought he was doing *that* well,' one of the men muttered.

'I shall move from the warehouse,' Josiah said. 'I shall take a new house for my wife.'

'Where will you live?'

'I shall buy a house in Queens Square,' Josiah said. Again he glanced towards the top table. The men there owned Queens Square outright; it had been built by the Corporation, to their design. They could choose whether or not to sell to him. Money alone could not buy him into their neighbourhood; but with Lord Scott's niece on his arm he would be welcomed in the elegant brick-faced square. Josiah would call them 'neighbour' and his new wife would visit their wives.

The men at the table nodded. 'And the lady . . .'

'Shall we return to business?' Josiah asked with a small triumphant smile. 'I think that is enough about the lady who is to be Mrs Cole.'

They nodded, as impressed by the triumph of his marriage as by his quiet dignity.

'About this voyage of the *Lily*,' one of them said. 'I think

I'll take a share after all. Will his lordship be coming in with us?'

Josiah smiled slightly. 'Oh, I should think so,' he said.

Mehuru's mission was going well. He went from town to town and even stopped at the councils of the larger villages as he worked his way north-west across the great rolling plains of the Yoruba nation. The villagers knew that he was talking nothing more than sense. For all the profits that could be made from the slave trade – and they were beyond the dreams of most farming communities – there were terrible stories, garbled in the telling, of rivers where no-one dare fish and woods where no-one could walk. Whole villages were desolate, hundreds, thousands of women and children abandoned and starving in fields which they could not farm alone. It was a blight spreading inland from the coast, a plague which took the young men and women, the fittest and the strongest, and left behind the ill, the old, and the babies.

This plague of slavery worked unlike any other. It took the healthy, it took the adventurous, it took the very men and women who should command the future. The guns and gold and fine cloth could not repay Africa for the loss of her brightest children. It was the future leaders who were bled away, along the rivers, down the trade routes.

'This is where it stops,' Mehuru said firmly in one town council after another. 'One nation has to refuse. One nation has to throw up a wall and say that it must end here. Otherwise what will become of us? Already the trade routes running north are unsafe, and the wealth of this nation depends on our trade. We send our leather goods, we send our brassware, we send our rich luxuries north, across the Sahel Desert to the Arab nations, and we buy our spices and silk from them. All our trade has always been north to south, and now the slavers are cutting the routes.

'The coastal forests and plains are becoming deserted. Who

26

will fish if the coast is abandoned? Where shall we get salt if the women cannot dry it in the salt pans? Where shall we get food if we cannot farm? How can a country be strong and safe and wealthy if every day a hundred, two hundred men are stolen?'

The men in the village councils nodded. Many of them showed the profits of the slave trade with ragged shirts of cotton woven in Manchester, and guns forged in Birmingham. But they were quick to notice that the vivid dyes of the cottons bled out after a few washings, and the guns were deadly to the users as well as to the victims when they misfired. No-one could deny that the slave trade was an unequal deal in which Africa was losing her brightest sons in exchange for tatty goods and shoddy wares.

Mehuru worked his way north, persuading, cajoling. He and Siko became accustomed to riding all day and camping out at night. Siko grew deft at building small campfires for cooking when they were out in the open savannah. The young man and the boy ate together, sharing the same bowl, and then rolled themselves up in their cloaks and slept side by side. They were fit and hardened by exercise and quietly companionable. Every time they stopped for Mehuru to tell the village elders of the new laws they heard more news, and all of it bad. The trade goods were faulty, the muskets blew to pieces the first time they were fired, maiming and killing. The rum was poisonous, the gold lace and smart hats were tawdry rubbish. Worse than that, the white men were establishing gangs of African brigands who belonged to no nation and followed no laws but their own whim, who cruised the rivers and seized a solitary man, a child playing hide and seek with his mother, a girl on her way to a lovers' meeting. There could be no rule of law where kidnappers and thieves were licensed and paid in munitions.

Some of the coastal nations now dealt in nothing but slaves. They had turned from a rich tradition of fishing, agriculture, hunting and trading, to being slaving nations, with only men

27

to sell, and gold to buy everything they might need. Nations of brigands, terrible nations of outlaws.

And the white men no longer kneeled to the kings of the coastal nations. They had built their own stone castles, they had placed their own cannon in their own forts. Up and down the rivers they had built great warehouses, huge stone barns where slaves could be collected, collected in hundreds, even thousands, and then shipped on, downriver, to the forts at the river mouth. There was no longer any pretence that the African kings were permitting the trade. It was a white man's business and the African armies were their servants. The balance of power had shifted totally and completely. The white men commanded all along the coast by the power of the gun and the power of their gold.

The more Mehuru heard, the more certain he became that the Yoruba states were right to stand against slavery. The wickedness of slavery, its random cruelty, no longer disturbed him as much as the threat to the whole future of the continent which was opening before him like a vision of hell: a country ruled by the gun for the convenience of strangers, where no-one could be safe.

'If slavery is such a bad thing,' Siko said one night as they lay together under the dark sky, 'I suppose you'll be setting me free as soon as we get back to Oyo.'

Mehuru reached out a foot and kicked him gently. 'You buy yourself out as we agreed,' he said. 'You've been robbing me blind for years anyway.'

He smiled as he slept; but in the night, under the innocent arch of the sky, he dreamed of the ship again. He dreamed of it cruising in warm shallow water, its deck misshapen by a thatched shelter, the sides shuttered with nets. In its wake were occasional dark, triangular fins. There were sharks following the ship, drawn through the seas by the garbage thrown overboard, and by the promising smell of sickness and despair. They could scent blood and the likelihood of death. The prow sliced through the clean water like a knife into flesh, and its wake was like a wound. Mehuru started awake and found that he was sweating as if he had been running in terror. It was the ship again, his nightmare ship.

He woke Siko. It was nearly dawn, he wanted the company of the boy. 'Let's go and swim,' he said. 'Let's go down to the river.'

The boy was reluctant to get up, warning of crocodiles and hippos in the river, and poisonous snakes on the path. Mehuru caught the edge of the boy's cloak and rolled him out.

'Come on,' he said impatiently. He wanted to wash the dream away, he wanted to play like a child in the water and then run back and eat porridge for breakfast. They had camped in the bend of a river and slept on the dry bank. Mehuru left his things by the embers of last night's fire and jogged, half-naked, to the river. Siko trotted behind him, still complaining. The coolness of the morning air cleared his head, he could feel his breath coming faster and the dark ominous shadow of the ship receding.

Ahead of them was the river, fringed with trees, the tall nodding heads of the rhun palm making a continual comforting clatter as the dried leaves pattered against each other. He ran between an avenue of locust bean trees, the broad gnarled trunks on either side of him, the fluttering feathery leaves brushing the top of his head. He could see the river, the green water gleaming through the thick undergrowth. A flock of plantain eaters swooped overhead, pied birds calling coop-coop-coop in a melodic chatter, and brightly coloured parrots flew up as Mehuru and Siko ran easily side by side. Mehuru's feet scrunched on white sand and he was pausing to catch his breath and to check the water for crocodile or hippo when he saw, from the corner of his eye, a shadow launch forward and in the same moment he was buffeted by a blow which flung him to the ground.

He struggled to get his arms free but he was winded and helpless under the weight of his attacker. He heard another man running forwards and saw a club rising above him and he cried out in terror, 'Siko! Run! Run!' as the blow crushed his head and flung him into fragments of darkness.

His last thought, as the dark shape of the nightmare ship rose up in his mind to blot out the sunlight and the gleam of the green water, was that he, of all people, should have known how far inland the slavers might have come.

At Mrs Daley's house,
Dowry Parade,
the Hot Well,
Bristol.

11th November 1787

Dear Frances,

I am Writing this before I leave for London as I Know you would want to Know at once my thoughts on Mr Josiah Cole.

I find him a Plain and simple Man, on whose Word I think we can Rely. I have had sight of his Company books and he seems to be well-established, tho' he is not a member of the Merchant Adventurers nor of the Africa Company, which is a regret to him. However, the Friends you can bring may Rectify the Omission.

He was Not demanding as to your Dowry and we have settled matters to our Satisfaction. I have taken a Share, on your behalf, in the cargo of one of his ships, the Daisy, which is loading off Africa in this Month. Another of his ships, the Lily, came into port while I was there and I watched the unloading of his Wealth in the Form of Sugar and Rum. It is a Risky business, but highly profitable. I have no Hesitation in believing that you will be well Provided for during your Marriage; and if Widowed, you will Enjoy an adequate jointure. We have Agreed that there is no haste for the Marriage and since you have to complete your contract with Mrs Snelling, and he hopes to Buy a house Suitable for his new Family, we have fixed it for the month of July next year. It is Not what your father would have wished, but I Agree with you that it is the best you can Anticipate.

As to the Pupils you were to teach, he made no Mention of them, except as a Scheme he had in Mind for later. My principal concern was your Sister-in-law, Miss Sarah Cole, who does not Seem to welcome the Match. However, you will have Dealt with more Intractable domestic situations at Home and with Mrs Snelling.

I shall be home within the Sennight, and will drive over to Mrs Snelling's house to discuss the matter with you then.

Yours,

Scott.

Mehuru regained consciousness with an aching head and flies buzzing about the blood on his temple. His arms were bound behind him and his neck was lashed into a forked wooden brace with rough hemp twine. At his side was Siko, whimpering pitifully, his neck-brace paired with Mehuru's so that they were bound together like some misshapen yam which sprouts a twin. They were whipped to their feet and then directed down the river path to where their captors had hidden their boats. Every stumble Siko made tore Mehuru's neck and knocked him from his stride. They fell together in a helpless embrace and were whipped until they stood again. Only when they fell into a slavish head-bowed shuffle could they move forward, and even then both their necks were rubbed through bruises into bleeding sores. 'I am sorry, sir, I am sorry,' Siko wept. 'I am sorry.'

'It is I who am sorry,' Mehuru said only once as they struggled to their feet. 'I brought you far from your home and mine, I should have taken more care. I did not know that they had come this far inland.'

He did not finish his thought: that it was not only Siko whom he had failed. If the slavers were raiding this far inland then the whole of Africa was open to them and Mehuru could not send a warning. 'The gods only know what will be the end of this,' he said to himself. He was worried for the Yoruba kingdom and for its plan to boycott the slave trade. He did not yet know enough to fear for himself.

Siko wept like a little child, but Mehuru stayed calm. He

31

knew that while they were within the borders of the Yoruba states his authority would be recognised. The men who had captured them were ignorant violent peasants of the worst sort. Mehuru tried to speak to them in all the African languages he knew but they answered him only with a threatening wave of a cudgel. He decided to wait until they reached their base camp. As soon as they reached their master, Mehuru would explain who he was and they would be released. In his more optimistic moments Mehuru thought what an excellent anecdote this would make back at the court, and what a hero he would seem: fighting slavery and personally endangered.

It took three days walking downriver to where the slavers' boats were waiting, and at every halt the slavers went out and hunted down another man, another woman, another little child. Mehuru's opposition to the slave trade had been theoretical; but when he saw the women sick with fear and the children too terrified to weep he knew that he hated the Trade and would be against it all his life. Then he longed to be back at court – not only to boast of his escape, but to add his voice to the counsels against slavery. He had heard it named as a sin but when he saw the whipping and the casual brutality, he understood for the first time in a comfortable leisured life what a mortal sin could mean.

And he was afraid – if the slavers had penetrated this far to the north and east then how far might they yet go? Africa was a massive continent, rich with people living well on fertile soil. Slavers using the river routes could penetrate deep and deeper into the very heart of nations. Mehuru had been in the borderlands of the Yoruba kingdom but even so, he was thousands of miles from the coast. How far would the slavers go for their Trade? What would it take to stop them?

They were twenty in all by the time they were loaded into the boats to travel downriver. They were made to kneel on the floor of rough wooden canoes, still bound neck to neck.

The sun burned down on their heads, and where the lashes of the whip had cut the flies crawled and feasted. With hands lashed tightly behind him Mehuru felt the skin of his back cringe at the touch of the insects, the little minute trampling of their feet against his eyelids, the probe of their tongues into the gash on his face. The men paddled the canoes out into midstream and caught the smooth fast current, but the flies were not blown away. They followed like a haze, tempted by the smell of fearful sweat and open wounds.

The heavily laden canoe slipped past green thickly wooded banks like a dream, rocking only slightly as the men held it in the centre of the river. Sometimes the water was so wide that you could hardly see from side to side, sometimes it narrowed and Mehuru looked longingly at the banks. The sun beat down on them, the boat rocked them like a cradle. The heat haze danced on the banks and the flies buzzed around their heads. Mehuru thought of the silent progress of his ship, his nightmare ship, and its wake of sharks and the stink which hung around it in his dream.

On the fifth day they rounded a bend in the river and saw before them a large stone building, which could only have been built by white men with their strange desire for block shapes and their disregard for the contours of the land. It was nothing more than a cube, with little slits for windows, the roof steeply thatched. Before it, sticking out into the river, was a wooden jetty which led to a stone quay. Behind it was a cluster of huts, a poor slovenly place with no women to keep it tidy and no men to farm the land.

Mehuru thought that here at least he would find someone who would see sense and release them. He was anxious for Siko, who had stopped weeping and was now like a man drugged. The boy sat in the boat in silence, his eyes downcast on the green water, and neither the pain of the neck-brace nor the discomfort of sitting in the heat of the midday sun prompted him to speak. His eyes had gone blank with fear, he would not eat. Mehuru wanted them both to be released promptly, before the boy fell sick. He readied himself to demand to see whoever was in charge.

But there was no-one on the landing stage. There was a big iron gate in the massive stone wall and their boat was simply unloaded with shouted commands and whipped in through the gate. The men ignored Mehuru's demand to see their master and pushed him into the entrance vestibule with the rest. When the outer gate clanged shut behind them, another was opened before them and they stumbled into a massive stone chamber ten times as big as the largest barn. A group of men pushed them into line and chained them, quickly and efficiently, with the chain running through their manacles, and fastened each end to rings set into the stone-work of the wall. Mehuru noted the clumsy cast-iron manacles and chains, nothing like the light well-crafted metal of his own people. But it was good enough to hold him, to hold them all.

Time passed. He tried to count the dawns with marks on the dirt in the floor but there was no space, they were packed too close, and every day another couple, another dozen of new captives were added. The food was scanty and often bad. Many people were sick, vomiting into the slop pail, or voiding uncontrollably on to the earth floor. The smell was dreadful. There was no water for washing and no change of clothes. Mehuru banked down the flickering panic at his own degradation. He refused to let the dirt and the humiliation touch him, and he spoke encouragingly to Siko.

'This is a mistake,' Mehuru said. 'They should not have taken us. When someone in authority comes I will tell them who I am. A Yoruban envoy cannot be so treated. When they realise who I am they will let us go.'

Siko did not reply. He would not look at Mehuru.

When new men and women were brought in Mehuru tried to speak to the jailers. Every time one of them came within shouting distance he called out to him, first in Yoruban, then in Dahomean, then in Mandinka: 'Tell your master that I am

34

an obalawa of Yoruba, on the king's business. Tell him the king will pay a high ransom for me. Tell him I demand to speak with him!'

They did not understand, or they would not listen. Mehuru knew he must be patient and wait until he could speak to their leader. Then he would be released and he could demand that Siko be returned to him. His main fear was that they would try to keep Siko when they released him; and Mehuru's duty to his slave, to offer complete protection in return for complete obedience, would be threatened.

He let himself worry about Siko, he let his concern for Siko be the principal, the only thing in his mind. While he could think of himself as a master, as a man of property with obligations, he could pretend that he did not belong in the nightmare storehouse, soiled with his own mess, with dirty hands and matted hair. He thought his sanity depended on him remembering that he did not belong there, that he was not a slave, he was a Yoruban envoy on a mission for the Alafin himself.

After about a month in which conditions in the storehouse grew worse and worse, there was a gathering, like some nightmare market. A new boat, a white man's boat, had come upriver from the coast, bringing two white men. Mehuru readied himself to explain to the men that he must be released. All of the captives were dragged one at a time from their prison and brought out to a white man, who lolled on a chair under a tree.

It was Mehuru's first sight of a white man, the race that was destroying his country. He had expected a towering demon or an impressive god – not this dirty weakling. His skin was pale, his clothes were grey and foul and the stink of him as he sweated in the sunshine was so bad that he could even be smelled above the stench from the storehouse. The man was wet all the time. He lounged on a chair in the shade but he did not sit still and consider his purchases. He shifted all the time in his seat, getting hotter and hotter and his terrifying pallor went an even more frightening flushed red colour and all his face grew shiny and wet with sweat.

When they pulled Mehuru forward by a twitch on the rope around his neck he was so shocked by the corpse face of the man, and the disgusting thick clumps of stubble hair on his chin and at the open neck of the dirty shirt, that for a moment he could barely speak. But then he drew himself up to his full height and looked the man in the eye.

'I am an envoy of the Yoruban federation,' he said clearly. 'I must be released at once or there will be severe reprisals.' He repeated the sentence first in Portuguese, the language of the slavers, and then in all the African languages he knew. 'I demand the release of my personal servant and my own freedom,' he said.

The white man turned his head to one side, coughed and spat a gob of infected yellow phlegm. He nodded to a second white man who stepped forward. Mehuru forced himself not to flinch; the man was rancid with the stink of drink and a sharp acrid smell of old sweat. Mehuru breathed in through his mouth and repeated the speech again in Portuguese.

The white man did not even reply. He put his filthy hands in Mehuru's face and pulled back his lips to see his teeth. Mehuru jerked back, and staggered over the chains at his ankles.

'How dare you!' he cried. At once two of the African slavers seized him from behind and held him in an unrelenting grip.

'Let me go!' Mehuru shouted. He bit off his panic and spoke clearly in Portuguese. 'You are making a serious mistake,' he said urgently. 'I am an envoy for the Yoruba federation.'

The white man nodded to the guard to hold him firmly, leaned down and pulled aside Mehuru's loincloth. He pulled back the foreskin of his penis to see if he were infected, and then nodded at the guard to make him bend over, to see if the flux had left blood on his anus.

Mehuru's outraged shout was stifled in his throat. When he felt the dirty hands on him he choked with shame. Siko was watching him, his eyes wide with horror. 'It's all right,' Mehuru called in hollow reassurance. 'We will get to their leaders and explain.'

It was bravado, not courage. That night when Siko had wept himself to sleep and was lying with his limbs twitching with dreams of freedom, Mehuru sat quietly, dry-eyed and horrified. The fingerprints of the white men burned on his skin, the recollection of their washed-out stares scorched his memory. They had looked at him with their pale eyes as if he were nothing, as if he were a piece of meat, a piece of Trade. They looked at him as if he were a nobody, and Mehuru thought that in their horrible transparent eyes he had seen the death of his individuality. He thought that if he lost his sense of who he was, of his culture, of his religion, of his magic power, then he would be a slave indeed.

Only the god, Snake, was with him in that long desolate night. Mehuru called on him to save him from the men who were as white as ghosts, and the Snake god laughed quietly in his long throat and said, '*All men are dead men, all men are ghosts.*' Mehuru did not sleep that night, though he was weary through to his very bones.

The next day the chosen hundred were herded into canoes and taken down the river. Mehuru no longer depended on his powerful status as a representative of the Alafin of Yoruba. He kept a sharp lookout instead for a chance to escape and run, run like a slave, for freedom.

But even that could not be done. Not on the river journey, not when they were unloaded on the beach at the coast. The slavers had done this too often. Mehuru saw that they were practised in the handling of many angry, frightened people. They never came within reach, they whipped them into line with long whips from a distance. Mehuru kept watching for a chance to order the whole line of them to run – run in a great line towards the market place of the town – and in the confusion find hammers to shear the chains, and spears to kill and then scatter. But there were too many too lame to run fast enough, and too many little children crying for their mothers, chained in the line.

He waited, pretending obedience and waiting for his chance. They were herded through the little village at the mouth of the river and down to the wide white-sand beach where boats, white men's boats, were drawn up with the waves washing around their keels.

When he saw the ship, the great ship, bobbing at anchor beyond the white breakers, his heart sank. It was the ship of his dreams come for him at last. The hot humid wind which blew steadily on shore brought the smell of death as clearly as if he could already hear the widows crying. Mehuru stared at the water around the ship and saw the swift movement of a shark's fin – just as he had seen it in his dream. He looked at the prow which he had dreamed slicing so easily through the water and knew that it would cut through miles of seas. Even the rope of his dream was stretched out tight, as the ship bobbed on her mooring. It was all as he had known it.

Mehuru embraced despair then. The ship had been coming for him for months, he had seen it set sail, he had seen it arrive off his own coast, and now here it was at last, waiting for him. He closed his eyes as a man will close his eyes in death and let them herd him, like a sacrificial goat, on board.

Chapter Three

Frances Scott, now Frances Scott Cole, closed the door of what was to be her bedroom and looked around her. It was a plain room bereft of any trimming or prettiness. The bed was a massive four-poster in dark heavy wood and had a small table beside it. The wash jug and ewer stood on another matching side table. There was a chest for her clothes and a mirror on the wall. It had been Josiah's; now he would use the adjoining room, except for the nights when he might choose to sleep with her.

The room smelled. The whole house stank of the mid-summer garbage of the dock. Only in a rainstorm or at high tide would the air smell clean to Frances, who had not been brought up on these fetid river banks.

Josiah still had not bought his house on Queens Square; but he had promised to find a house soon. As the date of the July wedding drew near, Frances had agreed to live for the first months of her wedded life over a warehouse on the Bristol quayside.

The room was in half-darkness. Only a little cold moonlight found its way in through the casement window, obscured by the brooding cliff which towered over the back of the house. Even at midday the room would be dark and damp. Frances put her candle down on the bedside table, went over to the mirror and unpinned her hair. Her reflected face looked impassively back at her. She had been a pretty child but that had been many years ago. She was thirty-five now and no-one would mistake her age. Her forehead was lined, around her mouth were the downward lines of discontent. Her pale skin was papery and dry, around her dark eyes were slight brown shadows. She suffered from delicate health, inherited from her mother who had died of consumption. Her great beauty was her dark hair which showed no grey. She looked what she had been only yesterday – a lady clinging on to fragile social status, of uncertain health, unmarried, impoverished, and ageing fast.

But now it was all changed. Frances smiled slightly and picked up her silver-backed hairbrush. She was a married woman now and an entirely new life was opening up before her. It seemed like a hard choice – matrimony at thirty-five – when many women were matrons already with a family around them. But anything was better than being a governess in a state of genteel servitude. Anything was better than watching her place move inexorably down the dining table until one day she would be asked to dine in the nursery with the children, and disappear from polite society altogether. It had been a hard choice, but in the end no choice at all.

Frances started to plait her hair in a thick hank, ready for bed. The wedding dinner had been better than she could have hoped. Lord Scott had been as kind as always, although his cold unfriendly wife had cast a cool shadow over the proceedings. Frances had dreaded that Josiah would be rowdy and jolly but the evening had been as dignified as a funeral. Only Sarah and Josiah represented the Cole family so Frances's other great fear – that there would be dozens of vulgar relations emerging from the Bristol woodwork – was stilled. The dinner had been well cooked, a little lavish for just the five of them. The wines – as you would expect in Bristol – had been excellent.

Frances had sat at the foot of the table in the tiny airless parlour and smiled without flinching. Everyone at the table knew that marriage to such a man as Josiah was not her first choice. Everyone at the table knew that she had no choice.

The coldness in her heart was reflected in the cool serenity of her face.

Her calm had been threatened only once. When Lord Scott took her hand on leaving he had whispered to her: 'God bless you my dear, it's the best thing you could have done ... considering.' This tactful acknowledgement that she was orphaned and penniless sent a shiver through her. 'I will pray it goes well for you,' he said.

There would be nothing he could do for her if it did not. Frances was owned by Josiah, body and soul. She had promised to obey him till death.

'But it will go well for me,' she whispered. She tied her nightcap under her chin and crossed the cold floorboards to the bed. She had wept the night her father died. She had wept the first night that she had slept in a strange house, far from the country vicarage, and far below the genteel status of the vicar's only daughter. She had raged then against the unfairness of a life in which a woman is dependent completely on a man. A woman who lacks a father must find a husband. Frances had not married when she should have done, in the brief bloom of her youth. She had aimed too high and her father had been too proud. He had not understood that a man, any man at all, was better than spinster hardship. Her father's death abandoned Frances to loneliness and to poverty and to the unending slights of the life of a governess.

She got into the broad bed, and rested her head on the plain linen pillow. She would not cry tonight. She was a wife and she had a dinner table of her own, even though it was only a little table and pushed to one side in a tiny parlour. The rest of her life would be spent accommodating her desires to her husband's fortune. If Josiah rose in the world she would rise with him; if he did not she must bear it with patience and be glad to have found such a haven as this little house. She pulled the covers over her shoulders as if the coldness in her spirit had chilled her very skin, despite the sultry night air. She felt as if tears or feelings would never touch her again.

41

She was heartbroken and exhausted by heartbreak; and she mistook it for the calmness of old age.

There was a tap on the door between Josiah's room and her own and her husband came in, carrying his candle. He was wearing a plain linen nightshirt. He set the candle down on the bedside table and stood, looking at her. He was clearly at a loss.

'I hope you enjoyed the dinner,' he said awkwardly.

Frances nodded. 'Thank you,' she said in her cool level voice.

Josiah's feet in Moroccan leather slippers shuffled on the wooden floor. He looked intensely uncomfortable. 'The wines were good,' he volunteered.

Frances nodded.

There was silence. Frances realised that Josiah was painfully embarrassed. Neither of them knew how a husband claimed his marital rights. Neither of them knew how a wife consented. Her dry little cough rose up in her throat and she cleared her throat.

'It's quite late now,' Josiah remarked.

Frances turned back the covers. 'Will you come to bed, husband?' she asked, as coldly civil as if she were offering him a dish of tea.

Josiah flushed scarlet with relief. 'Thank you,' he said. He stepped out of his slippers and slid into bed beside her. They lay side by side for a moment, taking care not to touch each other, then Josiah leaned over and blew out both candles. Under cover of the sudden darkness he reared on top of Frances and pulled her nightdress out of his way. Frances lay still underneath him with her eyes closed and her teeth gritted. It was a duty which had to be done. Josiah fumbled awkwardly for a few moments and then he exclaimed in a whisper and moved away.

'It's no good,' he said shortly. 'I have drunk too much wine.'

Frances opened her eyes. She could see only the silhouette of his profile. She did not know what she was supposed to do.

'It does not matter,' he said, consoling himself rather than her. 'It will come right in time. There is no need for us to hurry. After all, we neither of us married for desire.'

There was a long, rather chilling silence. 'No,' Frances acknowledged. 'Neither of us did.'

'Good morning, ma'am,' a voice said, and the curtains rattled on the brass rail as the maid drew them back and tied them to the bed posts.

Frances stirred and opened her eyes. The maid who had waited at the dinner table last night was standing before her with a small silver tray bearing a jug of hot chocolate and a warm pastry. Frances sat up and received the tray on her knees.

'Thank you.'

The maid dipped a curtsey.

'Master said to tell you that he is gone out early,' she said. 'But Miss Cole expects you in the parlour as soon as you are dressed. She is there already.'

Frances nodded. She waited for the maid to leave the room and then bolted the food and gulped down the hot chocolate. She sprang from the bed and went over to the ewer of water to wash her face. Then she paused, remembering her new status. She was no longer the governess who had to hurry downstairs for fear of keeping the mistress waiting. Frances smiled at the thought and poured water into the bowl. She washed her face and patted it dry, enjoying the sense of leisure. Her clothes for the morning were laid out on the heavy wooden chest: a linen shift, a morning dress in white muslin, embroidered at the hem, with a frivolous silk apron to denote Frances's intention of domestic work.

The dress was new. Lady Scott had given Frances whole bolts of fabric when the marriage contract was signed. Her entire wardrobe had been renovated and improved with gifts from her cousins and her aunt. Frances knew it was the last thing Lady Scott would ever do for her and she accepted the old gowns and yards of silk with nothing more than polite gratitude. Her husband would have to provide for her new clothes, and there was an allowance of pin money laid down in the marriage contract. Frances would never again darn and re-darn her silk stockings.

She slipped on the shift and turned as there was a tap on the door and the maid came in again. Frances sat at the dressing table and brushed her hair in steady sweeps of the silver-backed brushes, and the maid helped her plait it into two braids and pin them up on her head with a pretty scrap of lace for a cap. The woman was slow and not very skilful. She dropped the hairbrush.

'I am sorry, Mrs Cole,' she said awkwardly. 'I don't usually work as a lady's maid.'

'Does Miss Cole have her own maid?'

'She dresses herself.'

Frances hid her surprise. She had never heard of a lady dressing herself, she wondered how Sarah managed with the small covered buttons at the back of a gown. Even as a governess Frances had borrowed a maid to do her hair and help with the fastenings. For the first time Frances had a glimpse of her tumble in status. The maid shook out the morning dress and held it for Frances to put on, fastening the two dozen mother-of-pearl buttons up the back of the dress, and tied the ribbon of the apron. Lastly she set out the little insubstantial slippers of pink silk.

'Shall I show you to the parlour, ma'am?'

'Yes,' Frances said.

She followed the woman down the stairs. It was a dreadfully dark poky house, she thought, sandwiched between one large warehouse and another, with its front door giving directly on to the dock and its back door into a yard overhung by the glowering red sandstone cliff. The cliff was part of the building; the warehouse carved into its overhanging walls. The storerooms extended into caves deep inside it, running back for miles in a red sandstone labyrinth.

It was no house for a lady. It was crashingly noisy with the rolling of barrels on the cobbles of the quay. Costers and hawkers shrieked their wares, screaming to make themselves heard over the bawled orders on the unloading ships. Frances did not know if Josiah had a carriage and she did not know if she would be allowed to walk along the quayside outside her front door without endangering her reputation. She had a fine line to tread as the niece of a lord but the wife of a man whose house was no larger than a shop.

Bristol was not a genteel city; it was all port and no town, quaysides and no pavements. Every other street towards the town centre was a bridge with a river running beneath it. The town centre itself was crammed on the banks of the river with masts of sailing ships overtopping the chimneys, and the prows of the boats almost knocking on the doors. When the tide was full the boats rocked and bobbed and sailors in the rigging could see into bedroom windows and shout bawdy comments at the housemaids. When the tide was out the ships were dumped on the stinking mud of the harbour bottom and the garbage from the boats and the sewage from the town gurgled sluggishly around them.

The maid paused before the dark wooden parlour door, tapped lightly and stood aside. Frances turned the door handle and went in. Sarah Cole rose from her seat at the table, her face unsmiling under a plain morning cap.

'No need to knock,' she said coldly. 'You are the mistress here now.' She put her hand on a great ring of keys on the table. 'These are the household keys. My brother has told me to offer them to you, if you wish to take the housekeeping into your own hands.'

Frances hesitated, and Sarah Cole gestured to an ominous pile of dark-backed ledgers. 'Also the housekeeping books,' she went on. 'I think you will find them in order. I present them to my brother once a month for his signature. That will now be your task.'

'Gracious,' said Frances weakly.

The stern face of the older woman gleamed with pride. 'It has been my life's work to make this house run as smoothly as our trading company. The company books are no better than the household ones. I do them both.'

'He must be very grateful to you,' Frances said tentatively.

Miss Cole's face was stern. 'There is no reason why he should be,' she replied. 'I was doing my duty and protecting my fortune, as I trust you will do. It was my task to run the business and the housekeeping, for both my brother and for my Papa, for all these years ever since Mama died. Now it is my duty to hand the housekeeping accounts over to you.'

Frances went to the table and opened a ledger at random. It was written in perfect copperplate script:

'To Mr Sykes, butcher ... £3. 4s. 6d.' Beneath it was another entry, and another and another for page after page.

Frances turned the pages. They fluttered with the petty cash of many years. 'I have never done accounts,' she confessed. 'In my father's house it was done by the cook. I merely checked the totals at the end of each month. I am afraid I don't know how to do them.'

Miss Cole raised an eyebrow. 'You must have been badly cheated,' she said.

'Oh, no! Cook had been with us since I was a baby. She was devoted to my father and to me. She would not have cheated us. She was like one of the family.'

Miss Cole shrugged. 'I do not know about grand houses,' she said. 'I am a trader's sister and a trader's daughter. I do not have servants who are one of the family. I check their work and if I see an error then I sack them.'

'It was hardly a grand house. It was a little country vicarage on Lord Scott's estate.'

'I was born in a collier's cottage,' Miss Cole said sharply. 'I think your country vicarage would seem very grand to me.'

Frances paused. This woman would be her daily companion; when they moved house she would move too. They

46

would live together, they would meet every day for the rest of their lives. She forced herself to smile. 'There is much I do not know about your life and your business,' she said. 'I hope you will teach me, Miss Cole, and help me to fulfil my side of the bargain and be a good wife to your brother.'

The woman's face was stern. 'I do not know what bargain you have made. I do not know why he wanted a wife, and such a wife as you.'

Frances blinked at the woman's abrupt honesty. 'Well, this is frank speaking indeed!'

Sarah nodded. 'I speak as I find. I am a simple trader's daughter.'

'You did not wish him to marry?' Frances ventured.

'Why should I? We have lived together and worked side by side on the company for years. We have made it grow from one ship to a fleet of three. We have trebled our business and our profits. And now Josiah wants a town house, and a smart lady for his wife. But who is to pay for this? Are we to spend our money on houses rather than ships? What return will they make? What return will you make?'

Frances snatched a little breath. She could feel her heart pounding with embarrassment at the other's plain speaking. 'Really . . . Miss Cole . . .'

'You asked and I answered you,' the woman said stubbornly.

Frances put her hand to her throat. 'I hope you will not be my enemy,' she whispered.

Sarah Cole looked at Frances's white face and shrugged. 'What would be the sense in that?' she said. 'It is a business arrangement, after all. But you should not try to manage my account books if you do not understand them.'

'Would you prefer to do them?' Frances asked. 'Until I have learned how things are to be done? Would you prefer to go on as you have been, and I will watch you and study your ways?'

'I think that would be best if it is your wish.'

'I have no desire to push you from your place,' Frances

said hastily. 'Nor cause any quarrel in this house.'

'You don't look the quarrelsome type,' Sarah said with grim humour.

Frances suddenly flushed as she smiled. 'Indeed I am not! I cannot bear quarrels and people shouting.'

Sarah nodded. 'I see. You suffer from sensibility.'

Frances, who had never before heard it described as a disability, gave a shaky little laugh. 'It is how I was brought up,' she said.

'Well, I am not a lady, and I thank God for it,' Sarah said. 'But I will try to make allowances for you. You have nothing to fear from me. Now I will show you around the house,' she continued, rising to her feet. 'You have seen only this parlour and your bedroom so far.'

There was not much to see. The parlour was on the first floor. It ran the length of the house, overlooking the quay at the front and overshadowed by the cliff at the back. There was a small dining table and six hard chairs where Miss Cole worked during the day and where breakfast was served at mid-morning, dinner at mid-afternoon, and supper in the evening. There was a fireplace with two straight-backed chairs on either side. There was Miss Cole's workbox. The walls were washed with lime, empty of any pictures or ornament and the floorboards were plain waxed wood, with a thin hearthrug before the fire.

Josiah's office, the next room, was even plainer. It also overlooked the quay but it did not even have curtains at the windows, just forbidding black-painted shutters. His desk was set before the window to the left of the fireplace, a big wooden captain's chair before it. There was a chair by the fire and a small table beside it. There were three maps hanging on the walls. One showed the south coast of England, one the west coast of Africa, little more than a wriggling coastline and a completely empty interior, and the third was a navigation chart of the shoals and currents around the islands of the West Indies. Nothing else. Frances, looking in through the door of the spartan room, wondered what the Coles did for amusement, where they entertained their friends. There was nothing in either room to indicate anything but a life dedicated to work.

Miss Cole gave a longing glance out of the window before she turned away. On the quayside immediately below, the Coles' ship the *Rose* was unloading. Sarah Cole would rather have been entering profits into the ledger.

On the floor above the parlour were the bedrooms. Josiah and Miss Cole had bedrooms facing the dock; Frances's room was quieter, at the back, sheltered by the red sandstone cliff. If she opened her window and leaned out she could look down to the cobbled backyard outside the kitchen door, hemmed in by high warehouse walls, and beyond them, the twisting little streets which ran from the dockside up to the church on the peak of the hill: St Mary Redclift. On her left was the towering height of a lead-shot tower. To her right, overtopping the church spire, was the fat kiln-shaped chimney of the glassworks. All day there was ceaseless noise: the crash of the metalworks, and the roar and rattle of the furnaces. The sour toxic smell of lead haunted the Backs.

Above this floor was the attic bedroom for the servants and the linen and storeroom. Miss Cole showed Frances the bare poverty of the rooms with quiet pride and then led the way down the stairs to the front door and hall.

The hall was hopelessly dark, the only light seeping through a grimy fanlight over the front door. At the end of the corridor at the back of the house was the door to the kitchen. They could hear someone pounding dough on a board and singing softly. In all the shaded, sombre house, it was the first happy sound.

At the sound of Miss Cole's footstep the singing stopped abruptly, and the pounding of the dough became louder and faster.

Sarah Cole opened the door to the kitchen and ushered Frances in. 'This is your new mistress, Mrs Cole,' she said abruptly, surveying the kitchen. The cook – floured to the elbows – bobbed a curtsey, and the upstairs maid, Brown, rose from the table where she had been polishing silver and glasses. A little hunchbacked girl came in from the back-yard wiping her hands on a hessian apron and dipped a curtsey, staring at Frances. Frances smiled impartially at them all.

'The cook is Mrs Allen. The maid is Brown. Mrs Allen discusses the menus with me every week and shows me the housekeeping books.' Sarah shot a sideways glance at Frances. 'You should be there when we meet. I take it that Monday afternoon will still be convenient?'

'Perfectly,' Frances said politely.

The little scullery maid had not even been named to Frances.

'You can get on with your work,' Miss Cole ordered them brusquely and led the way from the kitchen, through the poky little hall and up the stairs to the parlour.

She seated herself at the table and drew one of the ledgers towards her. She took up a pen. Frances, rather at a loss, seated herself on the narrow windowseat and looked down on the quay.

The tide was in and the foul smell of the mud had lessened. The sunshine sparkled on the water of the dock and quick-silver water lights danced on the ceiling of the parlour. The quayside was crowded with people selling, loading and unloading ships, hawking goods, mending ropes, and caulking the decks of outbound ships with great steaming barrels of stinking tar. The Coles' own ship, the *Rose*, was still unloading her goods, the great round barrels of rum and sugar were piled on the quayside. The intense stink of a ship of the Trade wafted up to Frances and even penetrated the house: sugar, sewage, and pain. As she watched, she saw Josiah slap one of the barrels for emphasis and then spit on his palm and shake hands on a deal with another man.

Sarah's pen scratched on the paper. The room was stuffy

and hot, the windows closed tight against the smell and noise of the quayside.

'I should like to go out,' Frances said after a while. 'I should like to walk around and see the city.'

Miss Cole lifted her head, her finger on the page to keep her place. 'Brown will have to go with you. You cannot walk on the quayside alone.'

Frances nodded and rose to her feet. 'Very well.'

Sarah shook her head, not taking her eyes from the book. 'Brown is working in the house now. You will have to wait until afternoon. You can walk then.'

There was a short silence.

'I see Mr Cole down there on the quayside,' Frances said. 'May I go down to him?'

Sarah dragged her attention from her work again. 'He is engaged in business. He would have no time for you, and the men he is dealing with are not those he would wish you to meet. They are not gentlemen. You will have to be patient. You are no longer a lady of leisure,' Miss Cole volunteered spitefully. 'You cannot act on whim.'

'No,' said Frances, turning her attention back to the quayside, 'I see that I cannot.'

Most of the sailors had been paid off and had left the ship but the captain and one other man, his hair tied back in a greasy little plait, were watching the sailmakers pulling the ragged canvas out of the lockers and spreading it on the dockside. Josiah inspected the worn sails and nodded his agreement as the sailmakers bundled it on a sledge, took up the ropes and started to tow it away. Frances watched him from her vantage point above him, a curiously foreshortened view as if he were not a powerful man in a man's world, but a little man, struggling to cope.

'It is strange to see your money being made,' she remarked thoughtlessly and then flushed with embarrassment. 'I beg your pardon! I spoke without thinking.'

'It is not strange to me,' Miss Cole said. She did not take

51

offence as Frances had feared. 'I have lived in this house most of my life. I have waited for our ships to come in and I have known what profit or loss they made on every voyage. Since I was a child of nine I have cared for nothing else. That one you see there, the *Rose*, has done well for us.'

'What a pretty name,' Frances said.

Miss Cole showed her thin smile. 'All our ships have flower names since our first one, a captured French merchant ship called *Marguerite*,' she said. 'That means *Daisy* in French, you know. We have three ships: the *Rose* which you see here, the *Daisy* which should be at the West Indies, and the *Lily* which was in port a few months ago and should be loading off Africa, God willing.'

'You say that they "should be" . . . do you not know where they are?'

'How should I know? I know when they set sail and I know when they are due, but between their destination and their home port is the most vast and dangerous ocean. We have to wait. The largest part of being a merchant in the Atlantic Trade is waiting, and keeping your counsel while you wait.'

'Have you ever sailed with them?'

'No-one of any sense would sail to Africa,' Miss Cole replied. 'It is a death-trap.'

'Do you sail nowhere else?'

Miss Cole turned from the window and went back to her work. 'There is nowhere else,' she said irritably. 'What other trade is to be had?'

'I don't know,' Frances said foolishly. 'I thought perhaps you might sail to India, or to China.'

'This is Bristol,' Miss Cole explained patiently, as one might speak to a child. 'This is the heart of the sugar trade. We trade to the West Indies and to the Americas. It is on this Trade that my father made his fortune and on this Trade that we will make ours.'

'Only sugar?'

'There is no more profitable business,' Miss Cole said firmly. 'The Trade is supreme.'

'But so uncertain . . .'

'We trust in our abilities,' Sarah said piously. 'And we are all of us in the merciful hands of God.'

They did not know themselves to be in the merciful hands of God. They seemed very far from any god. They lay very close together, stacked side by side like logs in a woodpile. When the ship rolled they rolled hard one way, bumping and bruising, and then when it pitched back, they rolled again. When the ship reared up over a massive wave and crashed down it was as if they had been packed on their naked backs in a rough wooden case and dropped, over and over again. Within a day they were bruised from the planking, within a week the skin was rubbed away. When the sea was heavy the water poured in through the gratings on the deck into the hold where they lay, and the slop buckets overturned and sewage washed around them. They were not fed during bad weather and those that were not vomiting from seasickness or already dying from typhus went hungry. When the sea was calm they were ordered up on deck, staggering under the bright uncaring sky, and made to wash and dry themselves, sharing a soiled piece of cloth. A man watched them rinse out their mouths with vinegar and water and spit through the netting into the huge waves which rolled unstoppably towards the little ship, coming from the far horizon, as high as hills. It was a nightmare, a long unbelievable nightmare, which got worse and worse every day.

At first Mehuru had thought that the crew were ghosts, that he had died at sight of the ship and that this was some long punitive afterlife. The crew's skin was so pallid and their eyes were empty of colour or warmth. He could not at first accept their dreadful ugliness. They did not look like men and they did not act like men. They behaved as if they were a different species from Mehuru, from Siko, from the two hundred men they had on board. They prodded at them with

53

sticks, they whipped them with casual cruelty. They never looked in their faces, they never met their eyes. There was something so cold and unnatural in their indifference that Mehuru felt his very soul wither and shrink from them. These could not be men. No man could treat another man with such chilling indifference.

The Snake god's counsel was bleak on the voyage and the farther he went from his home, the fainter and fainter grew the voice until Mehuru had to face the dreadful prospect of losing his guide. He had no magic to bring him back, the gods go where they will, and Mehuru could make no offering. He had no pet snake to feed, he had no smoke to please the god, or bones for it to play with. All he could do was dream that he was making pleasures for the god and give him the thoughts of his mind. So he lay in the pitching blackness with his back rubbed raw against the sweating planks of the hold, the filth of the bilges washing around him, and made in his mind a perfect flower, a flower from the hibiscus bush, bright scarlet, frilled as silk. Then he pictured a jewelled snake and brought the flower to the snake in a bowl of white clay studded with tiny blue stones.

The three images were almost too much for him: the brilliant snake, the perfect flower, and the white bowl with the blue pattern. In the sodden sweaty torture of the black hold with people dying around him, Mehuru shut his eyes and summoned three perfect forms: god in a flower, god in an animal, and god in a man, guiding his hands to work with clay and with little blue stones.

There was no way to measure time in the darkness. Mehuru woke sometimes and thought perhaps he had died and that the Yoruban belief that you stay near to the people you loved, watching over them, was all wrong. The afterlife was a perpetual rolling and pitching, heat and smell, and the horror of being pushed against sickly men, unable to help them, and no emotion but hatred for their rough bumping against you, and hunger for their share of food.

Sometimes the sailors opened the hatches and bawled down into the darkness for the captives to come out. The sunlight hurt their eyes but they had to stand on deck and one of the sailors would beat a drum while another cracked a whip. Mehuru looked at them in utter wonder. The sailors wanted them to dance. As obedient as idiot children, with the guns all around them and the whips cracking out the time, they shuffled and hopped while others were ordered to clean out the hold and throw the dead and dying over the side. Mehuru sank deep inside his mind while his body hopped and pranced.

If the dancing were to keep them healthy Mehuru could not think why they were fed so poorly. If their jailers wanted them fit, Mehuru could not think why they let so many sicken for lack of water in the unbearable heat of the hold. They lowered buckets filled with stale warm water and bad yams which crawled with insects. Never enough water, never enough food. They had loaded about two hundred men and elsewhere in the ship they were keeping women and little children, perhaps another hundred of them. On Mehuru's shelf alone, five had already died. One had flung himself over the side, two had sickened, one had been whipped too hard and never came back to the hold and the last one had sealed his lips from food and water and had watched the others eat every day while he starved himself to death. Mehuru's imagination could not stretch to the scale of it. It never occurred to him that more than three hundred of them had been shipped but that only two hundred and forty or so were expected to survive. It was not necessary that they should all survive. It was a process so large as to be industrial. Mehuru had no concept that his life could be written off as wastage.

He started to dread the arrival of the bucket of food for only then, when they were ordered to gather around and share ten to a bucket, eating with their dirty hands, could he see how many of them were sickening to death. They were the ones who did not struggle and claw at each other to get to the food. Mehuru set himself the task of fighting for his share and then giving half of it to the neighbour on his right. He did it as an exercise, a discipline, not an act of love. He thought he would never love anyone, ever again.

When he had eaten, and the slowly dying man beside him had mumbled on his slabber porridge, Mehuru would shut his eyes and try to build a picture of a perfect tiny snake as an offering for the god.

He knew that his mind was going when the snake became very bright and easy to find. The snake became more important than the ship, more vivid than the clammy touch of the dying man beside him. The snake opened his mouth and sang to him as Mehuru felt his skin grow wet with sweat and his mind shift and slide away from the darkness. He knew he should stay in his waking mind and guard Siko; but he had not seen Siko, except for a glimpse on deck, since they had set sail. He knew he had failed in his duty to him. He knew he was guilty of a mortal sin in taking the boy into danger. But he could not keep himself alert, he could not stay on guard. As they went farther and farther west Mehuru sank into a deep deathly indifference.

He could not tell how long they had been sailing, but when they came on deck to dance there were more limp bodies thrown overboard, and there were fewer who could dance each time. Mehuru looked around idly for the children, the little ones who had been loaded on the ship as round as berries and as dark and shiny as the sacred wood of the iroko tree. They were thinner and many of them were sick, but worst of all was the way the bright life was draining from them. They no longer cried like desperate fledglings for their mothers, they were lost children. Whether they lived or died there would be a gap in their spirits which nothing would ever replace. How would they respect their fathers, and how love children of their own, if their most powerful memory was being abandoned to despair?

He thought that about forty had died, and two crewmen as well, when the sound of the ship changed one night. Then

56

came urgent noises of running on the deck overhead, and abrupt commands and anxious shouts and then the great rolling yaw of the ship ceased, ceased at last, and he heard the roar as the anchor chain sped out through the housing and the ship thrust a claw into the ocean bed and dragged herself to a standstill. They were brought up on deck as if to be ready for dancing, but then they were manacled, arms to legs, and chained from one neck to another. The captain, even whiter than before and thinner from the voyage, looked at each shivering black man or woman or little child before he waved them into the line and had them locked on to the chain. A few, a very few, he waved to one side under guard of a sailor who held a musket easily at their heads. Mehuru thought of the unreliability of the muskets on sale in Africa and thought it might be worth taking the chance and rushing the man. But when he looked around to see where he might run he felt sicker than he had felt in the whole long voyage. For they were not off the coast of Africa any more. Wherever they had come to, it was a land he had never seen before.

The last of his courage went out of him then and when the captain waved him to the little group he went as weakly as the children who were already chosen. The last time he saw Siko was when the boy hobbled obediently to the long chain and bowed his neck to the collar. Mehuru tried to find a voice to call to him, to wish him well, to promise to return to find him if he possibly could. He was dumb. Siko looked at him, a long look of reproach and despair, and Mehuru could find no words at all. He dropped his gaze and turned away and when they were ordered back down into the hold he went without looking back. When they chained him back on a strangely empty shelf he held his hands out for the manacles on his wrists like a foolish trusting child.

A great longing for his home, so painful that he thought he would die of it, sickened him to his very core. He lay in the darkness, refusing to open his eyes, refusing to take food. The little group was kept together in the hold, twenty of them. Two other men manacled with leg-irons like himself chained on the shelf, and five women with neck-irons and long chains so that they could move more freely, but not reach the men. The smallest children were allowed to go free; two of them could barely walk. The other children aged from four years to adolescence wore light chains from wrist to wrist and ankle to ankle.

One of the women called to Mehuru to eat, but he turned his head from her and closed his eyes. The smallest toddler struggled through the slurry which washed around the floor to bring him a bowl. Mehuru saw fresh fruit – the first he had seen in the long two months of the voyage – but he did not allow himself desire. He would not eat. He had been robbed of his home, he had been robbed of his people. He had been robbed of his servant and robbed of his duty to provide for him. He had been robbed of his life. He would live no more.

Days passed, and still the ship did not sail. They were ordered on deck and made to build a little shelter against the sun. They were kept there like hens in a pen, lying on straw. They laboured below to clean out the mess of two hundred men, stalled like animals for nearly sixty days. They baled out the excrement and the filth and then the master of the ship went below with his handkerchief over his face and lit pastilles of camphor which smoked all day and all night and still could not drown the stench.

Mehuru would not speak. He ate a little rice every day and drank some of the fresh sweet water. When the women asked his name or the men touched his hand in companionship and shared mourning he turned his head away. Nothing should tie him to life.

The sailors lived on board and worked during the day, loading the ship and making it ready for another voyage. They had long idle periods when they came and took the women away. The women came back bruised and sometimes blood-stained, with their heads in their hands. Mehuru, chained hand

and foot, turned his head away from the horror in their faces.

One woman did not come back at all, and after that the sailors were forbidden to touch them. The little children missed her, she had played with them and fed them and sung them songs. Without her they were a little more lost. One little girl sat beside Mehuru for the greater part of every day and banged her head gently against the deck. Mehuru lay with his eyes shut, the deck echoing beneath his head like a drum to the steady thud of the little girl's head against the planks.

The master came back on board and the ship was ready to sail, only half-loaded with large kegs of sugar and rum. The little girl disappeared, they took her away one day, but still Mehuru could hear the thud thud thud of her head on wood. It beat like a heart, it drummed like an accusation.

He closed his eyes and refused to eat rice. He drank only water. He felt himself floating away. There was none of the right things that an obalawa should have around him, and he could not warn his fathers that he would need their help in crossing over. He thought his tree that held his spirit had bent in some storm and was perhaps breaking, and he prayed for it to fall so that his spirit might flow out of it and he might die.

Mehuru readied himself to join the ones who had to die sitting down with their eyes staring out into the darkness. He feared he would not find his fathers, dying thus. Only the Snake god had seen him with his huge shiny eyes and would know where his son had been stolen far away across the great seas.

Chapter Four

Josiah came into his house for a pint of porter and a slice of pie at midday and Frances was waiting for him at the top of the stairs.

'I should like to go out for a walk,' she said. 'But Brown cannot escort me in the mornings.'

Josiah was absorbed in business, a missing hogshead of tobacco – a great round barrel packed with whole sweet-smelling dried leaves – and he looked at her as if she were an interruption, a nuisance. 'I meant to get you a carriage,' he said absently. 'You cannot walk along the dockside.'

'So I understand,' Frances said. 'But I wish to go out.'

He sighed, his mind still on the *Rose* and the question of missing cargo. 'Perhaps we can hire a carriage.'

'Today?'

'I am very busy,' he replied. 'And troubled over this ship. There is an entire hogshead of tobacco unaccounted for, and the captain can give me no satisfactory explanation. I shall have to pay Excise tax on it as if I had it safe in my bond, as well as carrying the loss.'

'I am sorry to hear that,' Frances said politely. 'Where would I hire a carriage?'

Josiah broke off with a sudden short bark of laughter. 'You are persistent, Mrs Cole!'

Frances flushed at his use of her new name. 'I am sorry,' she said. 'At home I always walked in the gardens in the morning. My health is not very strong, as you know, and the day is fine and I wanted to go out.'

'No, it is I who am at fault. I have not provided for you as I should have done,' Josiah apologised. 'I will hire a carriage for you myself and I will drive with you this afternoon and show you the sights you should see.'

'If it is no trouble . . .'

'It is an interruption to my work,' he said frankly. 'But I should have provided you with some amusement. Can you not do sewing or painting or something of that nature?'

'Not all day.'

'No, I suppose not.' Josiah thought for a moment, and then nodded at her and headed towards his office.

'At what time shall I be ready for the carriage?' Frances called after him.

'At two,' he said. 'Tell Brown to go around to the coachyard and hire a coach, a landau or something open.' He nodded to her again and shut the door firmly in her face. Frances waited a moment and then went back to the parlour.

Miss Cole's place was empty, her ledger open at the accounts of the *Rose*. Frances leaned over the chair and saw the meticulous march of figures down the page, showing the purchase of petty goods for small sums. Sixpence for gold lace, threepence each for small knives, fourpence each for brass pots. She shrugged. She could not imagine how Miss Cole could bear to spend the day on these trifling sums, nor what difference they made to an enterprise of any size. She did not know what a trading ship sailing to the Sugar Islands would want with gold lace or small knives. Frances returned to her seat in the window and waited for two o'clock.

The coach was prompt; it was standing at the door as Frances came down the stairs wearing a large picture hat crowned with two fat feathers. She had changed into a walking dress: a greatcoat dress with a wide collar and caped sleeves. Mindful of the plainness of Sarah's attire, Frances was rather relieved to find only Josiah waiting for her at the door, and Sarah shut up in the parlour.

'I was afraid you would have forgotten,' she said. 'Did you find your tobacco?'

'The planter in Jamaica cheated us, or made a mistake,' Josiah answered. 'And the captain had it wrong on the cargo manifest. They were loading in a hurry. I had ordered him to make haste, it was the last of the new crop, and this is what comes of it.'

'I am sorry to hear it,' Frances said uncertainly. She felt she should condole with him, as one would to a man who has suffered a loss. But her training to avoid the vulgar topic of money was too powerful.

'I shall write to the planter and send the letter by *Rose* when she sails,' Josiah decided. 'Within fourteen or fifteen months she will be back in port again and it should be set right.'

'Gracious,' Frances said.

'And I will carry the loss for the whole of that time,' he said irritably. 'Just as I have to offer credit to the planters for two years at a time.' He looked at her and his frown cleared. 'This means nothing to you. Let me take you for a drive.' He handed her up the little step into the carriage. Frances unfurled her parasol against the bright summer sunshine and tipped the shade over her face.

'Go to Queens Square first,' Josiah ordered the driver. 'This is where I propose we should buy a house,' he explained to Frances. 'We have to go round through the old town, but pay no attention to the dirt and the noise. Queens Square is very smart indeed.'

The carriage moved forward, jolting on the cobbles, sailors and dockers begrudgingly giving it room. The street sellers eyed Frances's fine clothes and one girl, hawking watercress from a tray, turned her head and spat on the ground.

They drove down the Back Lane, the overhang of the houses above their heads so close that the streets were in permanent twilight, in a fog of foul air. The sun shone in a brilliant stripe down the centre of the street but the houses and the foul-smelling middens were in dank shade. Great wooden beams over their heads braced apart the houses on opposite sides of the street, which looked as if they were ready to topple together. The broad gutter in the centre of the road was an open drain, thick with slops, mud and garbage, stinking in the heat, breeding swarms of fruit flies. People swore as the carriage lurched past, splashing them with slurry. The horses scrabbled to find their footing on the greasy stones and the carriage bumped and dipped; the road was almost impassable. Frances was afraid that the horses would founder. She gripped her parasol a little tighter and held one gloved hand to her face, trying to block out the evil stink of the lane.

Every doorway, every archway was an entrance to a workshop. There were woodcarvers and sempstresses, there were coopers and workers of metal. There was a wigmaker who also drew teeth, there was a small dingy apothecary shop doing a roaring trade in laudanum and neat opium. Every other house seemed to be a ginshop, every third house was a brothel. It was a mediaeval city of timbered overhanging houses suddenly crowded to bursting point with small dangerous industries.

Frances, who had spent all but two of her thirty-five years in the country vicarage, stared in horror from one ominously dark doorway to another. The white-faced occupants stared back at her, and someone shouted an insult at the carriage and threw a handful of mud.

'It is rough,' Josiah conceded. 'Bristol is a city of labour, my dear, not leisure.'

'How can people bear it?'

He gave a snort of laughter. 'This is a prosperous street, my dear. If I showed you the colliers at Bedminster *then* you would see something to shock you. They live like animals in their own filth and no person of any wealth goes near them. They live in a world of their own, without parson or magistrates – totally outside society, totally without law.'

Towering on the hill above them, in abrupt contrast to the clutter of roofs below it, was the ornate highly decorated church of St Mary Redclift at the head of a soaring flight of stone steps. But they turned away from the spire and back towards the city, passing over the bridge.

'It would have been quicker to go across the river by the ferryboat,' Josiah explained. 'Queens Square is directly opposite my dock. When we have our house I will take a boat over every day. The lad will row me over for a ha'penny each way.'

'I am sure these streets cannot be healthy,' Frances said. She tried to keep the dismay from her voice.

'They are pestilential, madam!' Josiah exclaimed. 'If you are not killed by some fool setting fire to your house, or felled by someone dropping something on you, or poisoned by some manufactory, you will be destroyed by cholera or typhoid or both. The foul water and the summer sun are a fatal combination.'

'I wonder that your family chose to live here,' Frances said faintly.

Josiah laughed shortly. 'We did not choose! We were not in a position to choose! We bought what we could, where we could. My father bought the warehouse and dockside from his profits as a privateer and that was where we lived. We were glad enough to have a business to run and premises to call our own.'

'He was a privateer?'

Josiah nodded and then laughed abruptly at her shocked face. 'Don't look so aghast, Mrs Cole, he was a privateer, not a pirate! He had a letter from the Crown licensing him to attack French shipping. He took out his one leaky old boat and captured a French brig. That was our first chance. She was called the *Marguerite*. We paid our dues to the Crown and kept her and traded with her. It was the founding of our fortunes, the founding of our trading line. When she sank we called our next boat *Daisy* after her.'

Frances nodded. The carriage rolled on to a wooden bridge. Looking down, she saw the water rich with waste. Litter, garbage, excrement, and all the flotsam and jetsam of a busy port bobbed around the pillars of the bridge on the rising tide. The carriage bumped along the quay on the northern side of the river and then the road ahead opened out with sudden surprising grace. There was an avenue of young plane trees ahead, their broad leaves still fresh. There was a smooth green lawn in the centre of the square, there was a proud statue of a man on a galloping horse. The stink from the river was less strong, and the noise of the Backs was left behind them.

'Queens Square,' said Josiah with satisfaction. 'As good as any Crescent in Bath, eh?'

He was exaggerating, it was not as good as Bath. It lacked the easy regularity of those fine terraces, it lacked their confident scale. Part of the square was built in the golden stone of Bath but part of it was red brick, and the profile of the roofs and the detail on the houses was idiosyncratic – each house an individual. But it was a well-proportioned square lined with young trees, divided into four by long avenues running north to south and east to west. At the centre of the square the paths crossed and the statue made a handsome centrepiece. The houses were new; some looked like London houses in smart red brick with pointings of white mortar and corners of white stone. At the east end was an elegant large building flanked by two wings in thick yellow stone: the Custom House.

The carriage drew up before the first house in the south-west corner, one of the biggest and most imposing in the square. 'This is where we shall live,' Josiah announced. 'This is where I have been aiming for years.'

Frances looked at him in surprise. She had never before heard of a man desiring anything more than to stay in the position to which he had been called. She had heard men complain of the decline of manners; but never to seek change. Her father had preached that it was God's will for a man to remain where he was born, a good Christian stayed where God had been pleased to put him. Josiah was the first man in her experience to express an ambition – to want something more than what he had been given. It was a revolutionary doctrine.

'You have been aiming for it?'

'My father was born on an earth floor in a hovel,' Josiah said. 'No more than a peasant. My sister in a collier's cottage, a coalminer's daughter. I was born on a stone floor in a warehouse. My son will be born in a proper bed, in a proper house. My family is on the rise, madam. Before the century is out we will be known as gentry. We will have a country house and a carriage. This is but a step on our way; not our final destination.'

Frances flushed at his mention of a son but Josiah had no idea that he was indelicate. He pointed to the grand house, the best house on the square, three red-brick storeys high with little attic windows let into the roof. Long white stone columns ran the length of the windows on each storey; above each window was a carved face. The double doorway was large and imposing, flanked by more pillars. Stone-carved gateposts and wrought-iron railings shielded the front of the house and emphasised its importance. 'This is it, Mrs Cole. This is our house-to-be. I happen to know that it is coming up for sale and I shall bid for it, you may be sure. And I shall have it. No-one will outbid me, cost what it will. It is generally known that you and I are wed. It is generally known that I am looking for a town house to establish my family.'

Frances looked around the square, trying to imagine what it would be like to live there. A curtain in a front parlour beside them twitched and dimly she saw a woman step back from the window. It would be a little community, ingrowing and inbred. There would be small feuds and long memories. Frances did not mind. She had lived in a country village, dependent on the good will of the lord, her uncle. She knew how small communities worked.

'We should drive on,' she said gently to Josiah. 'We will be noticed if we stay here any longer, looking.'

'So?'

'These people will be our neighbours,' she explained. 'We wish them to have an agreeable impression of us.'

He was about to argue but she saw him hesitate and then he nodded. 'You know best, Mrs Cole,' he agreed. 'You are the one to teach me. It shall be as you wish. Now, is there anywhere else you would like to see?'

'I don't know the city at all,' Frances said. 'I have never visited here. I had some friends who drove out to a picnic and looked at the Avon gorge. They told me it was sublime.'

Josiah leaned forward and gave the order to the driver. 'We can go and look at the gorge,' he said. 'You will not think it so sublime when you understand what it costs me in barge charges. We can drive to the Hot Well at the foot of the gorge. I have a particular interest in it.'

The carriage turned out of the square and bumped along yet another dockside beside another river.

'This is the Avon again?' Frances asked.

'The River Frome,' Josiah corrected her.

'It is as if we live on an island,' Frances said. 'Surrounded by water.' She nearly said, 'foul water'.

'The old city was a defensive site ringed by the two rivers, the Avon and the Frome – like a moat,' Josiah told her. 'Now it is all docks.'

They waited for the drawbridge ahead of them to be dropped and then the carriage bowled over the wooden planks and turned left, away from the docks.

Frances looked ahead as for the first time the city seemed something more than a dockside slum. The pretty triangle of College Green was before them, with two churches on their left. The College church was an imposing building with the Bishop's Palace behind it. Frances heard birdsong – not the irritable squawk of seagulls, but the summery ripple of a blackbird's call. Looking up, she saw swallows and housemartins swooping and wheeling around the high towers of the cathedral.

The thick foliage of the elms threw dark green shadows over the road and as they drove up the steep hill the air grew fresher and cleaner and the sun shone brightly on the new buildings.

'Oh, if we could only live up here!' Frances exclaimed. Set back from the track were occasional terraces of houses in soft yellow stone, built in the style that Frances liked – plain regular and square.

Josiah shook his head. 'It's a whim. One or two people are building here but no true merchant will ever move away from the city. The river is our life blood. Clifton is too far to go. It is country living – not city dwelling at all. There are people buying land and putting up houses but it will never be the heart of the city. We will always live along the river banks, that is where the city always has been. That is where it always will be.'

At the top of the hill they forked to the left, skirting a high hill and dropping down towards the river again.

'But if we had a carriage you could drive down to your work,' Frances observed, her voice carefully neutral. 'And these are handsome houses, and very clean air. I love to breathe clean air and my health needs it.'

Josiah shook his head. 'It is a whim,' he repeated. 'It will pass and those men who have bought land and built will have bankrupted themselves. Take my word for it, my dear, Park Street is beyond the limit of the city and Clifton will never be more than a little out-of-the-way village.' He craned his head to see a ship in the dry dock. 'The *Traveller*,' he said with quiet satisfaction. 'I heard she was badly holed. That will put Thomas Williams's nose out of joint.'

Ahead of them the river widened out and started to form sinuous curves between banks of thick mud. Dark woodland reared up from either side of the banks and then broke up around the lower reaches of white cliffs of limestone which towered above them. The little road clung to the side of the river, following the curve of the bank overhung by the cliffs.

It was spectacular scenery. Overhead seagulls wheeled and cried and dropped down to dive for little fish. A small fishing smack slipped downriver, moving fast on the ebbing tide, her sails filled with wind. The air was salty and clean, damp with the smell of the sea. A flat-bottomed trow crossed from one side to another and passed a ferryboat rowed by a man bright as a pirate in a blue jacket with a red handkerchief tied on his head.

'Sublime,' Frances said. It was Lady Scott's favourite word of praise. 'This is wonderful scenery, Mr Cole. So romantic! So wild!'

Josiah tapped the driver on the back with his stick and the man stopped the carriage. 'Will you walk, my dear?'

The driver let down the step and Frances got down from the carriage and took Josiah's arm. 'Above is the St Vincent's rock,' he said. 'It's quite an attraction for people who love scenery.'

Frances craned her neck to look upwards at the high white cliffs with wild woodland tumbling down. 'I never saw anything more lovely. You would think yourself in Italy at least!'

Slowly they walked along the little promenade which clung to the side of the river, tucked in beneath the cliff. An avenue of young trees had been planted in a double row to shade the road and form an attractive riverside walk. Ahead of them to their right was a pretty colonnade of shops set back from the river in a curving half-circle, lined with small pillars so that the customers could stroll under cover, admiring the goods on sale, on their way to and from the Hot Well Pump Room. It was as pretty as a set of doll's houses, a dozen little red-brick shops in miniature under a colonnade of white pillars.

Frances and Josiah walked along the flagstones, looking in the shop windows at the fancy goods and the gloves and hats, and the crowded apothecary shop. There was a small circulating library which also sold stationery and haberdashery goods.

'This is Miss Yearsley's library!' Frances exclaimed.

'Who is she?'

'Why, Anna Yearsley, the poetess, the milkmaid poet! Such a natural unforced talent!'

Josiah nodded at the information. 'I have not had much to do with poetesses,' he confessed. 'Or milkmaids. But I know about her library. This is a new building, all brand new, and she will be paying a pretty sum in rent. The Merchant Venturers have spent a fortune to make this the most fashionable place in Bristol.'

'I believe my uncle stayed at the Hot Well when he visited you,' Frances said. 'In Dowry Parade. He spoke very highly of the lodging house but he said it was dear.'

Josiah nodded. 'Whoever takes it on will have to charge a fortune to recoup his investment. Not just these shops but the spa itself has recently been improved. These trees are new-planted. For years the place has been open to anyone – you can take a cart from the city for sixpence to come here, and drink the water for free. Any tenant who takes it on will have to charge more and exclude the common people. A successful spa must be for the fashionable people only, don't you think? Will you take a glass of the water? I am sure you do not need it for your health but you might enjoy the experience.'

They walked towards the Pump Room which stood on the very edge of the river, its windows overlooking the water and the Rownham woods on the far side of the bank. Josiah paid an entrance fee and they went in. The place was busy. A string quartet positioned in a corner of the room played country dances. Invalids advertised their ill health with yards of shawls and rugs across their knees, but there were others, whose visit was purely social, flirting and laughing in the corners. A few people promenaded self-consciously up and down the length of the rooms, stopping to greet friends, and staring at the new arrivals.

Frances straightened her collar where it fell elegantly at the neck of her walking gown, and held Josiah's arm. He seemed to know no-one. No-one stopped to speak to them, no-one hailed him.

'Do you have no friends here?' she asked after they had walked the length of the room. They paused before the fountain of the spa. Josiah paid for a glass of water and the woman pocketed the coin and poured a small glass for Frances. It was light-coloured and cloudy, sparkling with little bubbles.

'My friends are working traders, not pleasure-seekers,' Josiah said. 'They will be at their warehouses at this time in the afternoon, not dancing and walking and drinking water. How does it taste?'

Frances took an experimental sip. 'Quite nice,' she said cautiously. 'Bland, a little like milk. And quite hot!'

'Very strengthening!' the woman at the fountain asserted. 'Especially for ladies. Very effective for skin complaints, stomach complaints and the lungs.'

Frances blushed at the frankness of the woman's language, and forced the rest of the glass down. 'I would not care to drink it every day.'

'Many people do,' Josiah replied. 'Some of them are prescribed a glass every couple of hours. Think of the profit for the tenant in that! Many come and stay for weeks at a time to drink it. And it is cried all around the city and sold like milk at the back doors. And bottled and sent all around the country. A very good business if one could afford to buy in.' He took her arm and walked her back down the length of the Pump Room. 'How does it compare to the Pump Room at Bath, in your opinion?' he asked. 'I have a reason for my interest.'

Frances thought for a way to tell him that would not seem offensive. 'Of course it is smaller,' she began carefully. 'And very much prettier. The scenery is wonderful, much better than Bath. But Bath has more ... Bath is more ... established.'

'Only a little place but I think it will grow,' Josiah said as they left the Room. 'But I am glad you like it. I am glad you

71

like the rocks of the Avon gorge even if you do not like the taste of the water.'

'One could not help but admire it,' Frances said. The carriage had followed them down to the Pump Room; she took the driver's hand and stepped in. 'I am a great admirer of fine landscape.'

'Do you draw or paint?' Josiah asked her.

'A little,' Frances said. 'I should like to come to try my hand at drawing this scene.'

'So you shall,' Josiah said. 'You shall hire the carriage whenever you wish and my sister will drive with you. You shall teach us how to enjoy leisure, Mrs Cole. And we will teach you about business!'

'I shall be happy to learn,' Frances said. The carriage turned back towards the city and to the dark little house by the noisy quay filled with the stink of the harbour. 'I shall be happy,' she repeated firmly.

Chapter Five

Josiah's attempts to buy the house at 29 Queens Square were
not at first successful. The building was owned by Mr Stephen
Waring, a Merchant Venturer and a member of the Corporation of the city. He was building a grand new house halfway
up Park Street in a new road to be called Great George Street.
Josiah approached him as he sat in the coffee house with his
brother-in-law – another Merchant Venturer – on one hand
and his cousin standing behind him.

'Good day,' Josiah said. He tried not to sound deferential
but he could hear the hint of inferiority in his voice – a tinge
of Somerset, a trace of servility. He sounded like a man who
had been born on the floor of a warehouse. 'Good day, Mr
Waring.'

The man looked up. 'Cole?'

'I wonder if I might speak with you on a matter of business?'
Josiah's plain three-cornered hat was in his hand. He felt
himself turn it, and tap the points, like a servant fidgeting
before a master.

'Yes?'

Josiah glanced at the other men. They were staring at him
with open curiosity. No-one made any movement away from
the table, they did not even trouble themselves to turn aside.
His business would have to be done before them all.

'I am interested in your house in Queens Square,' he said.
'I understand that you may be selling it? I am newly married
and my wife . . .'

The man laughed gently. 'I do not think you would like it,

Cole,' he said. 'It is the wrong side of the river for your little warehouse, and you would find my neighbours very poor company.' He smiled at his brother-in-law and turned his back on Josiah. The meeting was concluded.

Josiah flushed with embarrassment. There was nothing he could do but sketch a bow and go back to the table where he usually did his business, with the smaller traders and the unemployed captains. They had been watching him; everyone in the coffee shop had seen him rebuffed. Josiah pulled out a chair and seated himself, trying to look jaunty and hide his mortification. 'I have mentioned my interest in the house at Queens Square to Mr Waring,' he said to the table generally. 'I shall write him a letter with my offer.'

'He's a warm man,' Captain Legge warned. 'I've heard that he paid more than two thousand pounds for his new house off Park Street.'

Josiah blinked. 'That is a new house though,' he objected. 'New built and according to his specifications. The house in Queens Square must be nearly seventy years old!'

'And his father and the rest of the landlords made profits enough in the first year!' a small merchant commented. 'The leases on those houses were an extortion. Many a tenant was ruined in the first year if he was not a member of the Merchant Venturers, who had insiders' terms.'

Another trader nodded. 'How convenient it was that the Corporation chose to build in brick when the Waring family owned the brickyard,' he remarked slyly.

'That'll do,' Josiah said swiftly, glancing towards the top table where Mr Waring had summoned one of the masters of his ship and was examining a cargo manifest. 'The Corporation of Bristol and the Merchant Venturers have together brought this city to the highest prosperity. We all know that.'

'It's joining them that's the challenge, eh, Josiah?'

Josiah Cole flushed. 'Gentlemen,' he said. 'My future plans are my own concern, I think. Now, I heard that you were

74

interested in my sugar, Mr Williams. Shall I send you a sample?'

Frances was seated at the parlour table, the ledgers of the company spread before her. Sarah was teaching her the business, showing her the books of the ship *Daisy* due home in December.

'This page shows the cost of fitting out a ship,' Sarah explained patiently. 'See, here is every item, and along the line,' her finger traced the row of ink dots, 'here is what it cost. At the foot of the page is the total cost.'

'I see,' said Frances wearily. Outside the window the *Rose* was being fitted with new ropes and newly mended sails. There was a continual bellow of orders and screams of quay-side sellers. They had a pulley rigged on the mast which screeched every time it took the weight of a load, and then the crew started a chant to help them pull the ropes together. The sun burned in at the parlour window and the reflected light on the ceiling danced a dizzying ballet. The tide was coming in and the filth and sewage which had been draining downriver was now washing up and down the quayside wall. The wind blowing up the gorge brought the acrid stink of burning lime from the Clifton woods to mingle with the per-vasive smell of Bristol: boiling fat for soap, smoke from the furnaces. The window was tightly shut as usual. The parlour was hot and stuffy, the sun beating in through the glass of the panes. Frances had a headache; she sat very still and straight and did not complain.

'So the total cost of repairing and fitting out the ship was £907. 2s.'

Sarah Cole nodded. 'Correct. On the next page we show the trade goods supplied.'

Frances passed her cool fingers over her eyelids. 'What are all these names?'

'These are our four partners. Merchants and tradesmen who joined with us for this voyage. Here you see that they

75

supply the trade goods themselves. Here is a cutler – he supplied the knives and forks and tin dishes. We show the goods and the value of them. Here is a haberdasher. He supplied cloth and lace and some hats. The other things, some beads, Italian blue beads, and the guns, we bought direct. The other partners supplied the money to buy them.'

Frances looked down the page. There were many things listed but the greatest quantity of money had been spent on muskets, Bonny muskets at nine shillings each, gunpowder and flints. 'What a lot of guns,' she said.

'They are the most popular trade goods,' Sarah Cole said. 'And a great cost to us. They can only be bought from Birmingham and no Birmingham firearm maker will come in with us as a partner. They are quick enough to make a profit from us but they will not share the risk. Now, Frances, can you see how much it cost to send out the ship?'

Frances looked wearily to the foot of the page. The shifting light in the room seemed to be beating on her eyes. 'Yes, £5692. 16s. 0d,' she said. 'What a great deal of money!'

'Now you see!' Sarah exclaimed. 'Now you begin to understand. This is why I don't want a grand house. This is why I don't keep a carriage. I daresay Lord Scott himself could not find such a sum, and find it three times every two years! Every time we send out a ship!'

'I don't know,' Frances said unwillingly. 'I have never learned about money before.'

Sarah smiled in triumph. 'Well, you are a merchant's wife now,' she said. 'It is right that you should know where the money comes from. When you hire the carriage or want a new silk dress it all has to be paid for.' She smoothed the pages lovingly with the flat of her hand. 'It all comes from here.'

She turned the page. 'Now this is the record for the transactions in Africa,' she went on. 'I compose the books when the captain shows me his log on his return. See here: purchased over six months on the Africa coast – three hundred and twelve – at an average of fourteen pounds each. Wastage on voyage – sixty-two. Price in Jamaica, average fifty pounds each. First profit – £12500, minus the cost of buying – £8132.' She waited for Frances to speak.

'Very profitable,' Frances said.

'Apparently so,' Sarah said sourly. 'From this profit we buy sugar, tobacco and rum to the cost of £4830. We extend credit to the planters to the cost of £1750, and we pay off half of the crew at a cost of £130.' She ran her finger down the columns, Frances followed it with her eyes. All she could see was the neat fingernail and the black-ink numbers spooling away.

'Now you see,' Sarah Cole went on. 'When the ship comes into port she has to pay for a pilot up the Bristol channel, and then another pilot up the Avon. She has to pay a fee to every lighthouse, she has to pay a fee for the new bridge, she has to pay the rowing boats to tow her up the gorge, she has to pay a fee to the mayor and to the quay warden, and a docking fee.'

'Gracious,' Frances said weakly.

'No wonder the Liverpool merchants steal our trade,' Sarah Cole muttered to herself. 'They sail straight into a deep-water dock with cheap quay rates. No wonder they build bigger and bigger ships.' She turned her attention back to Frances. 'So, can you see the profit which is made at the end of the voyage?'

Frances looked wearily at the final page. 'Here, £2513.'

'Divided among the partners – five partners including ourselves,' Sarah prompted.

Frances looked at the final figure. 'That's £502 each.'

Sarah Cole nodded at her, waiting for some response.

'After all that work and worry?'

'And we own the ship and keep the warehouse, and allow credit to the planters in Jamaica and all the other costs that the partners do not see,' Sarah added.

'It does not seem very much for us when you put it like that,' Frances said.

Sarah got up from the table and went over to the window. 'It's a good profit on a two-year investment for the partners,' she said. 'For a little man with little savings it is good business. But the scale of it is not big enough for my brother now. He can double his money every five years on these figures, but he wants to advance in six months, by tomorrow. I do not see how we are to do it. I show you these figures because you should know our business, but you can see for yourself that we are not making the profits we need.'

'Why not?'

The woman shrugged. 'Rising prices all around us. It costs more and more to repair and equip a ship. The price of sugar is falling as more and more planters increase their land and grow a bigger crop each season. The American war made it dangerous even for civilian shipping and increased the cost of insurance. The French can import their own sugar from their own colonies, and now they are selling in England. I heard that a man is finding a way to make sugar from vegetables called beets. When they make sugar from carrots we are ruined indeed.'

She stepped towards the table and shut the ledger gently, passing her hand over the ship's name, *Daisy*, engraved on the front of the leather-bound book. 'The Liverpool merchants have ships twice the size of the *Daisy*,' she said. 'And they do the trip in half the time. That means they can make four times our profits. Just think of it! Twice the amount of trade in half the time!

'The big Bristol merchants are members of the Royal Africa Company and they do not have to wait off the coast, trading up and down at all the little stations, buying here and selling there. They anchor at a Royal Africa Company fort and they load food and water that is waiting for them, and the Trade that is ready and waiting for them. They halve the loss of life for the crew because they are away from West Africa within a month, while we delay for six months gathering cargo.

'When they arrive in the West Indies they have an agent

waiting on the quayside to greet them. He has already bought the cargo for loading, he has already arranged the sales. He has agreed prices while they were still at sea. They deal with the best planters and they have contracts arranged. When they give credit to the planters they bring home bills which are honoured in London at once, by the planter's agents, as soon as they are presented. So they get their money within the quarter. But *we* have to give credit and then wait until our ship is in the West Indies again, sometimes as long as two years before we are paid! The people we trade with do not have a London agent. They are the smaller planters, and they demand credit from us. It is no business for the little men any more.'

'Yet Josiah seems so confident,' Frances demurred.

Sarah's face was grim. 'Yes,' she agreed. 'He is very confident. He sees sugar in the storerooms of the Redclift, his bond is filled with tobacco and rum. He can see the gold coming in from one little sale after another, and he is down on the quayside doing as well as other little traders. But I spend my day with the books and I can see that the profits are slowly falling as the costs rise. The world is changing and we will have to change too.'

'My uncle thought that Josiah was a prosperous man,' Frances protested, clinging to hope.

Sarah shrugged her shoulders. 'What would he know?' she said disrespectfully. 'I imagine he has never seen a set of accounts in his life. He would see his rent rolls and nothing more. But I have spent my life with these books and I can read them as you would read a novel. And I can see that each voyage out, and each voyage back, is less and less successful. It costs more every day, the risks are greater all the time.'

'What can we do?' Frances asked. 'Can't we build a bigger ship? Or take up a different trade?'

Sarah Cole measured Frances. 'No,' she said with a little smile. 'We can never leave the Trade. It is the only thing we know. It is the foundation of our fortunes and it is our inheritance. Whatever anyone says, I will never countenance that we leave the Trade. We must stay with it – but do it in a new way.'

'What way?'

'We import slaves direct,' Sarah said very softly. 'We bring black slaves into England. We put a black slave in every household in England. We call them Scott slaves – named in honour of you – and we make our fortune.'

There was a loud crash from the quayside as something was dropped, followed by half a dozen shouts. Neither woman heard them.

'What?'

'We ship slaves already,' Sarah said sharply. 'You saw the accounts with me. You saw the figures. You saw that we bought three hundred and twelve on *Daisy*'s last voyage, you read it yourself. You saw wastage on voyage – sixty-two, you knew that meant that sixty-two of them had died during the passage. You saw how they sold in Jamaica – they went for fifty pounds each. My idea is to bring a sample of them on to England. To train them here to be house servants, to sell them for households in England. Isn't it the fashion?'

'Yes,' Frances said slowly. Lady Scott had a little black boy to carry her fan and run her messages, and every lady in London had a black maid or a handsome black footman to ride behind the carriage, and a little black girl to play with the children. But all the slaves that Frances knew had been imported singly from the West Indies, brought over by returning planters, sold by slaving captains. 'Can you train them in large numbers, and sell them in large numbers?'

'Why not?' Sarah demanded. 'It was done in the past. In the last century people imported slaves direct from Africa. I have heard of a Liverpool merchant who has imported a dozen this year. They take up little space on the ship coming home from the Sugar Islands, and they will sell in England for eighty or ninety pounds each. But if our slaves could become known for their manners and their training, we could command an even greater price.

'You shall teach them. They are the pupils you would have had, if you had come to us as a governess. Now you will take a profit rather than a wage but they will still be your work. They will be famous for their smartness and their training, and that will be your job.'

'I'm not sure . . .' Frances said.

'You can have no objection,' Sarah said coldly. 'You knew we were Bristol merchants. You accepted the Trade well enough when it took place at a distance. You came for a job with us.'

'I did not know I was to be governess to slaves . . . Josiah never said . . .'

'You can have no objection though. You knew where our wealth was earned.'

'I have no objection,' Frances said. 'Of course I have none. I know that it is a good thing to take the Africans away from their paganism and to teach them godly work and religion.'

'And they are not humans, not as we understand humans,' Sarah reminded her. 'They are animals. They cannot speak unless we teach them; otherwise they just grunt and moan. They are not fully human.'

'Oh,' Frances said. 'I had not realised. I have never had much to do with them. Lady Scott has a nigger pageboy, but I have never seen one fully grown.'

'So you will teach them?'

Frances nodded. 'I only hesitated because I do not know if I can. I have taught children, but they were human children. I wouldn't know how to teach niggers.'

Sarah nodded grimly. 'Then let me tell you, Sister, that you had better find a way to teach them. This will be the saving of our Cole and Sons and its key to the future. If we can train and sell slaves then we can make a fortune big enough to satisfy Josiah's ambition, and to pay for Queens Square. If we do not, it will not be Queens Square for you, you will stay

81

here forever, beside the filthy water of the dock – cold and damp in winter, deadly in summer.'

There was a long silence. Frances could feel herself becoming breathless and put her hand to the base of her throat to steady her pulse. 'You are not exaggerating?' she confirmed. Her little cough rose up and choked her for a moment.

Sarah waited until she had her breath back. 'The bottom is slowly falling out of the Trade,' she said. 'If, in a few years, our Bristol partners can get a better return in land and building, or in shops, or in importing cotton to Manchester, they will no longer put their money with us. Then we will not be able to send out ships at all and our investment – in our ships, in our warehouse, in the quay – will be thrown away. We have put so much money into the Trade that we *have* to trade, and we have to make the Trade pay.'

'I will try, Sarah, I will try my best to teach them.'

Sarah smiled a wintry smile. 'You were a governess, weren't you?' she asked. 'You replied to our advertisement for a governess? We planned all along that you should teach them. But now instead of working for a wage you are working for yourself. You shall be their teacher and you shall recommend them to their places and give them a character. You will make this plan work for us. You will earn the new town house. You want it, don't you?'

Frances looked around the tiny parlour and breathed the tainted air. 'Yes,' she said. 'Of course I do.'

82

Chapter Six

Josiah came in for his dinner in the mid-afternoon in thoughtful silence. Frances, new to his moods and weary herself from Sarah's long lessons with the account books, sat at the foot of the table and said nothing. Her cough was troubling her. She sipped water, trying to choke it back. Sarah waited until the tablecloth had been taken away and a decanter of port set at Josiah's hand before she asked:

'Trouble?'

He raised his head and smiled. 'Oh! Nothing. I have been all day seeking proper insurance for *Rose*. Ever since the *Zong* case it has been more and more difficult.'

'The *Zong* case?' Frances asked.

'Business,' Josiah said dismissively.

'She should understand it,' Miss Cole pointed out. 'It is her business too now.'

'Oh aye, you're probably right,' Josiah agreed. 'The *Zong* case, my dear, took place half a dozen years ago and concerned the good ship *Zong* which is still in dispute with the insurers.'

'Why?' Frances asked.

'Well, it is a long story, but basically the *Zong* ran short of water while sailing to Jamaica. There was much illness on board and the captain took the decision to pitch a quarter of the cargo overboard.'

'What cargo?' Frances asked stupidly.

'She does not understand,' Miss Cole said.

'It is simple enough,' Josiah said briskly. 'The captain of the *Zong*, fearing that a large number of his four hundred and seventy slaves would die of thirst, had them thrown into the sea to drown.'

Frances looked from Josiah's face to his sister's. 'To save the drinking water?'

Josiah allowed himself a small sly smile. 'Well, that is what the captain claimed. However, while they were in the midst of these kindly killings, it came on to rain and it rained for two days.'

Miss Cole hid a little laugh behind her hand.

'And the good ship *Zong* docked with full casks of drinking water in Jamaica.'

The two of them smiled at Frances, expecting her to understand the joke. She shook her head.

'It was a fraud,' Miss Cole said impatiently.

'The captain was lying,' Josiah explained. 'See here, Frances, he had a bad batch of slaves, very sick, dying on him, dropping like sick flies. Slaves who die of illness are a cash loss – a loss to the traders; but slaves drowned at sea are paid for by the insurance. Captain Luke Collingwood had the neat idea of slinging all the sick men and women over the side and claiming for them on the insurance.'

'He drowned them for the insurance money?'

Josiah nodded. 'In three batches, over three days as I remember. A hundred and thirty-one altogether.'

'And they say the big Liverpool shippers are better,' Miss Cole crowed. 'You never heard of a Bristol captain cheating like that.'

'He did not cheat, Sister,' Josiah reproved her. 'He ran his ship at a profit. Lord Mansfield himself sat in judgement and ordered a retrial.'

'The captain was tried for murder?' Frances asked.

The look the two of them turned on her was of blank incomprehension. 'Lord, no!' Josiah shook his head. 'It is no crime to kill slaves. This was a civil matter. The insurers refused to pay out. They argued that slaves are insured only against accident, not against deliberate drowning. They won the first round in the courts and then it'went to appeal. Lord Mansfield sat on the appeal, I remember. He said that it was exactly the same as if horses had gone overboard, and that the owners should be insured against their goods going into the sea for whatever reason.'

Miss Cole nodded in mild triumph. 'He said that slaves are property, Lord Mansfield himself said they were the same as horses.'

'But it has left us with great difficulties,' Josiah went on. He rubbed his hand across his face and his boyish exuberance suddenly drained away. 'Because his lordship ruled that all slaves lost at sea are to be paid for by the insurance, there is a fear that all captains running at a loss will simply drown their slaves and claim for them. The insurers do not trust us. I have spent all day trying to find someone to insure a cargo of slaves for me, and they put in so many requirements and conditions that it is hardly worth insuring at all.'

Sarah looked anxious. 'We dare not sail without insurance,' she said. 'What if the ship were to go down and we were to lose all? Or a slave revolt? Josiah, we *must* insure.'

'I know! I know!' he snapped. 'But now they will only insure against rebellions. They will not compensate for sickness, or for slaves who suicide. If a slave is whipped to death they will not compensate. If a slave starves himself to death they will not compensate. If they kill themselves what can I do? I cannot carry such losses.'

Sarah was grave. 'Someone must insure us.'

Josiah shrugged his shoulders crossly. 'They are all in a ring. If I could break into the Merchant Venturers then I could share my insurance with them. On the inside they all insure each other. It is the little fish left on the outside which bob about trying to snap at trifles. If I could get inside the Company then I would be safe.'

He broke off and looked at Frances, his mood lightening. 'We can do it, I know we can do it. With the house at Queens Square and with you, Mrs Cole, to give me some presence in the world, we will get there. We have been trading for two generations, we are respectable Bristol merchants. They will invite me to join, they must invite me to join soon.'

'It is an old trade,' Frances said. 'Respectable.' She was thinking of the ship in the drizzling rain. The one hundred and thirty-one men and women thrown over the side into the heaving water, clinging to the ropes and screaming as they went overboard, bobbing in the wake of the ship as it ploughed on without them, trying to swim after it in the buffeting waves, and then seeing, on the edge of their vision, a dark scythe-like fin as it came straight towards them, slicing through the water.

'*Rose* is nearly ready to sail,' Sarah said. 'We have to have insurance within the week. And we are still two partners short.'

'I will get it,' Josiah promised. 'I will get it in time, and partners for the voyage as well. I cannot have her sitting on the dock eating up my money doing nothing. I will get insurance for her and partners too. Trust me, Sarah, I have never failed before.'

Josiah was trying, but the mood of the city, as sensitive as a flock of little wading birds which scavenge at the edge of the sea, was against him. There was a whisper around Bristol that Josiah was losing his sure touch. He was spending too much time with his new wife, he was seen driving in a hired carriage to the Hot Well, to the Clifton Down. He was negotiating to buy a house on Queens Square. They said he wanted to be a man of leisure, soon he would be too grand to drive a hard bargain. The small traders who haunted the quayside coffee shops with their savings to invest wanted to place their gold with a man who knew the value of money as they did. They wanted a man who admired the chink of a hundred hard-won guineas in a little purse. They suspected Josiah of soaring too high for them. They did not know that he was trapped in the gulf between the two worlds of the hardest city in Britain. The great men, the Merchant Venturers, had no place for him. Their wives might murmur that the new

Mrs Cole had been Miss Scott and niece to Lord Scott and long to be her friend; but the new Mrs Cole was seen only at church and she attended St Mary Redclift, not the more fashionable cathedral on the north side of the river, on College Green.

They could not call on her in that dreadful little house on the dockside. The drive to the front door alone was more than most of the ladies could stomach. They sent their footmen to leave their cards, but they did not call in person, and Frances, reading the signs quite correctly, knew that she must wait until they moved into the big house in Queens Square.

At the end of the week Josiah decided to take a gamble. He would send *Rose* out with insurance only for goods. No insurer would cover him for shipping slaves. Josiah was too desperate for profits to wait. He threw down his hat, took Captain Smedley by the arm as they walked along the quayside and thrust him towards the ship.

'Go!' he exclaimed. 'And sail her as if she were your own. I tell you honestly, Captain Smedley, we have to see a mighty profit on this sailing, and we are taking a mighty risk.'

The captain nodded. 'I am ready. I will join her at the Kingsroad, when the pilot has brought her down the channel. I will do my best for you, Mr Cole, as I always have done.'

'There will be a note for you in your cabin.' Josiah's face was hungry. 'We may need to bend the law a little on this voyage, Captain Smedley. You would have no difficulty with that, I take it.'

'As long as the ship and my crew are safe . . .'

Josiah nodded. 'Keep the ship safe, whatever you do. I will see her set sail on the tide at dawn tomorrow. And your orders will be on your chart table in your cabin.'

The captain stooped and picked up Josiah's hat, and returned it to him with a smile. 'Cover your head, Mr Cole, I shall see you in the Merchant Venturers' Company yet.'

Josiah bared his brown teeth. 'Please God,' he said tightly.

* * *

Next morning Josiah was up early waiting on the quayside in thick cold fog. *Rose* was loading her final stores, extra boxes of trade goods carried swiftly and efficiently from Josiah's warehouse: crate after crate of Birmingham muskets with flints and shot and gunpowder. Josiah was pouring munitions into Africa, to feed their need of guns.

Captain Smedley was not aboard; he would join the ship at Kingsroad anchorage, when the pilot had guided her down the Avon gorge, with the rowing boats towing her. Josiah wrote one final letter of instructions to him and left it in his cabin.

4th September 1788

On this Trip above all Others I must stress that we have to show a Profit. To this End select the Very best Negroes you can find; but do not Delay too long off Africa. Ship Women and young children and Pack them very Close. I want you to carry as many as Six Hundred. The Extra deaths in passage will be paid for by the Extra profit in taking So many.

On this voyage, on this one Voyage only, you are to Go straight to the Spanish colonies and sell the slaves There, for Bullion. The papers to cover this Voyage make No mention of the Spanish colonies, and you will Destroy this letter when you have Read it. I know that this is Smuggling and you will see a Bonus on your Return. This will be the only Time I will ask you to Trade with the Spanish, and I will Reward your Success. Buy what Sugar they offer, provided it is of Good quality, but take No notes of Credit. I want nothing but Gold and Sugar. Do not Fail me, Captain Smedley – Ship as many as you can find and Pack them Tight!

The *Rose* was rocking temptingly on the tide, the waves slapping the quayside. The pilot came aboard as Josiah watched the barges attaching their lines.

'Take care now,' Josiah said under his breath. The ship was uninsured for the middle voyage and would be perilously overloaded. He dared not tell Sarah; he hardly dared acknowledge to himself what he was doing.

The dockers slipped *Rose*'s moorings and the rope snaked through the green water and was hauled up to the ship. The rowing boats moved slowly forward and the towing ropes sprang out of the water and quivered tautly, shedding drops of silver water along their length. There was the silent, precious moment as the ship hesitated, as if she could not believe that she were free, freely in her element after weeks of being tied to land, then slowly, almost reluctantly, the *Rose* moved away from the dockside and gathered speed as she glided down the channel towards the heights of the Avon gorge.

'God speed,' Josiah said under his breath. She was undercapitalised on this trip. She was financed by himself and only three other small partners. He had taken three shares to himself and the others had only one share each. He had borrowed to buy the extra trade goods, he owed more than a thousand pounds on her. She was undercapitalised and underinsured. Josiah had no choice but to send her outside the law to sell to the Spanish plantations. It was a risk he had never taken before; but the Spanish would pay highly and in bullion. Josiah was sailing very close to the wind. 'God speed,' he said.

As if to justify Josiah's belief in his luck, that very day, when the sun had risen, showing red through the smoke from the lead shot tower, Mr Waring took breakfast with his wife and finally decided to sell the house in Queens Square to the Coles. Mrs Waring had heard from the bishop's wife herself that the new Mrs Cole was the daughter of the Reverend John Scott who had held the living at Claverton Down. Stephen Waring was frankly incredulous that a Miss Scott should marry a man such as Josiah, and sleep above a sugar store, but Mrs Waring was more acute. 'I daresay if Josiah Cole is good enough for Lord Scott he is good enough to buy our house,' she remarked archly. 'And I daresay, Mr Waring, that you can name your price if Mr Cole has to provide a good house for his new wife.'

Mr Waring said nothing but when he retreated to his office he wrote a note to Josiah naming a price for the house that was high enough to discourage any but the most eager.

If Josiah had been a regular at the top table of the coffee shop, he would have known that other houses in Queens Square were about to come on the market. If Josiah had been acquainted with the wealthy men of the city, he would have been in no hurry to snap up 29 Queens Square when 18 and 31 would be on the market within the month. The richest merchants were moving from the square; the city centre was becoming too noisy, too dirty and too crowded for them. Their wives had ambitions to be ladies of leisure, they did not want a parlour which also did service as an office.

Park Street was paved almost to the crown of the hill and on either side of the street elegant town houses in pale honey stone were springing up. The first few houses in Great George Street had been sold and others were planned. The astute men were buying up land all around Great George Street, and on either side of Park Street, and architects were drawing plans for elegant terraces to rise one above the other all the way up the hill. Mr Waring was discreetly negotiating, through an agent, for land even farther from the dockside. He did not share Josiah's love of the city centre. Mr Waring was interested in Clifton.

Queens Square was falling from fashion and the prices would slide as soon as it became apparent. Mr Waring opened the paper again and added a note along the bottom.

I can Offer you this house at This price for a Week Only, Mr Cole.
I have had a Pressing enquiry from Another man to Whom I must
reply within Eight days.

90

He folded the paper over, dropped red wax on it, and pressed his seal on it.

Thoughtfully he took up another page.

Dear Tom,

Oblige me by Keeping your house Off the market for a Week.
I have a Buyer for mine and I do not want him Distracted.

He scrawled his initial and sprinkled sand over the note, rang for a footman to deliver them both, and went through to the parlour.

'I think you should call on Mrs Cole, my dear,' he said to his wife. 'Warehouse or no warehouse, I think she would reward an acquaintance. And certainly, I shall be happy to do business with her husband.'

Chapter Seven

'We have to rise,' Josiah said to Sarah, Stephen Waring's note in his hand. 'We have to move in the circles where capital is available. The little men are growing wary of risk and the bigger men want only large investments. You are right, the Trade is in a temporary decline. It will boom again – we have seen it come and go – and we have to ride out these doldrums. There are great chances in this city if we can but grasp them. We have to move in the circles of those that know.'

Sarah was pale with anxiety. 'We had only three partners for *Rose*,' she said. 'And she will not be home until late next year. *Daisy* will not be in until this December. We cannot over-extend ourselves, Josiah. Mr Waring's price is far too high for that house. We are carrying too great a risk on the *Rose*, and too much of our capital is tied up in her. We cannot buy a new house as well.'

'Then we must borrow,' Josiah said determinedly. 'Another house might not come vacant for months, even years. You know how sought-after that address is, Sarah. I have been waiting for a house for nearly a year. We have to buy it now, we dare not wait. We have to borrow.'

Sarah shook her head. She feared debt more than anything in the world. 'Is there nothing left from her dowry?' She nodded to the room above the parlour where Frances was lying down, sick with a headache, her curtains drawn against the noise of the streets near her window and the smell from the middens in the backyards.

'No, it was all invested in *Daisy*.'

'Please God that she comes in safe with them and we see a profit.'

Josiah bowed his head. 'Please God,' he said.

The Vessle Daisy,
at St Kitts.

15th August 1788

Dear Mr Cole,

I send this Letter to you by the Bristol ship Adventure which is leaving Port tomorrow, to Announce that I have arrived Safely in St Kitts, Praise God.

Tomorrow I shall arrange for the Sale of the majority of the Slaves who are generally Good in health and Well in appearance. Prices seem to be Lower than at my Last Visit but you can be Assured I shall do my Best.

According to your Instruction I have reserved Twenty slaves for your use. Three men, Five women, Four infants, Four girls and Four boys. I will bring them Home as you Instructed and will indeed take Care that they have Blankets as they may be Weakened by Cold.

I will Seek other Cargo tomorrow but I Fear we may be Disappointed this Late in the Season. Be Assured however That I will do my best as Per your Instructions.

With God's Will I shall Complete my business here within the Month and set sail for Bristol as Soon as may be Possible. I hope to convey my respects to you in person in the month of December 1788.

Your obdt servant,

Capt. William Lisle.

Josiah placed the letter before Sarah. She threw her needle-work to one side and snatched it up.

'Where did you have this?'

'From the master of the *Adventurer*. He had a good crossing. The letter is dated August, it has taken him only six weeks to get home. He does not speak well of the trade in St Kitts.'

'What does it say about the slaves?' Sarah scanned the letter quickly and then looked up. 'Twenty,' she said. 'And as I ordered, children, and he has even brought infants.'

'Infants?' Frances was at the table, making entries into the household ledger. A pile of bills was under a paperweight, and she was ticking them off as she entered the petty sums.

'If I could have bought babes in arms I would have done,' Sarah declared. 'They are bound to learn the quickest, and you have the more work from them.'

'Oh,' Frances said. 'When will they arrive?'

'January at the latest,' Josiah replied. 'It takes more than a month to load the ship in the West Indies, and then he will have to come home through the autumn storms. Please God they will make safe landfall by Christmas.'

'We will be in the new house by then,' Frances said. The end of the summer had brought an end to the dreadful smell of the dock and the continual fear of cholera and typhoid in the old town; but autumn wind and rain meant that Frances was confined even more to the little parlour. She suffered painful claustrophobia from the small rooms and low ceilings of the little house. It would never be anything more than a warehouse with rooms tacked on the side; the fireplaces were inadequate and the constant smoke made Frances cough and cough. The rainy weather made driving a rare pleasure, and she could not walk out among the dockside workers. She spent every day in the cramped parlour with Sarah, unless she chose to sit alone in her unheated bedroom. Nobody called at the little house on the quayside. No-one invited them to any parties. Nothing would breach the Coles' loneliness and isolation until they moved into Queens Square. 'Surely we should be in the new house by then!'

Josiah glanced at her. 'I am sorry for this delay,' he said. 'It is all the fault of Mr Waring. I have paid the deposit we agreed but his builder is taking longer than he promised and Mr Waring's new house is not yet ready. He has been delayed by the weather. We are all waiting on each other.'

'We would have been hard pressed to pay the whole in any

case,' Sarah pointed out. 'If we do not move until after *Daisy* comes in, we will have her profits to go towards the final payment.'

'Another two or three months!' Frances exclaimed involuntarily.

Sarah looked at her sharply. 'This house was a palace to my mother. I have always been proud to live here.'

Frances bit her lip. In the four months of her marriage she had learned that Sarah was defensive about their home. 'I did not mean to be impolite,' she said carefully. 'But I should like to be able to walk out of doors, and the noise from the quay is very disturbing. We will have no society until we move.' She glanced at Josiah. 'It was part of the agreement,' she reminded them. 'When Josiah first wrote to me, he promised that we would live in Queens Square.'

'She is right,' Josiah said fairly. 'And Queens Square is our side of the bargain. We will move as soon as we can and, if need be, I can find the money, with or without the *Daisy*.'

'You mean borrowing,' Sarah snapped.

'I mean forward selling,' Josiah said steadily. 'I can sell *Daisy*'s cargo while she is still at sea and complete the payment for the Queens Square house with the money.'

'It is a risk,' Sarah said. She glanced at Frances, hoping for support. 'If the ship sinks then we have to carry the loss and repay the buyers of the cargo. I am sure Frances would not want us to take such a risk just for her benefit.'

Frances gave Josiah a demure smile. 'If you think it is worth the risk, Husband, then I must follow your judgement. And if it ensures that we get the house . . .'

'Very wifely,' Sarah commented acidly.

'As soon as Mr Waring is ready to leave I will complete the sale and we shall move to Queens Square,' Josiah declared, closing the subject. 'But I am glad to have heard that Captain Lisle is well. The *Daisy* always was a lucky ship. God speed to her as she sets sail!'

*   *   *

When the *Daisy* was ready to leave, the little shelter that they had made on her deck was dismantled, and the slaves returned to the hold. Mehuru was not strong enough to stand, he lay on the dirty straw and watched the others hold out their hands for manacles and their feet for leg-irons.

The sun shimmered on the blue water, the quayside of St Kitts wavered before his dazed eyes. The dark green terraced hills melted slowly into the low beautiful grasslands of his home. Mehuru thought that soon his body would release its tenacious grip on life. Soon the pain would be over. Soon he would be home. If the gods were kind to him, if his ancestors sought his soul, he would be home and lying on the breast of the kindly fertile earth of Africa once more.

The captain, watching them as they were chained and sent below, noticed for the first time that Mehuru's skin and muscles were wasting away.

'What the devil is ailing him?' he demanded. 'Is he sick?'

They watched him when the food came and saw that he lay, his face turned away. Then they came and bolted an iron mask around his head with a funnel going into his mouth. Twice a day they poured scalding soup down his throat. The first day Mehuru felt nothing, he was floating and gliding down the sweet river of his home. But that night he was tortured with pain as his shrunken stomach griped on the food. Next day he felt the spiteful heat of the soup, burning his throat and his mouth. The third day he fought them, but they got it down despite his struggles. The fourth day they took the mask off and he knew he was hungry. He came back from his journey into darkness and he heard Snake's voice counselling patience and wisdom. He knew himself to be wiser for having risked everything. He tried to find within himself some power as a survivor, as a living ghost, since all his power as a man, even as a human being, had been stolen from him.

The ship set sail. Mehuru felt himself rolling on his shelf again and wondered if he was to spend the rest of his life in half-darkness with the wash of waves pouring through the grating, longing for his home and forever in exile. He would not fast again, he could not bear the grip of the white men and the sharp evil pain as the boiling soup threatened to drown him. Instead he ate his share of the common pot of food.

It grew bitter, colder than any weather Mehuru had known before. When they were ordered on deck to dance Mehuru could not recognise the sea, could not recognise the sun. The waters were a deep sullen grey, the wind had a smell behind it which was icy cold. He could not comprehend where the sun had gone, it seemed to be walking farther and farther away and it was losing its heat and strength. Every day it grew smaller and paler. Mehuru thought that the ship was sailing into permanent night. When the shadow of the grating moved across the floor of the hold the squares of sunlight were insipid and pale. Through the grille he could see the sky veiled, slurred with clouds. He had never seen a sky so thick. Even in the rainy season at home the storm clouds would suddenly part and the sun would burn through. He and one of the other men lay close together for warmth. Mehuru missed the others who had gone. They seemed very few in the echoing hold, and they were fearful and could not comfort each other.

One of the infants became sick. They thought she was dying of the cold. Mehuru saw that as the sun sickened and grew weaker the child sickened too. There was nothing they could do for her. She cried a little, very pitifully, and then died while a woman held her and rocked her. When Mehuru brought the little body up on deck for burial they took her roughly from him and tossed her over the side. Her arms and legs flew up as she went over and Mehuru had a heart-stopping moment when he thought she cried out. But the ship plunged down into the deep grey waves and her little black head bobbing in the water was hidden from him.

Days stretched beyond counting, weeks, and then months. They took the flux – dysentery – and one of the men died and another of the infants. The weather was too stormy for them to dance on deck, and besides they were all growing weaker. Mehuru wondered if they would sail on and on until they were all dead. When they were called up to empty the waste pail, two of the boys slipped through the nets hung around the rigging to keep them on board and flung themselves into the sea. Mehuru felt shame at their loss. He should have given them hope, he should have given them a reason to live. But there was no hope and there was no reason to live.

The bucket of food grew more and more stale but it did not rot. Unbelievably it was too cold for that to happen. Then in the night Mehuru felt the rhythm of the heaving ship steady and change. He heard the yell of the men dropping the sails. There was a long time of rocking gently as if they were anchored, and then a new jerky movement as the ship was taken into tow.

Mehuru waited in the darkness of the hold, listening for any clues which might tell him what was happening on deck. Once again he heard the urgency of the ship nearing port and the growing noise of a quayside. The others woke, the women clutching each other in fear, the children whimpering. There was a foul sour smell of dirt, like an old midden. It penetrated even to the fetid hold of the slave ship. There was a dreadful noise of people shouting, and a screech of machinery working. Mehuru gathered his blanket around his shoulders and trembled a little with cold and fear. Then the grating was lifted off, they were ordered on deck, and they climbed out unsteadily and stood, shivering in the cold, looking around them.

They could see little for it was not yet dawn and there were only a few lanterns lashed to the rigging and to the side of the ship. A chain was passed along their line, linking one neck collar with another, and they were ordered to walk down a ridged bridge of wood to the quayside. Mehuru, his insteps flinching from the cold hard cobbles, touched ground for the first time in six months. He had never felt freezing stone before, he could not believe the ache of coldness in the high arched bones of his feet. They whipped him and the others with light biting blows on his shoulders and his back, and they shouted at him, as men shout when they herd cattle. The cold air in his face and the cold hardness beneath his feet told Mehuru that he had arrived into some dreadful exile in the land where all the men were dead men; and Snake alone knew what they wanted of him.

Mehuru breathed deep, three, four times, of the icy dirty air, and tried to hold down his panic. Before him was a high building with no lights showing and arched doorways like gaping mouths leading to storerooms. A small door at the side of the building opened at their approach and they were ordered into a hallway, through another door into a kitchen. The warmth and the smell of cooking gave him a sharp pang of homesickness, but then a blow on his back forced him forward and they were through the kitchen before he had time to look around.

At the far end of the kitchen there was a stout wooden door standing open and four steps cut downward into rock. Mehuru and the others stumbled down, their chains jerking at each other's necks as they were pushed roughly into line around the walls of the room. It was part cellar, part cave. Mehuru saw a couple of old barrels of wine, and a rack which had once held bottles. Hammered into the soft red sandstone of the walls were new iron rings to hold their neck chains, and anchor points for their shackles. A new man, a stranger, whose clothes smelled of the land and not of the sea, came along the line, bolting each of them against the wall, and kicking clean straw around their cold feet. He took up the lantern and surveyed them carefully, like a good groom checks a stable before he leaves it for the night, and then he walked from the cave, taking the lantern with him. They heard the door at the head of the steps slam on the light and warmth of the kitchen, and they were left alone, buried alive in the damp cave, in the dark.

Then Snake spoke softly to Mehuru, and said one word to him:

'*Despair.*'

Frances learned that the *Daisy* had docked at dawn when Sarah sent a message with her breakfast tray asking her to come to the parlour as soon as she was dressed. The long anxious wait for the ship was over, and Frances's work was about to start. She dressed in a plain grey gown and wore her plainest cap, but she did not resent the slide back into governess work. The winter days in the little house on the quayside were very long, it was dark by four o'clock and too cold to drive out. The sides of the dock were lined with ice every morning and the smoke from the glass furnaces hung like a fog over the house. There was no birdsong, only the cry of seagulls, and only the frozen cold cobbles of the quay to watch. There were none of the amusements that Lady Scott and the Whiteleaze ladies took for granted, no walks in the winter shrubbery, no afternoons in the glasshouses.

Frances could remember an annual competition with her father to see the first snowdrops in the hedge at the bottom of the rectory garden. She could hardly bear a winter with no prospect of flowers, nor trees coming slowly into bud. She had read more novels than she could remember, she had sketched the view from the parlour window a dozen times: the shelf of the Coles' quay in the foreground, the gibbet profile of the Merchant Venturers' crane on the opposite side of the dirty river, the forest of masts, and the blank square face of the warehouse opposite. She had completed more darning and hemming than she would have believed necessary; and still there were hours to fill in every day.

The move to Queens Square would have diverted her, but Mr Waring still had not vacated the house. To Josiah's mounting anger he found that he had agreed to a high price for a house in a square where other properties were now coming on the market, and he was not even in possession of it.

Frances straightened her cap and went down the stairs to the parlour. Brother and sister were waiting for her.

'*Daisy* has docked with a good cargo of sugar and rum and the first consignment of your slaves,' Josiah beamed at her. 'I have a list here of them.'

'*My* slaves!' Frances exclaimed.

'They were bought with your dowry and will be trained and named by you,' Josiah said. 'They should certainly be your slaves and indeed, my dear, Sarah is right in thinking that they will command a better price if they are known to be your own.'

'We hoped to have twenty,' Sarah said. 'The losses have been very bad, I shall have words to say to Captain Lisle. He has delivered only thirteen.'

Josiah handed her the list. Frances read:

> '*Two healthy men*
> *Four healthy women*
> *Two boys aged seven and sixteen years*
> *Three girls aged between seven and fourteen years*
> *Two infant boys aged two and five years.'*

'I did not expect them all to survive,' Josiah said. 'Remember, Sarah, that although we lose twenty in a hundred crossing the Atlantic, another twenty-five in a hundred die in the first year on the plantations. We must prepare ourselves to lose even more during the first year here.'

'Still, it is an excellent mix,' Sarah said. 'I particularly wanted young children. They are easier to train and the fashion is for very young black pages.' Her eyes were shining, she was smiling. Frances had never seen her look so animated.

'How long will it take you to teach them to speak English?' Josiah asked Frances. 'They know none as yet. But that is all to the good, isn't it? They will have no rough accents, they have not learned the patois of the Islands. They will speak pure English if they are so taught, won't they?'

Frances laughed, catching their enthusiasm. 'I believe so. But I know nothing about niggers. And whether they can learn quickly or slowly I will not know until I have seen them. Where are they now?'

'The ship docked in the night and I had them unloaded and stored in the cellar,' Josiah said. 'I had it cleared out and some straw put down on the floor. I thought it best that they be kept there until they are trained to stay in the house without chains. It is safe, there is only one stout door that leads into the kitchen. Will you teach them here, in the parlour?'

'Yes,' Frances said. She looked around the room. 'But there are too many of them. I cannot teach them all at once. I will have just six for my first lesson and then the others in the afternoon.'

Sarah looked displeased. 'Speed is essential,' she said. 'The sooner they are trained the sooner they can be sold.'

'I have to have some time to get used to them,' Frances said.

'She is right,' Josiah agreed kindly. 'She needs to become accustomed. I have taken on a good man, my dear, who has handled slaves on the Sugar Islands. He is an experienced driver. His name is John Bates and he will feed them and clean them, and muck them out and beat them for you.'

'We can go and look at them now,' Sarah said eagerly. She was animated, her pale cheeks had two spots of red.

Josiah smiled. 'I saw them when they were unloaded, so I shall leave you to inspect them on your own. I have to go to my work, but I look forward to hearing your progress this evening.' He nodded to Sarah but he took Frances's hand and bowed low over it. 'If you can accomplish this I will be obliged to you,' he said formally. 'Our fortune depends on it.'

Frances shifted uneasily. 'I will do my best, Josiah,' she promised.

'I ask nothing more,' he said, and left the room.

Frances stood by the window and looked down, watching

Josiah's dark three-cornered hat moving among the labourers on the dockside unloading the *Daisy*.

'What a long way they have come,' she said. 'And what a terrifying voyage it must have been. All the way from Africa to the West Indies, and then all the way to England, in rough seas and sometimes becalmed, in heat and in cold weather. How frightened they must have been.'

'Oh, I doubt it,' Sarah Cole said. 'They do not feel as we feel, you know. And they do not understand things as we do. Even now they probably do not realise that they are far from home, and never going home again.'

Chapter Eight

Cook was standing by the kitchen table in offended silence. Brown was washing the second-best china dishes at the sink. She turned when Sarah and Frances came in and dipped a curtsey. The scullery maid backed away, her head down, wiping her dirty hands on her hessian apron.

Miss Cole nodded at them and led the way past the table to the massive door in the wall, bolted top and bottom and secured with a lock. Hanging by the door was a heavy key on a ring. Sarah lifted it down and turned it in the lock. Then she slid back the bolts.

'Have they been fed?' she asked. It was as if she were enquiring about the welfare of carriage horses.

'Yes, Miss Cole.' The kitchen maid bobbed. 'And Bates has taken out the slop pail.'

Miss Cole nodded and beckoned Frances to follow her. Frances went towards the doorway and then hesitated. Ahead was a narrow passage-like cave, carved from the dark red sandstone of the cliff, illuminated by the horn lantern which Sarah hung high on a peg hammered into the soft stone.

At its highest the roof of the tunnel was only about six feet; Frances could see the scrape marks of the picks and shovels where the cellar had been hollowed out from the cliff. The floor was bumpy, rutted in parts by the rolling of barrels of sugar and wine. A heavy acrid smell wafted towards her. A smell of old long-stored wine, and a new smell of men and women left for months in their own dirt, a smell of degradation and despair. She recoiled but Miss Cole took hold of her arm and drew her forward.

'This is where the money comes from to buy your embroidered morning dresses,' she said sharply. 'Money has to be earned in this world. This is how we earn ours. It's a good trade and an honest trade.'

'It was just the smell . . .'

'The ships smell worse than this and we send our sailors out in them. The lead works poison their workers and yet your uncle buys their shot. You have been hidden from the real things, the dirty things, Sister. But now you are the wife of a man who makes his living by the sweat of his brow, whose hands are dirty at the end of the day. And I am proud of it. I don't want to be a lady who knows nothing of the real world. I am ready to earn my daily bread.'

Sarah's face was exalted in the flickering light. Frances pulled her arm away. 'I am ready to play my part,' she said with simple dignity. 'I have taken a share in the prosperity of this family. I am ready to work, Sarah, and I was never a lady of leisure. You need not lecture me.'

'Good,' Sarah said briefly, and led the way, sure-footed down the familiar passage. As Frances followed, the smell of sweat and grief and infection grew stronger.

'There!' Sarah said avidly. 'Look at them! And in good condition too! I shall pay Captain Lisle a bonus!'

Frances blinked, trying to accustom her eyes to the darkness. The tunnel had widened into a circular cave, lined with silent people. She could dimly make out the gleam of the candlelight on shining eyes and there was a soft chink of a chain as someone moved. She had a sense of a mute crowd, filling the small cellar. They were chained like dogs to each other, and to rings in the walls. Each man, each woman, each child had a light iron collar bolted around their necks and above this shackle their faces were dulled with pain, weary with hopeless grief. She could see stains of pus on the collars where the blisters had gone septic, and bloodstains where they had worn their necks raw.

One ring on the neck collar held the chains for the manacles on the hands, another ring held the chain which roped them together in pairs, the links passing from behind their heads up to bolts on the walls. Their feet were in heavy leg-irons locked to the floor. The place smelled of excrement and the sweet sickliness of diseased flesh. Frances clamped a hand over her mouth to hold back the nausea and above it her face was white as a cave-fish in the gloom, her eyes as black as theirs.

None of them looked at her. None of them cared enough to look at her. Those whose eyes were open stared blankly at the space before them, or looked down at their feet, skin puckered from standing barefoot in the mulchy straw. Mostly they were sitting on the stone bench cut out of the wall of the cave, leaning against the wall, their heads tipped back against the damp stone with their eyes tight shut.

Frances found her breath and whispered: 'My God!'

Miss Cole looked at her pale face. 'What is it?'

'I did not know,' Frances said. She looked around the cellar at the thirteen black faces still as heartbroken statues in the shadows. The cruelty of the Trade suddenly opened before her, like a glimpse of hell beneath her feet. 'I did not know,' she said.

Miss Cole nodded briskly as if that confirmed her poor opinion of Frances. 'Well now you do,' she said, and turned to go up the steps again.

Frances started to follow her, but then she froze. She had a strange feeling of being observed. She felt it so strongly it was as if someone had put a warm hand on the nape of her neck. She spun around, forgetting the roughness of the floor, and had to put her hand on the damp wall to steady herself.

One of the slaves was looking at her. His skin was black, as dark as the skin of a ripe grape, his nose flared, his mouth a sculptured perfection. His cheeks were scarred with curious blue lines drawn in intricate patterns on his cheekbones. The same pattern was etched like a headband around his forehead.

106

He had been standing with his head thrown back against the wall, the blank look of all the captives in his eyes. But something about her had drawn his attention, and his head had come up, the chain attached to the collar around his neck chinked. His eyes met hers.

He looked at her as if he knew her. She felt a jolt – as tangible as a light slap in the face. She had a strange falling sensation as if she were about to faint. The moment seemed to last for a long long time as she stared at him and he looked back at her.

'Come along, Frances.' Miss Cole's voice was spinster-sharp.

Frances did not move. She stared at the man. He stared impassively at her.

Miss Cole came back a few steps to see what had attracted Frances's attention. 'Oh, you are looking at his tattoos, are you?' she said. 'Grotesque, isn't it? And pagan. One of our captains told me that the ones who wear those tattoos are the wizards and priests of their pagan beliefs. He would have talked with the spirits and foretold the future.' She laughed one of her rare laughs. 'He couldn't have been a very good fortune-teller!'

Frances looked at him. His face was still impassive.

'Do they not understand English at all?' she asked.

'They'll have to learn,' Miss Cole said, holding open the door at the end of the passage. Frances turned unwillingly and walked away from the man. 'The whip is all the language they know now.'

Frances paused at the doorway and looked back at him. She longed to touch him, just lightly, a soft touch with her fingertip on the inside of his wrist where his black skin was soft.

He turned his head to watch her go, until all he could see was the hem of her grey gown and the shadow of the closing door.

The door at the head of the passage closed abruptly,

shutting out the daylight and the sound of voices. The slaves were left in darkness.

Mehuru leaned his head back against the damp wall again and closed his eyes.

He did not despair. The Snake's counsel was ambiguous, not always to be obeyed. Like all gods he teased with false knowledge. Mehuru kept his mind turned inward and waited for the earth under his feet to stop rocking. One of the women was crying but the children were shocked and silent. They looked to Mehuru to advise them, to speculate about what would happen next. The smallest of the children was not yet three and he watched Mehuru's face with the large trusting eyes of a baby. Mehuru shook his head and looked away from the child. He did not know what would happen. He could be of no comfort to anyone.

In a little while the door opened again and the man brought them loaves of strange-tasting bread, slices of cooked meat that tasted like old dry beef, and some hard good fruit with a green skin and white sweet flesh. There was clean sour-tasting water to drink in a pan.

After a short time the man came back and made them stand, and prepared them to walk in a line. Mehuru did not look for a chance to escape. He realised he was defeated. He did not know where he was, he had never even heard of a place where the air itself was cold and grey and smelled of smoke and dirt. He could not run when he did not know where he should go. So he followed like one of the children in his pitiful obedience. The man had two pistols stuck into his belt and a long thick horsewhip in his hand, they had no chance against him. They lined up like herded cattle, and did as they were bid, straggling along the tunnel and up the four shallow steps into the warmth and poignant normality of the kitchen.

They were not allowed to linger. There was a lad waiting for them who steered them out of the kitchen door into the backyard. Mehuru was so afraid that they were going back to the ship and on another long dreadful journey that he did not look around him at first but watched his bare cold feet creeping slavishly on the cold cobbles; a man no longer, but a trained animal.

'Get on, you!' the man said gruffly, and tugged at Mehuru's chain. They were in a cobbled yard surrounded by high red-brick walls. Ahead of them and on each side were the glowering bulks of the warehouses with barred small windows. Mehuru gazed up and up the grim facade. He had seen stone buildings before, the city of Oyo had higher walls and greater buildings than this, but he had never seen such functional ugliness before. The blank redness of the walls held his eyes. He was afraid the stones had been coloured with blood.

The man shouted at him and Mehuru was pulled forward to the pump in the centre of the yard. The lad worked the pump until the water gushed out into a bucket and the big man threw buckets of water at their heads and mimed to them that they should wash themselves with a block of soap. The water was icy and tasted bitter. The soap stank of ashes from old fires and the fat of pigs. Mehuru shivered miserably and hastened to do as he was ordered.

Two of the women seemed paralysed with fear; they were certain they were being washed for the white men to eat them. They thought they would be safer if they remained dirty. They held tight to their loincloths and ducked away from the buckets of water. In the end the lad poked them with a pitchfork and laughed as they flinched between the icy water and the sharp prongs. He licked his lips at them and the slave driver guffawed when he saw how they looked to the manacled men for help. The two men looked back at them in passive misery, wishing they were blind.

One by one they washed and then rubbed themselves dry on the same rough cloth. Then the back door of the house opened and the scullery maid brought out clothes for them, tittering at their naked discomfort. The lad, tiring of the jest, pulled the clothes on one of the boys and left the rest to guess how the breeches should fit. The women kept their hands spread over their genitals, their dark faces blushed even blacker with shame. The lad grinned and slid a curious finger between one of the women's clenched buttocks.

Mehuru spoke softly to her and she disengaged herself with a slow speechless dignity. The lad glanced at Mehuru, his eyes drawn to the blue tattoos on his forehead and cheeks.

'What you staring at?' he asked aggressively, gesturing with the pitchfork. 'What you looking at, you beast, you?'

'Is it now?' Mehuru asked Snake curiously, in the quietest corner of his mind. 'Will he spear me and kill me now?'

Snake kept his silence.

Mehuru dropped his eyes to the ground and the lad put the pitchfork down, oddly dissatisfied. 'I hate them,' he said to the driver. 'Let's get them out of the yard and back into the cellar.'

John Bates shook his head. 'They're to go upstairs,' he said. 'The new mistress is teaching them to talk English, if she can. Then they go into service.'

The lad looked at them. 'They can talk?' he asked incredulously. He stepped closer to Mehuru. 'Can you talk?' he shouted into his face.

Mehuru flinched at the spittle. He had no idea at all what the young man was shouting at him. The young man stuck his tongue out at Mehuru.

'Got a tongue?' he shouted. 'Can you speak to me?'

A sigh of pure terror went through the others at the sight of that startlingly red tongue poking out from the obscene pink lips.

'Gently,' Mehuru said to the others in his own language. 'Be still.'

'He made a noise!' the lad said, delighted. 'Say some more, Animal! Say something more!'

Mehuru looked down into the face of the young man. The scaly grey-green eyes looked up at him curiously. The ghostly dreadful skin was speckled with spots of brown as if the youth had some strange sickness.

110

'Come on,' said John Bates the slave driver, weary of the lad's interest. 'You must have seen enough niggers before.'

'Not straight from Africa I haven't,' the lad replied. 'I've seen them when they're tame, from the Sugar Islands. I've never seen them straight from Africa. They eat each other, don't they?'

'They wouldn't eat you,' Bates said. 'Too smelly by half. Come on now, let's get them in.'

They split them into two groups by pushing them into place and prodding them with the pitchfork. One group they left chained in the yard but Mehuru, two women, two little boys and one youth they chained and led towards the kitchen door. Mehuru turned back to the other group, shivering in the coldness of the wind.

'The gods be with you,' he said.

The other man looked after him. 'May we meet again, in a better place,' he said.

They shuffled into the kitchen, stooping to accommodate the weight and cutting edges of the neck-irons. Mehuru looked more vulnerable in the ill-fitting breeches and shirt than in his own loincloth. It had not been thought worth while to buy them shoes so the new breeches ended just below the knee and he was barefoot. The women were wearing cheap gowns which reached their ankles.

Frances and Miss Cole were waiting for them in the hall. When Frances saw them she drew a quick breath of surprise. Close at hand she was struck at once by the tiny frailty of the little children. Their smocks and breeches were far too large for them, their little black necks were coldly exposed by the broad scoop of the collars. The smallest boy was about two, she thought, and the one who stood beside him and watched her with enormous black eyes was no more than five. They both looked at her solemnly, unwaveringly, with the open faces of children whose experiences of cruelty and loss have not yet wiped out the early memory of love. They were still capable of hope.

111

'They don't smell so bad now, ma'am,' John Bates said loudly. 'Will you have them in the parlour?'

'Yes, take them upstairs,' Miss Cole said. 'Are they safe?'

'Quiet as dead rats,' John Bates assured her cheerfully.

'We'll keep them chained for the first lesson,' Miss Cole decided nervously. She walked down the line as they stood, their eyes fixed on the ground. They trembled slightly as the ghostly woman went by.

'Come along then,' she said, and turned for the staircase to the upper floor. John prodded the woman at the head of the chain, and they followed her, their lips compressed tight so they did not cry out in their terror. Only the widening of their eyes revealed that they were afraid, and the slight sheen of sweat on their faces.

Frances watched each one as they went past her. The two women looked as if they had suffered the most. Their skin was lighter and they clung together; both were scarred on the back, and one had an unhealed cut on her cheekbone. They were followed by one awkward ungainly youth who tried to keep a courteous distance from them but was dragged forward by the shortness of the chain. Frances made herself look away and stepped back to let the line go by her. She did not look up again, not even when she heard the thud of someone struck with the butt end of a whip.

'He was lagging, ma'am,' Bates explained cheerfully.

Miss Cole led them up the narrow stairs to the little parlour. When the line walked into the room they hesitated, and did not know what to do. Miss Cole pulled out a chair but then could not bring herself to touch the leading woman to guide her to her seat.

'Bates,' she said shortly. He put a broad red hand on the woman's shoulder and thrust her into a seat. Then the other woman and the youth perched on the very edge of the hard chairs and looked at Miss Cole and Frances with eyes which were blank with terror. The little boys had to be lifted up on their chairs. John Bates stepped back from the table and set himself with his back against the door, two pistols stuck in his belt, and his whip held across him.

'Sit at the head of the table, Frances, and start their lesson,' Miss Cole ordered.

Mehuru kept his head down, but he noted the tone of command, and he saw that the young white woman obeyed.

Her looks were horrible. She was as smooth and as pale as polished ivory. But the worst thing about her was her hair, which was as long and as thick as weeds in the river and was piled upon her head with trails of it coming down around her shoulders and curling like water weed around her face. Unpinned it must stretch down to her buttocks like some dreadful smooth cloth. Her eyes were as dark as his own but she moved like one of them, with small steps and a hunched body as if she hated herself, as if she were trying to hide her breasts and her belly.

She was bony and small, like an ugly child. He scanned her body and saw the uselessness of her narrow pelvis and the skinny buttocks. She was too thin, a man could not embrace her and roll her over and over on the ground. She would not seize a lover and take him with laughter. She would not shout joyfully at the approach of pleasure. He thought of his woman at home and how he would thrust his shoulder against her open mouth to muffle her singing cries when she opened her legs wide to him. This ghostwoman knew nothing of this, could learn nothing of this. She moved as if she had denied herself of pleasure for many years, as if she had never known lust, as if she had never known desire. She held herself like a criminal, not like a woman at all.

Mehuru suddenly realised that she was looking at him, and feared that his thoughts were showing on his face. He flushed quickly and looked away from her.

Chapter Nine

Frances drew a breath. She seated herself gingerly in the chair at the head of the table. Sarah went to the windowseat and gazed avidly at them all. 'Go on,' she said impatiently. 'Teach them something!'

The noises from outside the window were very loud. Josiah was auctioning his sugar on the quayside, Frances could hear his excited shout as the bids went higher.

'Go on,' Sarah said.

Frances looked down the table. The children were whimpering softly, each stretching out for the woman seated beside him. Only Mehuru was looking at her, with his strange judging gaze. As their eyes met he slightly inclined his head. It was as if he had given her some permission. She felt an unexpected sense of humility before him. She looked at him more closely. His forehead was lined with raised tattoos showing dark blue against his black skin. Around his mouth there were half a dozen blue circles that drew the gaze to the wide sensuality of his lips. His eyes were dark and unfathomable. His nose was broad and flat. His skin was perfectly black and smooth. Frances wanted to touch him, to feel that he was real.

She dragged her eyes from his face and tapped the table with the flat of her hand. 'Table,' she said quietly.

They looked at her in silence. They were all of them frozen with fear.

She slapped the table again. 'Table,' she repeated more firmly.

114

Miss Cole glared irritably at her across the bowed black heads. 'They clearly don't know what you mean,' she said. 'You must make them speak.'

Frances drew a breath and paused. She did not know what to do.

'Begging your pardon, ma'am, *he* can speak.' John Bates pointed with the butt end of his whip at Mehuru. 'Spoke in the yard when the lad asked him to make a noise. Him with the drawings on his face.'

Frances looked at Mehuru. 'Say: table,' she said, without much hope. 'Tay-bull.'

'Day-bull,' Mehuru said.

Frances jumped. He had a pleasant confident voice, the voice of a man who is accustomed to being heard. She was as surprised as if the table itself had said its name to her. She had not expected him to speak – she had not expected him to have this strong clear baritone.

'Yes,' she nodded.

'Make the others say it!' Miss Cole came forward from the windowseat, her flat breasts heaving with excitement. 'Make them say it too! Make them all say it!'

'Now you.' Frances pointed to the woman seated at the foot of the table. She slapped the wood and looked at her. 'Table,' she said.

With the tip of his fingers the young boy pattered out a message on the table top in the ancient language of drumming. 'What?' the rhythm asked urgently. 'What?'

'Speak,' Mehuru tapped back. He glanced round the table and nodded at the frightened faces. 'Speak,' his fingers tapped again. It was not the warm-skinned talking drums of home which could send messages for miles and miles across country, but it was still a little power, a little secret they had left.

'Stop that!' Miss Cole snapped with instant anger. 'Make the next one speak.'

Frances pointed at the woman again, and slapped the table

115

with her hand. Her palm made a sharp unkind sound after Mehuru's seductive drumming. 'Table,' she said.

'Day-bull,' the woman replied in a voice as low as a whisper.

'Yes!' Miss Cole's shrill excitement frightened them all. They shot scared looks at Mehuru, who had his eyes fixed on the wooden shiny surface.

'Make them all say it!' Miss Cole commanded. She was standing at the foot of the table, her sallow cheeks burning with two pink spots. 'Make them speak!' she cried.

'Table,' Frances said. 'T . . . t . . . table.'

'Day-bull,' they repeated.

Mehuru was watching Frances though she did not know it. His eyes were still turned down to the table top, and he was watching the inverted reflection of her pale face in the polished surface.

'Day-bull,' he said with the rest; but in his head he called for Snake.

Snake would know who this ghostwoman was and what she wanted with them. He called for Snake and begged him for sight. As if from a distance, Snake chuckled in his long throat and said: '*Sight is easy*'. Then Mehuru saw this woman with her hair in a thick plait lying in a high bed with a great many white covers. She was lying on her back and her face was wet with tears. Mehuru sensed her coldness and her loneliness. He thought that he had never in his life known a woman with so much power – power over him and all these others – and yet such passivity that she should lie like a stone and grieve for nothing.

She was defeated and fearful, a woman who had thrown away her power. She was a fool who had chosen to know nothing. She had closed her eyes to her own feelings. She had denied her own nature. All she had left was the cold shell of her body and – weep-weep-weep – a constant flow of tears. The light in the room and the covers on the bed were very cold and white. Mehuru knew it was this land, but not, he thought, exactly this time. Snake hissed a laugh in his head

116

and said: '*What does time or place matter to you? You who are imprisoned in the here and now?*'

'Day-bull,' Mehuru repeated with the others. Day-bull? What did she mean, day-bull? Did she mean wood, or the sort of wood it was? Did she mean the polish which made the wood shine? Did she mean the name of the woodcarver? Or the god of woodcarvers? Did she mean the feel of the wood under her palm, or the noise it made when she slapped it so?

Frances looked down the table and saw Mehuru frown even as he repeated the word. She suddenly flushed with her sense of helplessness. If she could not teach them to speak then the experiment would be abandoned and they would be sent to the plantations. No-one lived long working on the sugar crop. A quarter of them would die before their first year was out, half of the rest would not live more than four years.

That was why the slavers went crossing and re-crossing the wide reaches of the Atlantic seas, pouring men and women and children into the plantations which ate them up as surely as they crushed sugar cane. They worked so hard, they lived so poor, that they could not even breed to replace the dead. Children died before they could reach adulthood. Women died before they could give birth. Men died before they could lie with a woman and give her a child. Every month, every week, every day, new slaves had to be captured and shipped and sold. Without them the plantations would collapse and the English people would have no sugar, tobacco, cotton or rum.

Frances had spent her life among events which never rose above the trivial. Now suddenly, she was responsible for the survival of thirteen people, and one of them a man who sat as if he were wrapped in a cloak of magic. She turned quickly to the sideboard.

'Glasses,' she said, showing them two wine glasses.

'Classes,' they repeated.

'Knives, forks, spoons,' she said, laying them down on the table.

117

They babbled the words in panic, she had gone too fast. One of the little children started to cry. Miss Cole was still standing at the foot of the table, her colour high, her breath coming quickly.

'That one,' she said abruptly, pointing to Mehuru. 'The man with the marks on his face. He understands the most, he is watching.'

The meaningless repetition of words died away into silence. 'Find out his name,' she demanded. 'You can teach him, then he can explain to the others in their own tongue.'

Frances turned towards Mehuru. She could smell his fear like smoke.

She put her hand on the base of her throat.

'Frances,' she said. 'Frances.'

Then she pointed at him. Mehuru gulped.

'France-sess,' he repeated. He felt as if he had a thrashing animal trapped in his brain. What did she mean now, France-sess? Was that the word for woman? Or for throat? Was it the word for thirst? Or for the scared thumping of his heart which he felt as he put his hand there, mirroring her action?

'Not you! You fool! Her!' Miss Cole said irritably, watching him gesture to himself and say 'Frances'. His dark eyes snapped towards her as if he were waiting for an attack but did not know which woman would spring first.

'I am Frances,' the young one said quickly. She pointed to the older woman. 'Miss Cole.' Mehuru noted the dislike in her voice. She pointed at the white man with the whip who had thrown water over them and laughed when the woman was assaulted. 'John Bates,' she said.

Mehuru nodded, he understood: they were names. He had four names. He gave her his public name, which anyone could use without summoning his soul or harming him. He put his hand on his chest and looked her in the eyes. 'Mehuru,' he said.

Frances's black eyes gazed at him, and widened. She leaned

118

forward a little closer, as if to hear him better. She put her hand to her throat and felt beneath her fingers her own rapid pulse.

'Frances,' she said again. Then she reached out across the table and put her hand on Mehuru's chest. He could feel the light touch of her fingers tremble as she touched him.

'Mehuru,' she said.

Her small white childlike face looked into his. 'Mehuru?' she asked, seeking confirmation. She could feel the warmth of his chest through the thin linen shirt. She could smell the scent of his newly washed skin. The tattoos on his face were fine delicate lines of blue. The skin beneath his eyes was faintly blue too with fatigue and sorrow. His eyelids slanted upwards, his eyes met hers. He was as wary as a trapped animal.

'Mehuru,' she said lingeringly.

A ripple of fear ran through them all. A new depth of terror went through them like hot wind through the grasslands. They heard the tone of a woman speaking to her beloved.

Mehuru heard it too. He lowered his eyes to avoid her penetrating, horrible gaze.

'Mehuru,' he said obediently. 'France-sess.'

Miss Cole was exultant. She would have kept them all day in the shadowy parlour, learning new lessons. But Frances refused.

'They'll be getting tired,' she objected. 'And I am weary. We've done enough for today.'

Miss Cole nodded unwillingly. 'Bates, you must keep them chained in their groups so we do not muddle them up,' she ordered. 'Bring these particular ones to do another lesson tomorrow.'

Frances bowed her head. Mehuru held himself with weary alertness. The two white women were talking together but their voices were cold with dislike. The older one had the sharp tone of command but the younger one had power too. The man at the door called Johnbates was their servant.

Mehuru had given orders in his own world and he knew the tilt of a head which was ready to bow. Johnbates might be dangerous, but he was only a cipher for the women.

'Take them back to the cellar,' Miss Cole said to John.

Mehuru shot a swift look at Frances and met her slanty dark eyes. Her skin coloured and Mehuru stared, fascinated, as a deep red blush rose up from the white fichu at Frances's throat to colour her whole face. 'Red as frangipani,' Mehuru thought. 'Red as a tongue.'

Frances cleared her throat. 'They should not go back in the cellar where it is so cold and dark and dirty,' she said. 'Not now they are washed and have clothes on.'

Miss Cole was looking out of the window, relishing her sense of achievement. 'What?'

'We should teach them to keep clean,' Frances said. She found herself tapping some secret reserve of female cunning, the skill which says one thing while thinking another. 'Now we have washed them, and dressed them, they should not go back into a dirty cave in the dark.'

Miss Cole turned from the window in surprise. 'Why not?' she asked.

'Because they will only have to be washed again, and because they must learn how to keep clean, and sleep in beds, and wear proper clothes,' Frances reasoned. 'They should have a light. They should have proper food on plates. They should have a clean floor, and benches to sit on.'

'But they're slaves!' Miss Cole protested.

Frances slyly bobbed her head. 'I am sorry. I did not understand,' she lied. 'I thought they were to be trained as servants.'

Miss Cole opened her mouth to argue and then hesitated. Frances was right. It could not be too early to start training them in the standards of a proper Christian household. And they could clean the cave themselves.

'You, Bates,' she said abruptly. 'Take them back to the cave and get them to muck it out. Scrub it clean and put down

120

some matting on the floor. Get some benches for them to sit on, and put a lantern high on a hook for light.'

'They should be unchained,' Frances added. She stretched out her hand towards Mehuru's clenched fists, touched the manacle on his wrist. Mehuru froze as if some unknown animal were brushing against him.

'Not yet, not yet,' Miss Cole said nervously. She looked around at the impassive black faces. 'Not until they are a little more tame.'

'I could give them some linen to go around the manacles,' John offered from the doorway. 'That'd stop them bleeding into their shirts. Help with the smell too. The sores get filled with pus if they wear irons for too long.'

'That will do,' Miss Cole said, revolted. 'Make whatever arrangements are necessary, Bates. Take these back and bring the others for their lesson this afternoon. And then bring these back tomorrow morning.'

The driver nodded and stepped to one side. Mehuru watched him carefully, saw the little bow towards the old woman and the more shallow nod to the younger one. So the old one was the senior, as he had thought. He rose from his chair and saw the old one flinch back from his height and strength.

The others followed him, on their feet and walking with their painful shuffle from the room. They crowded at the top of the stairs, finding the narrow wooden steps frightening. Mehuru touched his mind with the wisdom of Snake: '*All skin sheds at last*', and went down, like a ghostman, one foot after another, his body erect. The others followed his lead. Frances watched the top of Mehuru's head until he was out of sight in the kitchen and she could hear the rising litany of complaint from the cook.

'Now,' Miss Cole said coldly, masking her pleasure, 'there is an hour left before noon. I suggest that you apply yourself to the housekeeping accounts.'

Frances turned demurely. 'Yes, Sarah,' she said.

They went back together to the parlour. Miss Cole laid out the bills and the ledger, and directed Frances to the pen in the standish. Frances nodded, sat down at the desk and pulled the ledger towards her.

Miss Cole drew up a chair at Frances's elbow and watched the downward march of figures in the columns.

'Very well.' She gathered her sewing basket and announced that she would leave Frances alone with the ledgers. 'You will want to study them, I expect.'

Frances nodded, saying nothing. But as soon as Miss Cole shut the door she pushed the books to one side and laid her face on the coolness of the polished wood.

She felt very strange, as light-headed as if she had drunk some young fresh wine. The room no longer seemed stuffy or oppressive, the sparkle of the sunlight on the ceiling seemed to promise a bright wintry day, the noise of the working quay was cheerful. She felt as if she were a girl again, as if she were young and hopeful. In her early days when her mother had been alive Frances had been a pretty, petted, optimistic child. Under the cold carapace of her adult disappointments her spirit stirred, as if it might warm and come alive again. She sat very still for long moments, feeling her sense of inexplicable elation. She did not know why she suddenly felt as if joy were possible. She did not know why the air seemed a little cleaner and the house less oppressive.

'Mehuru,' she said thoughtfully to the open pages of the ledger.

She did not think about where he had come from. She had no notion of an Africa before the coming of the British, of a huge continent populated by a complex of different peoples and kingdoms, of trading and barter stations, of caravans of goods which crossed from one nation to another; of men and women, some living like peasants working the land, some living in towns and cities and working in industries, some established in hereditary kingdoms seated on thrones of gold and ivory and living like gods.

122

She had no interest in the slaves as people who had come from a living and potent culture. She felt powerful beside the black slave in a way she had never felt powerful before. She had always been a young woman in a world where male power was absolute. For the first time in her life she was able to look at a man and know that she could command him. For the first time in her life she could be a woman who could find and take her own power, and make a difference in her world. If she were clever and cunning she could keep him from death on the plantations. She nodded and felt her lips curve upwards in a smile. 'I can save his life,' she said softly. 'And he has to obey me.'

She rose from the table and went to the mirror above the fireplace. She almost expected to see the face of the girl she had been when her mother had been alive and her father had been prosperous and happy. She looked for that round-faced confident girl and was surprised to see the reflection of the drawn thin woman who gazed back at her.

But her eyes were very bright.

The lantern-lit cellar glowed a dusky red. The walls, quarried out of the ruddy sandstone, were red as brick, the lamplight reflected an ominous carmine glow on the faces of the slaves as they gathered around Mehuru. They were still all chained one to another, and the last one at each end was fastened to the wall. Mehuru – whose uncle was a blacksmith, a sacred worker in iron – was looking over the chain for faults in the metal. Sometimes, if iron was cooled too quickly it became brittle and could shear as easily as stone could chip. He looked at each link in the uncertain light of the tallow candle. Each slave stood waiting patiently in turn. Mehuru shook his head.

'The chain is perfect,' he said in his own tongue. For the two women who were from another nation and did not understand him, he put both fists together to indicate strength and shook his head sorrowfully. They nodded.

'We will have to wait until they release us before we can escape,' he said.

123

The others nodded solemnly. 'D'you know where to run, Obalawa?' one of the women asked. She bent her head a little as she addressed him, in the instinctive respect of a woman to a man; and that of a mere mortal to one who speaks with the gods.

'No,' Mehuru admitted honestly. 'I have no sight here. I am blind like you. I am lost like you.'

A shiver of disappointment ran through them. The women groaned softly. The two Fulani women looked from one anxious face to another, trying to understand what was being said. Mehuru resisted the temptation to smile at them, to reassure his own people. He could offer them only false comfort, and in this pit in the ground he did not want to play at magic.

'I have no power here,' he said. 'I have lost it, just as the sun has lost its heat. I know no more than you. At home I was a priest with the ear of the gods, I was high at court with the ear of the king. Here I have to learn to be nothing. I am not a man, I am a slave. I know nothing more than any one of you.'

'If we walk,' one of the women suggested, 'if we walk with the afternoon sun on our right we will get home. D'you remember, in the great ship after we lost the others, the afternoon sun was always to the left? We must walk south.'

'If there is land,' the other man, Kbara, warned. 'It may be water everywhere. It was many days sailing, remember; weeks and months at sea. Who would make that journey if they could walk? Who would build a ship like that unless they had to? These people have horses and carriages. If there was land they would have gone by land. Perhaps we have come from our world to this one by a great sea of time.'

Instinctively they looked to Mehuru – he knew the mysteries of one world and another, he should know.

Mehuru shook his head. 'I do not know,' he said. 'It will be enough for me if we can get away from this house and from these people. And from that woman,' he added very low.

'Somewhere there must be real people,' Kbara said desperately. 'They cannot all be white. They eat food, somewhere there must be real people planting crops and herding animals. They must be people like us working the earth. They eat meat, there must be herdsmen like the Fulani.'

Mehuru nodded. 'Perhaps.'

'At least they have given us clothes and water and now a light,' one of the women said hopefully. 'They cannot mean to eat us, can they? They would have started by now, wouldn't they?'

'I don't think they will eat us,' Mehuru said carefully. 'I think they are teaching us to speak their language for a reason.'

The others nodded. 'For what?'

'To serve them,' Mehuru suggested. 'If we ever had a slave from far away we would teach him our tongue.'

The younger woman shrank back against the wall in distaste. 'To serve them!' she exclaimed. 'To cook their food and clean their houses and touch them, and endure their smell and the coldness of their eyes! I could not do it!'

Mehuru looked at her and his face held a world of sorrow. 'I think they will teach us to do all that, and worse,' he said.

Then he turned from the circle around the candle and squatted down with his face to the damp wall of the cave, rested his head against the cold stone and let himself long for the heat and the scents of Africa.

Chapter Ten

Josiah sent a message from the coffee house that he would be bringing guests home for dinner, a gentleman and his daughter. Brown brought the news to Frances as she was lying down on her bed, resting after her lesson with the second batch of slaves. Frances pinned on her cap and hurried down to the parlour.

'We will dine at five,' Miss Cole said. 'I have already sent out to the pastrycook's for some puddings and ordered Cook to make a special dinner. Since you were resting again I thought I should make the preparations. I did not wish to disturb you. Are you ill again? Is it your cough this time, or your headache?'

'Neither,' Frances said. She felt well for the first time since coming to the little house by the foul-smelling river. 'I feel very well.'

Sarah raised her thin eyebrows. 'I am glad to hear it. You may take your tea now, in the parlour if you wish,' she offered. 'I have no time for it this afternoon. I am going to see Cook again and then to my room to change.'

'I shall change too,' Frances said obediently as she followed Miss Cole out of the parlour and up the narrow stairs to the second-floor bedrooms. 'Who are our guests? Did Josiah say?'

'Sir Charles Fairley and his daughter,' Sarah said. 'I met Sir Charles when he visited England before but I do not know Miss Fairley. He is a very important man in Jamaica and a good customer to us. We buy our sugar from him and he

126

pays a top price for slaves. His demand for slaves is almost beyond our ability to meet.'

'He has such large estates?' Frances asked.

'His use is very rapid,' Sarah answered carefully. 'He gets through slaves quicker than any other planter.'

Frances nodded. She was starting to recognise the euphemisms of the Trade.

'There is no need to wear anything too fine for dinner,' Sarah said waspishly as she reached the door of her room. 'Our guests know me and they know my brother as respectable traders, not gentry. I have only one evening dress in dark silk – I shall be wearing that. If you have anything simple it would be appropriate.'

'I have a sack dress in grey silk,' Frances said carefully.

'That sounds very suitable,' Sarah replied.

Frances nodded, went into her bedroom and shut the door. She saw her own smile in her dressing-table mirror. She looked pretty and girlish and naughty. 'I will *try* to be as ugly as a boot,' she said to the mirror. 'To keep you in countenance, Sister-dear.'

Frances and Miss Cole waited in the parlour for their guests, sitting either side of a large fire. Miss Cole was resplendent in an evening dress of dark blue silk with a small half-train. Frances had chosen a gown of grey watered silk with grey silk gloves. It was high-waisted with a long sweeping skirt and a loose panel at the back like a train. The sleeves were white silk trimmed with grey velvet, very fine. Brown had spent an hour with the hot curling tongs trying to make Frances's hair into ringlets which were supposed to cling around her face, but had settled in the end for a soft wave rather than the tight corkscrew curls dictated by fashion. Against the sheen of the silk Frances's skin was warm cream. Miss Cole eyed her without pleasure.

'I think we should sew while we wait for our guests,' she said.

Frances took a cambric handkerchief from her workbox and started hemming it with small even stitches. The two women sat in silence. Then they heard Josiah open the door and the sound of footsteps on the stairs. Frances put her work away and rose to greet the visitors.

Sir Charles entered the room first, his daughter behind him. He was a large red-faced man, his broad chest and stomach bursting against his brilliantly embroidered waistcoat. Dark knee breeches encased fat thighs, his high white stock was wrapped tightly around multiple chins, his blue coat was lined with sable which made him even more bulky.

'So this is the bride!' he said jovially to Frances after he had greeted Miss Cole with a kiss on her hand.

Frances dropped a small curtsey and let him clasp her hand in his two moist palms and then kiss it.

'Oh, Papa!' Miss Fairley exclaimed languidly in a strange rich accent.

'Here, Miss Cole, this is my daughter Honoria that you've heard me tell so much about, in England at last!' he said to Sarah. He turned to Frances. 'I am honoured to present my daughter to you, Mrs Cole.'

Frances curtseyed to the girl. She was pale and slim, wearing a silk gown of icy white which drained her mousy hair and pale face of what little colour she had. She had a shawl of silver tissue around her shoulders and large pearls at her neck and in her ears and on her wrists. She had a second shawl of warm white wool trailing from her right shoulder as if she feared they would not have heated the room.

'Honoured,' she said coolly. Her rich accent was oddly at variance with her strictly conventional dress.

Josiah Cole came in behind his guests. 'Sit down, Sir Charles,' he said. 'What will you have to drink? Dinner will be served shortly.'

'I'll take a glass of rum and water if you have any of my own excellent barrels in the house.' The fat man winked at Frances. 'That's the worst of the Sugar Island life, Mrs Cole.

You get a taste for all of it. The sunshine, the drinks, the company. You should come on a visit. We'd make you very welcome, wouldn't we, Honoria?'

The girl gave the smallest of nods. 'There's very little society for ladies,' she said, her voice lilting with the rhythm of the Sugar Island speech.

'But the weather!' Sir Charles took his glass from Brown. 'I tell you, I have not been warm since I set sail.'

'It has been very damp,' Miss Cole observed. 'I sometimes think December is the worst month of the year, always cold and often wet.'

'I am spoiled, Miss Cole, and that is the truth. If I came in midsummer I should still feel a chill.'

Frances sipped a glass of ratafia. The scullery maid hovered in the parlour doorway and whispered to Brown, who stepped forward and whispered in turn to Josiah Cole.

'Dinner is served,' he said. 'You must take us as you find us, Sir Charles. You know we are simple merchant people. We dine on the table, here in the parlour. Will you sit here, sir? And Miss Honoria here?'

They took their places. Frances, who had dined all her life at a table which never seated less than twelve, tried not to feel snubbed by Honoria's rude stare around the cramped room.

Brown took up a position at the door and collected the dishes from the scullery maid who could be distantly heard pounding up the stairs, carrying the hot and heavy platters. Josiah looked down the table to Frances with an uneasy glance, and she felt a sudden pity for his discomfort. He knew it was not being done correctly, but not how it should be done. Frances smiled at him and his face lightened at once.

'Are you well, Mrs Cole?' he asked. 'Have you had an enjoyable day?'

'I am very comfortable,' Frances assured him. She saw Sarah's glance of surprise at her determinedly bright tone. 'I am very comfortable indeed.'

'I am sorry not to be served by your slaves,' Sir Charles

observed. 'Josiah has been telling me that you have a dozen of them in training.'

'They will not be ready for some months,' Josiah said. 'My wife is teaching them to speak.'

Honoria turned on Frances a look of pale disdain. '*You* are breaking slaves?'

Frances nodded defensively. 'Yes.'

'It's a man's job at home,' Sir Charles said abruptly. 'On my plantation the old hands train the new ones. This is a man's job that you have given to your wife, Cole.'

'She has the help of a driver, and besides they are no trouble. We have only two men and the rest are women and small children.'

Brown circled the table serving soup from a large tureen. Frances recognised the best silver brought down from the storeroom for the occasion.

'It's not the wit that's required but the whip!' Sir Charles exclaimed. He laughed, a deep satisfied laugh. 'Did you hear that? Not the wit but the whip!'

Miss Cole tittered agreeably, Josiah smiled.

'They're like children,' Sir Charles explained. 'They can remember nothing unless it is beaten into them. And their spirits are surly and defiant. On my plantation we have a beating in the stocks every day. In the fields they are whipped as they work; but at least once a day I have one whipped in the stocks. And I have the blacksmith brand them at the forge, oh! time after time, and sometimes slit their tongues for insolence. I wear myself out trying to devise punishments which will serve as an example to the others, and yet not injure them so badly that they are spoiled for work or re-sale.'

'So stupid,' Miss Honoria said languidly in her high sweet voice. 'They are so stupid.'

'What's your death rate now?' Josiah asked.

Sir Charles shrugged. 'I suppose of our two hundred we lose about fifty or sixty a year. They hardly breed at all. We lose women in childbirth all the time, and the babies are often born dead. When I hear of men preaching that the trade in slaves should stop I wonder how they would have me run my plantation? How else can sugar be grown?'

Josiah nodded and signed to Brown to pour more wine. 'It's ignorance,' he said. 'And fashion. It'll pass. It's a few young prating clergymen and a couple of members of Parliament trying to make their career. Methodists and radicals! It will blow over. It's nothing more than a few grubby radicals stirring up bad feelings and signing petitions. The leaders of this country know the profits that the Trade brings, and they like to take sugar in their tea. We won't be driven by the mob.

'Look at Bristol! Before the Trade it was a little town; nothing to what it is now. The fortunes made in this town are a monument to slavery. And Liverpool has been built on the back of the Atlantic trade. Every day they build another great house or another town hall. People know where their interests lie. This is a milksop agitation, it will pass.'

'I hope so,' Sir Charles said heavily. 'I cannot tell you how alarmed we get when we hear the fools agitating and complaining. What of this Wilberforce, and his bill?'

Josiah scowled and poured himself another glass of wine. 'It comes before Parliament this May,' he said. 'But we are all prepared. Our men will call for more evidence and adjourn the reading, it can be adjourned forever they tell me. The great men of the Trade in Liverpool and London and here are all ready to act in concert and their pockets are well-lined. I don't think that a handful of clergymen and some ignorant working men can stand against them. There's not one member of the Houses of Parliament that does not have an investment to protect. They will hardly vote themselves out of business.'

'I pay two members a pension direct,' Sir Charles said. 'To guard my interests. But it makes me so angry when I hear of these radicals. They know nothing about the Trade. They know nothing about our difficulties. Every visitor we've ever

131

had to Clearwater Plantation has gone away convinced that we are working the land in the only way possible. You can't get white labourers, and all the Indians are dead now – not one of them lasted beyond the first few years of our arrival. How are we supposed to manage? And what would the slaves be doing in Africa? Hunting each other and burning each other alive! We have saved them from the most foul paganism and taught them work and discipline. Why I could tell you some tales . . .'

'Papa!' Honoria murmured.

'I beg your pardon,' Sir Charles said. 'My daughter is delicate in her tastes,' he explained to Frances. 'I should not mention these things before her.'

'I do hate niggers,' Honoria said quietly to Frances as the men talked across the table. 'I wonder you can bear to teach them. I won't have them near me.'

'Do you have no black servants?'

'Most of them are half-castes,' Honoria replied. 'Mulattos. We prefer to use them in the house.'

'Half-caste?' Frances repeated the unfamiliar word.

'Yes,' Honoria said calmly. 'Papa likes to mix the stock.'

Frances heard the genteel euphemism; but she would not examine what it might mean. 'And what is it like?' she asked. 'Living on the plantation?'

Honoria glanced at her father and at Josiah and Sarah who were listening only to him. 'Dreadfully slow,' she complained. 'There's hardly any society unless we go into Jamestown and even then there are only two balls a year. We've come home for me to buy some gowns and . . .' she gave a small smile '. . . make acquaintances.'

'Young gentlemen?' Frances hazarded, and was rewarded with another small smile.

'I have nothing to do all day except watch the sugar grow and torment the housegirls,' Honoria said. 'Mama spends all day in bed. She's delicate, she's dreadfully delicate. She has Nanny – my old black Nanny – running up and down for her

132

every half hour with one thing or another, sending dishes back to the cook, and complaining and carrying-on.'

Frances nodded, trying to imagine the large white house amid a sea of lush green forest, with three discontented whites, drinking rum or nursing hypochondria in the shade while outside two hundred exiles worked under the merciless sun, whipped if they went slow, mourning for their homes and their families.

Brown removed the soup and loaded the table with dishes: cutlets, a haunch of beef, a venison pie, and sweetbreads.

'You Bristol merchants spread a good table!' Sir Charles exclaimed. 'I always enjoy a visit to your house, Miss Cole.'

Miss Cole smiled her acid smile and asked for how long the Fairleys would be visiting Bristol. Sir Charles outlined an itinerary designed to net Miss Honoria a husband. They were to go shopping for clothes in Bath, attend the Pump Room, visit in the country during summer and then stay with friends for the London Season in the winter.

'We hope to be setting sail again by next spring,' he concluded. 'Unless Honoria here surprises me with other plans!'

Honoria turned her eyes down to the table and tried to blush. 'Oh, Papa!'

'And who runs your place while you are away?' Josiah enquired. 'D'you have a manager you can trust?'

'An overseer,' Sir Charles nodded. 'He's a man from Jamestown, working his way up. He's a brute but I can trust him with a shipful. He knows how to handle them and he'll give no quarter. I'll come home and there will be some sad faces in the slave quarters, and some new mounds in the grave-yard; but there will have been no trouble.'

'Surely on Clearwater you never have trouble?' Miss Cole remarked.

Sir Charles shook his head as his plate was cleared away. 'I never sleep without a gun at my bedside,' he said. 'You never know where you are with them, Miss Cole. You have to remember the numbers you are facing, all the time you have to be wary. Remember that there are only three of us, Lady Fairley, Honoria and myself, and there are two hundred of them, and more if you count the visitors in the slave cabins that I don't know about, and the runaways hiding in the forests around. I have to keep the upper hand night and day. They're always waiting – waiting for their chance. Who next, eh? Where next?'

He nodded at Frances. 'If you have the management of them you had best remember my warning, Mrs Cole. They are killers. They are all born killers. Never let your guard down.'

'Our slave driver watches the lessons and he has a whip,' Miss Cole said. 'And they are manacled.'

'Keep them that way!' Sir Charles recommended. 'Keep them that way until their spirit is broken, until their very will to live is under your feet. They have to long for death. If they are attached to their lives then they want to better themselves – that's when your trouble starts.'

Miss Cole looked thoughtful. 'We have perhaps already been too kind . . .'

Sir Charles shook his head. Brown put a large portion of syllabub before him and poured cream. 'Break their spirit and keep them low,' he advised. 'Separate the bucks from the women, keep them underfed, watch them losing weight. Keep their minds on pleasing you for little rewards, and if you see the least sign of unwillingness beat them near to death – or beat one to death if need be. The others will note it, I assure you.'

Miss Cole smiled at him. 'You are so kind,' she said. 'I will consider it very carefully.'

He beamed back. 'A sensible woman,' he proclaimed with pleasure. 'Josiah, you are to be congratulated with helpers such as these. Beauty, and brains. You will go far, I know it!'

Josiah smiled and raised his glass. Frances pushed aside her untouched dessert. She had a sour taste in her mouth, the conversation was making her nauseous.

134

The men talked of the Trade while the fruit and sweetmeats were brought in. Honoria nibbled a sugar plum, her pale brown eyes blank with boredom. Frances sat very still, her hands in her lap, her face a mask of polite interest, willing herself to be deaf to them both.

When Josiah nodded to her, she rose from the table and led the way for the ladies to sit at the fireside. It was a pathetic parody of the rituals of gentry life. Frances's face revealed nothing, she conducted Honoria to a place at the fireside as if Lady Scott herself always dined and sat in the same room.

'We'll go to my office,' Josiah announced. 'We'll take a glass there and join you later, ladies.'

They went unsteadily from the room, having already drunk the best part of four bottles. Honoria, Sarah, and Frances made thin conversation at the fireside and ordered tea. The men did not return. The conversation dwindled and died. Honoria openly watched the hands of the clock on the mantel-piece. When it chimed nine she asked if the maid might tell her Papa that she wished to go home.

Sir Charles appeared in the doorway, woefully drunk. 'So sorry, my dear,' he said, speaking with meticulous care. 'I shall send you home in a chair, don't you know. A chair. Brown has gone out to fetch you one and she shall see you home. I'll see you in the morning, my dear. In the morning. Josiah and I are setting the world to rights and finishing a very pretty port. A very pretty port indeed. I shall take my supper here.'

Honoria nodded and let Frances help her with her cape.

'I shall go to bed,' Frances said quietly to Josiah.

'Do,' he said pleasantly. 'We will make a night of it. No need to wait up.'

The men retreated to Josiah's study again, broached another bottle and ordered some supper. By midnight they were thoroughly drunk.

'Let's have one of the slave girls brought in,' Sir Charles suggested. 'Have a little sport.'

Josiah peered at him owlishly. 'We're not at Clearwater

135

now,' he observed. 'There are the servants to think of, and the ladies.'

Sir Charles laughed his rich happy laugh. 'Servants be damned. And the ladies know when to look the other way. Lady Fairley knows when she'd better look aside, you can depend on it.'

'I cannot,' Josiah protested. 'I don't keep the keys and anyway Mrs Cole would not like it.'

'She need never know,' Sir Charles said. 'Go on, Josiah. Don't be such a damned Methodist.'

Josiah was drunk but still reluctant. 'It's not the done thing in England,' he said. 'Assure you, my dear fellow. Let's go out and get a woman if you wish . . . but slaves in your own home . . . not done.'

'I know what the done thing is!' Sir Charles was starting to get unpleasant. 'I'm a damned baronet . . . a baronet! I should know the done thing, I hope. I'm good enough to buy your slaves at a handsome profit to you, and good enough to sell you sugar on the quayside at knock-down prices. I know the done thing then, don't I?'

'I just meant . . .'

'And here am I, offering to take a share in one of your ships, one thousand pounds' worth, I remind you, Josiah! I should have thought I know the done thing!'

'No offence, no offence,' Josiah said quickly.

'Well, none taken,' Sir Charles replied, his mood swinging back into sunshine. 'None taken. But let's have a girl, Josiah! Let's stir the stock.'

'They're in the cellar,' Josiah said. 'And my wife has charge of all the household keys.'

'Send her a message, tell her we want to see the slaves!' Sir Charles had the characteristic stubbornness of the drunkard. 'Come on, man! You can't be under the cat's paw in your first year of marriage! Who rules the roast here?'

'I do!' Josiah said stung.

'Then get us a damned woman!'

Josiah touched the bell rope and Brown came wearily to see what he wanted now. 'Tell Mrs Cole we want to see one of the slave women,' Josiah ordered. 'Ask her to send me the keys.'

Brown curtseyed and went out.

Sir Charles smiled in anticipation and poured himself another glass of port. 'I assure you,' he beamed, 'once you get the taste for it, you are spoiled for anything else. At home I take them whenever I fancy.'

Josiah hid his distaste. 'Do you not take African diseases, Sir Charles? African illness?'

The man nodded. 'Aye, and pass them on too! But I'm grown very reckless, you know. There is something about being master, complete master, of so many. There is something which stirs you, to know that every woman has to do your bidding, and that the others can do nothing but watch.' He blew out a plume of cigar smoke with a shaky little laugh. 'There is nothing like it. This empire of ours is a glorious thing, Josiah. It makes us Englishmen like gods.'

Josiah nodded, took a small sip of port and swallowed down his distaste. There was a tap on the door and Frances stood in the doorway, wearing a loose gown and with her cap hastily pinned on her hair. 'May I speak with you, husband?' she said.

Josiah rose and went to the door, half-closing it to shield their conversation from the guest. 'What are you doing downstairs dressed like this?'

Frances glanced at her wrapper, the usual morning dress for ladies in their homes. 'I had gone to bed,' she said reasonably.

'You come before a guest half-dressed?'

Frances gave a little laugh, and then looking into Josiah's face saw that he was serious. 'Excuse me, husband,' she said carefully. 'I had no idea that you would object.'

The gulf between his world and hers suddenly opened before them. Josiah knew that on all matters of etiquette she was bound to be in the right; but he was an ambitious man, anxious about his respectability. 'I do object,' he said, knowing himself to be in the wrong, knowing himself to sound foolish. 'I do.'

Frances bowed her head, wary of his drunken irritability. 'Shall I go and change my dress?' she asked.

'No. Tell me now what it is that you wanted.'

'Brown brought me a message.' Frances had been distracted by his disapproval; she tried to regain the initiative. 'I came to ask you . . . it seems so strange at this time of night . . . may I ask what you want to see a woman for?'

'No, you may not, madam! Sir Charles wishes to inspect the slaves. I sent for the keys which should be in your safe-keeping. There was no need for you to come downstairs at all and no call for you to question me.'

'It is just for him to see a woman?' Frances broke off. 'To look at her? It is not to – er – to trouble her?'

Josiah flushed dark red. 'I beg your pardon, Mrs Cole! You amaze me with your boldness! Please give me the keys and go to your chamber. I do not want Sir Charles to see you like this, nor hear such slander spoken against him!'

Frances stood her ground, scarlet with embarrassment. 'I cannot give you the keys,' she maintained, her voice shaking slightly. 'I beg of you, sir, not to ask me. I am supposed to be teaching them, they are in my care. You are speaking of my pupils. I cannot permit it. I have to have an undertaking from you.'

Josiah came out into the hall and shut the door behind him. He was trembling with drunken anger, his spittle flew as he hissed at her. 'You are shameless! Your insinuations are shameless! This is an honoured guest! A man who has done many years of very profitable business with me and my house. If he wishes to look at one of our slaves then of course we will allow it. Why not? Why on earth not? Go and fetch one of the women, Mrs Cole!'

Frances backed away from him until she reached the newel post at the foot of the stairs. She had the keys in her hand behind her back. 'I must ask for your assurance . . .' she insisted weakly.

'My assurance?' he repeated, ready to explode with anger.

She collapsed before his bluster, her breath coming short, her hand to her thudding heart. 'Very well. But you will just look at her, won't you?'

'Fetch one of the slave women, Mrs Cole,' he said angrily. 'You should have stayed where you were and sent the keys to me by Brown. I am much displeased. Since you insist on coming down you can fetch the woman yourself, and then go to bed!'

Frances's face was white as she turned from him and went slowly, very slowly, down the stairs to the kitchen.

Brown and John Bates were sitting either side of the kitchen range, waiting for the family to go to their beds so that they could lock up. At her step they rose to their feet.

'I am sorry to trouble you,' she said. Her lips were cold and stiff, she found it hard to speak. 'Bates, could you come with me to the cellar? Your master wishes to see one of the women slaves.'

Bates thrust his hands into the armholes of his jacket and straightened his stock. Frances went to the cellar door and turned her key in the lock.

The cellar below her was shadowy. As she went down the steps she heard the chink of the chains. One or two of the slaves had been sleeping, but as they heard the door open they stirred nervously and woke. Mehuru rose slowly to his feet, looking from John Bates to Frances, trying to read their faces.

She did not meet his eyes. She looked around the cellar in the shadowy unreliable light of the lantern and then pointed to the biggest woman, the one who seemed the most robust. 'Her,' she said.

John stepped forward and unchained the woman from her handcuffs. She flinched away from him as he came towards her and shot a look at Frances – a look which was both a question, and an appeal. Frances's face gave nothing away, she was like a cold stone statue.

'What does she want of me?' the woman demanded of Mehuru.

He shook his head, his eyes on Frances. He could sense her powerlessness. He could feel her sense of defeat and something more . . . a deep sense of shame.

'I don't know,' he said softly. 'Have courage, Sister.'

The woman trembled and would have fallen but John Bates grabbed her around the waist and pushed her towards the steps. Her knees buckled beneath her and she crouched at the foot of the steps. 'They will eat me,' she whispered. 'Look at her face. She has come for me and she will eat me.'

Mehuru glanced swiftly towards Frances and saw her horrid narrow lips bitten even thinner. 'No,' he said certainly. 'It's not her choice.'

'Save me,' the woman begged softly. 'Mehuru, save me!'

Mehuru stood very still and felt the depths of his helplessness wash through him and over him. He knew that she would be raped and all that he could do was watch her be taken. He was unmanned, perhaps forever. 'Have courage, Sister,' he said tightly. 'We are a proud people. Bear this proudly.' He heard the hollow bravado in his voice, even as he spoke. He was a proud man no more; he was less than an animal for he did not have even a safe lair.

She found her feet, managed to stand.

Bates, growing impatient, asked Frances: 'Shall I carry her upstairs? I don't think she can climb them.'

'Yes,' Frances said shortly. She did not dare to look at Mehuru. She kept her eyes on her feet. She had dainty grey silk sandals to match the gown she had worn at dinner. She pointed her toe to look at the sheen on the silk, and the twinkle of the paste buckle.

John Bates caught the woman up. She grunted as his meaty shoulder butted into her emaciated belly, but she was silent as he climbed the steps. She seemed to have fainted from her fear, her head lolled at each step, her arms dangled down. 'Shall I carry her to Mr Cole's office?' he asked.

'Yes.' Frances followed him up the steps and carefully locked the door behind them. Slowly Bates walked through the kitchen with Frances behind him. Brown watched them pass in silence. Frances kept her eyes on the worn heels of Bates's boots.

When they left the warmth and light of the kitchen and went into the dark hall the woman started muttering the prayers for death. Over and over again she called the name of her husband, who was still waiting for her, still hoping for news of her. Over and over again she called to her ancestors to prepare a place for her, and begged them to forgive her for whatever wrongs she had done that she had been sent away from her home to die in dishonour in exile.

Frances heard the babble of pleas without understanding. She did not know the woman was calling on her, demanding of her what was wanted, what they wanted her to do, if there was any way she might be spared. Frances walked behind Bates, nursing her ignorance, deaf and blind to pain.

She tapped on Josiah's door and then swung it open, her face impassive. Bates marched in with his burden and Frances closed the door on them all, and went steadily up the stairs to her bedroom. Through the closed office door she heard the woman call out suddenly and clearly: 'Day-bull! Day-bull!'

She was trying desperately to please them. To say 'table' as they had wanted her to say this morning. To do whatever it was they wanted.

Frances hesitated for a moment at that one despairing cry, and then she went on, slowly, slowly up the stairs, her face set and grim. She was seated before her dressing table looking at her white face in the pier glass when she heard one scream of pure pain, quickly muffled by a heavy hand.

Frances unpinned her cap and plaited her hair, pulled on her nightgown and got into bed. 'I made an agreement,' she said to herself. 'I knew it would not always be to my liking.'

141

She pulled the cold white sheets up to her chin and lay very still. She closed her eyes. From the floor below came a rhythmic grunting which went on and on like a clumsy machine at work, and at last, a loud satisfied groan.

Frances put both her hands over her face and pressed down as if she would suffocate herself, block out the air as well as the noise. 'I made an agreement,' she whispered. 'I was warned that it would not be like home. But I made an agreement. That was my Trade.'

There was silence from downstairs. Then Frances heard her husband's study door open, and someone walk downstairs heavily, carrying a burden back to the caves. No expression crossed Frances's white face, she did not move. She lay as still and as cold as an effigy of a lady in white marble and she heard nothing, she saw nothing, and she thought of nothing at all.

Chapter Eleven

John Bates heaved her down the stairs like a lumper on the quayside, and dumped her ungently back in her place. He felt the accusing wide eyes of all the others on him.

'Well, I did nothing,' he muttered, half to himself.

She crouched on the straw with her head between her hands, doubled up over the pain in her belly. Bates had trouble making her straighten up so that he could bolt on the neck-collar.

The little children, the two-year-old and the five-year-old, looked at him with big frightened eyes but they were too wise to cry aloud.

'Oh damnation,' John Bates said irritably, and took the lantern off the hook and stamped up the stairs, leaving them alone in the dark and silence.

In the office Sir Charles and Josiah broached another bottle of port. Sir Charles was sated and at peace with the world, and Josiah hid his discomfort. He had made his fortune from the Trade but he had never before abused an individual. All the pain and grief had happened far away, out of sight, out of earshot. Seeing a woman raped on the hearthrug of his office made him uneasy. He had sat in the window and pre-tended to watch the pitch-black quayside while Sir Charles had laboured over her, but he could not help but hear her half-suffocated whimper of pain, and he could not avoid the smell of her fear, and the dirty clotted smell of Sir Charles's unwashed body.

He reminded himself that she was an animal, with only

animal feelings, but he had not liked her agonised face when they had finally lifted her from the floor. Not even his best port could wash away the unpleasant taste from his mouth. He dared say nothing. Sir Charles was an important customer to Cole and Sons and, besides, Josiah feared that he himself was less of a man for his absence of desire.

It was nearly dawn, a grey sunless winter dawn, before the men parted. Josiah bade farewell to Sir Charles, climbed the stairs to his room and got into his bed.

Frances, lying awake, cold, and with her head buzzing with pain, heard him get into bed in the next room and the little puff as he blew out his candle. She did not know that he was lonelier than he had ever been in his life, and that he would have given a ship's cargo to be able to get into bed beside her and feel a little human warmth.

Frances woke later to the dark of a cold morning with her head a raging storm of pain. Small pinpricks of light danced against her eyelids. Her shoulders were rigidly tense, her neck was tight. The very skin of her face and the bones in her cheeks ached as if she had an ague.

The adjoining door to Josiah's bedroom opened. 'I owe you an apology,' Josiah began without preamble.

Frances barely opened her eyes. 'I am ill,' she said. 'Forgive me.'

Josiah checked. 'I wanted to speak with you,' he persisted.

'I cannot.' Frances's voice was a thin determined thread.

'Can I fetch you something?'

'My laudanum, in my writing table.'

He opened the lid of the little box. In the shelf at the back was a small bottle. 'How many drops?'

'Three.'

He measured three drops into the glass of water at her bedside and gave it to her. She drank without opening her eyes and lay back on the pillow, waiting for the pain to ease.

'Sir Charles's behaviour was not fitting for an English

144

home,' Josiah said precisely. 'You were right to object. I had taken a little too much drink and, moreover, I was bound to be hospitable. But when I awoke this morning I thought your objection should have been heeded. I apologise.'

'You need say no more,' Frances said. She turned her head away and closed her eyes.

'The woman took no hurt,' Josiah said. 'And Sir Charles returned to his hotel in the early hours of the morning. I fear that too long a stay in the Sugar Islands has made him forgetful of English courtesies.'

He waited, looking at Frances as if she should say something.

'I have apologised,' he said with increased sharpness.

'I am sorry,' Frances whispered weakly. 'My head . . .'

'You will feel better when you are up and dressed, no doubt,' he said without sympathy. 'I will leave you now for my work. I shall be home for dinner at the usual time. The maid will bring you your chocolate – my sister will expect you in the parlour at nine.'

'In the parlour?'

'For their lesson,' he said levelly. 'The slaves will be waiting for their lesson. Today. It is my wish that they be taught all together, every day. It will take too long otherwise.'

'I cannot do it,' Frances protested stubbornly. 'I am too unwell to see them.'

'Then do not work overlong,' Josiah replied promptly. 'But start at nine, teach them all together, and then send them away after an hour or so. I do not wish them to miss a day of their training. Sir Charles was convinced that they have to work daily or they will become unruly.'

Frances searched for grounds for refusal and could not think of one. 'I wish you had not fetched her to your office,' she said pettishly.

'I did nothing,' Josiah said awkwardly. He paused. Neither of them could discuss exactly what had taken place. 'The woman was not harmed,' he repeated. 'Indeed, at Clearwater, or any plantation, these things happen almost every day.' He hesitated, seeking refuge in generalities. 'It is not as if she were hurt. She would expect nothing else.'

There was a silence. Josiah went towards the door.

'I feel ashamed,' Frances said suddenly. Her headache thumped as if in recognition of a truth spoken aloud at last.

Josiah, closing the door softly behind him, was careful not to hear her.

They filed into the parlour, all thirteen, and took their seats at the table without looking at her. They were crowded. Frances was already at her place and did not look up as they came in quietly, but she sensed Mehuru's presence when he drew out his chair and sat on her right. Looking down at the polished table top, she could see his gently clasped hands. She longed for him to put his hand on her forehead where it throbbed and tightened. She longed for him to lay his hands on her hot eyes and tell her that he forgave her; that she might forgive herself.

She shot a swift painful glance at him. His dark dark eyes met hers in one long judging look and then turned away. He would not look at her, though Frances waited. The other slaves sat in silence around the polished table and watched her. Tentatively, Frances put out her hand and gently touched his clasped fingers with her forefinger. It was the lightest of touches, but one which lingered with her, the warmth of his slim strong hand under her fingertip.

'Mehuru,' she said softly.

He looked up at her. She put her hand on the base of her throat. 'Frances,' she said aloud, and then, very softly, too softly for Miss Cole or the driver John Bates, or any of the other slaves to hear, she said, 'I'm very sorry. I could not stop them.'

Mehuru looked at her with a hard, unforgiving glare, and would not hear her whisper; and if he had heard it, would not have understood.

The lesson went badly. Miss Cole sighed in the windowseat and picked her teeth with a silver toothpick which clicked against the stained enamel. She had painful indigestion from the night before and every now and then she shifted in her seat with a little grunt of discomfort. John Bates stood like a statue with his back to the door and his whip held across him. Mehuru would not meet Frances's eyes again. The woman who had been raped sat in complete silence, her head bowed so low that her face nearly rested on the table, hiding the dark bruise on her temple and the dead look in her eyes. The smallest boy cried continually, little half-smothered heart-broken sobs. He sat still on his seat, leaning forward, and his tears fell on his bare black knees where they peeped from his breeches. He was only two, he did not know how to endure in silence. Frances did not know how to teach simple nouns while the child shook with silent grief.

'Get them to say their names,' Miss Cole suggested, moving from her place in the window. 'That's where you left off yesterday. What is wrong with them today?'

Frances looked at her. 'Sir Charles disturbed them in the night,' she said.

There was a brief silence. Miss Cole understood perfectly. 'What for?' she asked, daring Frances to speak the truth.

'I don't know,' Frances replied, deliberately ignorant. Behind the words was Miss Cole's sharp comprehension of what had happened, and Frances's shame.

'Well, that is no reason for them to be dull,' Sarah said briskly. 'They should not object to being looked at. Ask them their names, all of them.' She pointed to Mehuru. 'He said his name last time. Ask the others what they are called.'

Frances nodded. She put her hand to the warm cambric of her gown at the neck and said her name, and then she pointed at one, and then at another. Today they would not speak. They shifted uneasily in their seats and stared at her with frightened eyes. When she pointed at the woman that Sir

Charles had taken from the cave the others gave a soft groan, as low as the creak of bending trees in a forest.

Frances touched the back of Mehuru's hand again. The warmth of the dark skin under her fingers encouraged her. 'Mehuru,' she said quietly. 'That woman. What is her name?' She pointed to herself. 'Frances.' She pointed to him. 'Mehuru.' She pointed to the woman. 'What name?' she asked.

'She wants your name,' Mehuru said to the woman. His voice was tender, as one would speak to a sister mortally injured. But his resentment burned beneath the quiet tone and Frances could hear it.

'My name is Shame,' the woman said quietly. 'My name is Shame. My name is Died of Shame.'

Frances frowned at the quick low exchange and then turned enquiringly to Mehuru.

'Shame,' he said in Yoruban. 'Died of Shame.'

Frances's stupid white face brightened, she nodded. 'Died of Shame,' she repeated, pleased. She pointed to the next. 'And who is this?'

Kbara did not raise his head. 'Despair,' he said in his language, Mandinka.

'Despair,' Frances repeated happily. 'Now we are getting on! And who is this?'

'Homeless,' the girl said in Wolof.

'Homeless!' Frances repeated carefully, mimicking the sound.

Mehuru closed his eyes for a moment at the horror of Frances's encouraging bright voice mouthing curses.

'And this?'

'Grief.'

'And this?'

'Accursed.'

'And this?'

'Lost.'

'You'd much better give them English names,' Miss Cole

148

interrupted. 'No-one will be able to say this gibberish. It doesn't mean anything. Tell them some new names, Christian names.'

Frances hesitated. 'I will, when I've learned their African names.' She smiled at them. Mehuru recoiled from the horrid paleness of her mouth and the white teeth against the pale bloodless lips. 'They need to trust me,' Frances said. 'We need to be friends.'

She rose from her seat at the table and went to the sideboard and rapped on the polished top. 'Sideboard.' She waited for Mehuru's response, sensing his unwillingness. 'Sideboard,' she said again.

There was a glass bowl in the centre of the sideboard, piled with expensive hot-house fruit from last night's dinner. Frances took a warm apricot in her hand. She brought the fruit to the table. She laid it before Mehuru like a woman of a village might lay a gift before the shrine of a difficult god. She had the same supplicating deferential smile.

'Apricot,' she said.

Mehuru looked from the fruit to her intent face. There was a ripple of unease from the others. Frances did not notice, she did not even see them. 'Mehuru.' She spoke his name like a caress. 'This is an apricot. Apricot.'

He could not bear the appeal in her face. He dropped his gaze to the polished surface of the table. 'Apricot,' he said, very low.

Frances exhaled slowly as if he had made some private long-sought agreement with her. She took the apricot up to her mouth and bit a little piece from it. She took the mouthful from between her lips and offered it in silence to Mehuru. Their eyes met, then his hand came up and took the piece of golden fruit from her hand and put it in his own mouth.

'Good,' she said and nodded at him.

'Good,' he repeated obediently. Then his eyes fell back to watching the table. His face revealed nothing.

Frances took a knife from the sideboard and cut the apricot

149

into small slices for the rest of the class. 'Apricot,' she said to each of them. When they repeated the word she gave each one a piece. They ate their share delicately and in silence.

'Good,' she said.

They repeated the word like automata, without understanding. They kept shooting glances to Mehuru for cues as to how to respond to this strange dangerous woman who could come for them like Ayelala the goddess of death and judgement in the night; but during the day was a supplicant, begging for forgiveness, speaking one nonsensical word at a time.

Frances pointed to the fruit plate. 'Plate,' she said. 'Knife.'

'Plade,' they said nervously. 'Knigh.'

Mehuru felt his consciousness back away from reality, like a wounded animal will retreat into its lair, lie in the darkness and long for death.

'Plade. Knigh.'

Frances looked around the table at the shuttered faces. 'Smile!' she suddenly commanded. She bared her teeth at them. 'Smile!'

They shrank back from her dreadful white face and the huge gaping mouth. 'Oh my fathers, save us!' one boy muttered. A woman gave a sob of fear.

'Steady,' Mehuru warned softly. He was still in his lair, his dark eyes watching Frances, his soul tucked safely away from her.

Frances turned to him, her eyes – dark like his own – imploring. 'I'm trying to help you,' she said. 'You have to learn and I have to teach you. Smile.'

'Mile,' Mehuru said softly to her. With dead unfeeling eyes he curved his lips up in a ghastly parody of joy. 'Mile,' he said.

Chapter Twelve

When the lesson stopped at half-past ten and the slaves were sent away Frances remained seated at the parlour table.

'Would you like a dish of tea before breakfast?' Sarah offered.

Frances shook her head. 'I shall not be eating breakfast,' she said.

There was a short silence. 'Frances . . .' Sarah warned. 'I hope you are not getting vapourish.'

Frances's head came up. 'Vapourish!' she exclaimed. 'I am not vapourish, I am sick to my heart! I don't believe I can do this, Sarah. I don't believe it should have been asked of me. I shall speak to Josiah. I don't think this scheme can work. They cannot be taught and certainly I cannot teach them.'

Sarah moved from the windowseat and took a chair opposite. 'You do not wish to work,' she said bluntly.

'I cannot do this,' Frances said. 'I cannot prepare them for a life of slavery where any master can abuse them as he wishes.'

'Not in England,' Sarah said quickly. 'They would not be abused in England. They would be treated as servants.'

'Then let them be servants,' Frances replied. 'With wages and the right to leave if they find themselves in a disagreeable position.'

There was a pause. 'Where would be the profit in that?' Sarah asked simply. 'You have forgotten why we are doing this, Frances. We are doing it to sell them, as we sell sugar and tobacco. We are here to sell them at a profit.'

Frances dropped her head into her hands and clasped her

151

thudding skull through the tight curls. 'I cannot do it,' she said miserably.

Sarah watched her for a moment. 'But you have no objection to slavery in principle,' she remarked quietly.

'Of course not,' Frances said.

'You have no objection to taking the profits and enjoying the goods which slavery brings us?'

'No.'

'Then your only reservation is that you do not want to do the work yourself.'

Frances raised her head. 'Yes,' she said.

Sarah shrugged and rose from the table. 'This is not principle, this is laziness. I warned my brother that a fine lady would not be prepared to work for his business as he works and as I work. But he believed that you understood the trade you were making. You wanted a family and a house of your own, and he wanted a working wife. You brought him aristocratic connections and he gave you a handsome settlement. He is keeping his side of the bargain, the house at Queens Square will be yours. But you wish to renege.'

'I am not lazy,' Frances replied, stung.

'Then keep your side of the bargain,' Sarah Cole said firmly. 'As we are keeping ours.'

Downstairs two women slaves were watched by John Bates as they took out the pail and slopped it on the midden. The girl who had named herself Died of Shame fell back as they went through the yard, snatched up handfuls of earth from the foot of the wall, and pushed them down the bodice of her dress.

When they were back in the gloomy light of the cellar John Bates brought them a pail of food – some bread, some potato peelings, the scraps and the bone from Sir Charles's roast dinner. They ate right-handed from the pail, taking it in turns to choose a piece of food and then putting it on the tin plates before them.

Mehuru took the piece of fruit out of his mouth where he

had held it under his tongue ever since Frances had given it to him in the lesson. Squatting, he put it carefully on the floor between his bare feet and looked at it for long minutes. The other slaves sat in silence around him. He was the obalawa, he could be talking with the fathers.

'Apricot,' Mehuru said softly.

At the thought of her saliva on the piece of fruit that had gone into his mouth his throat tightened with terror.

'Will you not eat?' one of the women asked softly.

He shook his head. He would not touch Sir Charles's leavings. He drank only water and watched the woman who called herself Died of Shame. When it was her turn to take her pick from the breakfast pail she tipped the earth from her bodice on her plate and ate mouthful for mouthful with them until her face was stained with mud and her breath smelled of death.

Mehuru did not stop her. He could not ask her to live. He could not reassure her that no harm had been done, that the husband who loved her would never know of it. That the little baby she had left behind her in Africa would never be insulted because his mother was dishonoured. That it was a new life, and new and dreadful ways were facing them all, but that they might survive. He had no right to persuade her against her own wisdom. And besides, he had no hope to give her, and no hope for himself. They sat in the half-darkness, all of them with their faces buried in their hands. When she started moaning very softly, they moaned quietly with her, in a gentle chorus of lament.

'Here,' Cook said upstairs. 'What's that?' She was making pastry for a pie.

'It's them!' the scullery maid said nervously. 'Groaning.'

'Mr Bates! Mr Bates!' Cook cried. 'What are they doing down there?'

John Bates listened at the cellar door. 'They're just singing,' he said. 'And sighing.'

'Why?' Cook demanded irritably. 'They never have before.

153

I can't work in a kitchen with sighing and singing in the cellar. I shouldn't be asked to.'

John paused. 'I'll beat them,' he offered. He took his whip, unlocked the door and surged down the steps. The slaves raised themselves up at the noise of his boots, their faces turned towards him and the light and the good smell of baking. He slashed the whip at random in the small space and heard it sing and crack as it found an arm, a face, an ear. Kbara cried out, a woman screamed. John Bates looked around for any challenge. They huddled together and watched his scarlet angry face and his popping eyes. 'That'll do,' he shouted at them, incomprehensible threatening words. 'Stop that noise.' He turned on his heel and marched up the steps again. They heard the door at the top of the steps bang and the key turn in the lock.

They sat in darkness and silence for a while and then Died of Shame put her hands over her mouth and groaned out her pain as quietly as she could. The other women drew closer to her, and they moaned with her, as soft as the cooing of plantain-eaters.

Mehuru started to recite, very softly, the prayers for the dead, calling on the forefathers of Died of Shame to take their daughter home, back over that long wide sea, so that she might feel the sun on her face again and lie on the fertile earth.

'They've started again,' Cook said sharply.

John listened. 'You can hardly hear them.'

'But I can hear them! I think I'd better tell Miss Cole I'm no longer suited. I could walk into any place tomorrow, the Cole table is well known in this city. I can't keep my pastry light with savages groaning in the cellar. They shouldn't ask it of me.'

John Bates turned in irritation to the kitchen maid. 'Find Brown and tell her to tell Mrs Cole that the slaves are moaning. She's supposed to be teaching them to speak. She can teach them to be silent too!'

The kitchen maid peeled off her grimy hessian apron, revealing a cotton pinny underneath, only marginally cleaner. She scurried for the stairs and found Brown polishing the little table in the hall. Brown thrust the duster into her hand, went up to the parlour and tapped on the door.

'Beg pardon, Mrs Cole,' she said. 'The slaves are moaning in the cellar.'

Frances looked to Miss Cole. 'Moaning?'

Sarah waited. 'Do you wish them to be left, Frances?' she challenged. 'If you will not care for them and I do not have the time then they will have to moan in their cave until my brother comes home.'

'Bates says he could beat them,' Brown volunteered.

'I'll come,' Frances said. She led the way down the back-stairs, Sarah following behind her. Cook was standing behind the kitchen table, banging the rolling pin down on a lump of pastry. There was a low soft sound from the cellar, like the panting of a hurt beast.

'I gave them nothing more than a little clip,' Bates protested. 'But they started again. They were quieter for a while. They know they're doing wrong. Shall I beat them again?'

'No,' Frances said quickly.

'Did they start for any reason?' Miss Cole asked. 'Have they been fed?'

'They had the pig pail,' Cook answered without turning around, her broad back expressing her total disapproval. 'And good food there was in it too. Then they started this noise. It's not right for a Christian kitchen. It's not what I'm used to.'

'Of course,' Miss Cole said rapidly. 'We'll stop them, Cook. We'll stop them at once. Frances, go down and see what is wrong.'

Frances shrugged resentfully. 'How should I know? I've had no experience.'

'I could beat them, ma'am,' John offered. 'That's what we always did in Jamaica. Beat them till they were quiet.'

155

'No,' Frances said. 'I don't want them whipped.'

'Then you must silence them some other way,' Miss Cole demanded. 'Either by teaching or beating, Frances, they must be quiet.'

Reluctantly Frances went to the head of the stairs. John unlocked the door, uncurled his whip. 'Perhaps I had best go first,' he cautioned her. Frances heard the note of fear in his voice.

'Are they chained?'

'Yes, ma'am.'

He preceded her down the stairs. Frances blinked, accustoming herself to the gloom. She saw the food pail in the centre of the cellar ringed with plates. On one plate she saw a dark smear, like mud.

'Fetch me that,' she said to John.

He stepped towards the four women who leaned away from him, like a field of rustling sugar cane leaning away from the wind. The woman called Died of Shame had tipped earth over her head, had covered her face, and was moaning, as soft as a breath, into her cupped hands.

John proffered the plate to Frances. 'Looks like earth, ma'am.'

Frances looked across at Mehuru. He met her eyes without expression. He had neither smile nor scowl for her. He looked at her as one might look at a cheating market trader – with a distant scorn.

'She is eating earth?' Frances asked. 'Why should she eat earth?'

Bates shrugged. The movement uncoiled the whip and the long tail of it hissed on the straw of the floor. The women shifted in one small movement, farther back against the wall, farther away from him.

Frances showed the plate to Mehuru. 'Died of Shame?' she queried, repeating the girl's name in her strange stupid voice.

Mehuru nodded.

'She is eating earth?' Frances asked.

156

Mehuru's face was impassive.

'I don't understand,' said Frances, who understood all too well. She turned to John Bates. 'I *don't* understand,' she insisted.

'They're savages,' he volunteered. 'Perhaps they eat it all the time in their own country. Perhaps she fancied a bit of Bristol dirt for a change.' He gave a little chuckle and then straightened his face when Frances scowled at him.

She turned and went back up the steps to the kitchen, taking the plate with her. 'It's the girl called Shame.' She carefully pronounced the African name. 'She has been eating earth. I think she may be sick.'

'Which is she? You know I can't remember their names.'

Frances flushed scarlet. 'She is the one ... she is the one ...' Frances could not say that she was the one she herself had sent to Sir Charles last night. Frances could not say such a thing before the servants.

'Oh.' Miss Cole understood at once. 'Well, that's no reason. It must be something else.'

'Should we call a doctor?' Frances asked.

Miss Cole shook her head. 'No, too expensive. Besides, how would a white person's doctor know what to do?'

'The farrier might know, ma'am,' Bates offered. 'A horse will eat earth sometimes. A farrier might know.'

Miss Cole tapped her teeth with her toothpick. 'Sir Charles,' she said finally. She turned to John Bates. 'Go to his hotel and see if he is at home. Give him my compliments and ask him if he would step over. We need his advice.'

John Bates gave a little bow, reached for his hat on the chair and went out of the back door. Miss Cole turned her attention to Cook. 'All this will be swiftly settled,' she assured her. 'Sir Charles is very experienced in the handling of slaves. It will be all over by dinner. And I shall see that my brother knows that you have worked through some disruption.'

Cook slapped the pastry on a brimming pie and abruptly trimmed the rim. 'I hope so indeed, Miss Cole,' she said ominously. 'I must say it's not what I am accustomed to.'

Miss Cole nodded to Frances to lead the way up the stairs to the parlour. She returned to her seat in the window and looked down at the quay, watching Bates as he waited for the little ferryboat to take him across the river to Sir Charles's hotel on the opposite side of the Avon. 'I hope Sir Charles is at home,' she said. 'Or we will have to send for my brother.'

Frances did not answer. She knew that they should not have sent for Sir Charles with his tainted expertise. She knew why the woman who had named herself Died of Shame was eating earth and pouring earth on her head, and streaking her face with it. Frances knew that she was inviting a rapist to order how his victim should be managed. She knew that she was being slowly and effectively corrupted by a system over which she had no control.

'How will he know what to do?' she asked.

'Clearwater is one of the best-run plantations on Jamaica.'

'But he said that a quarter of their slaves died within the first year, and another quarter within the next four, just through illness. He loses even more by punishments and selling on.'

'That's quite good actually,' Miss Cole remarked. 'Some plantations, especially those that are low-lying in fever country, lose every single slave within a couple of seasons.'

Frances seated herself at the table, and picked up the sheet she had been darning. 'Sir Charles said that of every ten slaves shipped out of Africa, two die on the voyage, two more die the first year, and then another two are dead by the fourth year,' she said, her voice carefully neutral. 'So for every ten that have been caught and shipped, only four are left alive by the end of five years.'

Miss Cole nodded. 'And this is why it is such a reliable trade,' she observed. 'That is why it is such good business for us.'

Frances inclined her head. 'I see.'

The two women sat in silence until Miss Cole, looking

down at the quay, said, 'Here he is,' as Sir Charles strolled up to the front door and hammered on it with his pearl-handled stick.

He came into the parlour behind Brown. He kissed Miss Cole's hand, he bowed low over Frances's hand and kissed it gently. He straightened up and gave her a little intimate roguish smile. He looked like a charming boy caught in an apple orchard with bulging pockets. He very nearly winked.

'Forgive me,' he said in his warm flirtatious tone. 'I should have presented myself with my compliments this morning. My daughter and I enjoyed a most excellent evening with you. Alas! I overslept – your wine was very fine!'

'We sent for you because we have some difficulty with one of the slaves,' Miss Cole interrupted.

He turned from scanning Frances's face and smiled at her. 'Anything I can do to assist – you only have to command me.'

'Frances has the managing of them,' Miss Cole said, allocating blame where it was due. 'And now one of them is behaving very strangely. They are all moaning and it is disturbing Cook.'

Sir Charles gave a little seductive laugh and flickered a smile at Frances. 'We cannot have that excellent cook disturbed for one moment. Would you like me to see them?'

'It is just one,' Frances said quietly. 'She will not eat food . . . She is eating . . .'

'Earth?' he guessed.

Frances's glance flew to his face. 'You knew?'

He shrugged. 'It's not unusual. A foul habit, isn't it? The women do it often. It makes them sick as dogs, they get the yaws and they will eat it till they die sometimes. It is their mad spite. They know they are robbing you of their purchase price. They are insane with spite. You will need to use a bridle, ma'am.'

'A bridle?'

He tutted in irritation. 'Of course, you will not have one to hand. I had thought myself at home! We put a bridle on them when they eat soil. A metal cage which goes around the face, under the jaw, with a gag of metal across the mouth. Their driver must take it off at mealtimes and watch her to make sure she eats her food. She must wear it all the rest of the time. They are cunning as monkeys. If they want to eat dirt they will get their hands on it somehow. The only way is to gag their mouths.'

'And you frequently use these devices?' Miss Cole asked, interested.

'We could not run the plantations without them. We use it on those who eat earth, and many people put their cooks and kitchen maids in bridles to stop them tasting as they work. This is a common problem for us, ma'am, and a common solution. I could draw one for you and a farrier could make it up. It looks like a scold's bridle from olden times – it has the advantage of making them dumb as well! Which one is causing the trouble, what size is she?'

Miss Cole looked at Frances. Frances wanted to say, 'the one you raped', but she found she could not. The man stood before her, smiling, assured, charming. She could not name him as a rapist. He had assaulted a woman and now she ate dirt and heaped dirt on her head, and Frances was dumb.

'The largest woman,' she said, cowardly.

'Well, you'll just want a medium-sized one then,' Sir Charles said comfortably. 'It has to be tight enough to cut into the mouth, to press against the lips, against the teeth and gums. They learn the lesson well that way. If she bleeds a little around the mouth it is no great loss. Here, I'll sketch one out for you.'

Miss Cole gestured to the parlour table and put paper and a pen before him. With swift confident sweeps of the pen he drew a little helmet with an open socket for the nose and a smooth plate which blocked the mouth, fastening behind the head with leather straps.

'Don't be discouraged,' he said kindly to Frances. 'One

160

little setback means nothing. I am sure you are making good progress.'

'Thank you,' Frances said stiltedly.

'Now, come back with me to my hotel!' he commanded. 'And take a glass of wine and a little luncheon with me there! Honoria will join us, she is longing to improve her friendship with you, Mrs Cole.'

Frances glanced at Miss Cole, who was flustered and flattered. 'You must give us a moment to put on our bonnets. Shall I need a cape or a shawl?'

'It's as cold as ever but it has stopped raining, thank God!' Sir Charles exclaimed. 'I shall wait for as long as you need to get ready, Miss Cole. It's not often I have the honour of a beauty on either arm. I would wait all day for the privilege.' He smiled at her and Miss Cole flushed with pleasure. His sideways gleam to Frances gave the compliment to her. His powerful maleness, his confidence of his own desirability filled the little room.

Frances went slowly to the door. She did not want to put her hand on Sir Charles's arm. She did not want to have luncheon with him. She did not want to see his knowing little smile or hear his half-shamed, half-bragging chuckle. She thought of him taking the black woman against her consent, and of all the other black women he had used, against their wills. She paused at the door, nerving herself to refuse.

'This is a great pleasure for me,' Sir Charles beamed. 'I have such little occasion for the society of English ladies. I can feel myself becoming more civilised minute by minute.'

Frances felt the traitorous weakness of her polite smile. 'Oh good,' she said.

Chapter Thirteen

The lunch party was not a great success although Sir Charles was a charming and expansive host and Miss Cole was delighted to be in his company. Honoria was as coldly polite as she had been the previous night. Frances could feel the sick thudding of her headache coming back.

'You are pale, Mrs Cole,' Honoria said in her rich languid accent. 'You are so lucky. I have to shield my face from the sun all the time at home. Mama is terrified of me getting brown – brown like the girls.'

'I don't feel very well,' Frances said quietly.

'The strains of new married life, eh?' Sir Charles interrupted, smiling intimately down the table at Frances. 'Running a house, teaching the slaves. You must tell Josiah that he must not work you too hard!'

'It is not the work,' Frances said. 'I worked harder when I was at home.' She felt a sudden pang of homesickness for the rectory and the little village where she and her father were well-known along every lane and track, and where she enjoyed a constant sense of self-righteousness. 'I used to walk in all weathers. I used to visit the poor, my father was the rector, and my uncle, Lord Scott, the landlord. It is the countryside I miss. My home was in the hills outside Bath.'

'And now you are cooped up in town!' Sir Charles exclaimed sympathetically. 'I wish I could take you ladies to Clearwater.' He included Sarah in his smile, but his eyes were on Frances. 'You could rest in a hammock and look out over two hundred acres to the sea, Mrs Cole! As lush and as thick and as fruitful as your heart could desire, and a dozen slaves to do your bidding, whatever you might want! That would bring the colour to your cheeks. And I myself should make you rum punch which would make your heart beat a little faster.' His voice held a caress. Frances glanced uncomfortably at Sarah.

'My sister is happy where she is,' Sarah said. 'And within a month we will be living at Queens Square. There is some delay with the purchase of the house but when it goes through we shall have the Queens Square garden for our enjoyment.'

'An excellent address,' Sir Charles agreed. 'But had you not thought of the heights of Park Street? I barely recognised the city, there has been so much building since I was last here. The whole town seems to be sprouting terraces.'

Miss Cole shook her head decidedly. 'No. We prefer to live in the town. My brother says that a merchant is happiest where he can see the masts of his ships.'

'I am sure he knows best,' Sir Charles said pleasantly. 'And so the next time I come to visit you I shall see you in a beautiful town house, Mrs Cole.'

'Yes,' Frances said thinly.

Sir Charles nodded at the black slave who stood behind him for more wine and the man stepped forward and poured. Frances shook her head. 'I drink only water at noon.'

'Why, that is why you are so pale!' Sir Charles exclaimed. 'You must let me give you a little of my own rum, in a punch of my own devising.' He nodded to the slave. 'Punch, Sammy. Punch. Quick-quick.'

The man bowed, unsmilingly. 'Yassuh.'

'Please don't bother,' Frances protested. 'I assure you, Sir Charles . . .'

He smiled and leaned towards her. He put out his hand and rested it over hers. Unseen by Miss Cole, his little finger slid beneath her wrist and caressed the delicate skin. 'You must indulge me,' he said. His voice was very warm. 'I have been spoiled in the Sugar Islands and I bring my luxurious

163

ways home with me. You must indulge me, Mrs Cole.'

Frances, thinking of his indulgences last night, and the woman who today smeared earth on her face and filled her mouth with dirt, took her hand away.

'You are a fine host,' Miss Cole said sharply, keeping a critical watch on Frances. 'My sister will be delighted to taste your punch and then we must go home. We have much to do in the afternoon, as you will understand. My sister is no longer a lady of leisure, she is the wife of a working merchant. She has duties now.'

Sir Charles shot a sympathetic look at Frances, then his slave came in with a silver punch bowl and he turned his attention to the drink.

'I must speak with Mr Cole on business this day,' he said, after he had squeezed the lemons and added the sugar. He nodded to the slave and watched him carefully as he handed around the silver cups of punch.

'My brother will be delighted,' Sarah replied instantly. 'Is there any way that I can be of assistance?'

'You can advise me, ma'am,' Sir Charles said pleasantly. 'I am dogged by the troubles of getting my moneys to England. There are investments I wish to make, I wish to buy land here. I shall return to live here one day, of course, and there is Honoria's dowry to think about. I don't like to send bullion on a strange ship and I have no agent in England to handle notes of credit for me. I even have some gold with me now, but I need the name of someone whom I can trust to handle it for me, to invest it.'

Miss Cole thought for a moment. 'You have no family here?'

He shook his head. 'It was all done by my brother, he was my factor. But he died two years ago, and I have no-one to take his place.'

Miss Cole cleared her throat. 'If I might be so bold as to offer our services . . .' she began tentatively. 'We have had a long and successful trading relationship, Sir Charles. I know that both my brother and I would be honoured . . . You could place your moneys with us and we could serve as your agents in England. We could purchase what things you needed and send them out to you on our ships. You could give us notes of credit for all the slaves you purchase from other traders, and we could pay them when they were presented to us.'

Sir Charles hesitated. 'I know trading companies do this. But mostly in London and, forgive me, they are all larger concerns.'

Sarah touched her tongue to her dry lips. 'We are expanding, as you know,' she persisted. 'And we have reserves of our own capital to draw on. We are experienced in the Trade.'

'But the purchase of land . . .' Sir Charles let his doubt trail into silence. He implied, but did not say, that a self-made Bristol trader would hardly know how to buy good agricultural land.

'You would want to choose your own estate, of course,' Sarah continued desperately. 'But we could collect the rents for you.'

'Yes,' Sir Charles said slowly. 'But land is a very different thing from the Trade, my dear Miss Cole.'

'I am sure my uncle Lord Scott would be happy to assist,' Frances interrupted suddenly.

Both Sir Charles and Sarah looked towards her, surprised. Frances felt irritated that they should assume that she had nothing to say in a conversation about business, that she was as much of a parasite as Honoria, who was gazing blankly out of the window.

'He told me that Josiah was to call on him at any time,' Frances said. 'And he owns much land in Somerset, and he also has a large estate in Scotland and a lot of land in Ireland.'

'Lord Scott himself would be prepared to advise me?' Sir Charles asked. He glanced towards Honoria. 'You would introduce us?'

Frances, who might know nothing of business, knew a great

deal about social values. 'My uncle Lord Scott would be delighted to assist you, and to welcome you and Miss Honoria to Scott House in London. My aunt and uncle are there for the Season. My aunt generally gives a ball. I could ask her for tickets.'

Honoria, who had been daydreaming during the business discussion, straightened in her chair and fixed her father with a meaningful glare.

'Well, well,' Sir Charles smiled. 'What an excellent idea! I should be honoured with Lord Scott's acquaintance. I should be happy to enter into an agreement with you, if Lord Scott were our advisor. It might be a very good idea indeed!' He beamed at Frances and shot an indiscreet wink at Honoria. 'I should be grateful,' he said. 'Grateful to make his lordship's acquaintance. And Miss Honoria would be glad of a ticket to the ball, I don't doubt! You are obliging, Mrs Cole. I appreciate it.'

'It is my pleasure,' Frances said coldly. She knew that she was a fool to be led into favours for Sir Charles, but her pride had been piqued at being neglected at the luncheon table, she had been driven by an unworthy desire to outshine Sarah, and by irritation at being excluded from the conversation. She did not know how to be his guest and yet keep her distance from him. And she had longed to put Miss Honoria in her place.

Sir Charles sent them home in his hired carriage as it had come on to rain. As they drew near to the quay Frances could smell the sweet nauseating stench of the river. The rain was washing smuts down out of the heavy sky. The dark dirty clouds of smoke from the glass furnace and from the leadworks hung around the spire of St Mary's, staining the intricate carvings and trailing tears of soot down the faces of the stone saints. It was growing dark with the early dusk of midwinter. Sarah was bubbling with suppressed elation. 'You did very well, Frances,' she said. 'Very well indeed. Sir Charles is a fine man to have as a friend.'

Frances felt her momentary excitement drain away. 'I do not like Sir Charles,' she said in a small voice. 'And I have a headache.'

'He is a most important man to us,' Sarah snapped. 'And your mention of Lord Scott was very helpful. Will you be able to bring his lordship up to scratch, d'you think?'

Frances stepped out of the carriage and went to the front door. A new ship was in port near to the Cole dock, and the Merchant Venturers' great crane was screeching as it swung out and hauled barrels up from the hold. The noise jarred on Frances's taut nerves. She was sorry that she had been persuaded to go to lunch, and angry with herself at her complaisance to Sir Charles. She had wanted to enter into the world of persuasion and business. With the return to the dirty little house on the quayside she realised that she had been exercising her social charm on a rapist to benefit a petty dockside trading company.

'Lord Scott has my interests at heart,' Frances said distantly. 'I am sure he will do anything I ask him.'

'If we can get him to come in then we can be Sir Charles's agents, and our problems of cash will be over.'

The door opened. Frances stepped inside before her sister-in-law. 'I hope so, indeed,' she replied, smothering a cough.

Sarah clicked her teeth together. 'You did offer,' she reminded Frances. 'You will have to come up to scratch. You cannot promise something and then renege. These are business matters, your word must be sacred.'

'It is not a religion,' Frances said tartly. 'You speak as if a contract was one of the ten commandments.'

Sarah nodded. 'It is. That is exactly what you must learn as a merchant's wife. You should break one of the commandments before you break your word. Everything this house has been built on depends on the reliability of our word.'

'I will try and understand,' Frances said with dull resentment. 'I am teaching the slaves, Sister. I will do everything else that is in my power to further our business. And if Josiah wishes it, I will ask Lord Scott for his advice, and ask him to invite Sir Charles and Miss Honoria to Scott House.'

'He is a fine gentleman,' Sarah insisted. 'He would be perfectly at home in Scott House, I don't doubt.'

'I do not share your confidence. But Lord Scott will understand, and make allowances.'

Sarah knew herself to be snubbed, but let it pass without comment. Brown closed the front door behind them as Frances started to climb the stairs.

'You will teach the slaves this afternoon,' Sarah reminded her.

'I will have a rest, and teach them at four o'clock.'

'I hope you will feel better then,' Sarah said grudgingly. 'You have done well today, Sister. I do recognise it.'

Frances nodded and went into her room, closed the door and leaned back against it. If it had been furnished with a bolt she would have locked it against her sister-in-law, and against the claustrophobic house, and against the imposing vulgarity of Sir Charles.

Sarah had not seen that tiny distasteful caress of his finger on her wrist and Frances did not know what would have been said. In her world – the world of the country aristocracy – a flirtation after marriage was a normal state of affairs. But in this anxious world of Bristol merchants where a fortune hung on appearances Frances did not know how she should behave.

She had no feelings to guide her. Even as a girl Frances had never fallen in love. She had watched her cousins' passing infatuations and agonies at balls and dances and picnics with mild amusement. When they declared that she was cold, she had not denied it. She lacked passion, and the years had made her cool and distant – even from herself. The death of her mother, and then a year later of her father, had taught her that the price of love is vulnerability, and she never wanted to feel the grief of loss again. She thought that all her feelings had died with her father, that she had wept them out of her heart, and that for the rest of her life she would see everything

168

through a thick pane of glass, and feel everything as though through gloves.

Frances rubbed her face, pressing her fingers against her temples where her headache drummed. She lay down on the bed and stared up at the ceiling. In the street outside her window someone was rolling barrels; the rumble of the wood against the cobbles seemed to shake the very house. She shifted her head on the pillow, seeking comfort but finding none, then she closed her eyes and slept.

Her bedroom door opened and Brown came in. 'Miss Cole said to wake you,' she said apologetically. 'She has ordered the slaves up from the cellar. Bates will take them to the parlour when you say.'

Frances yawned. 'I slept.'

'You'd have been tired out, late last night with Sir Charles at dinner, and then lunch with him today.' Brown moved around the room deftly folding laundry and putting it into the drawers, straightening Frances's silver-backed brush and comb on the ponderous chest of drawers. 'Even Miss Cole took a rest, and that's not a thing which happens often.'

Frances sat up in bed. 'I'll change my gown,' she decided, glancing down at the creased muslin. Nothing stayed clean in this city. At home she would wear the same gown all the day but in Bristol the continual drift of smuts and ash covered everything with a fine dark grit which soiled white linen within hours.

'There's the sprigged muslin, with a green silk sash, that's pretty. But rather fine for staying home,' Brown suggested.

'I'll wear it,' Frances said.

Brown shook the gown by the shoulders and spread it out for Frances to see. It was tightly fitted over a silk bodice with smooth close-fitting sleeves. The sprig in the white muslin was in the pattern of little flowers and the green sash was embroidered with matching flowers. It was a dress for springtime, a dress for walking on a warm well-clipped lawn in the country.

Frances nodded and stood with her arms out while Brown unhooked her at the back, helped her step from her old gown and then threw the afternoon gown over her head.

'Just tie my hair back,' Frances ordered. 'I'll wear it in a knot.'

'You have such pretty hair,' Brown said. 'I could put a little curl in it. There's the kitchen fire lit, I could have the tongs heated in a moment.'

'No,' Frances said, reaching for a warm shawl against the chill of the bedroom. She did not want to confide in a servant but she thought to herself that it was hardly worth curling her hair when there was no-one to see her but her sister-in-law and her husband. Mehuru would see her, of course. But Mehuru was hardly interested in whether her hair was curled or straight. For a moment she wondered if he saw her as a woman at all, or only as a slave driver, as an enemy. She hoped very much that he knew she was not his enemy. 'Tell Bates to take the slaves to the parlour. We can start at once,' she said.

She waited while Brown went downstairs and then she heard the slaves slowly coming up the backstairs from the kitchen. She heard their low frightened whispers from the hall before she went to the head of the stairs and walked down.

Mehuru, looking up at the noise of her bedroom door closing behind her, saw her coming down, almost floating, down the stairs, gliding like a ghost in a white mist of a gown. Frances, seeing his face upturned and watching her, paused on the stairs and put her hand to the base of her throat where her pulse was suddenly thudding. Mehuru saw the colour rise into her face and go again, leaving her even whiter than before.

'Mehuru,' she said.

'France-sess.'

She followed them into the parlour and watched them sit in their usual places. She gave them a small smile. 'Hello,' she said.

Their faces were smooth and unchanging, like ebony.

For once, Frances and the slaves were virtually alone. Bates stood at the door holding the whip across him, but he was not listening nor watching. He was a bored sentinel, standing at his post. Miss Cole's windowseat was empty. Frances gazed at Mehuru, disregarding the others. She felt restless and light-headed. 'Mehuru,' she repeated. He looked at her but said nothing.

She glanced around the room, wondering what she could teach them. She went to the window, took a handful of the curtain material and showed it to them. 'Curtain,' Frances said.

She looked at Mehuru. 'Curtain,' she said again. She nodded at him. 'Curtain,' she said more firmly.

Mehuru suppressed a small unhappy sigh. 'Curt-dane.'

'That's right!' Frances said brightly. 'Curtain.'

She tapped on the window. 'Window,' she told them. 'Win-dow.'

She took her seat at the head of the table and pointed to the back of her chair. 'Chair,' she said. They repeated it dully. Then she slapped the table before her.

'What's this?' she asked Mehuru. 'What's this?'

'Table,' he said easily.

She pointed to the curtain and the window and the chair. He repeated all the names, he had learned them instantly, he did not need a second reminder. He was learning nouns with the facility and speed of a linguist. He had always known a good deal of Portuguese; another European language was not difficult for him. He listened to the orders from Johnbates, he eavesdropped while he waited in the kitchen. He was putting together words and meanings all the time. Frances was teaching him single words like a child, while he was stringing together sentences and guessing at their meaning every time he was taken from the cellar.

Frances rose from her seat and went to the window. He

watched her carefully, without seeming to watch her, as a man will watch an animal when he is not certain if it is tame or wild.

'Come here,' she beckoned him. He rose and went carefully towards her, his bare feet silent on the boards and the rugs. She liked to command him. She liked the way he came silently to her side. In all her life she had been powerless before men; and now here was a man who moved like a dancer, in complete obedience to her smallest gesture.

'Look,' she said. She pointed out of the window. 'See, a ship. A ship.'

Mehuru had not seen the view from the front of the house before. He had seen nothing beyond the backyard but a small patch of dirty sky. Looking down from the parlour window, he could see, lying on the mud of the harbour at low tide, the ship that had brought them on the long long journey from home. She did not look so fearsome now, he thought. Beached and unloaded she looked vulnerable, not like the smooth devouring monster of his nightmare.

He could see the gratings in the deck, which had been his sky for those long months, lifted out and leaning on the railed side of the ship. He could see the hold, which had been his world, scoured clean and ready for re-loading. The sails were stripped from the masts. They were being re-sewn and repaired in sail lofts on the top floors of the warehouses. There were sailors seated on the dockside retying the ropes and cables. Mehuru recognised the cycle of preparation and readiness. Soon the ship would sail again, he thought. Sail that long journey over those grey dangerous seas and then wait off the coast of his homeland for people, his people, to be snatched in their twos and threes and gathered together in a dreadful poaching expedition and taken away to their death, or to a life so cruel that they would wish themselves dead many and many times.

'Ship,' Frances smiled. 'Ship. You know that ship, that is the *Daisy*, which brought you here.'

172

Mehuru nodded. He knew that ship. He knew it better than any sailor could know it, for it was the blood from his back in the timbers of the hold and his bare feet that had danced on deck, and his pride and his joy and his manhood that had drained down into the stinking bilges. He knew that ship.

'Ship,' he said coldly.

'Excuse me, ma'am,' John Bates said from the doorway. 'But the little ones are crying again.'

The smallest child was hunched in his seat, rocking himself. Unstoppable tears poured down his face. The little boy next to him, only five years old, was holding the sleeve of the Fulani woman to his face. His shoulders were shaking as he sobbed. The two seven-year-old children, the girl and the boy, were dry-eyed but anxious; they looked ready to weep at any moment. Frances looked around at them.

'Now!' she said brightly, taking up a plate from the sideboard. 'What is this?'

The lesson continued with the naming of things until Brown tapped on the parlour door and peeped in. 'It's the farrier, ma'am,' she said. 'He's brought the thing you ordered.'

'That will be the bridle,' Frances said. She glanced nervously at Mehuru. He listened carefully, trying to follow the inflections of her speech. He did not understand the words but he saw her quick guilty look.

'What?' Kbara tapped on the table urgently.

'Don't know,' he tapped back.

'Perhaps you had better take them away,' Frances said to John Bates. 'Put the bridle on her in the cellar.'

'I'll do it when they're chained,' he said. 'That big one, the pagan, he might cause trouble.'

'Very well,' Frances agreed. She wanted nothing to do with it. She did not want to see the bridle being fitted. She did not want to hear of any struggle.

'I'll take the lad down with me, and I'll wear my pistols,' Bates told her. 'If she struggles I may have to whip her.'

Frances hesitated. She looked at the woman. She was

173

lifeless, she had taken no part in the lesson, she had said nothing and made no sound. Her eyes were sunk in her head, she was blind with despair. She seemed to hear nothing and know nothing. 'Very well,' Frances said, abandoning her. 'Whatever you think best.'

Bates nodded and opened the door. He jerked the chain on the neck rings and the slaves formed up into a line. There was a spatter of rain on the parlour windows. Mehuru shivered at the sound of it. At home there was a short season of rains and a long season of dry hot weather. He could not understand a country where it rained chilly, damp rain every day. He thought he would never be warm again. Even if he were miraculously transported home, sprawled by the side of the river in the middle of the day, he thought he would still feel this deathly chill in his bones and smell this stink of decay.

He stumbled as he went down the steps into the cellar and jerked the chain on the neck ring of the smallest child who was following. The child did not even cry out against the pain. He seemed to be in a deep silence, too deep and too filled with despair for any protest. Mehuru put a hand down to him but the child did not look up. He was still crying silently.

The lad secured them to the wall, running the chain from each collar through the rings fixed on the wall. Then Bates and the lad came and unfastened the chain for Died of Shame. She did not protest. She did not look to Mehuru for help. She went dully with them, not knowing what they wanted of her, no longer caring what they might do.

'We could have her and no-one would know,' the lad said. He giggled, an odd lively sound in the quiet cave.

'Go on then,' Bates said, uncaringly. 'The gentlemen did, why not us?'

They laid the woman down on the floor and she lay still and turned her head away from them and closed her eyes. The lad took her first, quickly and fumblingly; then Bates followed him roughly. The woman said nothing except a grunt

174

when Bates first thrust inside her. Mehuru, watching this tableau of cruelty as it was enacted before him at his very feet, felt himself dizzy with rage, dizzy with pain, dizzy at his own helplessness.

The men got to their feet but Died of Shame lay still.

'Is she all right?' the lad asked.

Bates kicked her experimentally with the toe of his boot. She did not move.

'Sister,' Mehuru said. Slowly, slowly she turned her face and looked at him. He saw her eyes were glazed. She had gone to somewhere they could not reach her and it would be cruelty to call her back.

'You are in the keeping of your fathers,' Mehuru said to her blank unseeing face. 'They love you still.'

'Let's get on with it,' Bates said. 'I don't like him.' He jerked his head towards Mehuru. 'He's learning fast. It's not natural. She shouldn't be teaching them like this. It's not right.'

He picked up the bridle from the ground. 'You hold her down,' he ordered. 'Stand on the chains of her wrist and neck, and beat her with the butt end of the whip if she fights me.'

He knelt at the woman's head and forced her face roughly inside the mask. It was a plate of metal with a triangular hole cut away for her nose. A broad band ran across her mouth. The whole device was fastened behind her head with thick leather straps and buckles. Bates fitted it on her face and then pushed her head to one side to tighten the straps. She said nothing, she made no move to resist. Mehuru, watching them handle her as if she were a doll, wondered if she had fainted, her neck was so slack. But then they dropped her head back on the floor and he saw, gleaming on either side of the metal band, her blank black eyes.

'Chain her up,' Bates said.

They had to drag her to her feet and prop her against the wall so that they could pass the chain for the collar through the ring on the wall. It was long enough for all of the slaves to stand or lie as they wished.

175

'Now go and fetch their dinner pail,' Bates said.

'What about her? She won't be able to get anything to eat.'

'She can do without tonight, she'll be hungry tomorrow and then she can eat. Teach her a lesson.'

The boy sped away and came back as Bates put a new candle in the lantern, lit it and hung it on the high hook. Bates watched the lad put the food pail, thirteen plates and the pitcher of water with the tin mugs within reach of the slaves then he went out, locking the door behind him.

Chapter Fourteen

The candle had guttered into darkness and the smallest children had been asleep for some time. The women had gathered the crying babies into their arms for comfort and slept with them held close. Mehuru had been waiting and listening a long while for Snake but he did not come. He leaned back against the cold wall of the cave, closed his eyes and readied himself for sleep.

Something touched his foot. 'Obalawa,' a muffled voice said.

It was the woman who called herself Died of Shame. She was sleepless, her face half-hidden by the bridle they had put on her. It covered her mouth completely and her nose was bleeding on either side where it poked through the sharp edges of the roughly made hole. She had to speak through clamped lips, her speech distorted by the plate over her mouth. 'You are an obalawa, a powerful priest.'

'I have been trained,' Mehuru said carefully. 'I have dedicated my life. But I am losing my vision, Sister. This country is making me blind.' He could hardly make out her speech, but he knew what she would want.

'They have gagged me like a dog. They have shamed me and now they starve me.'

'I know, Sister,' Mehuru replied gently. 'I grieve for you.'

'Wish me dead, Obalawa,' she said simply. 'I must go to my fathers. They may forgive me.'

He paused. 'They may not allow us to bury you rightly. With your things . . .' He broke off. She had no things here.

No cooking pot, no piece of chalk, no beads for her hair, no bowl, no spoon, no sharp knife, no hoeing stick, no purse with coins or cowrie shells, no comb. No little pretty women's things that a young wife should have laid in her grave beside her, none of these things could go with Died of Shame to the other world. And her son, her young son who should be the first to say farewell to her, who should wash her face in the funeral rites and kiss her goodbye – she had left him before he could say more than her name, before he could do more than call and call for her, and never hear an answer.

She nodded. 'The fathers may forgive me.'

'It might get better,' Mehuru said. 'We might be freed. We might find a way home. To choose death is often a mistake as well as a sin against the breast of the earth.'

In the darkness her eyes gleamed alongside the gleam of the metal plate. She looked like a masked dancer summoned to dance at a funeral, she looked eerie, mysterious. 'What do you see, Obalawa?'

Mehuru fixed his eyes on the gleam of the metal bridle that gagged her mouth. He looked into its dull light as if he might picture some future for them in the leaden sheen. Then he shook his head. 'I do not see us going home,' he admitted.

'And I could not go,' she said simply. 'Look again. Look at me. Look into me.'

Mehuru leaned forward and took her in, the blank strange shapes of her masked face, the hunched shoulders of a woman in deep pain, the shapeless clothes which hid her round smooth breasts and the pure line of her hips, and then he leaned a little closer, sensing the start of new life. He sighed a small hidden breath. He could see Sir Charles's baby.

The woman nodded, but Mehuru did not let the sense of the embryo slide away from him. There was something wrong. He breathed a little deeper; if he had the smoke, if he had the water, if he had the polished tray and the cowrie shells for the complicated arithmetical divination he would have been able to know what was wrong.

'The baby,' he said. 'I think it is sick.'

'The man was diseased,' she answered. 'He was thick with illness, he smelled foul, like death.'

Mehuru nodded. The baby would not go full term, he would not be taking a viable life when he wished the woman dead with a baby inside her. And Died of Shame did not have a life worth living now.

'Can you wish me dead?' she asked. 'Without pain, but quickly?'

Mehuru waited for guidance, closing his eyes. Patiently, the woman sat beside him, watching his face. They were silent together for nearly an hour until Mehuru hissed a long slow hiss 'Yes.'

'The goddess will not eat you,' she said generously, freeing him of any guilt, absolving him of blame so that Ayelala the goddess who punishes lawbreakers would not come for him.

'Or you.' Mehuru returned the blessing.

He took one last look at her before she went back to her place beside the other women and lay down. He saw that his wishing would only complement her own desire. Her eyes were already dead, they were as dull as the metal plate across her mouth.

He heard her moving softly in the darkness, lying down and wrapping her arms around herself. He heard her muffled lips name the people she loved, her little son, her husband, her mother, and then the ancestors who might come to her, who might, despite all that was wrong in her life, forgive her. And then he heard the long long silence of a woman waiting for death.

Mehuru sat up and stared into the darkness and started the wishing.

In the morning in the darkness of the cave he heard the women stirring and then an abrupt exclamation. 'Aiee! She is dead.'

'Mehuru! Did you know? Died of Shame is dead!'

He rose to his feet and staggered a little from the stiffness in his legs. 'I knew,' he said.

Kbara, chained to the wall at the other end of the line, was awake. 'What shall we do? She needs to be buried here.'

One woman pushed back the straw and tapped on the cave floor. It was sandstone. 'Do they have no earth in this damned country?' she asked. 'How are we to bury our sister where she should be buried, under the floor of her own hut?'

'She knew,' Mehuru told them. 'She was prepared for it to be done wrongly.'

The woman who named herself Grief drew a little closer to him. 'She spoke to you?'

Mehuru said nothing.

'So how will we manage?' Kbara demanded. 'Shall we shout out for them?'

'Don't make them bring the whip,' the girl called Homeless said hastily. 'When we shout they bring the whip.'

'We'll sing to her very quietly,' Grief decided. 'And make her ready as much as we can. Then Mehuru can tell them. Mehuru, you will ask for Frances and tell her.'

He nodded. It was a relief to see a woman taking command. They knew what they should do, it was their business. They gathered around her. He heard their soft lament, a whispered song, and he heard the shuffle of their feet in the straw as they moved, straightening her torn clothes and washing the parts of her face they could reach around the metal bridle.

'It is not right,' the girl called Lost cried despairingly. 'How can we do it right here?'

Kbara, Mehuru and the older boy Accursed stood uneasily waiting. They should have been digging the grave for the woman, inside the door of the hut, at her own hearthside so that she might always be with her family. They should have been walking to outlying houses to tell them of the death. They should have been making a gift, or doing some task for the bereaved family. They should have been helping to prepare a feast to say farewell, they should have been priming

180

their guns to celebrate her passing with gunshots, they should have been practising their steps and preparing the grim masks to dance for her funeral. There was so much to do when there was a death, especially that of a young woman. And now they stood around like fools, like idle fools.

The opening of the door was a relief. John Bates came in, carrying a big pan of porridge. He recoiled as Mehuru went to the length of his chain to greet him.

'Now then, now then,' he said nervously. 'Shush shush shush, stay quiet.'

'Frances,' Mehuru said quietly. 'See . . . Frances.'

John Bates nearly dropped the pan in amazement.

'Johnbates,' Mehuru said gently. 'I . . . want . . . Frances.'

'My God, he's talking,' John exclaimed. 'He said my name!' He turned his head and yelled up the stairs. 'The darkie's talking. The big one! He's talking words!'

Cook appeared at the top of the steps. 'If you've finished I'll shut this door,' she said crossly. 'I won't have it open all day. Shall I shut you in?'

'Wait a minute, if you please.' He thrust the bowl into Mehuru's arms.

'See Frances,' Mehuru repeated.

'Frances,' the driver nodded. 'Mrs Cole. But I know what you mean. I'll tell her.' He opened his mouth and suddenly shouted very loudly. Spittle flew from his red lips into the porridge, Mehuru could feel it on his face. 'I'll tell her!'

He turned and went back up the stairs. 'Remarkable,' he said as he closed the door and went into the kitchen. 'Here, Mrs Brown, tell Mrs Cole that the big nigger is asking for her. He's never done that before. He said her name.'

Brown sniffed disapprovingly. 'She's not even awake yet,' she snorted. She was laying the tray with Frances's drink of hot chocolate and a bread roll with fresh-churned butter and plum jam.

'Well, tell her when you take her breakfast in,' Bates said. 'She'll want to know. She takes a deal of trouble over them.'

Brown picked up the tray without answering and swept from the kitchen. But by the time she had woken Frances, drawn her curtains and set her tray before her on the bed, she knew that Bates was right.

'The big slave was asking for you,' she said.

Frances paused with the cup halfway to her lips. 'He asked for me?'

'He said, "see Frances", according to John Bates. I said I'd tell you. I hope I did right.'

'Yes, of course,' Frances said. 'I'd better see him at once.'

'You'll have your chocolate first?'

Frances pushed the tray to one side and got out of bed. 'No, you can make me some more later.' She was now accustomed to ordering what she wanted. 'Fetch me a wrapper and tie back my hair. I'll see him now. Is Mr Cole at home?'

'No, ma'am. He's gone out. He went over on the ferry to see Sir Charles Fairley at his hotel.'

'Then I'll come down in my wrapper.'

Frances brushed her own hair, scrupulously pinned her cap and tied her loose gown. 'Tell Cook I'm on my way,' Frances said, mindful of the protocol of Cook's kitchen.

There was a stony silence as she went into the kitchen but John was waiting by the cellar door. 'He said your name, Mrs Cole, clear as a bell. Shall I come down with you? Shall I bring my whip?'

Frances was about to refuse but then she hesitated.

'You don't know what he's doing,' John warned. 'It could be a trap, ma'am. I'll fetch my pistols as well before you go down.'

An old dark fear touched Frances. The fear of a woman outnumbered by men, the fear of one species among several of another, the master's fear when he is surrounded by slaves, the driver's fear when he knows himself hated, the slaver's fear when he knows he is a criminal. She tasted the sharp tang at the back of her throat which is the taste of power over others, and the fear that they, in turn, will take power over you. Then she thought of Mehuru and the darkness of his eyes and her vision of him as an individual – not as one of a dangerous crowd. She had absolute trust in him.

'I'll go down alone,' she said lightly, opening the door and descending the stairs.

Mehuru stepped forward to greet her and she knew from his face that something important had happened.

'Frances.'

'Mehuru.'

He said simply: 'Died of Shame,' and Frances in her ignorance did not know that his words were more than a name – the name the woman had given herself – but also a diagnosis of her sickness; and now, finally, her epitaph.

'Is she ill?'

He shook his head slowly. He leaned his head to one side in a mime of intense weariness, and then he shut his eyes.

'Dead?'

He looked at her questioningly.

Frances repeated his mime, closing her eyes. 'Dead?'

Mehuru nodded. 'Dead,' he said in his low steady voice, the word added to his growing English vocabulary. 'She is dead.'

He stepped to one side so that Frances could see the still body and the women who sat at her head and feet singing very softly.

Frances went forward and recoiled. She had forgotten the bridle. The young woman's face was encased in metal. Blood and saliva stained her neck from where the gag had cut her mouth and gums. She looked like a victim of some barbaric mediaeval torture. And Frances had ordered this. And now the woman was dead. There was a stillness about her which was very final. She looked peaceful; even in the strange helmet with a collar and chain, manacles and shackles, she looked at rest. For the first time she looked as if she were free, as if she had escaped from all the constraints they had put on her.

Frances shook her head, denying the truth, denying her

responsibility. 'But she was well,' she said. 'Except for . . .' She broke off. She could not bring herself to claim that Died of Shame had ever been well. She had been a captive in a strange land, she had been the victim of a rape, she had been in such great despair that she had filled her mouth and her belly with earth, and then, despite the cruelty of the bridle, she had escaped her tormentors and fled to her death.

Frances suddenly did not want to excuse herself, not even to Mehuru. She knew that she was culpable, that she was guilty of this woman's capture and her death. She had colluded with her capture and her ill-treatment, with her rape. Frances, by trading her prestige for Josiah's wealth and comfort, had been a party to bringing this young woman far from her home to her death. She had been raped and Frances had lunched with her rapist and promised him tickets for a society ball.

'I am sorry,' Frances said. Her voice was low. Mehuru did not recognise the words, but thought it was the first honest tone he had ever heard from her.

He bowed his head in a strange formal gesture. In his own language he said: 'We all have guilt to bear.'

Frances said nothing, and they stood, facing each other in silence. When she raised her face to him he was shocked, her dark eyes were filled with tears. He watched, fascinated, as one spilled over and rolled down her cheek. He put his hand out and touched it, almost as if he wanted to know if it was real. The skin of her cheek was warm, the tear was real. Frances stayed very still as he touched her, his fingertip soft and tentative against her cheekbone, as light as the brush of a feather.

Slowly he took his fingertip, wet with her tear, and put it to his lips. It was salty and wet, like a real tear. He tasted it on his tongue and gazed into her eyes as if he would read her like the oracle of Ifa.

'I am so very, very sorry,' she said again.

Chapter Fifteen

They took the body of Died of Shame away. There was a ripple of distress when Bates came into the cellar and took her by the wrists and dragged her like a doll up the steps.

'Mehuru, she should be washed and wrapped in cloth,' Grief accused him. 'You did not tell Frances!'

'How could I tell her?' he asked. 'I do not know the words for a proper burial. I told her that our sister was dead. I thought she would know what to do. I thought she would do the right things.'

They watched anxiously but the door at the head of the steps banged shut.

'Perhaps they will bury her as they bury their own people,' Kbara said. 'They may treat her with respect. It may not be our way but it could still be a good way.'

The girl called Homeless looked at him with anger. 'She is our sister,' she said. 'Of course she should be buried in our way. How else can she find her fathers?'

Kbara caught the sense of the Wolof words and was about to answer but Mehuru shook his head. At home they had the Gelede festival – the festival for soothing the mothers – designed solely to direct the awesome power of women for good. For ten days they would feast and dance, and watch ritual theatre to harness the magical power of women. Here in this dark cave, ominously like a grave, ominously like a womb, the women would seethe with their suppressed desires. Missing their children, missing their mothers, anything could focus their grief and anger. In any case the girl was right.

185

Mehuru had failed Died of Shame in her death as he had failed her in her life.

'It is I who am at fault, Homeless,' he said gently in her language. 'Not Kbara. We are not men here, we have no power. I cannot provide for you, or hunt, or farm, or even guard. I could not tell Frances what was needed. She seemed grieved, and I thought she would do the right things for our sister. I had not realised that these people can feel one thing and do another. They are strangers indeed.'

'Was she grieved for Died of Shame?' the youth called Accursed asked him.

'She had tears in her eyes,' Mehuru said. 'I trusted her. I thought she must care.'

The woman called Grief shook her head. 'She is a dreadful woman. She had tears in her eyes and yet she sent that rapist to bury his victim?'

'Yes,' Mehuru said. 'Exactly.' He sat on the stone bench, drew his knees up under his chin and wrapped his arms around them, isolating himself from the world, from the others.

'Are you praying, Obalawa?' Accursed asked in his endearing husky voice which was just breaking into the male depths and yet could still go unreliably squeaky.

Mehuru shook his head. 'I can summon no god,' he confessed. 'He comes to me no longer. I am waiting for him but he does not come. I am waiting for understanding, but it does not come either. Perhaps some day something will come to make sense of all this pain. Perhaps some day I will understand why we suffer this.'

The death of Died of Shame was to make no difference to the routine of the day, Sarah Cole decreed. The corpse was taken up to the Redclift graveyard and buried in an unmarked grave. It was not a pauper burial; Sarah paid threepence for the site and entered the sum in the company ledger as a loss. She looked accusingly at Frances as she dusted sand on the ink and closed the ledger. 'A loss,' she said reproachfully. 'You had better start teaching them to obey commands. We need to show a profit on this.'

They came into the parlour in silence and sat in their accustomed places. The two youngest children were not crying today, they were too shocked. Frances saw their little faces at table-top height as blank and as empty as new black slates.

She had brought her sketch and watercolour books for today's lesson, and she put up the easel at the head of the table. The first picture was the long view down the avenue of elms to the house at Whiteleaze.

'This is a house,' she said. She nodded at Mehuru. 'House.'

They knew now what she wanted of them and they repeated the word without emphasis, without interest. She might mean the paper, she might mean the easel. She might mean the artist or the gods who made it possible for men and women to dream and create art. They did not care. They repeated the word as she wished.

'This was my house,' Frances explained to Mehuru. 'Well, it was my uncle's house. I stayed here very often, and we dined here two or three times a week.'

Sarah Cole in the windowseat leaned forward to look at the easel, her curiosity overcoming her irritation with her sister-in-law.

Frances gestured to herself and then pointed to the picture. She said to Mehuru, 'This was my house. My house.'

So she was an exile too, Mehuru thought. That accounted for the strange sense of loss which hung around her. It accounted for her powerlessness in this place. She was a new arrival, she had not yet made it her home. He thought of his country and the careful arrangements of introducing a bride to a new home. The senior wife would fetch the new bride and take her to her husband's house. They would wash her legs and send her to his room. She would live in the senior wife's house as her apprentice, to learn what should be done and the right way to do things. For three months she would visit her parents only at night, when the work of the day was done. It was almost a game, the sneaking back home to mother, and any troubles in the early months could be whispered in the darkness. After three months the girl had served her apprenticeship and knew her rights. But in any case, there were few troubles. It was a world where men and women knew their duties to each other, and where the gods were kind. Before the slavers had come, before the slaving nations had been armed and set upon their neighbours, it had been a world of particular good fortune: fertile, with good weather, and long, long-established political stability.

Frances turned a page to show a competent watercolour of a still life. 'These are fruits,' she said. 'Fruits.'

She pointed to the painted fruits and they named them after her. 'Apple, pear, grapes, peach.'

She turned another page. It was a picture of a King Charles spaniel sitting at the edge of a cornfield. The pale green corn was bright with flowers, scarlet poppies and blue love-in-a-mist. The hedgerows around the field were spotted with dog roses and the nodding heads of foxgloves.

'This was my dog,' Frances said. 'My little dog.' Her voice quavered slightly. 'I had to give her away when I went to work. She was a spaniel.'

Mehuru heard the distress in her voice and looked from the picture to Frances's face. She tried to smile at him. 'My little dog,' she said. 'My companion.' Her eyes were bright with tears. 'I know it's very silly.' She pulled a small handkerchief from her pocket. 'But she was a wonderful little dog, she used to go everywhere with me. And I lost her, and lost my home, and lost my Papa . . .'

The women glared at Mehuru. 'Her tears do not mean much, then,' Grief remarked bitterly. 'One tear for Died of Shame, raped three times and dead in a cave, and a dozen tears for a picture of a monkey.'

'No,' Mehuru said. 'I was a fool to trust her. Her tears do not mean much at all.'

'They are chattering amongst themselves,' Miss Cole interrupted from the windowseat. 'How will they learn if they go on talking their own language and don't even listen to you?'

Frances cleared her throat and dabbed at her eyes. 'I beg your pardon,' she said to the sullen black faces. She turned a page of the easel and showed a picture of a church. 'This is my father's church,' she said. She looked at Mehuru and pointed to the building. 'Church,' she said. 'Jesus. Church.'

The slaves repeated the words in a sulky murmur. Frances smiled, pleased. 'Later on I shall teach you stories from the bible,' she promised.

She turned another page. 'And these are flowers.' She pointed to sketches of flower heads and named each one. They named them as she did.

Frances left the easel and sat down at the head of the table. 'Now,' she said brightly. 'My name is Frances. I come from England.' She pointed to Mehuru. 'Your name is Mehuru, you come from Africa.'

He stared at her in dull resentment.

'Go on,' Grief taunted him. 'You are her favourite. You tasted her tear. You trusted her. Speak as she bids you.'

'Say: "My name is Mehuru, I come from Africa".' Frances repeated her command.

He stared at her, a long burning stare filled with reproach. Frances stammered, and lost the thread of the lesson. 'What is it?' she asked him in an undertone, glancing quickly towards Miss Cole. 'What is the matter?'

He turned his head away from her, there was no mistaking the snub.

'Mehuru!' she whispered urgently. 'What is it?'

'My name is Mehuru,' he repeated in clear perfect English, mimicking her precisely, his accent sharp with anger, his very obedience an insult. 'My name is Mehuru. I come from Africa.'

*　　*　　*

189

Josiah Cole came home in time for dinner in a sunny mood. Frances, changing into yet another gown, heard him talking with his sister as he climbed the stairs.

'Two pieces of good work today. Sir Charles is considering placing money with us for us to act as his agents. You did well to suggest it, my dear, and Frances is a credit to us. If she can get him and Miss Honoria tickets for the Scott ball I will be obliged to her. And even better – Waring has closed the sale of his house with me at last! I was beginning to wonder if he meant to let me down.'

'I was beginning to wonder if it were not better to pull out from the deal altogether,' Sarah said. 'Brown told me that number 31 is to come on the market. Two for sale in such a short time must mean that both will be cheapened.'

'Queens Square will always be Queens Square,' Josiah declared firmly. 'Prices may fluctuate from time to time but it will always be the best area of Bristol.'

'It may be,' Sarah said urgently. 'But have a little patience, Brother, and think! With two houses on the square you could bargain with Waring, you could force his price down.'

'The deal is done,' Josiah said stubbornly. 'And I have shaken on it. My word is my bond, everyone knows that. I have agreed a price. I don't go running back to ask for a discount.'

'And when do we move? When do you have to pay the rest of the money?'

Frances opened her bedroom door and the two broke off.

'Excuse me.' She felt suddenly shy, as if she had been eavesdropping on a private agreement. 'But I heard you mention the house. Have we bought it at last?'

Josiah beamed at her, came up the last few steps, caught her hand and kissed it. 'Yes indeed, it is ours!' he said. 'You can move in tomorrow!'

'Tomorrow!'

'My brother exaggerates,' Sarah said. 'It is his way.'

'I do not!' he contradicted her. 'The house is being emptied now. When Mr Waring moves, at least he moves swiftly. He and his wife have moved out to stay in a hotel and their servants are ordered to move all their goods. He sent me a note to tell me that we can have the keys and call the place our own from tomorrow.'

'And the money?' Sarah demanded urgently over Frances's cry of delight. 'When is it due? We do not have it in hand, Josiah, you know.'

Josiah took her hand. 'Have confidence, Sarah,' he urged her. 'You do not buy a house like Queens Square outright with saved shillings. I have a long-term loan, against *Rose*'s profits. I do not have to repay until *Rose* comes in at the end of next year. This is my first great investment. And I have others in my mind. I have been waiting for this chance for a long time.'

'You have forestalled on a cargo?' Sarah was shocked. 'We have never done such a thing before, Josiah! The risk . . .'

'But how wonderful!' Frances interrupted. 'Will we not have to buy a great deal of furniture? Does the house need wallhangings renewing, and repainting? Is there not a lot to be done before we can move in?'

'You shall see for yourself,' Josiah said happily. 'We will go first thing in the morning and you shall judge for yourself. But I believe that there is very little that wants doing. Mrs Waring had it done throughout in Chinese fashion only last year. If the style is agreeable to you then we can simply move in our furniture and take up our residence.'

Frances inwardly swore that however dreadful Chinese fashion proved to be she would not complain. 'I am certain it will be delightful! I so long to live on the square.'

'We are taking a risk,' Sarah interrupted. 'I *will* be heard. We are taking a risk in doing business in this way. We are trading on credit and we have never done such a thing before.'

Frances was quenched. She looked to Josiah.

'We have traded small,' he said firmly. 'We had small

191

beginnings, Sarah, and we had to keep to our limits. But there are great profits to be made for men who dare to take a risk. It is my judgement that it is worth it.'

Sarah clutched her hands together in an odd involuntary movement. 'It is too great a risk,' she said. Frances looked at her curiously. The woman was near to tears. 'If *Rose* founders then we are ruined overnight. We cannot stake the survival of this trading house on such a gamble.'

Josiah hesitated, thinking for a moment that he would tell her of the further risks he had taken with *Rose* – uninsured for the middle passage, overloaded and ordered to smuggle slaves to the Spanish colonies; but Sarah's white anxious face dissuaded him. He could not face her anger and distress. He stretched out and stilled her wringing hands. 'Peace, Sister,' he urged her gently. 'There is no need for this worry.'

She looked at him as if he did not understand at all. 'I was born on the floor of a miner's hovel,' she said. 'I have been poor, Josiah, as you were not. You were born when we were on the rise; you know nothing about hardship.' She looked at Frances. 'You neither. You think that having to work and living here, over the warehouse, is poverty. I know you do, I have seen you looking down your nose at our ways and thinking them very mean. But I have known hardship that neither of you can understand. I have gone barefoot for lack of shoes and hungry for lack of food and I cannot *bear* to hear you talking, Josiah, about gambling with our livelihood. As if poverty were not waiting beneath our feet every day of our lives, waiting longing to gobble us up.' She was flushed, her eyes were bright with tears. 'We are in a little trow on a great river of poverty,' she cried. 'And your debts and your gambles, Josiah, will overturn us!'

He was taken aback by her vehemence. 'Sarah . . . I . . .'

'Promise me you will not run us into debt,' she demanded. 'Promise me that we will make an agreement with Mr Waring and pay him what we owe from our profits, not from forestalling on our cargoes.'

Josiah looked uncomfortable. 'Be still, Sister,' he said awkwardly. 'I am sorry to see you so distressed . . .'

'Promise me!'

'It is too late,' Josiah admitted. 'I have agreed to pay Waring a lump sum, some borrowed, some from *Daisy*'s profits, and I have sold *Rose*'s cargo already. The gamble has been laid, Sarah. You will have to accept it.' The rest of the gamble – the missing insurance, the smuggling – he left to silence.

She lost her colour at once, and swayed as if she might faint with fear. Frances, a silent observer between the two of them, thought that the older woman looked as if she had lost the love of her life. Sarah was obsessed with financial security. Nothing frightened her more than debt.

She took a deep breath and rallied. 'I am sorry to hear it.'

'It is signed and sealed and done,' Josiah said, impressing her with the finality of the deal.

'Then I can say nothing more,' she said with dignity. 'Except that I wish you had talked it over with me first, Josiah.' She carefully avoided looking at Frances. 'You would have discussed it with me, in the old days. You should have discussed it with me, even now.'

'I would have discussed it with you,' Josiah placated her. 'But it all took place in the coffee shop, it was quickly and easily done. And there is no great risk, Sarah. *Rose* is a good ship. There is no reason to think she will not come home safe.'

Sarah at once knocked on the wooden banister and Frances saw Josiah tap his foot involuntarily on the wooden tread of the stair.

'We had to buy the Queens Square house or throw away the deposit,' he reminded her. 'And I had promised a new house to Frances in the marriage settlement.'

'This house was our father's pride,' Sarah observed.

Josiah turned on the stair and smiled at her. 'It has been a good house for us,' he agreed. 'We have made our start from here. But now we must go upwards in the world.' He stopped

193

himself and laughed. 'Here! I must go upwards to my bed-chamber and wash before dinner. I am famished. I did not stop to eat at noon, I have been so busy this day.'

'Why?' Sarah asked, following him up the stairs. 'Have you found partners for *Daisy*?'

'Sir Charles is in for his share, of a thousand pounds, of course; and I have other partners to hand,' Josiah said happily. 'Money breeds money. Now it is known that Sir Charles has bought a share the others want to come in too. And when we are living in Queens Square it will be even easier. Have you had a good day?'

'We have done badly,' Sarah told him. 'Frances has lost one of the new slaves.'

Josiah looked quickly at Frances and saw her stricken face. 'One here or there does not matter,' he said kindly. 'Sarah, you must not reproach her. We are bound to lose two or three from a batch. It does not matter.'

He came up the last few steps, took Frances's hand and led her into her room.

'I am sorry,' Frances said. 'I do not think I should have the care of them. It was a woman, it was the woman . . .' She wanted to put the blame on Sir Charles, but she could not bring herself to speak of what he had done. 'It was one of the women. She ate earth and I let her be put in a bridle and now she is dead.'

Josiah seated her gently before her looking glass and stood behind her, his hands on her shoulders. 'It does not matter,' he said gently. 'I promise you, my dear, do not fret. One here or there makes no difference. This is an experiment. If we do well and sell at a profit we will repeat it on a grander scale. If they all die tomorrow then we will have learned that it cannot be done. Don't fret, my dear, you are doing the best you can and it is a difficult business, breaking slaves.'

He loosened the pins in the back of her head and Frances's coils of hair started to tumble down around her shoulders.

Frances felt lulled, as if she were a little girl again with her mother plaiting her hair. 'I do not know that I can teach them, Josiah. It is not like teaching children. They are so different from us, and the man who understands the most, Mehuru . . .' She broke off. 'He is not like a slave,' she said inadequately. 'I cannot think of him as a slave. I keep thinking of him as a civilised man.'

Josiah took up her silver brushes and gently brushed her hair. 'This is nonsense,' he said gently. 'You are overtired. Just do your best, my dear, it is nothing more than an experiment. We have to try, and we have to take chances. I cannot make the life for us which we desire without taking chances. We have to learn to take risks. I am a venturer, Frances! Not a shopkeeper!'

He swept the hair back from her forehead and from her temples where her pulse throbbed. It was a soothing gentle caress, the pressure of the soft bristles on her head and then the clean sweep.

'It makes me uneasy,' Frances confessed. 'To think of them all in my charge.'

'It is the nature of the Trade,' Josiah comforted her. 'You must not think of them as people or you will get distressed. They are commodities, my dear, they are goods, and English merchants have been trading in them for more than a hundred years.'

'So long? I did not know it had been so long! Why, how many slaves have we taken?'

'Oh, my dear! Who can say? English ships have grown bigger every year. The Trade has doubled and quadrupled.'

Frances saw in the mirror that her face was shocked. 'Hundreds of slaves? Thousands?' she asked.

Josiah shrugged. 'More. Many many more. Millions. It is an enormous business – three million slaves taken by the English in this century alone, and all the other European countries are slavers too.' He smoothed her hair away from her face. 'I see you are surprised,' he said. 'It is a mighty Trade, it is the very backbone of Britain, there is not a port

195

that does not deal in it. There is no family in the country that does not feel the benefit. We all profit from it. It is the greatest trade that the world has ever known. It crosses and recrosses the Atlantic, it makes massive fortunes. We *all* profit.'

'I did not know,' Frances said. She thought of the light easy conversation at her uncle's dining table, of her father's gently reproachful sermons against the sin of laziness, or gluttony. No-one had ever questioned the ethics of the slave trade in her hearing. No-one had even thought about it. She had heard nothing but complaints of radicals and abolitionists who wanted to threaten the prosperity of Britain, ruin the colonies and overpay idle working men. 'But it must have destroyed Africa,' she exclaimed suddenly. 'Taking so many people, and all of them young, and most of them men. It must have emptied villages, it must have ravaged whole countries.'

She tried to imagine what it would be like in England if three million young men and women had been stolen away in only a hundred years. The country would be devastated. There would be no wealth, no farms, no industries, no roads. It would be a blow to the very heart of a nation. And the absence of three million people would mean that children were not conceived, that babies were not born. In the next generation seven million would be missing, in the next fifteen. There would be a gap, a gulf into which poverty and despair would flood. Inventions would not be made, industries would not develop, farms would lie idle, the whole fabric of society and order would collapse.

Josiah nodded. 'Africa is our farm, my dear. The farm produces the stock, we ship the stock to where it is needed. Africa is a slave-farm to serve the civilised world. It is a most elegant and efficient system.'

Frances leaned forward and let her hair hide her face from Josiah's easy smile. She felt dizzy with the view of the world suddenly opened before her. She could not imagine how she had known none of this, how successfully it had been gilded over. And now her livelihood depended on its successful continuance. 'It must be wrong,' she said. But she spoke without conviction. 'It cannot be right for us to farm a whole continent for our own use. And they are not stock, Josiah. The men and women I am teaching, they are not stock. They are people and they feel as we do – at least I think they do.'

'Who knows?' Josiah asked comfortably. 'When you have taught them to speak and civilised them perhaps you will teach them Christian feelings too, Frances. That would be a fine thing to do. I am sure you are doing well, far better than most ladies could.'

Josiah brushed softly and steadily and then his hand came under her hair and caressed the back of her neck. Frances sat still and let him do what he wished. She thought of the thousands of deaths he must have caused and the heartbreak in those hundred, thousand, million homes. She looked up and met his kind face in the mirror.

'I fear it is not right Josiah,' she said.

He smiled at her. 'You're looking very pretty,' he said gently. 'I love your hair let down.'

Chapter Sixteen

Josiah awoke Frances early. He came into her room himself and drew back the window curtain and the half-curtain at the head of her bed. The fire had been lit in skilful silence by the scullery maid before dawn and the room was warm.

'Up and awake, Mrs Cole!' Josiah cried joyfully. 'I have a carriage ordered for us at eight. I am taking you to see your new house today!'

Frances sat up in bed and laughed at his eagerness. 'But the Warings will still be packing their goods!'

'I shall throw them out of the back door when you enter the front!' Josiah exclaimed.

There was a tap on the door and Brown stood hesitantly in the doorway with Frances's tray in her hands.

'I'll take that!' Josiah said, bustling forward. He put the tray on Frances's knees. 'Now eat up, Wife, and meet me downstairs in an hour. No later, mind!'

Frances smiled at him. 'I shall be prompt,' she promised.

Josiah bent to kiss her forehead. Obeying an impulse, Frances lifted her face and their lips met. Josiah's kiss was very gentle. Frances felt tender towards him, he was so exuberant, like a little boy about to open a gift. In Lady Scott's eyes he might be nothing more than a vulgar trader, but Frances acknowledged that he was her husband and that her future wealth and happiness depended on him. And besides, she was coming to like him.

'An hour,' Josiah said ebulliently, and went from her room.

*   *   *

The carriage was waiting on the cobbled quay outside. Frances was dressed in her best dark blue velvet gown and pelisse with matching blue hat and muff.

'You look very fine,' Josiah said. He did not know that it was an old gown, carefully unpicked and resewn with the bald patches of the velvet folded inside where they would not show. 'You look very grand. You look like a proper lady.'

Frances winced at that. 'I should hope so, indeed.'

Josiah heard the slight reproof in her voice. 'Of course, of course,' he said hastily. 'Shall we go?'

Sarah was at the top of the stairs. Frances hesitated. 'Are you not coming, Sarah?'

'There are things that have to be done to ensure that the *Daisy* sails on time. Cargo to be ordered and checked, papers to be made ready. All the permits have to be entered. I shall spend this morning at work.'

Frances wavered a little at the reproach but Josiah was cheery. 'Excellent!' he exclaimed. 'And do not think that we are gallivanting, Sister. There are many ways to make money in this town and one of them is to be seen to be prosperous. This move will be the making of us, I swear it!'

'And will she teach the slaves this afternoon?' Sarah asked rudely.

'Yes, yes,' Josiah said. He opened the door, led Frances to the coach, and handed her in. 'And tell Brown that the slaves can start to help packing. I want us to move in as soon as possible. They can start today.'

Frances settled herself in the carriage and smiled half-apologetically at the dark house and Sarah's irritable glare. Josiah swung himself into the seat beside her as the carriage jolted on the cobbles and lurched forward. 'Sour as lemons,' Josiah said cheerfully under his breath. 'Now, Mrs Cole, you shall see something!'

The house was indeed furnished in Chinese fashion. Frances had to close her eyes when she first saw the best parlour, which

199

was gloriously ornamented with plasterwork that sprawled magnificently from the top third of the walls to the central rose in the middle of the ceiling, rich with dragons, cherubs, swirling leaves, wild vines and the ultimate vulgarity of long-beaked ho-ho birds. The walls were lined with plush red silk – an eccentric choice given that the carpet, all twining vine leaves and fruit, was blue, and the curtains were green.

'Very grand,' Josiah said with satisfaction. 'Very fashionable. Colourful! I doubt there is another house like it in Bristol!'

'I doubt it too,' Frances said. She stepped from the room and peeped into the second parlour opposite, which was slightly smaller and plainer. 'And this is a very pretty room.'

'You won't sit here,' Josiah ruled. 'The best room is surely the morning room at the front of the house? This back room will be my office, and tradesmen can come and see me and enter from the back door. We shall have two doors now, Mrs Cole! No more working men tapping at your front door! No more tradesmen marching through your hall.'

Frances smiled. Despite the excesses of the plasterwork and the exuberant colour schemes it was a fine house, built in simple rectangle shapes; four rooms on the ground floor, four above, four above them, and then the attic rooms fitted into the roof. The kitchen and domestic rooms were crammed into the rear courtyard, the cellar stored wine and goods. As they stood in the hall they heard a crash and muffled oath from above as one of the Warings' servants dropped something.

'We will need to take on more staff,' Frances thought aloud. 'There is too much to be done for Brown and the scullery maid in a big house like this.'

'Aye,' Josiah said with satisfaction. 'We will use the slaves for now. And we will have to buy furniture to fill the place up a bit. Shall we buy all Chinese goods, my dear? I have a man in mind who imports very good copies from India, I swear you would not tell the difference.'

Frances managed to smile. 'I think I would prefer some simple English furniture.'

200

'But Chinoiserie is all the rage!' Josiah expostulated. 'It is the very thing! And with the house already so designed!'

Frances gave him a small sideways glance.

'Is it a little ornate for your taste?' he asked. He was immediately unsure. 'I thought it very fine? Is it not any good?'

Frances touched his bare hand with her gloved finger. 'Mr Cole, it is very fine indeed,' she said. 'And it is the very height of fashion. But I think we will look a little less . . .' she hesitated, trying to find a word that would not hurt his feelings '. . . a little less new if we buy some furniture which is not at the very top of fashion but which will give us a little background.'

'Background, is it?' Josiah asked. 'But not second-hand. I'm not having other people's goods furnishing my house. I'm not a bailiff to sit on other men's chairs.'

'My parents' furniture was kept at Whiteleaze,' Frances offered. 'They had some very fine pieces and it is good to have things in a house which are not all new. They give a house a sense of . . . belonging.'

'Old stuff?' Josiah said, still ready to argue. 'We don't want old stuff.'

'From the Scott family,' Frances added quickly. 'Heirlooms.'

'Oh, heirlooms!' Josiah cheered immediately. 'I thought you meant old rubbishy stuff. Heirlooms is excellent. And with the Scott crest? Does it all have the Scott crest? Or we could put the Scott crest on anything we buy, couldn't we?'

Frances was about to refuse but then she saw the eagerness in his face. 'Oh well,' she said, thinking that no-one who would matter would ever know. 'Why not?'

'But we'll buy some China stuff as well,' Josiah persisted. 'Great vases and that.'

'Yes,' Frances said. 'I shall write to Lady Scott for my father's furniture this afternoon. When we see what we still lack, we can buy it.'

'But we will have a great vase or two,' Josiah insisted. 'Whatever furniture you have. We will have a great Chinese vase or two. And porcelain dragons. I have seen them in red porcelain. We will have a pair of dragons!'

Frances giggled. 'I could not live here without!' she told him. 'I am depending on it.'

Josiah gave her his half-ashamed rueful smile. 'You think I am a fool. But I am assured that China stuff is the thing.'

'It is,' Frances agreed. 'And as long as we do not have too much then the house will look very lovely.'

'You will make it nice?'

For the second time that day Frances was prompted to show him affection. She reached up and put a dry kiss on his cheek. 'I will,' she promised. 'I will make it lovely for us.'

He was surprised at her caress, and they stood in embarrassed silence for a moment.

'I should like to see the upstairs rooms.' Frances moved away and up the stairs, Josiah following.

Only when she had seen all over the house, from the attic bedrooms to the kitchen with the new-designed range for cooking, did Josiah agree that they could leave the Warings' servants to take the last of their things out and close the big front door behind them.

Just as they were leaving, a carriage drew up. It was Mrs Waring.

'Mrs Cole.' She stepped down to shake Frances's hand. 'You must forgive my informality but I so wanted to see you and wish you well in your new house. It has been a happy house for us, I trust it will be good for you too.'

'You're very kind,' Frances replied, taking the rather grimy kid glove in her hand. 'May I present my husband? Mr Cole.'

Mrs Waring turned to smile at him and gave him two fingers to shake. 'And will you be moving in at once?' she asked. 'And will you be entertaining? Shall we see Lord and Lady Scott here soon?'

Frances nodded. 'We shall move in the New Year. My uncle and aunt will be constant visitors, I don't doubt. Perhaps you would like to come to tea when we are settled?'

Mrs Waring smiled. 'I shall be delighted.'

'Thursday is our day at home,' Frances said easily. Josiah, who had not known that he had a day at home until this moment, opened his mouth to say something and then closed it again. It was apparent to him that Frances was as skilled at this, her work, as he was on the dockside.

'And Mr Waring?' Frances enquired smoothly.

'He is very well. He will be delighted to accompany me. And your sister-in-law is well?'

'Miss Cole is in excellent health,' Frances replied. 'But I must not keep you talking here in the street.' Her tone implied the slightest of reproofs.

Mrs Waring bustled at once towards her carriage. 'Oh no! Of course! Thursdays, then!'

'I shall be so pleased to see you,' Frances said sweetly. 'Good day.'

The carriage moved off and Frances raised a hand in a very small wave. 'By George,' Josiah said, impressed. 'You handled her very sweetly, my dear, you handled her like a tickled trout.'

Frances tried to look at him reprovingly but for the second time that day she could not contain a giggle. '*Not* a tickled trout,' she said. 'Please don't say that, Josiah. Not ever. Not a tickled trout.'

He grinned. 'Oh aye. Now come away, Mrs Cole. I have something else to show you before we go home.'

Frances climbed back into the carriage and Josiah ordered the driver to go once again to the Hot Well. They drove up Park Street, and then dropped down to the road which ran alongside the river. The tide was in and the bright sunshine danced on the water. The air was warm and smelled salty. Seagulls wheeled over the river, the sunshine bright on their white plumage as they dived for garbage in the water. Frances let down the window of the carriage and looked out over the river to the Rownham ferry on the far side.

'In summer I should like to cross the river and go for a picnic,' she said.

'You may have work which keeps you this side of the river,' Josiah warned her portentously.

The carriage rolled up before the little colonnade of shops which led to the Hot Well Pump Room.

'The Merchant Venturers who own the Pump Room, this row of shops and indeed half the lodging houses, are looking for a tenant to take the whole lot off their hands,' Josiah said.

Frances gasped. 'Not you?'

Josiah gave her a little conspiratorial smile. 'Now not a word to Sarah, who would rather die. But I think that I might venture it. Not the whole of the property, not by a long way. But I think I might make some money from the Pump Room and the spa, don't you?'

'You have planned this for some time,' Frances observed acutely. 'When we came here on my first visit you were thinking of it then.'

'I heard rumours, but the whole property is owned by the Merchant Venturers,' Josiah said. 'I cannot buy in to the lease without their consent. There is no way to get into the business without their blessing.'

Frances nodded, staring out at the pretty diminutive row of new shops and the towering square Pump Room building.

'If I got it, d'you think we could make it a great success?' Josiah asked. 'I thought that if you advised me on the fashionable world and things that we needed to do, and if Lord Scott could be prevailed to come, and Lady Scott . . . if we made it as grand a place as Bath?'

Frances nibbled the tip of her glove, thinking.

'It would have to be as good as Bath,' Josiah went on. 'People visit here but the season is too short, and we need to draw in more customers. It is dead in winter, we need local Bristol society to come too. And I do not know what it lacks. Would you know?'

'Yes,' Frances said finally. 'I think I know what we would need and how it could be done. And certainly I know the people that we would invite to make it fashionable. All of that

204

'I could do. But it would take a lot of money, Josiah, I don't know how much.'

He nodded. 'With the lease in my pocket I could borrow. But I have to buy the lease from the Merchant Venturers' association.' He gritted his teeth and then, in a sudden gesture of frustration, thumped his fist into his open palm. 'Everywhere I go in this town they confront me,' he groaned. 'I cannot get insurance at their rates and on their terms. I cannot get my ship unloaded without hiring their crane. Everything I do, I need their blessing. I *have* to be in with them, Frances. I have to have it.'

'I see it,' Frances concurred. 'I have seen it from the beginning. But will they not invite you? Surely now you are a big enough trader?'

'With the house in Queens Square, and with you, and with Lord Scott backing us, and with Sir Charles investing with us, surely then they will ask me?'

'Mrs Waring.' Frances named the key to their social success.

'Her, and her friends, and their husbands,' Josiah agreed. 'It is all part of a pattern which we have to make around us. We have to make ourselves one with them. We have to get in.'

Frances nodded and then smiled at him. 'I can do that,' she declared. 'I can do that for you, Mr Cole. Mrs Waring, her friends and their husbands can be managed. I can get us on the inside, as you wish.'

Sarah remained silent and sulky for the rest of the month of December. The festival of Christmas came and went in the little house on the quay with no greater acknowledgement than an extra visit to church, a day off for Cook and Brown – so a cold collation was laid at midday for them to eat at dinner time – and an early night. Frances, eating cold dried-up ham for her Christmas dinner, with cold boiled potatoes and a cold chicken pie, consoled herself with the thought that next month they would be in the house on the square, and she would have the ordering of dinner. She tried not to think of the noisy jolly dinners at Whiteleaze and at the little parsonage when her mother and father had been alive. She went to bed with a shawl wrapped tight around her, and found in the morning that she had been clinging to her pillow for comfort. There were stars and flowers of frost on her window on the morning of Boxing Day, and they did not melt until long after breakfast. At Whiteleaze they would be hunting, the hounds meeting on the lawn before the house and Lord Scott resplendent in his pink coat. Or the family might be in London, and there would be a continual parade of morning callers showing off their winter furs and smart boots.

Frances wore her warmest gown and sat as close as she could to the parlour fire. Inside her boots, her toes stung and burned with scarlet chilblains. In the stuffy room she felt her breath come short and laboured. On the other side of the fire, Sarah sat straight-backed, wreathed in woollen shawls, nursing a cold. She sniffed. Frances estimated that she sniffed three times every minute. They spent the long winter evening sewing, reading sermons, and waiting for the clock to show nine o'clock so that the tea tray could come in, and then they could go to bed.

The move to the new house in January was not as smooth as Josiah had confidently predicted. The house on the quayside was turned upside down with the confusion of packing, and then unpacking things that were needed at once. The plan was to move everything, furniture, goods, wine, food, and all the stored letters and papers of years over the bridge to the square on the other side of the river. But even with the slaves working under the command of John Bates and his lad, it took several days before the furniture and the goods were shifted, and in the two nights of confusion Frances slept in a bedroom bare of anything but her bed, and took her breakfast off kitchen china.

Frances selected only the very best pieces of furniture from the warehouse to send across the river. The Coles' furniture was old and shabby, most of it badly made. Frances left almost all of Josiah's office furniture; his worn desk and the captain's chair were riddled with woodworm. Sarah took a pride in insisting that all the bedroom furniture should be moved, and the parlour table and chairs. 'I chose it myself,' she told Frances, smoothing the cheap walnut wood. 'In the year that we bought the *Lily*.'

'Lovely,' Frances said.

The carters came from Whiteleaze with Frances's stored furniture and a note from Lord Scott wishing Frances every happiness in her new house. Lady Scott sent her card and Frances, who expected little affection from her ladyship, blessed her for that chill courtesy and put the card on the silver tray in the hall so that other visitors leaving their cards would be sure to see it.

In all the business and confusion Frances remembered to order a livery and shoes for the slaves. 'They cannot go bare-foot up and down the road to Queens Square,' she insisted when Sarah complained of the expense. 'They will get sick if they are too cold, and their feet are already bad with chilblains. It will do us no good if they are ill, but it will help us a great deal if they are seen smartly dressed and looking the part.'

The slaves were to have two attic rooms at the top of the house, one for the women and girls and young children, and one for the men and boys. They were to have straw pallets and blankets. They were to have jugs and ewers for washing, and proper chamber pots for their use. They were to be treated as servants and to be freed from their manacles and chains.

'But locked in at night,' Miss Cole specified. 'And stout bars on the windows.'

Frances nodded. The move to the new house had conferred on her, at last, the status of the senior woman in the house. She took the decisions for the new place, and only conferred with Sarah out of courtesy. 'We would have to release them sooner or later,' she pointed out. 'We would have to trust them not to run away. Besides, where would they run to?'

'There are many people who would be only too pleased to kidnap them for sale,' Miss Cole said. 'Captains on their way back to the West Indies, visitors to England. Or English families who see the chance of getting a servant for free. Or they might simply escape and live free.'

'Are they free men – those black men who work on the quayside?' Frances asked.

'Most of them,' Sarah replied. 'Their masters may have died and freed them in their wills, or they may have earned enough to buy their freedom. Or they may have escaped. There are many free blacks now; in London there are tens of thousands. And every port has more and more of them.'

'So our slaves could be free one day.' Frances spoke her thoughts aloud. She was thinking of what Mehuru would do with his freedom if he were one day to be released. She did not know what he wanted, his dark face was inscrutable now when he turned it to her. In the hurry of moving there had been only short lessons most days, and some not at all.

Even without lessons they were learning many words, words of command and words of abuse. Mehuru in particular listened intently to all the conversation around him and Frances, watching him as he took the weight of a load of bedding on his back, could see the comprehension in his face. But however fluent Mehuru might become, Frances could not command his speech. Nothing could make him want to talk to her. His gaze was veiled, he could act incomprehension. It was his final defence. It was a problem Frances had not anticipated: that Mehuru might understand almost everything but refuse to speak. When she asked him a question his face would become deliberately dull and stolid. Sometimes she thought he might know a million words of English, might speak as fluently as Josiah, and still hide behind an assumed ignorance, and act dumb.

She knew he had not forgiven her for the death of Died of Shame. She knew he blamed her for betraying the woman to Sir Charles. But as the days went on and Frances ran from the top of the house to the kitchens several times a day, supervising the unpacking and the placing of furniture in the new rooms, she put it into a corner of her mind and began to forget all about it. As Josiah had said, it was only one slave among many, and they had always known that they would be likely to lose two or three within the first year. If the woman had not died in the cave she might have died of the cold, or of some disease. There was much for Frances to do, it was easy for her to forget her sense of guilt. It was easier for her to forget than to remember.

Mehuru did not forget Died of Shame and the others did not forget either. The bustle around the new house they regarded with anxious suspicion, not knowing what it might mean. The stockings and shoes were intolerably uncomfortable for the first few days; feet hardened by walking barefoot did not fit into the stiff cheap leather. But after a few days they learned to like the comfort of warm feet, and when they walked along the Redclift quay up to the bridge and back again on the greasy cold cobbles around frozen middens, they were glad to be dry-shod.

Without the weight of the collar and the constant clink clink of the chains, Mehuru tried to straighten up and look about him. But he found the muscles of his neck were knotted tight, he was used to the weight of the collar. For days he could not teach himself to walk like a man, he could not rid himself of the slavish shuffle of a dog whose neck has always been chained to a tether. In his shoes and stockings, in his warm breeches and grubby shirt, Mehuru crept from the dockside to the new house, carrying goods and pushing a cart, and knew himself to be walking head bowed, neck bent, like a man without pride, like a man without hope, like the slave he was.

Chapter Seventeen

They completed the move to the house on Queens Square by the end of January and Frances was able to preside over her first day 'at home' on the following Thursday.

Mr and Mrs Waring came, and Mrs Waring brought her sister, Mrs Shore, who was married to one of the senior traders in the Bristol Merchant Venturers. While they were taking a dish of tea Mr Woolwick was announced, calling to present his compliments to his new neighbour.

'You'll forgive me bursting in on you,' he apologised. 'But since we live next door I thought I might intrude when I saw the carriages.'

'Of course,' Frances said. She nodded at Brown to bring another teacup. 'I am delighted that you have called. Do you know Mr and Mrs Waring and Mrs Shore?'

Mr Woolwick nodded at Mr Waring and bowed to the ladies. 'Aye. I'm afraid we are a tight-knit little group. Mrs Shore's husband is my cousin.'

Frances smiled. 'Then it is you who should introduce me,' she said pleasantly. 'For I am likely to be the only stranger here.'

'Newcomers are very welcome,' Mr Waring declared gallantly. 'Especially such a lady as yourself. Do you have no friends in Bristol, Mrs Cole?'

'Only my dear sister-in-law,' Frances said tactfully. Sarah Cole, sitting behind the tea tray, smiled thinly. 'I was born and bred in the country near Bath.'

'At Whiteleaze?' Mr Woolwick enquired.

'Oh, do you know my uncle, Lord Scott?'

'I have heard of him, of course. And we are members of the same club in London, but we are not personally acquainted.'

'I hope he will call soon with Lady Scott,' Frances said. 'And my cousins, the Miss Scotts.'

'Is Mr Cole not at home?' Mrs Waring asked.

Frances smiled at her. 'I do not know about Mr Waring, but I find that my husband is curiously reluctant to take tea. It is as well that he is not a tea importer.'

Mr Waring and Mr Woolwick chuckled ruefully.

'I, for one, take tea under protest,' Mr Waring admitted. 'But on this occasion, and with this hostess, I was easily persuaded!'

'Well, I hope I can tempt you to supper on another day,' Frances said easily, turning her head to look up at him. 'I find I can command my husband with the promise of a good table more easily than I can summon him to tea.'

'Gentlemen often prefer to work during the day,' Mrs Waring agreed. 'Though what they find to do in the coffee house all day long is a mystery to me.'

'Why, they drink coffee and we drink tea, and we all of us use sugar!' Frances exclaimed.

'Mrs Cole, you have learned all there is to know of trade.' Mr Woolwick beamed at her. 'Mr Cole is a fortunate man.'

Frances suppressed any thoughts of what her parents would say at such a compliment to their daughter. Their one concern in life had been to cling to the precarious status of intimacy with Whiteleaze and keep a distance from trade, and now their daughter was seated in a parlour flirting daintily with Bristol merchants and being complimented on her grasp of business.

The door opened and Josiah came in. He was looking very smart, dressed as Frances had requested in buff riding breeches and highly polished boots with a well-cut brown coat with deep dark brown cuffs and collar. He had wanted to wear his best suit but Frances had dissuaded him. He looked

211

better in riding clothes, he looked more established, he looked more at ease. 'But I don't have a horse,' he protested.

'You don't have one yet,' Frances corrected him. 'Anyway, they are not to know that you have not been riding for pleasure.'

'On a working day?' he demanded.

Frances held up one admonitory finger. 'Riding breeches,' she said, and Josiah had obeyed.

'Why, here is Mr Cole now!' Frances exclaimed in well-simulated surprise. She introduced him to the ladies, and he greeted the men. 'And I was complaining that I could not tempt you to tea, Mr Cole!'

'Indeed you cannot,' he said. 'But I have ordered punch for the gentlemen in my parlour if they would like to take a glass?'

Stephen Waring and George Woolwick rose to their feet at once.

'Well, run along,' Frances said indulgently. 'But do not kidnap my guests for long, Mr Cole!' She turned and smiled at the ladies. 'At least we can have a comfortable gossip on our own. You must tell me all the people I must meet in Bristol, and, if I may ask, Mrs Waring, would you tell me who does your hats? I thought you wore such a pretty bonnet the other day, and that cap is enchanting!'

Under Sarah's amazed gaze Frances slipped easily from charming the men to charming the ladies. Josiah abstracted the men from the room as easily as a pickpocket dipping for shillings, and led them off to drink punch and talk business. No-one could have suspected that the whole campaign had been planned and executed by Frances, but when Brown closed the front door on the last of their guests Josiah called for a bottle of champagne, popped the cork in the best parlour and spilled it on the hearthrug.

'Here's to you, Mrs Cole!' he cried, pouring Frances a brimming glass. 'And here's to you, Sarah! And here's to me, because I have just been offered insurance for *Daisy* at the Merchant Venturer rates. I was afraid I would have to send

212

her out uninsured. Now she can sail, and *Lily* is due in any day, and they will insure her too. And I am well on the way to being invited to join the Venturers.'

'Not already?' Frances asked, taking a glass and sipping.

'In the parlour just now!' Josiah confirmed. 'I could hardly believe it myself. They had a glass of punch with me, they asked me about Lord Scott and Sir Charles and I was just as you said I should be – discreet. I said nothing at all and they understood far more than is the truth. They are certain that both his lordship and Sir Charles are my partners, and the next thing I know is, do I need an insurer for my vessels? – yes please, says I – and then would I like to go to a little supper party – just for gentlemen – at the Custom House next week? – yes please, says I!'

Frances crowed with delight and clinked her glass against his. 'What a campaign! And so quick!'

Josiah shook his head. 'I knew we would do it,' he said. 'I knew you could do it. But I never thought it would tumble into our laps on our first night!'

Frances found herself laughing for joy, for the first time in long long years. 'And all I have to do is to buy a dreadful bonnet from Mrs Waring's milliner!'

'I shall reimburse you,' Josiah promised swiftly. 'I will buy it for you myself and you can fling it in the dock.'

'I do not understand,' Sarah said slowly. 'I thought you did not want to attend Frances's tea party.'

'A ruse! A ruse!' Josiah huzzahed. 'Frances thought of it all, tea for the ladies and punch in another room for the gentlemen. And now you see how right she is, Sister. We have made more progress in one afternoon than we made in a lifetime of trading.'

Sarah put down her glass of champagne with unnecessary force. 'I see that we are pretending to be what we are not,' she said sharply. 'I see that we are pretending to partners we do not have. I see that we are trying to live above our station in life and claiming kinship and partnership where they do not exist. I am the daughter of a man who was not ashamed to be a collier, and proud to own one little trow. Now I find I have to pretend that I am on calling terms with Lady Scott of Whiteleaze whom I met once, and did not much care for.'

Frances turned a shocked face to Josiah.

'Sarah . . .' he began.

'We were traders,' she said fiercely. 'Frances is making us over into mountebanks.'

'You are tired with the move and all the changes . . .'

'I am not tired,' Sarah contradicted him. 'I was never tired when I worked all the hours of the day on the company papers and accounts. But when I have to sit in the parlour and tell a string of lies to women who know nothing – yes! then I am weary of the turn our business has taken. I have been clerk, and factor, and ship's husband in this trading house. And now you expect me to simper in the parlour among a gaggle of women!'

Josiah was stunned. 'You still have your place in the company, Sarah.'

'I cannot lie and chatter about bonnets,' she said bitterly. 'I cannot do the pretty as Frances does.'

'I don't ask you to . . .'

'You do! You do!' she exclaimed passionately. 'I have sat here listening to nonsense all afternoon while you have been talking business in your study. It is *my* business too! It is *my* inheritance too! Da never spent a penny without checking with me. I knew every transaction in the books. I knew every guinea we made. And now you leave me with the women while you talk business with the men.'

'It has to be done!' Josiah exclaimed. 'We can't stay as we were. We can't be a little dockside trading house with you at the books and me on the quayside. We'll employ proper clerks, we'll open an office. We have to rise,' Josiah said exasperatedly. 'We have to be ladies and gentlemen.'

'I am not a lady!' Sarah screamed at him. 'I am the daughter of a working man, and I am proud of it.'

There was a stunned silence.

'I am so sorry,' Frances said feebly. She swallowed down her fear at Sarah's anger and choked. Her nervous consumptive little cough sounded very loud in the room. 'I did not mean to offend you, Sarah. I did not mean to embarrass you.'

Sarah shrugged her shoulders rudely, her face still trembling with anger. 'You can't help it. It's the way you were reared. But I can't pretend to it. And I won't pretend to it. I am the daughter of a trader and the sister of a trader. This is the business I was brought up to do. This is the business I understand; an honourable business done by hard-working merchants. Pushing in among our betters, mixing with the gentlemen of the Corporation, claiming kinship with lords and ladies and trading on their name ... that is not my business and I cannot do it.'

Josiah said nothing. Both women waited for him to speak. 'It has to be done,' he said at last. 'I have to join the Venturers, you know this, Sarah. I cannot get the capital, I cannot get insured, I cannot get the trade unless I am in.'

'They would have invited you on your own merits in the end,' she replied, not looking towards Frances. 'You did not have to marry and claim kinship with lords.'

'Never,' he said bluntly. 'You do not know what it was like, Sarah, in the coffee house and on the quay. They would never have had me without this house, without Frances. We would have stayed there forever.'

'There are worse places,' she said bitterly. 'You don't remember, Josiah, you don't remember where our family came from. There are worse places to be than the storehouse of a prosperous trader.'

'And there are better,' he argued stubbornly. 'We are on the rise, Sarah. Frances knows how to do it. I know how to profit from it. You must be glad of it. You *must* learn to be glad of it.'

Her bony face was white and stubborn. 'I fear it,' she said bleakly.

Josiah made no reply.

'I bid you both goodnight.' Sarah moved to the door. 'I shall dine in my room.'

At the doorway she hesitated, as if she expected Josiah would call her back, but he stood with his back to the fire and let her go.

The door closed behind her with a firm click. Josiah and Frances were silent.

'I am sorry . . .' Frances repeated awkwardly.

'It is not your fault,' Josiah said. 'We have moved too fast for her, we have got on too quick. And she is old-fashioned and stubborn as a grandma.'

'But this *is* the right thing?' Frances confirmed. 'This is the way ahead for you? You do not risk springing up too fast?'

'This is not a bubble which will burst,' Josiah said, his confidence returning. 'This is the direction in which I have aimed for years. Even my father would have been a Merchant Venturer if he could have had the chance. My family is on the rise and this is where the crest of our wave will take us. Drink up your champagne, Frances, we have done good work this afternoon. Whatever Sarah says!'

It was strange dining together. It was the first meal they had eaten alone in six months of married life. It was the first time they had ever been without Sarah's critical observation. Frances, looking down the long table at Josiah seated at the head, thought that for the first time she felt truly married to him. They had plans and ambitions in common, they had shared the excitement of their first success. They had chosen a house together and it was furnished by them both. The rooms might fluctuate violently, sometimes garish, sometimes elegant, but this reflected the nature of the marriage, and the compromises they had both made for the sake of harmony.

She saw him seated at the head of her father's dining table and for once she did not fear what her father might have thought. If anything, she was irritated by her father's imagined distress. This was not the son-in-law he would have chosen; but Frances thought that her father had been reckless with

216

her life. He had made no provision for her – neither a suitor of his choice, nor an independent fortune. Josiah was the only man who had offered. He might not be situated as her father would have wished, he might not speak correctly, he might wear the wrong clothes and his taste in furniture and decorations might be garish, even by Bristol standards; but he was working, he was trying as hard as he could to make them a proper place in the world. And she could not help but respect him for his dogged determination to rise, and to take her up with him. Her father had failed to provide for her and she had been forced to accept Josiah. Josiah's single-minded vision of wealth and prosperity for them both inspired Frances to gratitude. At last she had someone who would care for her.

She smiled down the table at him and Josiah, always responsive to her approval, smiled back.

And so that night, when Josiah came to her room, Frances turned back the sheets of her bed to invite him in beside her, and for the first time she did not flinch as he moved towards her. Josiah blew out the candle before he reached for her and for once his embarrassment did not eclipse his ability and he was able to do his duty with less pain for Frances and less awkwardness for himself.

It was not love, it was still a very long way from love; but it was better than it had been, and better by far than either of them had ever expected.

Mehuru in the attic room above them was sleepless. The room was lit by a little window set square into the slates of the roof, barred over by stout nailed planks. Lying on his back he could see the stars, like silver pin heads against indigo silk. If he had been a woman he would have wept for loneliness.

His three companions were asleep: Kbara, the youth who had named himself Accursed, and the boy called Sad. The two little pickins were next door with the women and the girls. Mehuru called to Snake to give him sight for the

217

future and tell him what would become of them all.

Nothing came. Mehuru thought that the coldness of the air had entered his body, and the dark mornings and grey afternoons had bleached the colours from his imagination, and would bleach the pigment from his very skin. Every day Snake slid further away from him, until one day he feared he would be an Englishman, as dull and as slow as any of them, and not an African at all.

He thought of his house in Oyo: its coolness in the morning and the way the sun gilded the walls and the paving stones of the street, the scarlet and black Barbary shrikes gathered around the well, waiting for Siko to spill water for them to bathe and drink. He thought of the cool interior of his home, shadowy and restful even when the sun outside was burning hot, and the comfortable warmth of the outside stones when he came home from a journey and leaned back against them. He thought of his wardrobe of clothes, the intricately embroidered court robes of billowing bright silk, the smooth cotton house robes, the softness of the pure wool travelling capes. He went over every stone in the door lintel in his mind, counting each one with a passionate homesickness. He reviewed the skyline of Oyo, the high walls of the palace, the imposing towers, the great proud sweep of the city wall which guarded every citizen and encircled a city that a man could be proud of.

He turned it all over in his mind, loving every stone, every corner. He thought of it as a man will think of the woman he adores, every little detail of her. And he fixed his gaze on the little distant star which he could see through the skylight and wished that this new life was a dream and that he could wake at home and find himself in his own bed, and Siko coming in with a brass cup of mint tea, and everything in the world to look forward to.

Insured, and with her full complement of partners, *Daisy* was at last ready to sail. Josiah went to see her off on the twentieth day of February. Captain Lisle was on board, going downriver with the ship.

'I will bring you back another two dozen slaves for your wife to train,' he promised. 'Are you sure you don't want more?'

Josiah shook his head and laughed. 'This is a little venture, not my whole business,' he said. 'Sell the slaves and bring me good sugar!'

'I will,' Captain Lisle promised. Josiah shook his hand and stepped down the gangplank.

They ran it ashore and cast the ropes off as the rowing boats took the strain. Josiah raised his hand to his departing ship. She had brought him in a profit of a thousand pounds on her last voyage and she was likely to do as well again. He owed more money than his father had earned in all his lifetime; but he was confident. He was investing large sums and he was earning large sums.

'God speed,' Josiah called over the widening grey water.

Daisy dipped as the rowing boats pulled her away from the quayside, as if she were saying farewell. Josiah watched the wedge-shaped stern of his ship move slowly away from him. Above her, a flock of seagulls wheeled, hoping for scraps from the galley. Josiah's last sight of her as she went round the curve of the river was a silhouette of clean rigging, the strong workmanlike shape in the water, and the cloud of seagulls wheeling and calling like mourning angels around her.

In the handsome town house the slaves were working as domestic servants. There was much for them to do. Every day the big rooms needed sweeping, the large windows needed dusting, the panes of glass had to be washed daily to rid them of the grease and grit of the constant Bristol smog. Curtains, carpets, all the linen of the house had to be continually laundered against the filth of the uncontrolled industries.

Every room was heated by an open coal fire, and every morning Kbara and Mehuru heaved full scuttles of coal from the cellar at the back of the house to each room where the women, under the scullery maid's nervous supervision, cleaned the grates, laid the fires, and struggled with a tinder box to light them. Frances liked to have a fire lit in her bedroom before she woke, and the fires were lit in all the downstairs rooms by mid-morning. The slaves swept the floors and scrubbed them with buckets of cold water and thick slabs of soap. They got down on their hands and knees and scattered used tea leaves and brushed the carpets clean. Kbara and Mehuru carried Frances's handsome Turkish rugs into the yard and beat them with cane sticks. Mehuru looked carefully at the quality of the weave. They were vastly inferior to the carpets on the stone floors and walls of his home. He guessed they had been bought from Arab traders and, in his opinion, the white people had been robbed.

Mehuru took to domestic work like a thoroughbred horse harnessed to a cart. He could manage it with ease, but he felt himself ground down by the dirt and the drudgery of labour. He had to take out the kitchen garbage and burn it in the backyard. He had to pour the slops from the chamber pots into the night-soil cart when it came to the backs of the houses every morning. He did tasks which his own slave Siko would not have done. He felt his hands harden and grow callused and his fingernails, which had once been so carefully manicured, split and broke down to workmanlike stubs rimmed with grime.

His English improved daily. He learned a dozen curses from John Bates, he learned streams of scolding from the cook. He even learned to distinguish one English accent from another: the affected gentility of Brown's parlour voice, and the Somerset burr of the kitchen and at the back door.

Lessons with Frances were resumed. Morning and afternoon the slaves were summoned to the dining room and seated around the large table under the ornate ceiling. All the slaves could now name things, and understand short clear sentences. In one lesson Frances surrendered to Sarah's demand and all of them were given new names, English names. Frances chose them without any care, almost at random, from Bible stories.

She started with the children. The two smallest boys she called James and John, the three girls were named Susan, Ruth and Naomi. The two young boys were Matthew and Mark. The three women were Mary, Martha, and Elizabeth. Kbara, she called Julius, then she looked at Mehuru.

'I shall call you Cicero,' she smiled. She reminded him of a little girl naming her dolls.

Mehuru felt a slow burn of anger, an unusual emotion for him in these days of servitude and endurance.

'My name is Mehuru, I come from Africa,' he said, reminding her of the lesson she had taught him. He would not take a strange name. It was as if she was robbing him of the last thing he had been able to bring from his home, his name, his identity.

Frances nodded. 'That's very good,' she said. She was still light-hearted, she did not realise the depth of his opposition. 'Very good indeed. But all of you are to have new names, English names. That will be nice for you. And you and Julius have special, classical names. It is the fashion. Julius will be Julius and you will be Cicero.'

Mehuru shook his head. 'My name is Mehuru,' he repeated. His voice was soft but there was a warning note to it. Frances's smile died. She turned to the others. 'You can go,' she said. She nodded to John Bates. 'Take them to the kitchen and see what work Cook has for them,' she ordered.

'I should perhaps stay with you here, ma'am,' Bates said. 'If he gets cheeky I could whip him.'

Mehuru looked at Bates, his face like stone.

'Just because he can speak proper doesn't mean he can't be whipped,' Bates said, aiming the words at Mehuru. 'There's no law that says he can't be whipped even if he can speak Chinese!'

'I know,' Frances said. 'But I don't need you, Bates. Take the others downstairs.'

The slaves shuffled out, leaving the two of them alone, still seated side by side at the dining table.

'I want you to be called Cicero,' Frances told him quietly.

Mehuru measured her determination. 'Not my name,' he said. 'I have a name. I will not take other.'

'English people do not like African names,' Frances said.

'Then they should not . . . take African slaves.'

She gave a little sigh of impatience. 'Slaves have to do as they are ordered.'

Mehuru said nothing.

'I want to call you Cicero,' she continued. 'He was an admirable man, a very fine Roman. It is a compliment to you to name you after him.'

She had spoken too fast for him to follow and he did not understand what she meant by 'admirable', 'Roman' or 'compliment'. But her meaning was clear.

'My name is Mehuru,' he repeated.

Frances reached out and slapped his hand as it rested on the polished table, an impetuous, playful gesture. 'Cicero! I want to call you Cicero!'

He caught her hand the moment she struck at him, snatched at it in the air, and she gasped in shock. The very room seemed to freeze, and she was suddenly still, her lips slightly parted, her eyes alert.

He thought she would scream but she was frozen. He did not move, he did not release her. His face was close to hers, his eyes black with anger. They were as close as lovers, caught in a lovers' quarrel. Her eyes were dilated. When she breathed out he could feel the warm sigh on his cheek. Slowly, slowly, Mehuru exhaled and the tension left his face and his neck and his shoulders. His fingers uncurled and he let go.

Frances sprang to her feet and fled to the closed door, but she did not fling it open and call for John Bates. She stood before it, her face turned from him, her hand wrapped around her wrist where he had held her.

'Please,' he said, as humbly as she could wish. 'You steal all. Leave my name.'

Frances turned slowly and met his eyes. He did not look suppliant, he looked very grave. She went back to the table

222

where he was still seated, and put her hand gently on his shoulder. He looked up at her; but still there was no pleading in his face nor in the tilt of his head. He looked steadily at her, without fear or tenderness.

'You *are* my slave,' Frances said, as if to remind them both. 'I can call you what I wish.'

'Yes.'

'Then I shall call you Cicero. It is a lovely name.'

Mehuru rose to his feet and Frances took an involuntary step backwards.

'Very well.'

He waited before her, his hands by his sides, his eyes on her face. The plain dark green livery which Frances had chosen enhanced the darkness of his skin and the blue tattoos around his mouth and eyes.

Frances's colour flowed into her cheeks and drained away again. She put her hand out to him.

'I *shall* call you Cicero,' she repeated. It was as if she were asking some kind of permission from him.

Her finger touched the inside of his palm. He did not respond at all. Frances looked down and saw the contrast of her white hand against the smooth darkness of his skin.

'Cicero,' she whispered.

His hand did not clasp hers, he moved no closer. He stood like a rock before her and though she took a step, a tiny half-step, towards him he did not respond at all. He did not even look at her but stared over her head at the blankness of the wall, as if he were trying to see the open free plains of his home in the silk wall covering.

Frances turned away from him and went to the window. 'You can go, Cicero,' she said abruptly.

He went towards the door without looking back.

'We will have another lesson tomorrow,' Frances continued, trying to make him acknowledge her. 'Cicero? You will come to another lesson tomorrow.'

Mehuru bowed his head, and went silently from the room.

Chapter Eighteen

Josiah took the ferry back to the north bank after he had seen his ship slip away downriver, but he did not go home for breakfast. Instead, he went to the coffee house where the traders met. Although it was early the place was already crowded. Josiah glanced around for a friendly face and started to make his way to his usual table.

'Josiah Cole! Hey! Josiah!'

He turned. At the top table Stephen Waring nodded to him and George Woolwick beckoned him. 'There's a place for you here!' he called.

Josiah, his heart swelling, nodded casually to his friends at his old table and strolled as nonchalantly as he could manage through the busy room to the best table in the coffee shop: the table laid with white linen, the table served first, and served with the very best of things.

'Cousin, this is Josiah Cole,' George Woolwick said to his neighbour. 'Josiah, this is my cousin, John Shore. You met his wife at your wife's tea table the other day.'

'Of course.' Josiah nodded to the man, who moved his chair over to make space for Josiah.

'Mrs Shore told me all about it,' John Shore said. 'She had her eye on that house, I have not heard the last of it I know. She said that your wife had some very fine furniture and would I ask you where she got it.'

'The Chinese pieces?'

John Shore frowned slightly. 'No, she didn't mention

Chinese. I thought she said old stuff. But I wasn't properly listening.'

'Oh.' Josiah thought fondly of Frances's resistance to Chinese. 'I think the best pieces come from Whiteleaze. My wife was a Miss Scott of Whiteleaze and she has some pretty things.'

'No chance of buying them then?' John asked gloomily.

Josiah shook his head. 'They're heirlooms,' he said. 'Priceless, I should think. You know what these old families are like, priceless heirlooms with the Scott crest on them.'

'Well, I shall tell Mrs Shore that we can't buy that,' John Shore said with finality. 'But she won't thank me for it!'

Josiah managed a commiserating smile. 'The ladies like to have things just so,' he said. 'Mrs Cole would have the ordering of her house whatever I might say to her.'

'And it's a devil of a house to run,' Stephen Waring interrupted. 'Have you had to take on many new servants?'

'Not a one,' Josiah said smugly. 'I imported some niggers for domestic work a little while ago, and my wife has been training them. They are doing the work to perfection.'

'By jove, that's a good idea,' Stephen Waring exclaimed. 'But I thought your maid was English?'

'Oh, I have kept her on for now,' Josiah said airily. 'But if my wife has her way we will employ none but slaves. They are quick and obedient and if they are well-trained they are better than English girls.'

'What race are they?' George Woolwick asked. 'I always think that men from Dahomey are very unruly.'

'Bonny slaves *will* kill themselves,' Stephen Waring said. 'They get melancholy and just die, just lie down and die.'

'These are hand-picked, mostly Yoruban, two Fulani women, a Mandinko, and a Wolof,' Josiah said. 'But the skill is in their education. They are not melancholy and they are not suicidal because they have been continually trained in England by my wife. They've never seen a plantation, they've no idea of anything but the way we do things here. These plantation house servants are spoiled by the time they come to England. But my slaves are fresh from the coast, they have been broken as I want them.'

'And you say your wife trains them?' Stephen Waring confirmed.

Josiah hesitated. Frances had coached him in what he had to say until he was able to sound convincing. She had warned him never to mention her period of work as a governess. 'She has had the ordering of very large houses,' he explained easily. 'At Whiteleaze, and at her father's rectory. She is experienced in handling a large number of servants. A dozen slaves are no difficulty at all to her.'

Stephen Waring nodded and the other men looked impressed. Josiah glanced around and signalled to the waiter to bring him a pint of small beer and a plate of bread, ham and beef for his breakfast.

'And will you keep these slaves for your personal use?' George Woolwick asked.

'I shall sell most of them,' Josiah said. 'When we are established in the new house, and when they are completely trained, I shall sell them as English servants. The men will be footmen, or even butlers. The women can serve as upper servants or ladies' maids.'

'Mrs Shore would want one,' John Shore said hastily. 'Please reserve your best manservant for her. I know that she would want one.'

Josiah nodded. 'I will make a note of it,' he said. 'The best one is to be called Cicero, I think. I will reserve him for you.'

'Any children?' Stephen Waring asked.

'Two little boys, two youths of about seven and fifteen, and three girls,' Josiah replied.

'I'll take one of the little boys,' Stephen Waring said. 'My wife wants a little playmate for our children, and when he grows he can be a pageboy.'

'One of them is a very pretty child,' Josiah said.

'No diseases?'

Josiah shook his head. 'They have been in my house for more than a quarter,' he said. 'By the time they are ready for sale they will be as fit as English children. As I say, bringing them from the coast and training them in my house, I can vet them before I sell them on.'

'By God! It's a pretty piece of business,' John Shore said enthusiastically. 'How much are you charging, Cole? I did not think to ask.'

'One hundred and ten each.' Josiah named Frances's astronomic price.

There was a stunned silence. 'Good God,' said Stephen Waring. 'Where did you get that price from, man?'

'From my wife,' Josiah confessed simply. 'She tells me that is what Lady Scott expects to pay for the slave we are training for her. These are the best prices for the very best slaves.' He hesitated, measuring their eagerness. 'Each is, in every respect, an English servant; but one which never asks for wages, or time off, or can move to another employer. Think what you pay in wages to your servants – and how they behave! Then think what value a slave is!' He paused and shrugged lightly. 'But if you wish to cancel your orders, gentlemen, there will be no hard feelings. I can sell them over and over again as you will imagine. The London ladies are wild for them.'

'No, Mrs Shore is bound to want one,' John Shore said with even greater certainty. 'If Lady Scott herself has ordered one, you say?'

'Yes.' The waiter put a mug of ale before Josiah and brought the joint of beef to the table and started to carve succulent pink-hearted slices and arrange them, fanned out on the plate. Josiah glanced past him to the table where he used to sit. His old friends were gazing at him in his new elevated position. Josiah grinned at them.

'And Mrs Waring must have her pageboy,' Stephen Waring agreed. 'One hundred and ten, I think you said?'

'Guineas.' Josiah took a gulp from his ale and smiled over

227

the top of the mug at Stephen Waring. 'Guineas if you please.'

'You are an astute businessman,' Stephen said pleasantly. 'I wonder if you would be interested in a venture I am proposing. I want to sink a deep shaft at my colliery at Bedminster and I need some extra capital to finance the work. It would be a loan at, say, four per cent over two years.'

Josiah accepted his plate from the waiter and bent over it to hide his elated face. 'Possibly,' he said. 'What sort of capital sum?'

Stephen shrugged. 'Not more than five thousand pounds. I don't know if you have that sort of sum by you?'

Josiah lifted his head and his expression was calm. 'I could have,' he said steadily. 'It would depend on the project, of course.'

'Indeed!' Stephen nodded. 'Perhaps you would like to ride out with me and see the mine. It's good quality coal, if we can get down to reach it. Are you at liberty this afternoon?'

Josiah buttered a slice of bread and loaded it with meat. 'Perfectly, Mr Waring. I should be glad to come out and see it.'

'Very well,' Stephen Waring said. 'And now let us have a look at these figures for the port charges. The town clerk suggests that we raise the harbour dues to amass some capital to build a floating dock. Of course we have needed a floating dock for years but nothing has yet been done. Here are the plans.' He pulled a sheet of paper from a roll beside his chair. 'It will mean that the port charges have to go up again . . .'

'But not for us,' John Shore added rapidly. 'Not for Merchant Venturers.'

'Not for us,' Stephen Waring confirmed. 'The smaller men can carry the cost. There will be no additional charges for us.'

Josiah came home at midday to change into his riding coat and breeches. Frances had ordered a horse to be waiting for him at the livery stables and she saw him off from the front door.

'I shall not invest,' Josiah said. Frances handed him his gloves and held his hat. 'Unless it is very advantageous indeed. I would have to borrow it all and I doubt I could get a rate to make it worthwhile.'

'Don't say one way or another,' Frances advised him. She did not understand about interest rates but she knew that it was wise not to disappoint a new acquaintance. 'Leave it until he has made you a member of the Venturers. Leave it until your supper party and then see which way the wind is blowing.'

'I do not have the capital,' Josiah said. 'I would have to borrow to invest it with him. But I have not said that. I spoke as if I had thousands sitting under my bed.'

'That is the way to do it,' Frances said encouragingly.

'I wish you could have seen me in the coffee house,' Josiah grinned. 'Sitting at the top table and taking my breakfast with them all. And then I saw the plan for the new dock, and discussed port charges with them. And selling the slaves – why, I made more than two hundred guineas this morning before breakfast!'

Frances smiled, catching his enthusiasm. 'We are on our way,' she assured him. 'But do not spend your two hundred guineas before you have it!'

'It is your two hundred,' he said fairly. 'They were bought with your dowry, and they have been trained by you. You are their owner. They are Miss Scott's slaves.'

'Then keep my two hundred guineas safe for me! I am not sure that I want a mine shaft!'

'Anyway, I do not think it would pay. I would not want us to be overstretched. And he was a fast customer over this house. I will not forget that. I heard today that there are two other houses coming up for sale on this square. I would have done a better deal if I had waited.'

'Two more houses for sale?' Frances was instantly on the alert. 'Why?'

'Oh, different reasons. There is nothing wrong with the buildings, my dear, never fear.'

'No, I did not think that there was. But why are the other houses for sale?'

'One family is moving to Clifton, and the other is building off Park Street, I think.'

Frances looked thoughtful. Josiah took his hat from her. 'They are foolish,' he said easily. 'This will always be Bristol's best address. Clifton is too far away and the Park Street houses are a jumble of designs, there is no elegant square like this one.'

'No,' Frances agreed politely. Then she saw a shadow of self-doubt pass over his face. Josiah was not always as confident as he seemed, and he trusted in her judgement more and more. 'I know you are right,' she reassured him. 'And this is a beautiful house! I would not live anywhere else!'

'It *is* the best,' Josiah repeated. 'The biggest and best on the square. There is not another of better proportions. It is a very good investment.'

Frances nodded. 'I know it.'

Josiah opened the door and nodded his farewell. 'I'll be back before dusk,' he said. 'By five.'

'We will dine late then. Enjoy your ride.' Frances waved him off and went indoors to sit in the best parlour.

Sarah was seated at the table with the book for *Daisy*'s accounts laid out before her. Frances hesitated in the doorway, but Sarah looked up. 'Come in,' she said. 'I wanted to speak with you.' Sarah closed the book and waited while Frances pulled out a chair and sat, rather nervously, opposite her.

'I am about to start the afternoon lesson,' Frances began defensively.

'It's not that.'

'Is it still the tea party?'

'No, it's more important than that.'

There was a little silence.

'You are a powerful influence on my brother,' Sarah started. 'Since we moved to this house especially. He admires your taste, he takes your advice.'

Frances nodded, saying nothing.

'You should be aware of our situation,' Sarah said.

'Is it no better?'

'How can it be, when we have trebled and quadrupled our expenses by moving to this house and our earnings have remained the same?'

'Is it very much more expensive here?'

Sarah bit her lip to contain her temper. 'Instead of one fire burning during the day we have four,' she said. 'You have bought curtains and wallhangings for five rooms. You have bought chinaware – those Chinese vases, and the porcelain dragons – and much furniture. I am aware that you brought many of your own things to furnish the house, but even so, the carters had to be paid. Today Josiah has hired a horse, three times this week you have hired a carriage. I imagine that soon you will want to buy a carriage and then we shall have to buy horses and set up stables, and pay a coachman to drive them for you.'

'Josiah hired the horse to ride to Mr Waring's coal mines to look at an investment,' Frances observed. 'We are not wasting money, Sister. We are keeping a house in the style that Josiah's station in life demands.'

Sarah folded her lips together, and placed her hands gently in her lap. She was determined not to lose her temper. 'I am aware of my brother's ambition,' she said quietly. 'And I know that you support him. But I must remind you, Frances, that we do not have the money to spend on high living. The housekeeping bills have more than doubled. Your dressmaker's bill arrived today. You have spent more in a month than I spend in a year. The business cannot support this kind of spending.'

'Josiah has taken two orders for the slaves only today,' Frances countered. 'From men who were at my tea party. At one hundred and ten guineas each!'

'Then let them be sold at once. And let us have the two hundred and twenty guineas without delay. I have bills at the

231

chandler's for *Daisy*'s stores, and a bill at the sailmaker for her sails which I cannot meet.'

Frances shook her head. 'They are not ready,' she said reluctantly. 'They can do simple tasks but only Mehuru – Cicero – is fluent.'

'They must be sold as soon as possible,' Sarah said. 'All but two women. Now we have such a large house we will have to keep two of the women to do our work. After Easter, I shall let Brown and the scullery maid go. We cannot afford a staff of so many.'

'Yes.' Frances suddenly thought of Mehuru's hand, the warmth of his palm under her finger, the fascinating tracery of brown lines against the paler skin of his palm, the turn of his head, and that charged moment between them when he had snatched her hand. 'I wish . . .'

'What?'

'I wish we could keep them longer. There is so much that they will have to learn. It is such a strange world to them.'

'You are not teaching them for their convenience,' Sarah said. 'You are teaching them to increase their value. And *Daisy* will bring you a dozen more on her return.'

'It won't be the same,' Frances murmured half to herself.

'You have not forgotten that they are slaves?' Sarah reminded her sharply. 'They are Trade goods, Sister, the same as sugar or brass kettles.'

'I have not forgotten,' Frances said quickly. 'I am not likely to forget my place with them. I have commanded servants all my life.'

'These are not servants. These are goods.'

'I don't forget it,' Frances said.

Josiah stood with his hands thrust deep into the pockets of his new winter coat and watched his ship, the *Lily*, sail into port on the last day of February.

It was a cold raw day, but nothing could shift the beaming smile from Josiah's round face. The rowing boats brought her carefully to the side, the quayside workers fended her off and caught the ropes to make her fast. The gangplank came down and Josiah strolled on board.

'You made good time,' he said to the captain.

'We did,' the captain replied. 'And a good profit also. Slave prices are high in the West Indies again, for a couple of the best of them I got seventy pounds!'

Josiah's grin broadened even further. 'And the sugar price? And tobacco?'

'Fair,' the man said. 'I think you will be pleased. I have the books to hand.'

'Do you carry much gold?'

The captain nodded to his cabin. 'I have three hundred pounds' worth in my strongbox. It's all accounted for.'

'Unload it now,' Josiah said. 'I'll have it at once.'

'There's the crew to pay, and the bonuses,' the man demurred.

'Pay them tomorrow,' Josiah said. 'I'll see to it. You'll get your share, don't worry.' He whistled for one of the sailors and the captain let him take the strongbox down the gangplank to the old empty warehouse.

'I've never seen him do that before,' the captain said to himself. 'Usually it's the books or the cargo he wants. I've never seen him rush the strongbox ashore before he's even tasted the tobacco.'

He shrugged his shoulders and yelled to the crew to start the unloading. They lashed a wheel to the mast and began to haul the heavy hogsheads of tobacco out of the hold and on to the dock. The hold was foul with the stink of slaves; the men wore their scarves pulled up over their mouths. Not even the powerful scent of new tobacco and the rich heavy smell of molasses could overcome it.

Josiah in his office was counting the money and setting it into heaps of coins balanced on bills. He had not yet settled all the *Daisy*'s bills, though she was more than a week out of port. He owed the carpenter and the plasterer for the Queens

Square house. He owed the sweep and he had not yet paid for the new curtains and carpets. The profits of *Lily*'s voyage – which usually paid for her refitting and victualling – would be spread among Josiah's debtors, and he would seek extra partners for her next trip to meet her costs.

'Damnation!' Josiah had rung a coin on his desk and found it to be false. It did not ring true. It was lightweight base metal, gilded to look like gold. He was only a guinea short, the strongbox held more than three hundred pounds and his ship was well loaded with sugar and tobacco; but for a moment, knowing himself to have been cheated, Josiah looked absolutely afraid.

Scott House,
London.

Friday 20th March 1789

My dear niece,

This letter is to bring you my very Best compliments and to inform you that the Family will be arriving at Whiteleaze at the end of May.

You will be pleased to hear that your Sir Charles Fairley and Miss Honoria presented their Cards to Lady Scott and – as you asked – were invited to our Ball. Despite some little roughness of tone they Acquitted themselves Moderately well and Sir Charles in particular Endeared himself to my Guests by Losing heavily at Piquet. I have introduced him to my Club where his inability to Win makes him a Constant favourite.

On a more Serious note he tells me that he is considering Cole and Sons as his agent and I have Promised him that I will make myself Busy in seeking out a Suitable house for him and Consult with you. He has described to me the size of Establishment and the Extent of land and I am Certain that I can Find him such a place – and under terms which are Advantageous to all of us. I am Delighted to find that you have Become such a shrewd Woman of Business – since Your destiny has called you to be such. In Sir Charles you have a Customer to be Proud of, Generous and Indeed, feckless. I think we will all benefit from the Association. He is Extremely wealthy.

Forgive my speaking plainly but I know you will not Take offence.
You have done your husband a Good turn Indeed by winning Sir
Charles's fortune to your Trading house. I am happy to do all I can to
help Yourselves – and indeed to help Myself to the Benefits of such
an association. That Sir Charles benefits also Cannot be in Doubt. I
will keep you Informed of all opportunities of Investment which come
my way and of which you should be Informed. My favourite project
at the moment is a building scheme in London of Which I shall
reserve a Share for Cole and Sons, if I think fit. Also, there is a New
scheme for Wet Docks at Liverpool which is seeking investors. I will
keep you informed.

Forgive me this Odd mixture of Business and family Matters, but
I am anxious that you and your Husband continue to Prosper. I
imagine that it Would help your standing with your New neighbours
if Lady Scott were to Drive over for Tea? I will take the Liberty of
promising her Attendance on you as soon as she is in the Country.

You will have heard that the Abolitionists, headed by Mr
Wilberforce, are planning to bring a Bill before Parliament in this
session to Abolish the Trading of Slaves. I am assured that he will
Fail. There are Too many men in the House whose fortunes depend
on the Trade. However, for the Future, you would be well Advised to
move Some of your Business away from shipping Slaves. A Law to
limit the Numbers of Niggers packed into the Holds is almost
Certain to pass which must make Shipping less profitable. If you
could find Another such as Sir Charles you could move your Business
from Shipping to Agenting – The movement of Money, my dear, is
So much Easier than that of Goods, or even People!

I Trust you are well Established in your new House and that the
furniture all Arrived safely. I think of you Often and your Happiness
and Prospects are always Dear to my heart.

Your loving Uncle

Scott of Whiteleaze.

Frances put down the letter and looked into the red embers of the fire. Josiah was home late. It was a supper party of the Bristol merchants; they rarely finished before midnight, and Josiah was rarely home sober. The excesses of the Corporation were legendary even in a hard-drinking city. Josiah would return red-faced and smelling of strong roast meat and sweet rum, hoarse from singing bawdy songs and shouting jests.

Sarah might be tight-lipped with disapproval at breakfast, but Frances believed Josiah was carousing his way into the very inner circle of the Bristol Corporation and Merchant Venturer power – the unholy alliance which ruled Bristol completely. Besides, however drunk Josiah had been the night before, he was never late to work. He was always on the quayside at the usual time, before any other trader. He was always last in the coffee house for breakfast, he was always alert and ready for the small sale, for the little investor with a bandbox of money.

Frances looked at her uncle's letter again. If he was right, and if their business could develop, then Josiah's scramble for the capital of small men might be over. The ceaseless worry of insurance and ships, of storms and broken masts might be replaced by the easy transition of capital from one money-making scheme to another. She shook her head. Nothing would wholly wean the Coles away from trade, nothing would make them feel as secure as their bond house full of tobacco, their storeroom full of barrels of rum, of sugar. The handling of notes of hand was too distant for them. They liked goods they could taste and wealth they could weigh.

The rest of Bristol had moved away from the slave trade – abandoned it to the quicker, more efficient Liverpool ships. But the Coles had clung to it, and clung to it still. Even Josiah's dream of buying the Hot Well was not to replace his main business as a trader, but to supplement it.

Sir Charles's money left with them for safe-keeping when he had gone to London had not been fully used. If Josiah had

had his own way he would have stowed it all securely in a locked chest under his bed, bought only those goods Sir Charles required, paid Sir Charles's bills from it, and kept it safe for him. He would have invested only on his own ships, borrowed from it with his own note of hand. It was Frances who insisted that it be used to buy a share in a ship leaving for the Americas for cotton, and Josiah had watched unhappily as another trader left port with Sir Charles's money invested in a rival voyage.

Josiah was as jealous of Sir Charles's capital as of his own. But Frances would be proved right. The good ship *Endeavour* would show a profit of more than fifty per cent and a handsome forty per cent of that could go straight into the coffers of Cole and Sons.

Frances heard Josiah's knock on the front door, and Kbara going wearily down the hall to open it.

'Mrs Cole is there,' Kbara said.

Josiah came down the hall and put his head around the parlour door. 'My dear,' he said, blinking owlishly at the light. 'I am so glad you are still awake. I am obliged,' he nodded. 'Obliged to you.'

Frances stifled a giggle. 'I think, Husband, you have been drinking well.'

'A little punch,' he said seriously. 'And port, and wine, and sherry and a good deal of my own excellent rum, and a little brandy as well.'

'Would you like tea?'

'Certainly not,' he said. 'I fear it would give me a headache tomorrow.'

Frances laughed aloud. 'You are cautious.'

'As a Methodist,' he confirmed. 'Now, madam, cease laughing at a poor man, I have news for you which will make you wish to drink my health many times over too.'

Frances half-rose from her chair. 'The Venturers?' she asked. 'You are invited to be a member?'

Josiah opened his arms wide. 'At last!' he exclaimed.

Frances rushed across the room and hugged him. His warm breath reeked of alcohol. 'I am so glad!'

'I feel as if I have waited a hundred years,' he exclaimed. 'At last! And now I am excused dock charges, and lighthouse charges, and I can take a share of the fees and fines for others using the port. Now I can see the private plans for the new docks and know where to build a warehouse. Now I am privy to the very heartbeat of the town. At last, Frances! At last!'

Frances hugged him close, his rumpled stock under her cheek.

'And it is thanks to you,' he said in her ear. 'Your name, your position, the way you played them, your training of the slaves, Frances, you have made me!'

'I've done nothing . . .'

'You've made me!' he insisted. 'I knew where I wanted to be, but not how to get there. You knew how we could do it, and together we have done it. From now on, my dear, there is nothing that we cannot achieve. I shall buy you a carriage and pair, I shall buy you a riding horse. We can take a house in London for the Season, we can buy a house in the country. I can buy the lease for the Hot Well and you can work your magic there too. You are a ruby, my Frances, your price is above rubies!'

'Josiah!' Frances was smiling, overwhelmed with praise.

'We shall have sons,' he announced grandly. 'And leave them a fortune, a fortune apiece! We shall found a family! I shall buy a baronetcy and we shall have a title! You will not be humbled by marrying beneath you. I shall rise, Frances, and you will be where you belong again!'

'I did not feel humbled . . .'

There was no stopping Josiah. 'I shall build new ships,' he predicted. 'As big as the Liverpool ships and faster. And the first ship I shall call *Frances* and the second ship I shall call *Ruby* and the third ship I shall call *Virtue* and the fourth ship I shall call *Wife*.'

'Josiah,' Frances said fondly.

He dropped to the sofa. 'I shall close my eyes for a moment. And then you shall make me a glass of punch and we will drink your health.'

'I think you had far better go to bed,' Frances suggested hesitantly.

'Lemons,' Josiah ordered sleepily. 'Fresh lemons and lots of my sugar . . .'

Frances moved slowly to the bell, but by the time she put her hand out to ring for Kbara, Josiah was already asleep.

Chapter Nineteen

Even Sarah was pleased with the news when Frances met her at breakfast. But the promises from Lord Scott threw her into spinsterish anxiety again. 'We should not be too hasty to spend,' Sarah fretted anxiously. 'Sir Charles's money is for safe investment, not for risks. We know the risks of the Trade. What do we know of London buildings? And Liverpool docks?'

'That is why Lord Scott must advise us,' Frances said patiently. 'Sir Charles has chosen us as agents and Lord Scott as his advisor. Sir Charles wants us to invest in schemes for him.'

'We know the Trade,' Sarah said stubbornly. 'I can find him good investments in Bristol. I can find him voyages that pay five, even ten, per cent!'

It was pointless to argue that Lord Scott's investments might pay thirty or forty per cent. The prospect of huge profits frightened Sarah almost as much as the prospect of insolvency. Frances nodded. 'I shall write to Sir Charles for his instructions.'

There was a clatter from the sideboard. One of the slaves, Mary, had dropped a cup.

'Tell her to be more careful,' Sarah said.

'She understands perfectly well,' Frances replied. 'You can tell her yourself if you wish.'

'Careful!' Sarah ordered loudly. 'You! Be careful!'

The woman dropped a curtsey, as she had been taught to do. 'Sorry,' she said. 'Sorry.'

Frances looked at her. For a brief moment she did not see her as a careless slave who should be corrected, but as a woman, a little younger than Frances herself, uncomfortable in a plain green dress with a white cap on her head, always too cold, always hovering between exhaustion from the constant drudgery of her work, and the boredom of repeated meaningless tasks.

She was a Fulani, one of the nomadic people of Western Africa. If she had been at home she would have been gathering firewood and roots, beans and berries, watching the cattle, pounding millet in the big stone churn, hauling water from the well. She would have lived in a hut, set in a circle of huts, carelessly made; because next year, or the year after, the family would move to new pastures and build again. But inside the humble round hut would be her bed, draped in deep-dyed cotton, gorgeous with colour, and a woven palm-leaf basket carrying her clothes. At the foot of the bed would be a hand-carved cradle and a fine-boned chocolate-coloured baby blissfully asleep. It was a life that any English countryman would have recognised – a herdsman's life. It was a life that followed a seasonal round of moving across a broad plain, as light and as free as a herd of antelope. It was a life that turned in tune with the earth, that followed the rains, that chimed with the seasons. It was as alien to slavery as a silver-winged flight of cattle egrets to a moulting hen in a coop.

'Shall we keep that one, or the other?' Sarah enquired.

Frances was shocked from her reverie. 'We'll sell them both,' she decided. 'We'll keep Elizabeth. She is in the kitchen now. She is Yoruban like Cicero and some of the others. I think it is easier if they can speak amongst themselves.'

'But we'll only keep three,' Sarah said. 'A lad and two women.'

'Yes,' Frances said. 'They will be sold in summer. As soon as they can speak properly and follow orders.' She turned and smiled at the woman. 'Tell the others to go to the dining room,' she said and pointed to the door. 'I will come and teach them.'

The slaves were waiting for her when she entered, seated in silence around the table. Frances was alone in the room with them. John Bates had been dismissed. They no longer needed watching with a whip, they were thought to be safe. They no longer needed teaching domestic tasks, they had learned how to run a house.

Indeed, they were safe. They no longer spoke of walking back to their home, they no longer tested their imprisonment. Mehuru had not even checked the strength of the bars on the skylight window. They had ceased plotting for freedom. They were too overworked and weary to think of anything more than their survival. And also, fatally, they had lost their courage. They did not plot to escape because they feared the sprawling streets more than the drudgery of the house. They were very far from happiness, but they felt safer staying in slavery than running away into the unknown.

Mehuru was tired and drawn. He woke at five every morning and by six he had emptied the great bath tubs, brought coal for the fires and the kitchen range, cleaned the grates and emptied out the ashes, laid the fires afresh and taken out garbage for the cook. He was given no breakfast until the cook was ready and she made a policy of feeding the slaves last, with the leavings of the family food. He was cold when he woke in the morning, and cold while he worked all the day. Not even the heavy labour of house and yard warmed him through. He was losing weight though his muscles were leaner and harder than they had ever been before. The women were overworked too, and even the little children were set to sweep the floors and tidy the rooms. One of the children had a dry nagging cough which kept them all awake.

'Very soon,' Frances said clearly and slowly, 'we will have the feast of Easter. This is the day when we celebrate the death and the rising from death of Our Lord. He is our god.'

She looked around the table. The slaves looked blankly

242

back at her. She directed her speech to Mehuru. 'We worship the Lord Jesus,' she said. 'He was born on earth to save us from our sins.'

'A man?'

'He was a man, he lived many years ago. He died for our sins and after he died he went to heaven. He lives now and cares for us all.'

There was a silence as Mehuru took in the words, and tested them against his own certainties. 'Where is heaven?'

Frances glowed with pleasure at his interest. 'Heaven is not a place on earth,' she explained. 'It is the best of everything. The best of places. If you are good,' she said carefully, 'you go to heaven when you die.'

'Another place?'

She nodded. 'Far away.'

'How is this?' Mehuru asked. He searched for the simple words to express the complexity of his concept. 'The best is home.'

Frances shook her head. 'Your home is not important. Not compared to the love of God. Your home, your family, nothing matters as much as obeying Jesus and going to heaven.'

Mehuru paused, thinking. If Frances thought that the love of your home and the company of your family mattered less than a man who had died long ago then she was more of a fool than he had imagined. If she thought that the best of all places was exile, then no wonder she could take slaves from the heart of their country and expect them to sing and dance on the voyage. 'Do you all think this?' he asked incredulously. 'All white people?'

Frances nodded. 'And I hope you will come to think it too. Then you will be free from the burden of sin and death.'

'I will be free?' Mehuru asked, tasting the word.

Frances saw her mistake. 'You will still be a slave,' she corrected him. 'But you will be free of sin.'

'A free slave?'

'Yes, I mean . . . in a way . . . yes.'

243

Mehuru looked at her and she saw a sudden springing laughter in his eyes. Despite himself he smiled and then he laughed. 'Oh, Frances!'

Frances found she was smiling in return. In the face of his pagan wrong-headedness it was almost impossible to explain as she should explain. 'I am serious,' she protested. 'This is serious.'

Mehuru's rich chuckle was infectious. The others, not understanding all that was being said, but hearing the triumph of Mehuru's common sense over Frances's garbled theology, smiled too. Mehuru reached forward and put his hand over Frances's hand as it lay on the table.

'First make me free,' he said, still smiling.

Lord Scott sent a box of daffodils from the woods at White-leaze as an Easter gift for Frances. She arranged them in a large crystal bowl in the hall and they scented the stairs and the whole of the house with their clean green fragrance. Mehuru brought the water in a large enamel jug.

'These smell sweet,' he said.

Frances hung over the bowl, inhaling the perfume. 'They smell of spring,' she said dreamily. 'When I was a little girl we always had a big bowl of these flowers on the breakfast table on Easter morning. I used to get up early and pick them for my mother. They smell like hope, like being young and hopeful.'

'They are free flowers?'

Frances hesitated. 'You mean wild flowers? Yes. That's the great beauty of them. They grow in floods along river banks and under the trees, and every year there are always more.'

He smiled a little, watching her face. It was the first time he had seen her enjoying a sensual experience. He was oddly touched to see how rapt she was in the scent of the flowers. Her face above them was golden with their reflected colour. She had a smudge of yellow pollen on her cheek. He had a sudden insight into her joy at the free richness of the flowers:

244

that every year there were always more. The flowers were a complete contradiction to the house, to the Company, to the Trade itself which depended on scarcity and hunger. The earth itself was a generous giver of wealth, of this river of gold. It was the Trade which was mistaken, it was the Trade which was unnatural.

'Always more?' he asked and had the reward of seeing her dark dreamy eyes turned towards him.

'Yes,' she replied. 'Isn't that wonderful? When they grow from the ground they are just leaves, and then slowly you see the thicker leaves, fat little buds, and then suddenly the flowers have burst through and the ground is alive and bobbing with gold. And the wild cherry trees have thick white blossoms which bob in the wind and rain down white petals, and the birds start singing and singing, and the cuckoo calls.'

'Mmm,' he said. Many of the words she used were unfamiliar, but he could understand her tone of delight. Suddenly she looked years younger. The greyness had gone from her face, the daffodil glow was all around her. He put his hand to her cheek to brush away the pollen.

At his touch she froze, almost as if she were afraid, her face still turned towards him. His black finger lightly touched the smudge of yellow, and he showed her the dust on his fingertip. Her colour rose, he thought she looked young and desirable, and he wondered if she knew it.

Frances stepped back. 'You may go, Cicero,' she said.

Easter Day itself was a disappointment. Josiah and Sarah had no plans other than to eat goose instead of mutton at four o'clock and leave the company account books closed for the one day. There was no tradition in the Cole family of foolish sports like rolling coloured boiled eggs down hills, or egg hunts, or even a walk in the country.

'Do you receive no company?' Frances asked.

'No,' Josiah said uncertainly. 'We always spent Easter in the house on the quay. And no-one called on us there.'

'Did you not visit your friends or your family?'

'Our family live in Wales,' Sarah explained. 'And when we moved to Bristol we lost touch with them. They were a colliery family, in the coal mines of South Wales. My father did well to leave the valley; he never wanted to go back.'

'So what shall we do today?' Frances demanded.

Brother and sister looked equally bereft of ideas. They exchanged an uncomfortable look.

'I assumed you would go to church, to take communion,' Sarah volunteered. 'I shall attend chapel.' Both women looked to Josiah. Before his marriage he had always gone with Sarah to the Unitarian chapel. The cold clean walls and the simple creed suited many of the men in the Trade. There was no pretension in the chapel. A good straight sermon and a few bawled hymns. Frances, daughter of a Church of England rector, regarded the chapels with some disdain as the haunt of enthusiasm, evangelism, and labouring people. She had tried unsuccessfully to conceal this from Sarah, while Sarah had made little secret that she saw the richness and beauty of St Mary's church on the Redclift as being halfway to idolatry and papacy.

Josiah, caught between the convictions of the two women, sometimes went to church twice on a Sunday, accompanying Sarah in the morning and Frances in the evening. But he found, as Frances had shrewdly predicted, that the ambitious men in the Venturers attended the cathedral on the green, north of the river.

'Of course I will go to the cathedral,' Frances said. 'But shall we take a holiday for the rest of the day? We could drive out into the country?'

'I would not drive on a Sunday,' Sarah said piously. 'You must do as you please. I shall go to chapel, eat my dinner, then read my Bible, and then eat my supper and go to bed. I see no reason for excessive expenditure on a day which is set aside for thought and prayer.'

Frances closed her lips on a retort.

'The servants take a holiday after they have served us dinner,' Josiah intervened. 'We have a cold supper so that Cook can take the evening off. They have their own Easter dinner.'

'Brown and the scullery maid used to go home to see their mothers,' Sarah said. 'But since they are leaving tomorrow anyway I expect they will eat at our expense tonight.'

Frances nodded. When she had been a girl the Whiteleaze rectory was full of company for the Easter season. Her father and mother would invite friends from London to stay for a week. They would walk in the hills around Bath and pick armfuls of wild daffodils. They would sketch the trees, just thickening and budding into leaf. If the Whiteleaze family were at home they would ride out, far into the countryside, taking advantage of the warmer days and the lighter evenings. Even after her father's death and the gradual slow chilling of her happiness Frances still found her spirits lifting when the sky was light when she woke in the morning, and dinner was served in the yellow glow of sunset.

'I should have planned some treat for us,' Josiah said unhappily. 'Next year I shall do it better. I am sorry, Frances, it is not a season we have paid much attention to, in the past.'

'My father did not believe in it,' Sarah stated. 'He said the Lord's ascension should be celebrated with thoughtfulness and gravity.'

'Well, *my* father was a rector, and I suppose he should know!' Frances snapped. 'Next year I shall plan a party.'

Sarah raised her thin eyebrows and said nothing more.

The day was as thin of joy as she had feared. Josiah attended the cathedral with Frances, and Frances wore her new bonnet from Mrs Waring's milliner. The Easter Day service was longer than usual and the worshippers, leaving the gloom of the building with relief, gathered on the green outside in the sunshine. Frances was pleased to be greeted by all the major

247

figures of Bristol society and saw that Josiah was at ease with the important men.

That little elation did not last long, and when the goose had been cleared from the table, and the puddings and sweet-meats were gone, the afternoon seemed very long and dark and dreary. The sun had gone in and it was starting to rain, a steady misty drizzle which created a premature twilight, as cold and dark as winter. Sarah settled herself before the parlour fire with a book of sermons and seemed well content. Josiah dozed on the sofa. Frances sat on a chair facing them both, feeling as lonely as she had ever felt in her life.

Very faintly, from the very floorboards beneath her feet, came a soft insistent thudding, and then the half-heard snatch of song. Frances glanced across at her husband. He was fast asleep. Behind her book of sermons Sarah's head was nodding. Frances got to her feet and went to the door.

With the parlour door open a crack she could hear better. There was a patter of drumming, like rain, coming from the kitchen. Frances went into the hall and then pushed the green baize door which led down the corridor to the kitchen. As soon as she stepped through the sound hit her like a dark fast-moving wave.

It was a thud-thud-thud of drumming, and above the deep rhythm a patter, an exciting patter, of a contrapuntal rhythm. The two sounds chased each other, like laughter, like play, and Frances felt her feet tapping to the insistent dancy rhythm of the noise. A voice started a song, a deep confident voice – Mehuru – singing in Yoruban, a song about love, a song about the wantonness of young women and the pleasure there is in satisfying them. It was a song about magic – the magic of a woman's hair and the dark sideways glance of her smile. And at every verse-break, at every line-break there was a chorus of assent, in half a dozen tuned voices.

Frances crept slowly down the corridor and peeped around the half-open door, like a little child trying to watch a party. Mehuru was seated at the kitchen table with an upturned

248

wooden washtub and a couple of wooden spoons before him, a hastily improvised bass drum. He had thrown the spoons aside, their hardness gave no resonance, and he was drumming barehanded, using his strong fingers to call out a deep echoing rhythm, almost a tune, from the hollow bell of the wood. Kbara, beside him, standing barefoot on the stone floor and swaying in time, was pounding on a brass saucepan, sometimes using a metal fork, sometimes the flat of his hand. Mehuru was singing, his head thrown back, his eyes half-shut to hear the music, his wide sensual lips smiling and his whole face happy, in a way which Frances had never seen before.

It was a transformation. He was changed from a powerful brooding unhappy man into a man at ease with himself, singing from the depths of his belly, smiling at the joy of the rhythm and the excitement of the pounding noise.

And the women! Frances craned forward. The women were like a chorus in a Greek play. They were grouped together, swaying and singing, drawn by Mehuru, entranced by him. Every now and then one of them would step forward and dance towards him, for herself alone; and also completely at his bidding, and for him. When one of them stepped forward Kbara's treble drum would pound invitingly, the tone sharper and sharper as the fork rattled on the brass, piercing notes raining around her. Mehuru would speed his drumming, faster and faster, as if he were calling to her to dance and dance and dance for him. And the woman – Mary or Martha or Elizabeth – bunched up her skirt in her hand to show her bare feet and lovely black legs and pounded the floor with feet moving so fast that they were a blur to Frances, peeping around the door. Bent over, haunches moving, the women hammered into the floor, their feet making a new beat, a new quick erotic rhythm of their own, and then they would drop the hem of their skirts and sway back to the others, laughing and disclaiming praise, and Mehuru and Kbara would shout applause, and resume the slower pace of their song.

Frances stared disbelievingly at this explosion of strangeness into her English kitchen. She looked around for the other servants and then saw that the heady potency of the drumming had caught them too. As she watched, Cook, who had waged a campaign of bullying against the slaves since their arrival, was dragged forward by two of the little children and she too held her skirt from her feet and jiggled from one foot to another. And for her too Kbara and Mehuru speeded the music, called encouragement, pounded the rhythm.

Cook flushed rosily with a sudden sense of her own desirability. 'No, no!' she said, pulling her hands from the grasp of the two little boys. 'My dancing days are over!'

Mehuru shook his head and pounded his drum. 'You are a fine woman!' he called. 'A fine woman!'

Cook beamed at him. 'You ask Brown to dance a jig for you!' she said. 'She had an Irish mother!'

Mehuru rose to his feet and hefted the washtub under his arm. He snatched up a wooden spoon and walked towards Brown, smiling, drumming as he advanced. Frances thought that there was not a woman in the world who could have resisted him.

'I can't dance,' Brown protested, but she looked up at Mehuru as if he were a god, and she could not stop her colour rising.

He said nothing, he let his music call her. Brown's feet were tapping. 'I can't,' she repeated. 'I can't dance like you do.'

Mehuru stepped back, his long slim feet drumming on the ground in time to the music, his body swaying. Brown rose to her feet, stood before him and followed his movements like a thin white mirror of his potent image. He shuffled and stamped, and she followed him, he drifted to the right and she moved as he did. He turned and strode forward and she was behind him, then he whirled and hammered on the drum and called out to her and Brown hitched her skirts up in both hands and let her feet pound into the rhythm of an Irish jig, as wild a dance as could ever be – the deep irresistible drumming of Africa with the lightning heel-tapping toe-stamping dance of a Celt.

Mehuru laughed aloud at Brown's sudden abandon and pounded the drum in her praise as he turned to the other women. Cook rose up from her seat again, the scullery maid danced behind her, the slaves clapped rhythmically, swayed and sang in a compelling unending melody, in an incomprehensible promising language.

And Frances, watching this sudden explosion of joy and sensuality and passion on the stone floor of her cold empty house, sprang from her hiding place and whirled away from them, from the rich seductive drumming and song. She dashed to the hall, and then up the stairs to her chilly bedroom, with loud unladylike sobs choked back until she could slam her door and fling herself face down on her bed and cry out against her coldness and her loneliness. As she pushed her face into her pillow to weep without restraint for the first time in her life she acknowledged at last her vision of Mehuru as the only man in the world who could save her from the icy death-in-life of ladylike English behaviour, and she knew that for the first time in her life she had fallen, irretrievably and completely, in love.

Chapter Twenty

Next morning, Mehuru tapped on the parlour door. Frances was sitting at the round walnut table, another chair placed opposite her. A bowl of hyacinths stood in the centre of the table, their white waxy flowers scenting the room. Mehuru saw in one quick glance that this was not a lesson, when the table was swept bare; but he could not read Frances's set face. She was very pale and there was a bluish shade under her eyes as if she had lain sleepless. He wondered if she were ill. A second child had taken the nagging cough; they were all finding the slow turn to warm weather arduous and long. Maybe even white people, whose skin was suited to sodden days of mist and long grey afternoons, dreaded the long darkness and the pale disappointing coolness of the midday sun?

'Please sit down,' Frances said. Her voice quavered slightly.

Mehuru drew back the chair and sat before her, his hands clasped lightly on the table before him.

'I realise . . . I realise . . .' Frances started and then broke off. 'I have taught you for months, and I hardly know you at all,' she faltered. 'I have taught you to speak and never asked you anything about yourself, about your life before you came here.'

Mehuru's face was an ebony mask, carefully held from expression. He could not follow Frances's train of thought. He did not know she had heard his drumming. He did not know that for the first time and painfully, Frances was feeling emotions stir and warm into life.

'You want to know about me?'

252

'Will you tell me about your home, Cicero?'

He flashed a look at her at once. 'Cicero is an English slave,' he said precisely. 'Cicero was born here, in this room. You named him then.'

She bit at her upper lip, sucking it down so that her face was momentarily distorted and ugly. 'Very well. Just for now I will call you Mehuru. Where were you born, Mehuru? And where did you live? And what did you do?'

He hesitated, thinking to refuse this sudden, surprising curiosity. Then he relented. He could not resist the pleasure of talking of his home, even to Frances. 'I was born in the city of Oyo,' he said. 'My mother was a companion to the mother of the king, my father was one of the Eso –' he broke off, searching for the English word. 'I don't know what you call it –'

'What did he do?' Frances was smiling, thinking that the 'Eso' might be a little band of singers, or farmers, or some primitive group.

'He leads fighting men,' Mehuru replied. 'Those on horses.'

'Cavalry?' Frances asked, surprised. 'You had horses?'

'Yes. An army of horses.' Mehuru hesitated, gathering the words. 'A hundred horses to a lord, each lord obeys a higher. At the top a commander, and he reports to the Alafin – the king.'

Frances blinked. It all sounded rather complicated for a tribe of naked cannibals. 'Who else reported to the Alafin?'

'The prime minister and the council of nobles.' Mehuru thought. 'Seven lords who choose the Alafin. And then there is our church – a chief priest who keeps the oracle with chiefs under him. I worked for him.'

'You were a priest?'

Mehuru nodded. There was a distant look in his eyes as if he could barely remember. 'I was a diviner of the oracle, I spoke on grave matters. The oracle spoke against slavery. I took the message.'

'But niggers are slavers. You keep slaves yourself,' Frances protested.

'Not like you,' Mehuru told her gently. 'A criminal may be sentenced to work as a slave, or a free man may sell himself . . .' He had an abrupt vision of Siko who had sold himself into Mehuru's protection, and had been betrayed. He would never find the boy now, he was far away in the Sugar Islands. It was most likely that he was already dead. He had been a slight boy, not strong enough for backbreakingly cruel work in the fields or in the sweltering heat of the boiler houses, or feeding the roaring cane-crushing machines for ten, twelve hours a day. Mehuru looked away, his throat suddenly tight. 'I cannot tell you.'

'But human sacrifice . . . you do human sacrifice with your slaves . . .'

Mehuru stared blankly at her. 'I don't know what you mean,' he said with immense dignity. 'I think you must be thinking of another country. Murder is a crime in any of the Yoruban countries.'

Frances felt snubbed. 'I was told that all of Africa was a pagan country, practising human sacrifice and . . .' She paused. She could not mention bestial sexual practices. She flushed scarlet. 'And . . . impropriety.'

'Africa is a very large country,' Mehuru explained patiently, as a man might speak to a stubborn and stupid child. 'There are many different nations and many different ways of doing things. In Yoruba we live in cities cleaner than this one, we have laws which forbid actions which your laws allow, we trade, we farm, we hunt, our brassware is famous, our gold mines are wealthy, our leather and art goods are sold miles away, even across the Sahel desert. Why, you have some of our leatherwork here.'

'African leather?' Frances queried disbelievingly.

'Mr Cole's leather slippers,' Mehuru replied.

Frances thought of Josiah's beautifully worked leather slippers. 'Those are Moroccan,' she corrected him. 'From an Arab country.'

Mehuru shrugged. 'We sell leatherwork to the Arabs and

254

they sell it on. You have named it for the trader, not the makers. That leather is certainly Yoruban work.'

'It's not possible,' Frances protested. 'For Yoruban leather to get to North Africa would be a most tremendous journey. Thousands of miles across Africa, and across the desert.'

Mehuru nodded. 'We have very great trade routes. And mighty cities along the routes.' A shadow crossed his face. 'We *had*,' he corrected himself, his voice very low. 'When the slavers came the routes became unsafe. I am afraid that all that may be finished.'

He paused. Frances was looking down at her hands, pleating the fabric of her gown between her fingers and then smoothing it out. She was wearing a morning gown of muslin threaded with a blue velvet ribbon with a matching blue velvet jacket. It was one of her prettiest dresses, she rarely wore it. The skirt was creased from her fiddling, and as he watched she spread it out and put a hot hand on it.

'Mehuru,' she said very softly.

'What is the matter?'

She looked up quickly at the kindness in his tone and he saw her lip was trembling, and her face was filled with some suppressed emotion, her hands, her whole body was shaking. 'Mehuru,' she whispered.

'Are you ill, Frances? Shall I call one of the women?'

He got to his feet and she put out a hand to stop him. He checked at the touch on his arm, suddenly understanding her. Drawing in a breath, he froze, looking at her intently.

Mutely, she raised her white face to him, her trembling lips were pitiful. He scanned her expression from her dark eyes to the neck of her gown where he could see the thudding of her pulse in the hollow of her collarbone. And as he looked her breath came faster, the colour rose and rose into her cheeks and her eyes filled inexplicably with tears.

Silently he drew back. 'I shall call one of the women for you,' he said and left the room.

*   *   *

255

Josiah took his breakfast in an expansive mood at the top table of the coffee shop. He had a message from *Rose* who had passed a Bristol privateer off Africa. Captain Smedley wrote that they had made good speed and were off Goree Island, on the coast of West Africa. He was too discreet to refer to Josiah's illegal order to sell slaves to the Spanish colonies, he merely promised that he would ship as many as he could buy and pack them tight. Already the holds were half-filled. Josiah was to repose every faith in him and to know that he understood exactly what was required.

'You're early, Josiah,' Stephen Waring remarked, taking a seat beside him.

'The early bird . . .' Josiah said.

'Have you thought any more about my colliery?'

Josiah shook his head. 'It's a likely venture, I agree, but I have another project that must have first call of my capital. And you are the man to advise me if you will.'

Stephen nodded, snapping his fingers for a plate of ham and a pint of ale. 'If I can,' he said, smiling his sharp smile. 'You are a Merchant Venturer now. You have only to ask and there are a dozen men who will assist you.'

Josiah glowed slightly. 'I don't forget it. And it is that which makes me bold enough to ask you what the Venturers plan for the Hot Well. I hear that you seek a tenant to take over the lease. Is that right?'

'Indeed,' Stephen said cautiously. 'I don't know for sure. I have heard some rumour to that effect but I don't know. Would you be interested in the lease?'

'I would!' Josiah said. 'On the right terms, of course. But I think that with a little investment and with the advice of my wife and her family, I could venture to take the lease on.'

'I had no idea that you would ever shift from shipping, Josiah.'

'A man can spread his investments,' Josiah proclaimed boldly. 'It makes sense to spread your investment in these days.'

Stephen nodded. 'I shall enquire,' he promised. 'And then, if you wish to pursue it you could bring it up at the monthly dinner. I would be prepared to support your bid to buy the lease.'

'You would?'

'My dear fellow, why not?' Stephen smiled. 'A new member, and a new colleague? I would be delighted to be of service to you.'

'I would certainly make a bid,' Josiah said, abandoning his usual caution. 'I would need to see the figures of the investment in the Well, and the profits.'

'Very misleading,' Stephen murmured. 'I can tell you in confidence, Josiah. The Venturers have poured money into the premises and left no capital to run it. We have built a magnificent building, established an excellent name, there is now every reason in the world for it to prosper. The Venturers want rid of it, they want nothing more than a return for their money and someone else to take on the day-to-day expenses.'

'And so a man coming in fresh . . .' Josiah said excitedly.

'Would find all the work done for him,' Stephen supplemented. 'All of the rebuilding, the new colonnade of shops, the new pumping station, the filtering of the water, all done, all ready to run at a profit. The one thing against it is the ready funds. If you have those – you have only to pay your wages and you will make money in your second month of trading.'

'Just wages and trading money?' Josiah confirmed.

Stephen smiled. 'I would do it myself but it is so far out of my usual line of business. And I lack a wife with the friends and acquaintances of yours. You are a lucky man, Cole. This opportunity could have been made for you.'

'Will no-one else take it up?'

Stephen shrugged. 'They will snap it up as soon as they see it. But if you had the money to put down on it and my support, I would think it would go to you. There will be the lease to buy, of course, and an annual rent.'

257

'How much would that be?'

'As I say, I have not seen the figures. I should think you would need about two thousand pounds.'

Josiah looked aghast. 'So much?'

'It's an expensive purchase. And a handsome profit. But I would not advise it, Josiah, unless you have substantial sums to hand.'

'I do have,' Josiah said stubbornly. 'I do have substantial sums. If the terms are right.'

Stephen speared a forkful of ham and ate. 'Your judgement is sound. Shall I get the figures for you to look at?'

'Yes,' Josiah said. 'I would be interested if the terms were right.'

'Of course,' he smiled pleasantly. 'I only wish I had the skill to take it on myself.'

The cook had mellowed towards the slaves since their Easter party. The kitchen seemed very empty after Brown and the scullery maid had left, and Cook had only the slaves for company. In the evenings they all sat together in the kitchen and Mehuru, Kbara and the three women dined at the kitchen table with the children seated at a smaller table by the fire. Since John Bates had left Cook ordered all the work in the kitchen, now that Brown had gone Elizabeth ordered the work which needed to be done in the house, and Mehuru took overall responsibility for the security of the house and backyard.

Slowly, the division between enslaved and free was melting, and the kitchen was a home and a workplace to them all. The warmth of the kitchen range made it more comfortable than the cold attic bedrooms and after supper the boys would clear the plates, the girls would wash them and the children would put them away while Kbara, the three women and Cook drew up their stools to the fire and talked. Mehuru stayed at the kitchen table, reading. Frances had joined the circulating library at the Hot Well and once a week she sent Mehuru to change her books. He brought back the novels she wanted, and for himself he brought back histories and studies in geography and long difficult books on political economy. He was desperate to learn more about the world than Frances could tell him; and he suspected the glib simplicity of Frances's explanations.

The little boy who had been named James coughed constantly, and Elizabeth called him from his work to sit at her feet at the fireside. He had been only two when he was taken from Africa. He could not remember the warmth. He thought now that he had been cold forever, and he had forgotten his mother's face.

'You should tell Mrs Cole about his cough,' Cook said to Martha. 'Tell Mrs – boy sick.'

Elizabeth nodded. 'Both boys,' she said. 'I will tell.'

'Could be nasty,' Cook said. She looked thoughtfully at the child whose eyelids were heavy. 'Course you can't tell if he's pale or not under the black.'

'I can tell.' Mehuru looked up with a half-smile. 'He is pale and he is very hot in the evenings, and he coughs often.'

'Better tell Mrs Cole,' Cook repeated. 'She won't want to lose him. Not when he's learning to talk and waiting on her in the morning so prettily.'

'Yes. He has to be fit for sale,' Mehuru said coldly.

Cook looked down at the boy. He was sitting on the floor staring into the range, leaning back against Elizabeth's knees. The door of the firebox was open and the embers made a dream landscape, as intricate and lovely as the winding path of a river at home.

'Doesn't seem right,' Cook said, suddenly dissatisfied. 'I wager his mother misses him.'

'It will be as if he is dead for her,' Elizabeth said suddenly. Her English was slow and stilted, but they could understand her. 'He was her only child, he told me.'

The little boy was not listening to them, far away in a dream of a place where it was always warm, where he could remember a taste, a haunting taste: the sweet bland softness of mango. His eyelids drooped, his head nodded. Elizabeth bent down and lifted him into her lap. His body lolled in the sweet collapse of childhood.

'Doesn't seem right,' Cook repeated. 'Shall you all be sold?'

'I don't know,' Mehuru replied. 'They will need some of us to work in the house. She has not said which she will keep.'

'I don't want a new set,' Cook grumbled, getting to her feet. She shut the fire door and untied her apron. 'I'm for my bed,' she said.

Elizabeth gathered the little boy closer. He was half-asleep, limp with his fever, his forehead hot and dry. Mary picked up the other little boy and they walked together to the kitchen door, each one with a child on their hip. Mehuru watched them go, walking as easily and as steadily as if they were in their own country, on their own earth, with their own babies held close.

'It's not right,' Cook said. She looked at Mehuru and saw his face set with bitterness. 'Aye,' she said. 'It's not right.'

Frances lay on her back in bed and watched the cold light of the moon walk slowly from one side of the room to the other as the hours slid away. There were no clouds to shield the sharp sickle of the spring moon. The fire in the grate had died into soft white ash. The house was still and silent.

She could not sleep. She lay without moving, listening to the steady thud of her heartbeat. She thought that she would never sleep again. She knew that on the floor above, in the attic, Mehuru was asleep. If she called out, he might wake. If she crept from her bed and went softly up the stairs and opened his door she would see him. For a moment she let herself imagine that she could go to him – imagined her feet on the cold floorboards, on the creaking attic stairs, imagined the door swinging open and him sitting up in bed, his dark eyes opening and saying to her – 'Frances?'

And there she stopped – she could not think what she could

say to him. She could not acknowledge to herself what need, what absorbing need could take her, a married woman, in the middle of the night to the bedroom of a servant – lower than a servant, a slave.

Frances stared, as blank as a corpse, at the ceiling. There could be no reason that could take her looking for Mehuru. Not the moonlight, not the coldness of the night, not her growing awareness of his own tragedy – of the urbane culti-vated society which he had exchanged for this drudgery in her house – not her own loneliness, not her own inexplicable desire to hear his drumming, to hear his laugh, to see his smile. Frances lay in her own bed, imprisoned by her code of behaviour, by the powerful habit of denying her own desires, still and sleepless and waited for the morning when she might see him again.

Chapter Twenty-one

29 Queens Square.

2nd May 1789

Dear Uncle,

Thank you for your daffodils, we enjoyed them very much. Of all the things I miss most, living here in the Town, it is the trees and the Flowers of Whiteleaze. I hardly notice One season change to Another. Now it is Spring and soon it will be Summer and only One little Plane tree to show me! Josiah and Miss Cole are well and send their compliments.

The Weather here has been very grey and cold and the society here is very Quiet. Neither Josiah nor Miss Cole Dance, and apart from the Assemblies there is little Society. For some reason, I am not as Satisfied as I should be with my Situation. Since Easter I have felt Restless and Unsettled.

I am sure you will wish to remind me of my Duty of Obedience to my husband and Loyalty to his Life and his Business. I do not forget my Duty. Ours was a Marriage of convenience and I do not Regret it. I have promised myself that I will never Regret it. In the Trade a man's word is his bond – and I gave my word to Josiah. Fancies may come and go but Duty and Loyalty Remain Forever.

I remain your devoted niece,

Frances Cole.

Frances re-read the letter, crumpled it up, and added it to the others in the wastepaper bin beside her little writing desk, one of Josiah's Chinese purchases, elaborately carved with dragons breathing fire and little drawers hidden by sampans, bridges, and sinuous rivers. Frances leaned forward and put her head on her hands.

'You warned me,' she whispered. 'But I did not listen. Anyway . . .' Her voice trailed away as she thought of what her life would have been if she had refused Josiah's proposal.

She sat down and drew a piece of the hot-pressed notepaper towards her again, dipped her pen in the ink and wrote in plain spiky letters, quite unlike her usual elegant hand.

> *Dear Uncle,*
>
> *I have made the Dreadful mistake of falling in love with a man who is, in all probability, quite indifferent to Me. He is worse than a Servant, he is a Slave. He is in my Employ and I am bound to sell him for a profit to Another owner. Everything I have ever been taught about the Behaviour and natural Feelings of a lady tell me that this Cannot Happen. It cannot happen. It Cannot happen to me.*

She crumpled the letter and took it, with the others, to the fireplace which was laid with kindling and small pieces of coal. Frances scattered the letters on the top and then fetched the sealing-wax candle from her desk. She put the flame to the half-dozen pieces of paper and watched the pages darken, crinkle, and then burst into flame. She stayed on her knees on the hearth-rug, watching them crumple into fragile ribbons of ash, watching the words drift up the chimney in harmless smoke to gather with the smog which hung always in the skies above Bristol.

'I can never tell anyone,' she said softly. 'I shall never again acknowledge it even to myself. This is where it ends. It is over. It must be over.'

She got up from the hearthrug wearily, as if she were very very tired. She turned back to her desk, blew out the candle, and closed up the drawers. She turned the little key in the lock as if she were shutting away forever her youth, her new desire, and her hopes.

'Over,' she said with finality. And then she sat down in the chair, before the dirty cold grate, and took up some hand-kerchiefs to hem, and worked as if she could see her stitches through her blurred eyes.

Josiah found her there when he came in for his breakfast. Something in her frigid composure aroused his notice. 'Are you well, Mrs Cole?' he asked.

Frances smiled. 'I am perfectly well, thank you. Were you looking for me?'

'I have booked a little treat for you, my dear,' Josiah said. 'I remembered you telling me that you used to ride at Whiteleaze, and the stables have a lady's horse to hire. I have booked it for you this afternoon. One of the servants can go with you. One of the men can ride, can he not?'

'I think Cicero can ride.' Frances's voice was level. 'But I will ask Julius.'

'And you would enjoy it?' Josiah asked. 'You are looking a little pale today.'

Frances nodded. 'I thank you for a kind thought,' she said calmly. 'I should enjoy riding again very much. I will ask Julius if he can ride now.'

She went out into the hall. Kbara was coming downstairs with a heavy tray in his hands.

'Julius, can you ride a horse?' Frances asked.

He frowned. 'A horse?' he repeated. 'No, Mrs Cole. I never do.'

'Oh.' Frances turned. Mehuru was behind her. He had a scuttle full of coal in one hand and his livery was shielded from the dirt with a coarse hessian apron.

'Can you ride, Cicero?'

'Yes,' he said shortly.

'You should say, "Yes, Mrs Cole",' Frances corrected him.

Mehuru nodded at the information but did not repeat the sentence.

'I am going riding this afternoon,' she said. 'You will accompany me. You must go to the stables and pick out a riding horse for yourself, and borrow some riding clothes. You will need boots also.'

He did not look grateful. He stood leaning against the weight of the heavy bucket of coal, waiting for her to dismiss him.

'We will ride out on the Downs,' she said. 'In the sunshine. It will be like a holiday.'

Still he said nothing.

'Do you not want to ride with me?' she asked, suddenly impatient of his silence. 'I should have thought you would welcome a change from your work, from the continual drudgery here?'

Mehuru inclined his head only slightly. 'Yes, Mrs Cole,' he said.

The stable sent two fine hunters around to Queens Square. Frances, coming out of the front door in her old grey riding habit, saw Mehuru standing at the animals' heads, talking to the groom. She had to shield her eyes from the bright sunlight; the profile of his tall slim body was like a black cameo. It was just after noon and the square was bright and warm. The branches of the little trees were nodding with the bursting weight of new shoots. The grass of the gardens was springing green and ripe and was starred with white daisies in pink-tipped buds. One of the houses had a cherry tree in a tub at the doorway and the blossom was like a pink gauze scarf flung across the golden sandstone. The birds on the rooftops and in the saplings were singing and singing at the sunshine, a long ripple of sound. Frances bit her lip against the sudden welling of joy.

The stable had loaned Mehuru a pair of breeches and boots. He looked very tall and English in the handsome high boots and fawn breeches, the white shirt and stock and the dark brown hacking jacket. Against the high white stock at his throat his face was very black. When he saw Frances at the door he turned and smiled, and held her horse as the stable lad cupped his hands to help her mount and threw her up into the side-saddle.

Mehuru mounted and moved with the horse as it side-stepped and curvetted. 'He is . . . dancing,' he said. 'I do not know the word.'

'Dancing is a good word,' Frances agreed, watching Mehuru seated easily on the animal. 'We would say – he is fresh – meaning that he is eager.'

'I thought fresh was food?' Mehuru brought the horse under control and rode alongside her as she moved off, out of the square towards Park Street.

Frances found she could not think straight with him so close at her side. 'Sometimes,' she said unhelpfully. She gathered her thoughts and explained, 'Fresh food is new, prime food. A fresh horse is new out of the stable and in prime condition.'

'I see,' he said. 'It is an interesting language.'

Frances, who knew only conversational French and a lady-like smattering of Italian, had thought English the only language in all the world – not an option. 'How is it different from your language?'

A wagon went past them and Mehuru's horse threw up its head and sidled. He held it firmly and stroked its neck, murmuring softly until the wagon had passed. 'You have some words we do not know. And we have shades of meaning you do not have.'

'Like what?' Her voice was cool. She had herself under control.

'Oh, you have a word "beauty" – we do not have that.'

'You don't believe in beauty?'

'We believe in it, anyone can see it. But we don't have a word for it as you do. We have words which mean that something is good, or the rightness of things, the right thing for

266

the right place, the right colours. We have a word that you do not have – it means – that it lacks nothing. But we don't call a thing beautiful, we call it complete.'

Frances shot a small flirtatious smile at him. 'So if you loved a lady would you not tell her she was beautiful?'

He looked away from her, refusing to see the line of her cheek or the downward sweep of her eyelashes. 'No,' he said shortly.

They were riding side by side up Park Street. On either side of the street wooden scaffolding had sprung up, pale yellow stone houses were growing from foundations which marched like ascending steps up the hill. Gaps in terraces where a site had not been bought or where a builder had stopped work, short of cash, gaped like missing teeth. The city was being built piecemeal, all planning and order thrown aside in the rush for profit.

'So what would you say?' Frances persisted. 'If you wanted to tell a lady that you loved her, that you thought she was beautiful?'

'A man would tell her that he wanted her as his wife,' Mehuru said simply. 'He would not tell her that she looked as well as another woman. What would that mean? He would not tell her that she was enjoyable – like a statue or a picture. He would tell her that he longed to lie with her. He would tell her that he would have no peace until she was in his arms, until she was beneath him, beside him, on top of him, until her mouth was his lake for drinking, and her body was his garden. Desire is not about "beauty", as if a woman is a work of art. Desire is about having a woman, because she can be as plain as an earthenware pot and still make you sick with longing for her.'

Frances choked on a cry of outrage. She kicked her horse forward and rode ahead of him in shocked silence, looking straight ahead, her cheeks burning, her colour high.

Mehuru came up alongside. 'What now?' he demanded, exasperated. 'What's the matter now?'

267

'You should not speak to me like that,' Frances said, muffled. She would not turn her head to look at him.

'You asked!' Mehuru exclaimed. 'You asked me how I feel desire. And so I told you.'

'You should not speak like that,' Frances repeated in a small voice, her face still turned away.

'And how should I feel?' he demanded. 'You order everything. How should I feel, Mrs Cole?' He reined his horse back and rode a little behind her, like a servant.

They rode up the length of Park Street in single file in silence. Frances held her head high, she could feel her heart pounding with anger and desire: a breathless mixture of passions. Mehuru raged on his horse, watching her slim straight back leading the way. At the top of the hill the road petered out into a cart track and on either side there were builders' sheds and store yards of stone and piping and wood. There were stone cutters working under temporary wooden shelters, shaping stones to size and carving ornamental friezes and decorative heads and pillars. For long sprawling acres at the top of the hill it was nothing but a series of builders' yards for a city gripped with building fever. The sense of the city growing and re-making itself was almost tangible.

Frances and Mehuru rode on, Frances holding a handkerchief to her mouth to keep out the pervasive dust from the stone cutters, until they left the yards behind and the track became lined with little market gardens, and then fields with dairy cattle. Mehuru gazed around him as he rode, looking at the thick glossy coats of the cows, the incredible lush greenness of the grass. Even the hedges in this warm springing month of May seemed to glow with the sweetness of the constant rainfall. Bushes trembled with catkins as yellow as the primroses at the foot of the hedge. Whitebeam, hornbeam, and hawthorn flowered in a white mist. The beech trees were hazy with the greenness of their buds and the silver birch coppice at the edge of one field was a brilliant luminous budding green.

In Mehuru's home it was only in the brief spell of the wet season that trees glowed and dripped and oozed sweetness like this. He knew from Cook that this country was always wet. It always rained. No wonder they had fields as rich as forests and cows with pelts as glossy as lions. He glanced at Frances. In a country so ripe and rich and easy, how could a woman be taught to be sour and dry, so punitively cold to herself?

Frances felt his eyes on her. 'I am sorry. I should not have asked,' she said.

He waved it away. 'It does not matter. Do the cows always stay in these little fields? Do they not walk out to feed?'

Frances threw him a sideways look, amused and half-mocking herself. 'You are more interested in the cows than in my apology?'

He moved his horse close so that his knee was brushing her horse's flank. She could have reached out and touched him. He answered her with a smile which was singularly sweet. 'Frances,' he said gently. 'How can we speak truly one to another, when I am your slave and you can order me as you wish? Anything you say can mean everything or mean nothing. If I offend you, you can beat me or sell me. If I please you, you can give me a sweetmeat or a word of praise. I am your dog, I am your horse. You do not say "I am sorry" to a dog or a horse. You behave as you wish and they suffer as you please. Nothing else between us is true.'

'I do not wish it to be so,' Frances answered, her voice very low. 'You are not a dog, you are a gentleman, a nobleman in your own country, high in the government. I do not wish you to be my slave. I should like you . . .' She broke off. 'I should like you to be my friend.'

There was silence for a moment. The horses pulled gently on their bits and pricked their ears forwards as the country opened out before them, a little hill and the track curving upwards, an avenue of trees and from somewhere the faint salt smell of the sea.

'Then set me free,' Mehuru said simply. 'Only a free man can give his friendship. If you wish us to be friends I have to be free. Anything else is slavish devotion – it means nothing. You have to set me free, Frances.'

She let her horse trot and then ease into a gentle canter. Mehuru's horse followed, speeding up. Mehuru sat easily in the saddle and watched Frances lean forward and let her horse go faster. They breasted the hill side by side and burst out at the top of the Downs. Frances's horse lengthened its pace from a canter into a gallop across the close-cropped green turf. The sun was bright and the wind was light and keen, smelling of salt and the early buds of wild thyme. Mehuru let out a wild hunter's yell and his horse caught his sense of excitement and sudden feeling of freedom. Its ears came forward and it chased after Frances's hunter. Neck and neck they thundered on until Frances pulled her horse up and shouted, 'Woah! Woah!' and called out: 'Be careful! Be careful! The cliff edge!'

Mehuru pulled his horse over beside hers. There was a rough wooden fence marking the edge of the cliff and then a precipitous drop of white limestone rocks hundreds of feet down to the sluggish curves of the dirty river below, winding between banks of slime. On the far side equally high cliffs were tumbled with woodland and white dramatic outcrops, right down to the river edge. It was a staggering sight, a mighty gorge leading onward, westward, out to the distant sea.

'Is this the way we came in?' Mehuru asked. 'Our boat, up the river?'

Frances nodded. 'They have barges to tow the boats. It's very difficult to sail up the gorge. The winds are uncertain and the channel is very narrow.'

He nodded, looking down the deep chasm to the river below. 'I am glad it was night and I was below and did not see it,' he said. 'I would have thought it the entrance to a prison for life – these high walls.'

'I cannot set you free,' she suddenly said.

'Who is my owner?'

'I am. But I cannot set you free.'

He was gazing westward. The river curved out of sight, he could not see where it flowed into the sea. He wanted very much to see the waves and the clean water of the sea and know that on the other side of that ocean, miles and miles away, the waves of the same water were breaking on the white beaches of his home.

'What would you do, if you were free?' Frances asked.

'I should go home,' he replied instantly. 'I am needed there.' He thought how much he could tell them about the white men, how much he knew. He thought how much they needed his skills and now his grasp of the English language to keep them safe through these most perilous times. 'And I need to be there,' he added, his voice very low.

Frances, watching the longing on his face, said nothing. He glanced across at her. 'I can never be happy until I am home,' he said simply.

'I cannot let you go,' she repeated, and for a moment he thought she sounded more like a possessive woman deeply in love than the owner of a slave. 'I cannot possibly let you go.'

Josiah had the figures of the Hot Well before him in his office, the back parlour at Queens Square. Stephen Waring had obtained them for him and told him, with a wink, to read them and return them quickly before the May monthly meeting. Josiah understood that they had been borrowed for his benefit, that he was already gaining from Stephen's friendship and from his membership of the Merchant Venturers.

The figures went back to the earliest days a century before when the spring was first discovered. It was underwater for all the day except for a brief hour at low tide when it could be seen bubbling out, hot and sparkling, showing a clean ripple of water in the brown of the river. A businessman had opened a bath-house and later bottled the water. Josiah nodded; as soon as the site started to show a profit the Merchant Venturers took an interest. They bought it, and started to lease it out to speculative tenants.

The last tenant, Mr James, had seen the boom of interest in spas and mineral waters and determined on capturing the gentry trade from Bath. He had done well. The spa was now running in parallel with Bath. Convalescents were notoriously restless and many would decamp from Bath to the Hot Well. Desperately ill people would pay anything for a cure and the Hot Well's reputation for curing diabetes, skin complaints, stomach troubles, and even pains in the heart and lungs, gave them hope. The Methodist preacher John Wesley himself had been cured by the treatment. Endorsed by him and by other more worldly invalids, the business was thriving and the Merchant Venturers decided to expand it yet further.

The figures showed the spending – a two-thousand-pound investment in the Pump Room, making it the largest assembly room in the country. A thousand pounds on the pretty colonnade of nearby shops. A double avenue of trees leading to the rooms, and a complicated system of pumps and filters to get the water away from the contaminating river which was daily more of a threat to the health of the spring as the river water grew dirtier and dirtier with the outfall from Bristol sewage and industries. The Venturers had done everything to establish a thriving business, but they did not want the trouble of running the spa themselves. They wanted to hand it over and to see a return on their investment.

Josiah chuckled and rang the bell. Kbara came, light-footed and smart in his livery. 'Yes, sir?' he asked.

'Rum and water,' Josiah ordered.

He pulled a sheet of paper towards him and scribbled down some figures. He thought he could borrow two thousand pounds for the lease against the cargo of *Daisy*, who should be loading at the efficient Africa Company ports and due back in December. If Josiah's captain bought well and crammed on sail Josiah would make a small fortune on her.

He would need it. The vagaries of the Trade meant that sometimes all three of his ships were away from Bristol at the same time. There was a fallow period in which Josiah could do nothing but wait. From April to July all his ships were loading off Africa while the debts mounted steadily at home. He could not clear a penny until they came back into port again. The Hot Well's profits would smooth over the dramatic fluctuations of the Trade in which a man could be bankrupt one day and then see his ship sail, heavy-laden, into port the next.

Josiah had a loan outstanding of a thousand pounds for the Queens Square house and five hundred for furnishing. He had borrowed a thousand pounds against the *Rose* herself and he owed for half the cargo instead of splitting the risk with equal partners. By deciding to take women and children, pack them tight and sell them to the Spanish, Josiah had made the voyage at once more risky and more profitable. Selling to the Spanish plantations was smuggling, breaking the laws which limited trade with the competing plantations of Spain. But since it was contraband cargo it was paid for in gold. Josiah would not have to offer credit to the planters which could not be redeemed until a year or two later. *Rose* would come home in November and bring him sellable sugar and gold. She would reward one of the greatest risks he had taken in his commercial life – sailing without a full complement of partners, and without full insurance – with the greatest profit he had ever seen. She would be followed into port by *Daisy* in December, and two months later by *Lily*, and Josiah would be acclaimed as a wealthy man.

He needed that public success. Even with Merchant Venturer friends Josiah found his ships were not attracting investors. The returns on the slave trade were too risky compared with the guaranteed profits of land. The three markets where a profit or a loss might be made, in Africa, in the West

Indies, and in England, no longer fired men's imaginations. The men who used to gamble on the slave trade to give them a triple profit now preferred to buy and sell sugar direct – trading to and from the West Indies. Prices were easier to calculate, and profits came quicker. By cutting out two legs of the three-way journey they diminished the risk by two thirds, they speeded the return of the ship – and thus the profits. Only the traditionalists, who had always dealt in the Atlantic trade, and the little savers who were welcome nowhere else, were still investing in slavery and Josiah's ships.

But Josiah was confident. His membership of the Merchant Venturers was already showing him benefits. Through the Company he would obtain full insurance on all future voyages, even including the loss of slaves except by death through illness. He could reassure future investors that their money was safe, completely insured.

Best of all, as a member of the Merchant Venturers he was a member of the Royal Africa Company. For the first time ever Cole and Sons ships would not have to trade up and down the fever-sodden coast, searching for individual slaves, bartering with coastal chiefs, haggling for one man here, for another there, exposed to illness, threats from the shore, and mutiny on board. From now onwards a Cole and Sons ship would moor at a Company fort, where she would take on supplies of food and clean water. Slaves would be waiting for purchase in the huge dungeons. The captain could take his pick of the prisoners, and if he wanted more, he could send a message to the Company warehouses further upriver to send down as many as he wished. The turn-around of the ship could be as swift as if she were in the dock at Bristol. The gathering of the slaves was as efficient as an industry. At last Josiah would leave the uncertain, chancy old days behind. As long as the seas were kind, he could guarantee a profit on each and every voyage. When the investors saw the account books of his ships under these new circumstances

Josiah was certain they would put their money with him again.

Against all these fair omens were only Josiah's debts on the house and on *Rose* – three thousand pounds altogether – and his soaring living costs. Neither of them troubled him yet. The value of the house justified his debt, the loan on *Rose* was investment capital, and living costs were bound to increase. He thought that a man aspiring to the status of a gentleman had to be generous about his housekeeping bills.

He drew a sheet of paper towards him and wrote to Stephen Waring.

Dear Waring,

I return these papers to you at Speed, as you requested, and with my Thanks. I shall certainly bid for the Hot Well lease Provided that I can have an Undertaking that the Rent for the lease will be Agreed for a Minimum of Ten years and not be increased During that time. I thank you for your support in this Matter. I shall see you at the Dinner when I will Make this offer to the Honourable company.

Yours etc.

Cole.

Josiah dripped sealing wax on to the fold of the letter and pressed his ring into the hot liquid, rang the bell and told Mehuru to send one of the boys round to Mr Waring's accounting house with the letter and the parcel of papers.

Mehuru hesitated.

'What is it?'

'I shall go myself.'

'Very well, very well,' Josiah said impatiently. 'As long as one of you goes and comes straight home.'

Still the man hesitated. 'If I see a seller of flowers shall I buy some for Mrs Cole?'

Josiah turned in his chair. 'What?'

'The flowers in the hall are dead. Mrs Cole loves flowers.

275

There are flower sellers outside the house every day. Shall I buy some flowers for her?'

'Oh!' Josiah was genuinely surprised. He heard the cries of flower sellers as he heard the cries of knife grinders or muffin men. He had never thought that they might be selling a commodity he would want. 'She likes flowers, does she?'

Mehuru thought of Frances's dreamy sensual delight over the daffodils and kept his eyes down so that her husband would not see his amusement. 'Yes, she does.'

'I'll give you a penny, get her a bunch.'

Mehuru took the coin. 'She would prefer many,' he said carefully. 'For the big bowl in the hall.'

Josiah tutted, thrust his hand in his pocket and threw a handful of coins at Mehuru. 'Here! Take half a crown, take a crown and bring me the change! Make sure you bring me the change, mind!'

Mehuru bowed swiftly, took the letter and vanished from the room before Josiah's innate caution with money could defeat his grand gesture.

He put on his hat and coat and slipped out of the back door, walked briskly to Mr Waring's warehouse on the northern, Bristol side of the dock, delivered the letter and then found a flower seller shouting her wares on the quayside near the bridge over to Redclift.

She had a tray hung from her neck filled with flowers. She had fat bunches of wood violets, picked in Rownham woods that morning, with their leaves still damp and their scent potent. And she had late-flowering daffodils by the hundred with their fat buds bursting into pale yellow petals and the trumpets opening in the morning sunshine.

'How much?' Mehuru asked.

'Ha'penny a bunch.'

Her Bristol accent was so strong that he could hardly understand her. 'Where do you come from?' he asked curiously.

She made an impertinent face at him. 'Closer to home than you,' she said.

He smiled at her. 'I don't want a bunch. How much for all?'

Startled, she stared at Mehuru. 'All of them?'

'Yes, quickly, I have to be home.'

'I've never sold all of them at once.'

'I want the tray too, to carry them.'

She stared at him open-mouthed. Mehuru had to laugh. She was as slow and as stupid as any peasant in a village in his own country. 'No-one has ever bought them all before,' she said.

'I see,' Mehuru said patiently. 'But *I* want to buy them all. How much would they all be?'

'Are you from London?' she asked, as if only that could explain his eccentricity.

'It doesn't matter,' Mehuru said. 'Look. When you get home in the evening and you have had a good day and sold nearly all, how much do you have?'

'Half a crown,' she answered promptly. 'But I never have.'

'Well, I give you three shillings for all the flowers, and you can come with me to my home, carrying the tray, and then I will take the flowers into the house,' Mehuru said patiently. 'Then you get some more flowers to sell, or you take the rest of the day off.'

She blinked at the concept. 'If you gave me four shillings I could buy a good dinner,' she said hopefully.

'Why not?' Mehuru declared, generous with Josiah's hard-won cash. 'But now!'

'All right,' she suddenly decided.

Mehuru set off at a brisk pace, the flower seller trotting behind him.

'Is it for a lady?' she asked slyly. 'A lady that loves flowers?'

'Yes,' Mehuru said, without turning his head.

'And do you love her?' She bumped into him as he stopped at the backyard gate.

277

Mehuru hesitated on his denial. He thought of Frances and the contradictory feelings which were growing between them. He knew it would be easier for him if he did not love her and safer for him if the word was never mentioned between them. 'I don't love her,' he denied stoutly. 'I am just getting flowers.'

He tipped Josiah's coins into the flower seller's hands and gathered up the armfuls of daffodils. The bunches of violets he packed carefully into the deep pockets of his coat.

'You'll smell like spring,' the flower seller said, looking at him and noticing for the first time his broad shoulders, his lean well-muscled body, and the deep soft blackness of his skin. 'Does she love you?'

Mehuru shook his head at her and smiled. 'Goodbye,' he said firmly. 'Enjoy your dinner.'

The kitchen was empty except for Cook, who was stirring a pan on the stove and did not turn round and see him, his arms full of buds, his pockets bulging with posies.

He slipped into the hall and then up the stairs to Frances's bedroom. Her bed was made, the room was tidy. He was struck by the cold elegance of it all. The hairbrush and comb were precisely positioned on the dressing table, the small pictures hung carefully on the pale silk walls, the pale blue carpet, the little blue silk chair placed at a right angle to the empty grate. He had meant to put the flowers in vases around her room, but something in the spinsterish tidiness of the bedroom made him feel anarchic and playful. He thought of the trickster god dressed in dark indigo blue studded with white cowrie shells who throws the destinies of men and women into gambling disorder. He laughed at the thought, and at the madness of flooding Frances with flowers.

He ripped back the covers of the newly made bed, and flung down the daffodils pell-mell on the white linen sheets. He studded the pillows with violets, dozens and dozens of bunches, and then he stood back and surveyed the disorder with delight.

Already the room was smelling sweet as the crushed violets

poured out their essence and the opening daffodils exhaled their subtle insidious perfume. Mehuru gave another little laugh and crept from the room, closing the door behind him with a sense of having released something troubling and dangerous and wild in the orderly house.

So it was that when Frances came upstairs at noon to change from her morning gown, she found her room filled with a heady golden powerful scent and her bed drenched with flowers.

She did not think, she did not hesitate for a moment. In some archaic, intuitive part of her mind, as yet unfrozen and untamed, she knew precisely who had brought her the flowers. No-one else in the house would have bought them with such spendthrift abandon. No-one else in the house knew that she loved daffodils and that this spring had released her wild young greening desire. She stripped off her dress and her shift, recklessly, like a young girl, and fell, naked, into bed with them. She buried her face in their cool passionate green-ness, and bathed in the watery pale scent of them. She rolled around on them and among them, swimming like a diver in a green pool, until her body was slick with the juice and her hair was tumbled over her bare shoulders and filled with petals. White sap from the daffodils smeared on her skin and was slick on her lips, sharp and bitter to the taste, staining the white purity of her sheets – and Frances was laughing and breathless and wanton, at last.

Chapter Twenty-two

Josiah was at his desk waiting to be called for dinner but whiling away the time in adding figures. He had half a dozen sheets of paper before him and each displayed a different calculation. *Rose* was due home first, but Josiah had already borrowed against her cargo to buy the Queens Square house. She should bring an extra profit in gold from her smuggled slaves; but Josiah could not borrow against contraband goods; they must remain a closely guarded secret. *Daisy* should only be a month behind her. Loading and unloading with the efficiency of a Merchant Venturer vessel, she should come into Bristol at the end of December, and *Lily* would be only two months behind.

Josiah hoped to raise money against *Daisy's* expected profits. He wanted to offer them as security for a loan on the Hot Well. On each page he calculated how much the repayment would be if he could borrow at three per cent, and then the further calculation if *Daisy* came in late . . . a week late, two weeks late, a month. The difficulty of Josiah's work as a long-distance shipper was its unpredictability. The voyage took, on average, fourteen months. But storms could delay a ship, a wrecked mast could mean that she put into a strange port for repairs and was delayed for months. The captain was authorised to buy repairs in such a crisis, but he could be cheated, or the work expensively done, and he could come home carrying no gold at all, forced to sell cargo to cover his costs.

Josiah never knew, until his ship docked, whether he had made a fortune or lost one. There was no way for a captain to get a message home unless he met another Bristol ship on the voyage and it got home before him, and that happened only rarely. There was never anything to do but wait, and try not to borrow against profits which even now might be tossing in a storm on a sinking ship.

There was a tap on the door and Frances looked in.

'Am I disturbing you, Josiah?' She was wearing her hair in a new way, combed simply over her shoulders. Her face was radiant, and she looked pretty in a way that Josiah had never noticed before.

'New gown?' he asked.

'No.'

'Oh.'

'Is it you I must thank for my flowers?' she asked carefully.

'I sent Cicero to buy you a bunch,' Josiah said. 'Did he find a pretty bunch for you?'

Surprisingly the colour rushed into Frances's cheeks. 'He bought a lot,' she said. 'They are beautiful. Thank you.'

Josiah waved his hand. 'What can I do for you, Mrs Cole? It's not dinner time, is it?'

Frances shook her head gravely. 'I wish to send for a doctor for one of the children. The smallest boy is very feverish. He has had a cough since before Easter and he is getting worse.'

Josiah looked thoughtful. 'Can we not give him a poultice or something? A few days' rest in bed?'

'He has been resting,' Frances said. 'And Cook has done all that she can. She wants him to be seen by the doctor, and I think she is right.'

'I'm very sorry for the boy,' Josiah said awkwardly. 'But we are running a business here, Frances. We cannot care for him as if he were our son. The doctor charges for every visit and then there are medicines to buy as well. I would rather we waited until we were sure it was essential.'

'The child is very ill,' Frances insisted.

'I daresay, and I wish him well. But a couple of visits from the doctor and we will start to run at a loss on him.'

Frances turned to go, the prettiness drained from her face. 'But I may send for him if the child gets worse? It will be a greater loss if the little boy dies, after all, Josiah.'

'I don't wish him to be neglected,' Josiah said. 'But we have to measure our costs against our likely profits. Otherwise it is not a business venture but a mission. We are not in business to take little children from Africa and bring them up in civilised homes and spend a fortune on medicines for them. They have to earn their keep.'

'I know,' Frances conceded. 'But I cannot help but feel for him.'

Josiah smiled at her. 'You have a tender heart. Oh, send for the doctor if you insist; send if it worries you! But remember that we must keep costs down.'

'I will,' Frances said. She gave him a quick smile and slipped from the room. She went upstairs to the top floor where the slaves slept. James, the smallest boy, was on his pallet bed, Elizabeth beside him. She was sponging his hot face with vinegar and water. He was tossing his little head from side to side, his black eyes glazed, seeing nothing.

'Very sick,' Elizabeth said as Frances came into the room. 'No better?'

'No.'

Frances bent down and put her hand against the child's forehead. His skin burned under her touch. His little close-cropped curls were damp with sweat, his smooth black skin flushed darker with the fever.

'I will send for the doctor this evening if he is no better,' Frances said.

Elizabeth shook her head. 'No better.'

'You do not understand,' Frances said, irritated. 'I said: "I will send for a doctor if he does not get better".'

Elizabeth shook her head again. 'No better.'

'It is you who do not understand,' Mehuru said softly from the doorway. 'She is saying he is no better, and he will not get better.'

282

Frances looked shocked. 'Of course he will,' she cried. 'This is just a fever. Children get fevers all the time. By later today he will have probably sweated it out and the fever will have gone. In a few days he will be up and running around playing.'

'He did not do much playing,' Mehuru observed. 'Even when he was well.'

Frances flushed. 'If he had gone to the plantations he would have been weeding in the sugar cane every day from dawn to sunset,' she pointed out. 'He has an easier life here.'

Mehuru nodded. 'And if he had stayed in Africa he would have been safe on his mother's back while she worked in the fields. And in the evening when she cooked his supper he would have played in the dust with the other children. And at night she would have tucked him up in bed beside her.'

Frances said nothing. In the silence they could hear the hoarse sound of James's breath, rasping through his closing throat. 'I know he would have been better left at home,' Frances said very quietly.

James turned his head restlessly on the pillow, seeking a cool place. Frances leaned forward and lifted his little head. Elizabeth turned the pillow over and Frances let him lie down again on the cool new cotton. 'I'll send for the doctor now,' she decided.

'I'll go,' Mehuru said. 'Where is his house?'

'Trenchard Lane, near the hospital. Dr Hadley. Wait, I will give you one of my cards to take.'

Frances went downstairs to the parlour for a card from her case, Mehuru following. She scribbled a note on the back of it. 'There,' she said. 'Ask him to come as soon as he can.'

Mehuru took the card, went down to the kitchen to throw on his jacket and snatch up his hat, went out through the back door and set off at a steady jogging run along the quayside of the Frome to John's Bridge.

The doctor was not at home. Mehuru tracked him around the city from one fashionable address to another and found him, coming from a lying-in at Culver Street. He was a young fair-headed Scotsman, notoriously free-thinking and politically radical. He was only tolerated by the conservative citizens of Bristol because of his remarkable abilities and his degree in medicine from Edinburgh University. He took Mehuru up in his phaeton and drove down to Queens Square.

'Are you a free man?' he asked curiously.

'No,' Mehuru said. 'Mrs Cole owns me.'

'You seem to be a man of education. You speak well.'

'Mrs Cole taught me to speak and I have taught myself to read.'

'Read, eh? Do you read the newspapers?'

'When I can see them. I have no money to buy newspapers or books.'

'You could go to a reading room or a coffee house.'

'I have no money,' Mehuru pointed out. 'And no time off. I am not a servant, I am a slave. I am not allowed out of the house.'

The doctor muttered something brief and impolite. 'Ever heard of Granville Sharp?' he asked.

'No.'

'He's a Londoner. He lives in London. He's made a bit of a name for himself, championing the people of your race.'

'Slaves or free?'

The doctor clicked to his horse as they turned into the square. 'Slaves,' he said. 'He defended a black runaway slave – what was his name now? Strong, Jonathan Strong, and another, James Somerset – their cases went to court and the judge ruled they could not be sent out of the country against their wishes. If they try to send you to the plantations you can refuse to go, slave or not. Did you know that?'

Mehuru jumped down from the seat and ran to the horse's head. 'I did not! I thought they owned me completely.'

'Not completely,' the doctor said with sharp irony. 'Even in Britain, in the land of freedom, you have some few rights. For instance, they can beat you but not to death.'

'Can I speak with you again?' Mehuru asked urgently.

'I dine at the Crossways coffee shop on Mondays,' the doctor told him. 'I talk to a number of friends there. We would be pleased to see you, if you could get there.'

'I'll get there,' Mehuru said.

'Don't get yourself shipped out before Monday,' the doctor warned wryly, lifting his bag out of the carriage. 'There's always a ship going to the West Indies and you won't be the first negro stolen away.'

'I'll be there Monday,' Mehuru promised.

The doctor nodded and ran up the steps.

The door opened at once, as Martha had been watching for him. She took him to James's little room at once. When he came down again Frances was at the foot of the stairs.

'Is he very ill?' she asked.

'He may pull through,' Dr Hadley replied. 'It's a violent fever and a putrid sore throat. But he's underweight and very sick. I've given the woman some pastilles to burn in his room, and some syrup to bring down the fever.'

'I did not know he was so ill.' Frances could hear the exculpatory tone in her voice.

'He's only a little boy,' Dr Hadley said abruptly. 'What is he? Three? Scarcely more than a baby. He should be with his mother. What's he doing here anyway?'

'It is a scheme of my sister-in-law's,' Frances explained. 'We import slaves direct from Africa and train them here for domestic work . . .' Under his sharp blue stare her voice died away. 'It is better work for them and a better life than on the plantations,' she finished feebly.

'I am sure of it,' he said ironically. 'I should think death itself is preferable to work on the plantations.'

'You are against slavery,' Frances accused him. 'You are an abolitionist.'

'In this town?' He raised his sandy-coloured eyebrows. 'A man would be lynched if he acknowledged such beliefs. I am a professional man, a doctor. I attend where I am summoned and I generally keep my opinions to myself.'

'Shall you come again?'

'I will call later to see how he is. The woman tells me that there is another little boy who is also unwell.'

'I did not know,' Frances said. 'Will you please see him too?'

'When I come tonight. He has gone out now to carry a message for your husband.' Dr Hadley glanced out of the window at the scudding clouds. 'A nasty day for a little boy with a fever to be running errands around town,' he observed. 'I will not delay you any more, Mrs Cole.' He made her a brief bow and strode to the front door. 'Good day.'

Stephen Waring was in his accounting house discussing his colliery with two other men. As they turned to go he called one of them back into the room as if he had suddenly remembered something.

'Oh! Green! I had forgotten to ask you. You are planning to give up your houses at the Hot Well, are you not? And move your business to Clifton?'

The man closed the door swiftly behind him to prevent eavesdroppers. 'Why yes, I am going to sell the lodging houses in Dowry Parade at the Hot Well. I am sure that Clifton is the coming place; such pretty buildings and such good company.'

'Perhaps you are right,' Stephen Waring said smoothly. 'But I know of a man who might be interested in taking on the Hot Well. He might be prepared to buy your place also.'

'Does he know what the lease for the Well will cost?'

'I believe so. But he thinks he can make it pay.'

'I thought they would never get someone to take that lease,' Green exclaimed incautiously.

'The Merchant Venturers have too much money tied up in the Hot Well,' Stephen said smoothly. 'I for one should like to see that money released for other projects. And if the Hot Well can be made to pay we would all benefit. The debt should be cleared, and this is the man to clear it for us.'

Mr Green hesitated. 'If it can be made to pay,' he said. There was a hint of warning in his voice. 'Fashionable society is moving up to the heights of Clifton, not down along the river. However elegant the Assembly Room – it is in the wrong place. If he is a friend of yours, you may wish to warn him. It is a fine building but I think Clifton is the place to be.'

'It is a venture like any other,' Stephen observed pleasantly. 'There is always risk where there is profit to be had. He is a trader – he should know that.'

When Dr Hadley came back to visit James late that night the child was worse. His fever had broken but the boy was no better. He was cold now, instead of hot. He lay very still and quiet on the little bed, his rasping breath coming slowly and sluggishly. When the doctor took the little dark wrist he could hardly find the pulse. The doctor looked at the black woman sitting at the head of the bed. She had the soft fringe of her shawl in her hand and she was leaning forward and gently stroking it against the boy's cheek. His head was turned to her and his eyes were shut.

The doctor raised an eyebrow to her.

'No better,' she said softly.

He opened his bag and took a small bottle of laudanum and mixed four drops in a glass of water. 'If he cries,' he said simply, 'if he cries for pain he can have this, a little at a time. I can do no more for him. He's sinking fast. He's going now.'

'Going home,' she said simply.

Stuart Hadley found that his eyes were smarting. He bent down and put his hand against the damp little cheek. The boy was so small that the white hand cupped his entire face from curly hair to rounded chin. He was little more than a baby.

'Going home,' he agreed softly.

He snapped his bag shut and went from the room.

Frances was waiting for him in the hall. 'Is he better?' she asked.

He looked at her coldly. 'He is dying, ma'am. He will be dead by tomorrow.'

She staggered slightly and went white.

'It is a risk you will have to carry,' he said precisely. 'If you bring slaves into England. They are susceptible to English diseases, just as white men quickly die in Africa. They are susceptible to the English cold and damp. Is this the first one you have lost?'

'No,' Frances admitted. She remembered the woman called Died of Shame, and the unmarked grave in the Redclift churchyard.

'What did that one die of?'

Frances shook her head wordlessly.

'Was she sick?'

'She ate earth,' Frances said, her voice very low. 'And she was found dead one morning. She died in her sleep.'

'How awkward,' he observed savagely. 'Well, I must be getting on. I send my bill to Cole and Sons, do I? It is a commercial loss, is it not?'

Frances flushed. 'I shall pay.'

The doctor bowed and went to the door.

'You despise me because we own slaves,' Frances accused.

He looked into her face. Her eyes were filled with tears and she was trembling.

'No,' he said with sudden honesty. 'That would not be fair of me. I used to take sugar in my tea, and I still love sweet puddings. I smoke tobacco, I wear cotton. I benefit from the Trade as much as you do but I manage to keep my hands clean, I take my profits from the Trade at a distance. How can I measure what good it does me? My university is endowed by rich men who draw their wealth from the colonies. My patients are all Traders. We all profit from the thieving in Africa. If we stopped it tomorrow we would still be rich from their loss.'

288

'Would you wish to see slavery abolished?'

'I believe the Trade will be ended,' he said certainly. 'And I pray to God that I will see it ended this very month in Parliament. But the cruelty we have learned will poison us forever.'

The parlour door behind Frances opened and she gave a guilty start. 'Oh! Sister! This is Dr Hadley, he is just leaving.'

'Is the boy better?' Sarah asked.

Frances shook her head. 'Dr Hadley thinks he will die.'

Sarah nodded brusquely. 'Thank you for calling anyway, Doctor.'

Doctor Hadley bowed to them both and let himself out of the front door.

Sarah looked crossly at Frances. 'Another burial,' she said pointedly. 'They all cost money, you know. I shall order the undertakers to call tomorrow morning.'

'When the undertakers come I will see them,' Frances said.

'It's not necessary.' Sarah went around the parlour blowing out the candles, without asking Frances if she were ready to go to bed.

'I know it is not necessary; but I want the little boy to be buried as he should be buried.'

Sarah took her cup and threw the dregs of the tea on the fire to damp down the last smouldering small piece of coal which she had been sitting over since supper. 'They know their business. You can leave it to them.'

'He is an African boy,' Frances protested. 'There will be things which they will want to do for him. The woman who has been sitting with him, Elizabeth, she nursed him as if he were her own child. She will not want him taken from her and thrown into a grave. She will want to say farewell to him, in her own way.'

Sarah straightened up, her face full of suppressed anger. 'You can make a big parade of your feelings over this,' she snapped. 'I heard you talking with that doctor. You can attend the funeral, you can hire a hearse. It is throwing bad money after good. The child is dying, and you knew when you started this that at least two or three would die during the first year. It is natural wastage. It is the natural loss of stock. If we have to go into mourning every time a slave dies we might as well grieve for a broken barrel of sugar.'

'He is a child,' Frances cried passionately. 'A little boy . . .'

'He is our Trade,' Sarah said. 'And if we cannot make this Trade pay then we are on the way to ruin. Wear black crepe if you like, Sister. But get those slaves trained and ready for sale.'

Chapter Twenty-three

In the morning Frances did not summon Mehuru to ask him how the slaves would want to say farewell to little James. She went down the corridor to the kitchen and found Elizabeth, her head in her arms, half-asleep on the kitchen table.

'May I come in, Cook? I want to speak to Elizabeth.'

Cook bobbed a stiff unwelcoming curtsey. 'Of course, Mrs Cole. This poor girl is worn out. I don't think she's slept for more than a few hours in these last two days.'

Frances pulled up a stool and touched Elizabeth gently on the arm. Elizabeth started awake at once. Frances saw that her eyelids were swollen from lack of sleep and from weeping.

'The men are coming to bury James,' Frances said, speaking slowly and carefully, watching Elizabeth's face. 'But I have said that you may make him ready and see it done as you wish. Would you like that?'

Elizabeth nodded.

'I shall tell Mehuru to spend the morning with you and the men to make sure it is done as you wish,' Frances promised. She rose up from the stool. 'I am very sorry,' she said softly. Her eyes were on Elizabeth's face as if she were asking for forgiveness. 'I am very sorry that James was ill, and that we lost him in the end.'

Elizabeth nodded, her face grave.

Frances went to the hall to find Mehuru. He was on his hands and knees in the parlour, sweeping the grate.

'Cicero, the men are coming to bury James. You are to stay

with Elizabeth and see that they do what she wants. He is to be buried as she wishes, as far as it is possible. You can tell them that I will pay for anything extra.'

Mehuru rose to his feet and wiped his hands on the rough apron protecting his livery. 'How do you want it done?' he asked.

Frances looked into his face for the first time. 'In your way,' she stumbled. 'However you wish. In the African way.'

He shook his head, his eyes on her face. 'Elizabeth is Yoruban, as am I, James was Sonke. Kbara is Mandinka. How do you wish him to be buried?'

Frances shook her head in frustration and clapped her hands together. 'I don't know!' she cried. 'I was just trying to make it better, Mehuru! I was just trying to make it right!'

He caught her hand and held it gently. Coal dust smeared her hand as black as his. 'There is no little way to make this right,' he said gently, almost tenderly. 'It is as wrong as it could be. But I will see him buried with care.'

Frances stepped back, their hands parted. 'Thank you,' she whispered, and slipped from the room.

Mehuru chose not to ask for permission to go out on the Monday night, a few days after the funeral. Instead he put his arm around Cook's broad waist while she was bolting the back door and whispered in her ear. She slapped his hand away. 'Impertinence!'

'I'll be in by midnight,' he cajoled. 'And I promise to lock up safely.'

'And what if we are all murdered in our beds between now and then?' she demanded. 'With the back door left open for any passing thief?'

'I'll ask Kbara to sit in the kitchen and wait up for me,' he said. 'You'll be safe enough.'

'And what if Master comes down and finds you gone and Julius out of his bed and waiting for you?'

'He never comes down to the kitchen, Cook. You feed him

too well for him to hunt for food in the night. Such a wonderful cook that you are.'

She slapped him again. 'That'll do. Where d'you want to go anyway?'

'Just to a coffee house for some talk,' Mehuru said. 'You get a night off, why not me?'

She nodded. 'All right then,' she agreed reluctantly. 'But mind you don't get press-ganged, or kidnapped. The slaver captains will steal anyone away to serve on their ships, remember! And the press-gangs for the Navy are not choosy! And don't get drunk! And don't go with a woman, half of them are diseased and the other half will take you round a corner and hand you over to be beaten.'

Mehuru threw up his hands, laughing. 'I will go to the coffee house and come straight home. I swear it.'

She opened the back door a crack for him to slip through. 'You have no money,' she said. 'Here.' She rummaged under her apron in her pocket and drew out a purse. She offered him a sixpence.

'I cannot repay you.' Mehuru hesitated. 'I have no money at all, and no chance of earning.'

'I know,' she said. Her powerful sense of dissatisfaction with the Coles made her push the coin, and then another, into his hand. 'It isn't right. It can't be right to work a man all day as hard as you do, and then not even have the price of a drink in the evening.'

The coffee shop was noisy and crowded, a pall of smoke hung at head height, the windows were running with condensation. When the door was opened steam and smoke billowed out into the dark street. Mehuru paused in the doorway, uncertain. But then he saw that a number of the men inside were black-faced like him. With a surprised exclamation he stepped over the threshold and saw Dr Hadley seated at a table with four other men, one of them a negro.

'Dr Hadley,' he called. 'I have come.'

'Cicero! Sit down,' the doctor said. He looked rumpled and

informal with his jacket off and his hair tied carelessly back and unpowdered. 'Here is a countryman of yours, Caesar Peters, and Edgar Long, and James Stephenson.'

Mehuru hesitated. For a moment he could not believe the sudden joy of meeting men as an equal, of being among men who looked him in the face and nodded a casual greeting. For long months now he had been invisible, a piece of cargo, an animal to be tethered and fed and trained. Only among his fellow slaves and the women – Cook and Frances – was he seen as a man, a real man. What he had missed was the casual company of strangers, the easy conviviality of free men. The constant pain of homesickness and the constant ache of injustice was suddenly lifted from him. He felt that he stood taller, his shoulders square. He remembered that when the weight of the slave collar was taken off he had learned to walk again, to free himself of the slavish shuffle.

He pulled up a stool to the table and smiled around at the men. 'Good evening,' he said. 'I am glad to be with you. My name is Mehuru, Cicero is a slave name.' He glanced at the black man. 'Are you Mandinka?' he asked.

The man smiled. 'I am Jamaican,' he said with a little irony. He spoke with a lilt to his voice, a rhythm almost like music. Mehuru found him hard to understand. 'I was born and bred on a plantation, and taken from my mother when I was small. I have never seen Africa. I cannot speak any African language. I'm told I look like a Mandinko – but it means nothing to me.'

'Are you free now?'

He nodded. 'I was press-ganged on to a ship. They didn't care whether I was a slave or free, they needed crew. I was paid off at the end of the voyage in London, and I now work there for a printer. I have brought these gentlemen some pamphlets.'

'Are there many free black people?' Mehuru was trying to adjust his view of England. He had thought it a country inhabited solely by white people.

'Thousands,' the man said. 'There are more than ten thousand in London alone. I live in a house owned by a black landlord with black neighbours.'

'Thousands?' Mehuru was astounded.

The man nodded.

'But what are they – what are *we* all doing here?'

The man chuckled, a deep rich chuckle. 'Some are slaves, brought from Jamaica and the West Indies when their owners came home to England. Some are free men, who have bought themselves free. Most have escaped. A good many are American slaves, freed or escaped during the war.'

'Don't you want to go home?' Mehuru asked incredulously.

'Home? My home is Jamaica and there's nothing there for a black man but beatings and labour. I'd rather stay here and earn a living.'

Mehuru shook his head and Dr Hadley laughed at his bewildered expression. 'Did you think yourself the only black man in England?'

'Very nearly,' Mehuru said ruefully. 'I have seen one or two men working at the docks but only from the window of the warehouse.'

'You must have been very lonely.'

Mehuru nodded.

'Well, you're among friends now. We're a radical society.' He lowered his voice, but no-one could have eavesdropped above the hubbub of the coffee house. 'Mr Stephenson here is a wheelwright and Mr Long writes for a newspaper. We are the Bristol Society for Constitutional Information – committed to the reform of Parliament. We're in touch with societies all around the country. We're collecting names for a petition to Parliament. The time has come for the suffrage to be widened, every man should have a vote to choose his government. The laws are made by the landed gentry and they oppress the working men. And –' he nodded at Caesar and Mehuru '– we *must* abolish slavery in Britain and in the British colonies. How can we progress towards true liberty when we are a nation of slave takers and slave users? Black or white, men must be free.'

'The pace of the abolition campaign is increasing,' Caesar said. 'They are holding meetings everywhere in the country and preparing petitions. The debate has been postponed once, but Wilberforce will bring a bill before Parliament on the eleventh – next week. Pitt, Burke, Fox all support it.'

'But the government is very fearful,' Edgar Long cautioned. 'We will have to take care to stay inside the law. First the Americans and now the French have grown so radical – they are making our masters uneasy.'

'We are outside the law already,' Dr Hadley said briskly. 'With so many offences on the statute books, just being in company with more than two other men is a crime if you criticise the government.'

'The London Society is being watched,' Caesar said. 'There is no doubt that our letters are opened.'

'It is not the government I fear but the mob.' Edgar drained his pot of beer and called for another round. 'The gentry call out the mob against us, get them drunk and set them on us. These are dangerous times.'

'They are times of opportunity.' Dr Hadley disagreed. 'America, France, change is in the air and we are in the thick of it. The world is changing, and we are at the head of it. I am not afraid of the mob. More and more the people will come to see that Reform is the way ahead. Proper wages, proper conditions will follow the vote. Look at France! It is a fine and noble thing they are doing there, bringing the power of the people to bear on a dissolute and tyrannical regime. I tell you, the work I do in the City Hospital would make a radical out of the king himself.'

A serving man came over and dumped five pint pots of ale down on the table. Mehuru realised that it was the first time anyone had served him since he had lost Siko. For a moment the warmth of the coffee house and the cheerful noise faded away. He thought of Siko, and his quick smile and his impertinence. Mehuru grimaced, and took up the tankard and tasted the beer. It was warm and watery but it made a pleasant change from the slop of the small ale of the kitchen and Cook's unending pots of weak tea.

'And the bill for the abolition of the Trade?' demanded Edgar Long. 'What do they say are the chances of the bill?'

'It must come,' Caesar said. 'It cannot fail. The mood of the country is with us, the leaders in the parliament are with us. Wilberforce has twelve resolutions to put to the house to ban the capture and shipping of slaves.'

'They will oppose,' Edgar Long warned. 'There is a lot of money in this country tied up in the Trade. The opposition is hidden because it is ashamed – but it is there nonetheless.'

'It is not ashamed,' Stuart argued. 'I meet these people, Edgar, as you do not. They are shameless. They live off the profits and they dine off gold, and they manage to forget that every penny they earn is paid for in torture and blood.'

'It cannot fail,' Caesar repeated. 'There is a majority in favour. We have canvassed the members of Parliament and they have faithfully promised their support. Slave trading will be abolished, and then we can go on to abolish the whole business of slavery, and my people . . .' he glanced at Mehuru with a smile '. . . *our* people, Brother, will be free.'

Mehuru had no reply, the man had taken his breath away. 'I did not know . . .'

'You shall see your home again,' Caesar said. 'And have an African son.'

Mehuru's face suddenly crumpled and he put his hand over his eyes. 'Forgive me,' he said softly. 'I had almost given up hoping.'

Stuart slapped him on the back. 'We are on the turn of the tide. You will be free to come and go as you please.'

At the thought of coming and going Mehuru glanced at the clock. 'I cannot stay now,' he exclaimed. 'Though for the first time in this country I feel that I am among friends. I promised the woman who works in the kitchen that I would

297

be home to bolt the back door before midnight and I will not break my word to her.'

'Can you come out again?' Edgar Long asked him.

'It is difficult,' Mehuru said. 'I would take the risk willingly, but the cook is responsible for locking the doors and she is a good woman. If they found I was missing she would be in grave trouble.' He downed his beer in four greedy gulps. 'But I will try. You can be assured that I will try. Are you here every week?'

'They are here every week,' Caesar confirmed. 'I am here once a month or so.'

'I'll walk home with you,' Dr Hadley said. 'Gentlemen, I'll see you next week, when we have had a chance to read Caesar's pamphlets. And we will meet on Tuesday night for news of the debate.'

The night air was cold when they stepped out into the street. Mehuru shivered and drew his cloak closer around him.

'I brought these for you.' Dr Hadley produced a handful of pamphlets from under his cloak. 'Abolitionist pamphlets. One of them is written by a countryman of yours, Equiano – a freed slave.'

'How did he gain his freedom?'

'He bought himself out. He is married to an English woman, he has written a fine book which I can lend you, if you wish.'

'He is married to a white woman?' Mehuru demanded. 'I had not thought it was possible.'

'There's no law against it. Most of your countrymen marry white women. How else are they to find companions?'

'There are no freed African women?'

'Most of the slaves brought back from the Sugar Islands are pageboys or footmen. And of course only men are press-ganged, or serve as soldiers. So only a few black women come here to England. But your countrymen marry well enough with white women. They have very pretty children, of a pale colour.' Stuart Hadley gave a short laugh. 'In a couple of hundred years you will not be able to trace the African descendants. But every Englishman with black hair or black eyes will have to wonder if his great-grandfather was a slave. Perhaps that will be your revenge on us – by the year 1900 there will be no pure white men at all.'

'I don't want revenge,' Mehuru said softly. 'I want to go home. I am needed at my home, and if I wanted to marry, the women of my nation would be my first choice.' He thought for a moment of the line of Frances's pale cheek and the way her skin gleamed like buttermilk.

'There is a scheme to take men back to Africa,' Dr Hadley said. 'Some land on the coast has been bought and named Sierra Leone. There are many black men in London who feel as you do, who want to go home to Africa. They are pioneers, they have grants of land to farm.'

'No,' Mehuru chuckled. 'You misunderstand me. I am not a farmer, I am not a pioneer. When I say I want to go home I did not mean that I wanted to camp out in the bush. I want to go home to my house, to my work, to my own country.'

Dr Hadley hesitated. 'Forgive me,' he said. 'I had thought of all Africans as living off the land, in – er – I suppose mud huts.'

Mehuru thought of the great high stone walls of Oyo and the architecture of the great houses and the palaces. 'I might as well suppose that all Englishmen lived in warehouses beside stinking rivers,' he said bitingly.

They were at the back of Queens Square. The Merchant Venturers' great crane threw a shadow like a giant gibbet over the quayside.

'You are right to correct me,' Stuart Hadley said. 'It is hard for white men to imagine your country.'

'That's all right,' Mehuru replied bleakly. 'Sometimes it is hard for me to remember it too.'

Kbara was dozing in the chair when Mehuru slipped in through the back door. He started awake and Mehuru clapped

299

his hand over his mouth. 'Sshhh! Fool!' Mehuru said swiftly in Mandinka. 'Is everything quiet?'

'The little boy is sick.'

'Like James?'

'The same.'

'Is he as bad?'

'Elizabeth says not yet, but she is worried for him.'

Mehuru thought. 'Should we fetch the doctor now?'

'Elizabeth said you were to go to her when you came in.'

Mehuru stepped out of his shoes, took them in his hand and crept up the stairs. Kbara stayed behind to lock the kitchen door and shoot the oiled bolts.

Mehuru hesitated on the landing. The two grand front bedrooms were Josiah's and Frances's. From the one on the left came a rumbling snore – Josiah – which meant that Frances was sleeping alone. Mehuru paused. He had a great desire to see her asleep. He wanted to see her without her knowing he was there, standing at the foot of the bed. He wanted to see her as a sleeping woman, innocent of her power as his slave owner. He wanted to see her warm and half-naked in her bed. He went towards her door, his feet silent on the Turkish rugs. He turned the handle and took one step inside her room.

Her window curtains were only partly drawn and the moonlight bathed the room in pale colours. Mehuru came a little closer to the bed. Frances was asleep on her back, one hand outflung. Her long hair was twisted into a careless plait. She was wearing a white nightgown of pure lawn, embroidered and pin-tucked around the neck. In her sleep one of the buttons had come undone and he could see the long pale column of her throat and the two smooth lines of her collar bones.

Mehuru swallowed. She was a lovely woman in the moonlight. Pale as a woman made of white flour, pale as a woman sculpted from frozen cream. He thought of what Dr Hadley had told him – that many black men had married white women – and he wondered if he would ever lie with a woman again. He could not believe that he must not go closer to Frances,

300

he could not believe that he was not allowed to touch her outstretched hand nor put his lips to where the pulse beat slowly and steadily at the base of her throat.

He heard Kbara's stealthy tread on the stairs and he slipped back out of the door, closing it quietly behind him, and met him on the landing. They went up the next flight of stairs together and tapped softly on the women's door. It was locked, of course. One of Cook's jobs before she bolted the back and front doors was to lock the slaves in their rooms. Kbara took down the key from its hook, unfastened the door and Elizabeth opened it from the inside. Her face was strained and tired. She had grieved for the death of James, her little foster-son, and watched them take him away and bury him in the cold alien ground. Now John was coughing as badly and his fever was rising.

'Should we fetch a doctor tonight?'

She nodded. 'He is a good man. Ask him to come.'

'I shall have to ask Frances,' Mehuru said.

'Do we have to wait until she is awake?' Kbara asked. 'Wait till the morning?'

The temptation to wake Frances was too much for him. 'I will wake her now to ask her,' he decided. 'I will go. Kbara, you go to bed. I will fetch the doctor. Frances will give me the front-door key.'

He went quickly down the stairs before they could argue, tapped very softly on Frances's door and went into the room. She opened her eyes as he came in and for a moment she thought she was dreaming, and that he had come to her in a dream of desire. Then she blinked herself awake, and there was no mistaking the expression on her face. 'Mehuru!' she said and her voice was full of joy.

He touched her outstretched hand and in a movement too quick for either of them to consider they clasped hands and he bent down to her bed, snatching her to him. Her arms went around his neck, he kissed her throat, the warm hollow where the pulse was now thudding, a line of kisses up to her mouth which was warm and sweet and opened under his. Her skin smelled of rosewater. He rubbed his face against her neck and felt beneath his moving lips the smooth swell of her breasts.

Her hands pulled at his stock, at his jacket, and he moved to throw his jacket aside but suddenly checked. 'Frances! No . . .'

'What is it? What is it, Mehuru?'

'I must not – I came to tell you – it's John. He's sick.'

Her eyelids fluttered for a moment, and then a cold closed look spread over her face. Her years of training shut down upon her desires like a trap. Her hand went to the open neck of her nightgown and pulled it close. 'Oh. Oh. I see.'

'Elizabeth wants him to see the doctor. May I go for him?'

She threw back the covers of the bed. He had a brief glimpse of her pale long legs. 'Frances . . .'

But she had herself under control. She would not even look at him. She threw a shawl around her shoulders and when she finally turned to him her face was icy. 'Mr Cole does not want the doctor called except in an emergency.'

'The child is sick.'

'Is he seriously ill?'

Mehuru exclaimed with impatience and reached out to her but she stepped back. The coldness of her face forbade him to come closer. He felt his quick anger rise at once.

'I beg your pardon,' he said bitingly. 'Excuse me, Mrs Cole. Yes, he is sick. He is sick like little James. Do you want him to be left to die, or shall I fetch the doctor?'

She flushed at the insult in his voice. 'You can fetch the doctor.'

He went to the door and hesitated, wondering if she would call him back. His mouth was still hot with her passionate kisses. He could not understand how she could suddenly summon such iciness and distance.

'The front-door key is in the drawer in the table in the hall,' Frances said precisely.

'Yes, Mrs Cole.'

*   *   *

302

Stuart Hadley was reading in his study when Mehuru arrived, breathless and hatless. He grabbed his bag and washed his face while Mehuru put his horse between the shafts of the phaeton and drove it around to the front door.

'Same symptoms?'

'Symptoms? I don't know that word.'

'Signs, signs of illness.'

'Yes. I think so.'

Hadley nodded. 'Better pray it's not typhoid.'

The clock in St Mary Redclift struck two and was answered by the cathedral clock on the other side of the city.

'Get into the house all right?'

'Yes.'

The carriage wheels rattled over John's Bridge and Mehuru turned the horse sharply to the right to drive down the bumping cobbles of the quay. The tide was out and the mud steamed with fresh sewage. Even in the cool night air the smell was overpowering.

'It's a wonder anyone survives,' Hadley said shortly.

Mehuru turned the carriage away from the quay and into the clean white enclosure of Queens Square.

'Will the horse stand?'

'He's used to it.'

Mehuru looped the reins over a railing and led the way into the house, up the stairs, past Frances's bedroom and up to the servants' rooms.

Stuart Hadley took in the overcrowding at one quick glance. The other women and girls had pulled their blankets over their heads, from tiredness and modesty, and were sleeping. Only Elizabeth watched by the bedside of the little boy, so like her own baby who had been left in Africa and now could not remember his mother at all. She looked up when the doctor came in.

'John,' she said, pointing to the little boy.

He was hot but fully conscious. He looked up in surprise as the white man came in and Mehuru whispered quickly that this was a good man come to make him well. Stuart smiled at him, took his pulse, and touched a hand to his forehead and his cheek.

'Not too bad yet,' he observed. He opened his bag. 'Here are the pastilles to burn again. They should stop the rest of you catching the illness. I wish that you were better housed. I will speak to Mrs Cole in the morning. There should be no more than four in a room of this size. And here is something to help him sleep. Keep sponging him with vinegar and water to keep the fever down and let him drink all he wants of clean water.'

Mehuru nodded and translated for Elizabeth.

'If anyone else feels sick you are to call me at once,' Stuart said to Mehuru. They closed the door of the women's room and went quietly down the stairs together. 'I do not think it is typhoid but I cannot be sure.'

'What is typhoid?'

'A very bad illness, a high fever, many people die.'

Mehuru nodded. They walked quietly along the landing, past Frances's closed bedroom door, and on down the stairs.

'I'll call tomorrow, in the morning, to see how the boy does,' Stuart Hadley promised on the doorstep.

'She may not want you to call,' Mehuru said tightly. 'They don't want to pay.'

The two men exchanged a look of mutual anger. 'She'll want me quick enough if she's got typhoid in the house,' Stuart replied. 'I'll call.'

He swung himself into the phaeton and gathered up the reins. 'Good night again,' he said softly, and turned the horse out of the square towards home.

Mehuru watched the carriage go, enjoying the silence of the night-time square and his rare sense of freedom. Overhead the blue-black sky was rich with stars, hundreds and thousands of them. Mehuru slowly turned to go back inside and closed and locked the front door and returned the key to its place.

He went quietly up the stairs and paused outside Frances's

bedroom. He could not tell if she were sleeping or awake. He felt an irresistible temptation to open her door and see if she would again come to his arms, but then he thought of the sudden coldness of her face, and how, whether she was warm or cold, he could never reproach her. She could be exactly as the whim took her, and he could do nothing but obey. At night, in her bedroom, with Josiah sleeping next door, he would not dare to speak louder than a whisper.

He made a muffled exclamation of anger and turned from her door. At once it opened, silently, and she was standing before him.

Her long dark hair was brushed over her shoulders, in the half-light of the hall her eyes were dark pools of shadow. He turned and stepped towards her and saw that she was smiling. He knew at once that for some reason, inexplicably, they had broken through the many boundaries which separated them, and that Frances had plunged through the restraint of her training. For this night, they were free to love each other as equals.

Frances, waiting for him to move, half-afraid and half-delighted, stood quite still. She thought for a moment of her bed of daffodils and whether being held by Mehuru would be like that sudden abandoned dive into freedom and sensuality.

He reached out his hand to her and put his finger against her cheek. Frances closed her eyes and leaned towards him. His desire for her rose up and he caught her to him and held her, feeling the warmth of her body against him, and the pleasure of her lips under his as she returned and sought his kisses. Mehuru lifted her easily in his arms, went into her bedroom and tumbled her on to the bed as recklessly as he had thrown the flowers.

Chapter Twenty-four

Early next morning, Stuart Hadley's phaeton drew up outside 29 Queens Square. Frances was waiting for him in the hall, her hair piled high, wearing a rich peach gown. 'I think he is better,' she greeted him.

'You have seen him yourself?'

Frances gave him a small sideways smile. 'I am not completely a slave driver. Of course I have seen him. And I think he is much better. Elizabeth is with him now, do you want to go up?'

Mehuru came halfway down the stairs. Frances glanced up at him and quickly looked away.

Mehuru made a little bow, his eyes on her face.

'Take the doctor to the room, Cicero,' she said carefully.

Mehuru bowed with meticulous politeness and led the way up the stairs. Stuart Hadley quickly glanced back at Frances and caught such a radiant smile from her as she looked up at the two men that he checked on the stairs, and hesitated. 'Mrs Cole?'

Frances blushed a deep rosy red. 'I am sorry,' she said. 'I was thinking . . . I was thinking . . .'

Mehuru too had paused. 'What were you thinking of, Mrs Cole?' he asked, his voice warm with suppressed laughter.

Frances blushed rosily, tried to say something, and then ran into the parlour and shut the door.

The two men were silent for a moment. 'I see,' Stuart said, understanding everything.

Mehuru glanced at him. 'You see nothing.'

They climbed the stairs to the attic bedroom in silence. Stuart put his hand on Mehuru's arm before he opened the door.

'I hope you are not putting yourself in very great danger, my friend,' Stuart said quietly. 'This is a perilous road for you and for her.'

Mehuru nodded. 'I cannot help but walk it. It is my Ifa – my fate.' He stepped back to let the doctor precede him into the bedroom. The little boy was seated on Elizabeth's lap and taking gruel from a spoon. She looked up and smiled as the doctor came in.

'Well, this is very much better!' he exclaimed. 'The fever broke in the night, did it?'

She nodded and put her hand against John's face. 'Cool,' she said. 'John is well.'

'Keep him in for the next few days,' Stuart advised. 'And don't let him go running errands in the rain. Plenty of food to build him up again. I think we have been lucky this time.'

Elizabeth smiled.

'And you get some rest,' Dr Hadley said gently. 'No point you getting overtired and making yourself ill too. Sleep.'

Her glance slid to Mehuru. They both knew that a slave only rested with permission. 'I will tell Frances,' he said. 'You rest with John today. I will tell Mrs Cole. She will allow it.'

The two men left the room together and went downstairs. Mehuru tapped on the parlour door and stepped to one side.

'The fever has broken,' Stuart reported briefly. He did not step into the room, he stood on the threshold and addressed Frances and Sarah without preference. 'It is not typhoid. You were lucky with this one.'

Frances smiled. 'I am glad,' she said.

'The woman who has been caring for him should have a rest today,' Stuart continued. 'She was at his bedside all night.'

Sarah looked as if she might argue but Frances nodded. 'Of course,' she said. 'And thank you for coming out in the middle of the night, Doctor.'

He bowed briefly to them both and went out into the hall. Mehuru, who was waiting, handed him his hat and went with him to his phaeton.

'I want my freedom,' Mehuru said suddenly. 'Whatever else. It makes no difference. I still want my freedom.'

The doctor nodded. 'I agree. You have no future here, like this. And slavery corrupts you all, spoils all your lives, hers as well as yours. That's what they can't see, the traders, the owners. When you use another person you are both enslaved, both corrupted. And by next week, by Tuesday when Wilberforce's bill is agreed, you will all be on the way to freedom!'

He climbed into the driving seat. 'Tuesday night!' he said softly to Mehuru, and the horse moved on.

29 Queens Square,
Bristol.

7th May 1789

Dear Uncle,

I have Heard this day from Sir Charles. He is coming to See us on his Way to stay at the Home of Lord Bartlet. He has Decided to Buy Shelby Manor from You and he wishes to Sign the Lease here. We are to Act as his Agents in this Matter also: Investing his Rents and settling Debts at the Manor. I understand there is a Land Agent to Manage the Day-to-Day running of the Farms. I therefore Await the lease from You and will Return it to You signed, and with the money for the Purchase Price.

The Weather here is still very uncertain, the winter seems to have lasted forever. The City is Prone to Fogs and low-lying clouds and the Smell from the Manufactories is very Bad. Josiah and Miss Cole do not Notice it, being Accustomed. I Drive out on fine Days to enjoy the Cleaner air of the Downs. Despite this I am very happy. I feel so Full of joy and I have Never been in stronger Health. I Wake every morning so Easily and I am Never tired.

An Acquaintance of Mine has asked Me for some Advice on which I Should like your Opinion. She has made a Marriage with a

Bristol Merchant but Finds herself very Attracted to a Visitor to Bristol – a Nobleman in his Own Country, and most Handsome and Tender to her. He tells her that he Loves her and She Believes it is the Truth. She tells me that she has Never felt Happier, as if her Life depends on him. She has Asked me What she Should do. I Wonder what Your Opinion is? There Can be no Future for them, of Course? I have told her My opinion: that the Bonds of Matrimony can never be Loosed.

I Hope you are in Good Health, my Dear Uncle. I remain your loving niece,

Frances.

Mehuru tapped on the parlour door and came into the room as Frances blotted her letter and sealed it.

'May I speak with you?'

Her quick colour rose at once, she smiled at him and whispered: 'Shut the door.'

He pushed it closed, but came no nearer.

'I wonder if we might be paid a wage,' he said.

'What?' She recoiled as if he had slapped her. 'A wage?'

'We work as Cook works,' he went on persuasively. 'She is paid wages and has time off. We are servants as she is.'

'But you are slaves!'

'I wish we could be servants. I could be content as your servant. I could serve you and have my pride.'

'It's not possible . . .'

'No, Frances,' he said quickly. 'It is *this* which is not possible. I cannot be owned by you any longer. I have to have my freedom. I cannot be with you as I want to be with you, unless I am a free man. Anything else shames us both. I want you to pay me, to pay all of us, and then at least I would be here by my own choice, I would be my own man.'

'Josiah would never agree . . . Sarah would never allow it.'

'If you paid me enough, I could rent a room and you could

309

come to me. We could be together under my roof, not hidden, not secret.'

She shook her head. 'It is not possible, my dear. It is not possible.'

'You are the owner.'

'In name alone. Everything I own, from my clothes to my father's dining table, became Josiah's when we married. It is his scheme, he bought you and the others. If you and the others were freed who would pay? Sarah keeps the accounts, there are the shipping costs and your food and livery . . .'

'We could pay you back, out of our wages.'

She shook her head. 'Mehuru – you have been sold and John has been sold for a hundred and ten guineas each! You could never earn that amount! Cook is paid only thirteen pounds a year, and she is trained. This is all part of a scheme, you are the first consignment and then there will be other slaves coming and they . . .' She trailed off at the thunderstruck look on his face. 'What is the matter? What is it?'

'Did you say I am sold? And the little boy John is sold?'

She nodded.

'You have sold me?'

Her eyes flickered from him to the door as if she wished someone would interrupt them. 'Cicero, I –'

'Don't call me that!'

'What?'

'Don't call me Cicero!' he said in a sharp undertone. 'In your bedroom you called me Mehuru! I won't be a free man in your bed and a slave in your parlour.'

'Mehuru . . . the sale has not gone through. It was an offer only, and Josiah has accepted it. It was before Easter . . . before I knew . . . It was before we . . . I did not think . . .'

He turned sharply, strode over to the window and glared out into the backyard. It was a warm sunny morning. A rose bush, sprawling over the backyard wall, was slowly opening its buds. He watched a bee land and struggle through the rich parcel of petals to the orange centre.

310

'You will sell me?'

She could not see his face, and did not know what the tight tone in his voice might mean.

'No,' she protested. She could feel a sense of panic rising. She had never argued with a man before, she had never faced a man's anger. 'Please, Mehuru, be patient. You know I could not bear to be without you. You know that. I will tell Josiah that we have to keep you, and we will sell Julius in your place.'

He turned on his heel. 'Until you are tired of me,' he said bitingly. 'When you have had your fill of me you can sell me then. You could sell me to a woman who wanted a man, with a special recommendation. You could tell her I am not fit to be paid a wage for a decent day's work but that I can be played with and . . .' in his anger he stumbled over the English words, but he made an obscene gesture with his hand '. . . used like a bull to a cow.'

Frances went white and dropped into a chair. 'It isn't like that . . . it isn't like that . . .'

He stalked to the door. 'Excuse me. I have not carried the nightsoil pail down from the women's room. It will be stinking. I have work to do.'

'Mehuru!' she called. But the door had slammed behind him and he was gone.

Frances rose from her chair, ran to the door and flung it open. But in the empty hall she hesitated, her hand on her heart to still its painful racing. She could not cry out for him, she could not chase him around the house. He was her servant, he was lower than her servant; he was her slave. To betray for one instant that she had forgotten her position and his would be a disgrace so total that death itself could not be worse. If Josiah knew, if Sarah knew . . . Frances shuddered at the thought and went back into the parlour. She seated herself again at the table and stared unseeingly at the notepaper.

Anyone coming into the parlour would have seen a Lady of Quality, fashionably dressed, writing letters. Frances, as still and as elegant as if she were sitting for her portrait, listened, in case Mehuru relented and came back into the parlour. She listened and she waited all morning. The rapid fluctuating beat of her heart raced every time she heard a footstep in the hall; but he did not come.

Chapter Twenty-five

At midday Josiah came home from the coffee house where he had been forward selling the cargo of *Daisy*. She had been seen loading off Africa and should be home in December. Josiah wanted to raise money to give him some ready cash for the housekeeping costs. He was gambling that she would be home on time and with a good cargo of sugar. He met a friend of Stephen Waring's, Mr Green, who was enthusiastic about the Hot Well lease. He assured Josiah that it was a fine piece of business, and only his commitment to building in Clifton meant that he himself was not in the running for it. In the meantime, he offered Josiah a Hot Well lodging house at a price which anyone could see was attractive. He complimented Josiah in seeing the opportunity of the Hot Well for what it was, a potential gold mine. Josiah came home excitable, and with a sense of moving in the circles of the highest power in Bristol where a whisper could make or break a man.

Frances hastily sent down a message to Cook that Josiah was home and wanted some luncheon. Within half an hour a cold collation was laid in the morning room. Sarah joined them.

'You are pale, Frances,' she observed. 'Are you unwell again?'

Frances shook her head. 'I am perfectly well,' she said. A small niggling pain at her heart contradicted her but she ignored it.

'Will you take a little rum and water?' Josiah offered.

Frances refused. 'No. I will have a glass of ratafia and just a piece of bread and butter.'

He helped her to her place and rang the bell. 'I had an enquiry for one of our boys. The surviving one is promised to Mr Waring. He is well enough to be sold now, is he not?'

Frances caught her breath. 'Oh no,' she said hastily. 'Not yet. I don't think so. And he is very little.' She glanced over at Mary who was serving them from the sideboard and who knew enough English to follow the conversation.

'How old d'you think he is?' Josiah asked around a mouthful of bread and ham.

'About four years, perhaps five,' Frances answered.

'Old enough then to run errands. He could go as a pageboy.'

'I am not yet happy about his health,' Frances said desperately. 'It would look very bad if we sold him and then he was sick or even died. We must make sure he is well before we let him go.'

'Yes,' Josiah agreed. 'But we could use the money, Frances.'

'What news of *Rose?*' Sarah demanded. 'Have you had bad news, Josiah?'

He shook his head. 'No, no news at all, Sister. I was thinking merely that it is time that the slaves were sold. We have had them for more than half a year. We always thought they would go within six months.'

'Their training was so interrupted, with moving house and everything,' Frances insisted breathlessly. 'You must give me longer. If they are to be a credit to us . . . They don't all speak well . . . and we have to keep Mehuru, I mean Cicero, to run the house and train the others . . .'

'Very well,' Josiah said pacifically. 'No matter. Whenever you think fit, my dear.'

Unseen under the table, Frances pushed her fist against her ribcage where she could feel a sharp, growing pain.

'And what have you been doing this morning?' Josiah asked, making ponderous conversation.

314

'I have written to my Uncle Scott,' Frances said. 'He is staying with some friends in Yorkshire.'

'Yorkshire, eh?' Josiah exclaimed. 'I have no friends in Yorkshire, I am sure. That's where that blackguard Wilberforce comes from, they're very hot on Abolition in Yorkshire, it is a nest of agitators.' Josiah nodded at Sarah. 'I think we have no cause for concern as yet. The Venturers say that it will all blow over. Wilberforce has the support of only a few men, and we are a powerful lobby. All the main cities of the kingdom and all the manufacturers are against him.'

'When is the vote?' Frances asked. 'It is this month, is it not?'

'The eleventh,' Josiah replied heavily.

'What would we do if the Trade were to be abolished?'

Josiah gave her a small smile. 'Beg, borrow or buy ships and do as many voyages as we could. The profits on slaves would go through the roof.'

'If it were banned?'

'No ban would be immediate,' Sarah explained. 'Any ban on the Trade would take several years to come in, and during that time prices would be at a premium. Everyone would want to stock up while they could.'

'And compensation would be paid to slavers,' Josiah supplemented. 'The greater profits one could show the greater the compensation. But in any case, I am not afraid of Abolition. We have too much power. This is our Parliament chosen by our electorate and stuffed with our placemen. Of course it will serve the interests of honest Traders and landlords.'

Frances nodded.

'I shall drive out to the Hot Well this afternoon,' Josiah said. 'Will you come with me, Frances? I want to see how busy it is mid-week. This is the prime season, it should be coining money.'

'Certainly,' Frances replied. She had a swift thought that now she would not be able to see Mehuru until the evening. But Josiah's wishes must come first. 'I would like to see it.'

'You can take a glass of the water,' Josiah said cheerfully. 'Will you come, Sister? You must come and see it. I am serious about buying the lease, I have had sight of the books and they show that the major expenditure has all been made. Stephen Waring is sure that we can earn a return from it.'

'A return such as a voyage to Africa and the West Indies will make?' Sarah demanded. 'I doubt it.'

'A different business with different costs and different benefits,' Josiah assured her. 'We have to move with the times, Sarah. All the great Merchant Venturer companies have shipping but they have land and collieries and building interests too. We have to be like them – we have to have some of our money out at sea and some of it safe home here on shore. And it is steady, Sarah. There is not the long wait for your profit. Now that we have high and steady expenses we need a business which pays us every month, not once every two years.'

Sarah cleared her throat. 'You can go, Mary,' she said. Mary curtseyed and left the room. Sarah waited until the door had closed behind her. 'I did not want to speak before her but, Brother, I must speak to you and Frances frankly.'

Josiah looked deeply unhappy. 'Speak, Sarah. You know I always value your advice. This is your company as much as it is mine, and your fortune as well as mine depends on it.'

Sarah glanced at Frances. 'I am not against Frances, or you, Brother,' she began. 'But I must question what is happening to the company. In my father's day and in the early days when you and I ran the company we took a pride in trading with cash in hand. We bought trade goods with cash, we bought slaves with trade goods, we sold slaves for gold, we bought sugar with gold, and we sold sugar at a profit on the quayside for more gold which then paid for the next voyage.'

Josiah nodded.

'When we realised that the Trade was slipping away, that fewer and fewer large investors were taking a share on our voyages, we decided to sell slaves direct into England. You

316

married Frances to obtain her dowry to finance their purchase and so that she should teach them for free and sell them to her friends.'

Frances, who had never before heard Josiah's proposal explained in such bald terms, blinked, but could not disagree.

'Why do we now think of changing everything?' Sarah demanded passionately. 'The money we earn from the sale of these slaves should buy more slaves. The money we earn from each voyage should equip another voyage. But instead it is being wasted on this house and high living, and all I hear from you is one scheme after another. We do not need schemes. We already know how to make a profit. Trade is what we have always done and trade is what we should do – trade with cash in hand.'

Josiah and Frances were silent.

'There is another thing,' Sarah continued more quietly. 'I know that you have longed all your life to be a Merchant Venturer and I congratulate you on your election to the Company. I believe it was bound to come to you in time, as an honest, profitable Bristol Trader. But I would remind you, Brother, that these are new friends, they are not tried and tested. If Mr Waring advises you of an opportunity or wants to borrow money, you should treat him with as much suspicion as an out-of-work captain in the coffee house. He cheated us over this house . . .'

'Now, Sarah! He never did!' Josiah exclaimed.

'He did! He did!' she cried passionately. 'Three houses on the market the moment we paid him the deposit. All of them friends and neighbours of his! All of them cheaper than this! He told them to hold off until he had landed his fish, Josiah. And you are so besotted with becoming gentry you will not see it.'

She had caught him on the raw. His voice rose to match hers. 'How dare you say such a thing! In all my years trading I have never been bested but I have always seen chances which you would have missed. You've never moved on, Sarah.

317

You've always looked back. You were happiest living with Da over the warehouse and with one racked old boat. You think small, Sarah, and you want to cut me down to your size!'

Frances ducked her head down and sliced bread and butter into tiny slivers, longing to be out of the room and away from the loud voices.

'I think as you should think,' Sarah hissed. 'I think that you are a small trader and now you are swimming in a large pond with greedy men who will gobble you up, Josiah. I do not trust Stephen Waring. I do not trust his ideas. And I certainly do not trust the Hot Well if it comes with his recommendation! Why can you not see that! Why can you not keep to the Trade you know?'

Josiah pushed his plate away and strode to the window, his face flushed, his feet stamping on the floor in anger. He glared out of the window and a street seller who had been about to set up his pitch and sing his ballads picked up his tray and hastily moved on.

Josiah gripped the windowsill until his knuckles showed white. He fought his anger until he had it under control. Then he cleared his throat and turned back to the table. 'Now, Sarah,' he said kindly. 'Don't rant at me. I am trying to do my best. Let me explain my thinking to you and let us be friends.'

She was still quivering but she nodded that she would listen. Brother and sister glanced down the table to Frances. Her head bent low, she was pleating and re-pleating the napkin in her lap. Brother and sister regarded her with mild irritation, and then returned their attention to each other.

'When we buy goods – trade, slaves, whatever – we move them to make our profit. We take them to another market where they command a better price.'

Sarah nodded.

'And it costs us to move them. We can never be sure what damage a ship will suffer. It can lose a mast, it can lose its

318

sails. If the worst occurs we can lose the whole ship and the crew and cargo.'

Sarah nodded again. 'So?'

'But when we buy land – such as the Hot Well spring – we can work it where it is. We know the risks. Nothing can go wrong with it. It's not like a ship tossed about by the wind and the weather. The water comes out of the ground hot and bubbling and we bottle it and sell it, or we sell it at the spa. It's safe money, Sarah. Safer than your ships. And there's another profit, a hidden profit.'

'How?' she asked reluctantly.

'Everything is costing more,' Josiah said. 'It was his lord-ship, Lord Scott himself, who showed it to me. We were talking about his rent rolls when Frances's dowry was to be paid and he showed me. They are using new methods to farm, the land is yielding more, and so every farm, every farm in England, is more valuable than it was twenty years ago. The ground beneath our feet, even here in the city, is more valu-able. When we come to sell this house we will get more than we paid for it. When we come to sell the Hot Well we will get more than we paid for it. Every day, everything we own becomes more valuable.'

Sarah shook her head at the incredible concept.

'It is like a miracle,' Josiah breathed. 'A miracle, Sarah. Everything we own is becoming more valuable. Even the warehouse, even the rock of the caves. Everything is growing in profit. All we have to do is to turn the warehouse, the rock, the land under our feet into cash.'

Sarah would have interrupted but Josiah was entranced by the prospect of self-generating wealth. 'Look at the prices for land on Park Street. If we had bought land either side of the street ten, twenty years ago we could have had it for ten pounds an acre. Do you know what it is worth now?'

Sarah shook her head.

'Hundreds,' Josiah said. 'You could name your price.'

'But we did not buy it,' Sarah maintained stubbornly.

'Because we did not know that it was going to become fashionable. We did not know it would be valuable. We could not have predicted it. You have never looked beyond a house here, in this square.'

'Yes, but now we can make predictions,' Josiah said. 'We did not guess that people like the Warings would move up the hill to Park Street because we did not know them. I did not hear them speak of it, I was not invited to their table in the coffee house. But now I *am* there, Sarah, and I *do* hear the rumours. Now I *know* where the fashion is taking hold. And I tell you, it is the Hot Well, it is Park Street. We are too late for Park Street. But we can snatch at the Hot Well and in ten years' time we can sell it for ten times what we have paid for it, as well as running it at a profit now.'

Sarah was almost convinced. 'But if this is so,' she asked slowly, 'if it is such an excellent deal then why are the Merchant Venturers selling it? Why is Mr Waring not buying it himself?'

Josiah slammed his fist into his cupped palm. 'Because I have hit it right! I have! Me! This is my moment! This is my time! Waring is buying land in Clifton – but there will be no development of Clifton for fifty years, he is in too early. James – the tenant of the Hot Well – was in too soon. The Company has done all the improvements and want their money repaid. I have caught this fashion on the bough – Clifton may be the very place in twenty years' time, Park Street was tempting ten years ago – but the time for the Hot Well is now! And here I am now! I am ready to buy in now!'

'What with?' Sarah demanded. As ever she went to the very heart of the question.

'I shall borrow against *Daisy*'s cargo, and two thousand pounds against *Rose*.'

She nearly moaned. 'Borrow more against *Rose*? You have forestalled her cargo already to buy this house. If she fails we will be ruined!'

'I own half the cargo,' he confessed. 'I could not get partners for her and now I am glad of it. I shall borrow every penny I can against her profits, and *Daisy*'s too.'

'Two ships carrying debt?' she demanded.

'Yes,' Josiah said defiantly. 'Look around you, Sarah! No-one trades with their own money any more. All the big schemes are done with loaned money. All the coal mines, all the foundries, all the industries are launched on borrowed money. You know that is the truth.'

'It is not our way.'

'No, and our way has been slow and sure. But I want to go faster, Sarah. I want the Hot Well. I can show you the figures and you will know I am right. We have to borrow to buy into the lease. I am determined that we should do it.'

Sarah turned from his stubborn face. 'Frances!' she appealed. 'This is your fortune too. Do you want to see Josiah borrow against a ship which has not even docked?'

Frances had relaxed when Josiah had controlled his anger and they had stopped shouting. She was thinking of Mehuru and wondering when she could see him again and how she could divert him from his demand for wages. She gave a little start and used her usual excuse. 'I am sorry. I know so little about business.'

Sarah turned back to her brother. 'I see you are determined,' she said. The colour had drained from her face.

'I am.'

'You will go ahead with this scheme, whatever I say?'

He nodded.

Sarah paused for a moment, measuring her will against his. 'You promised my father that I should share in the running of his business,' she reminded him bitterly. 'You made a death-bed promise, Josiah.'

'I did, and I have never broken it.'

She glared at him. 'You are breaking it now, when you will not listen to my advice, when you run headlong into debt and into schemes that we know nothing about.'

'I promised you should share in the running of the business,' he said. 'I never promised that you should rule the roast. I never promised that you should stand in my way and so ruin me.'

'I!' she exclaimed. 'I! Ruin *you*!'

He was quick and biting. 'Yes, you. You still keep the household books, you see how much money we spend every month. Where is it to come from, Sarah? We will be ruined if we do not find new ways to make money, new ventures. Not even you can wish us sold up and back at the dockside.'

She was silenced.

'We have to go forward,' Josiah insisted stubbornly. 'To hesitate is to be wrecked.'

They were both silent. 'I have not seen the ships' books since we moved house,' Sarah said. 'I have not brought them up to date. I shall need to enter these debts you are incurring, I shall need to show that you have sold their cargoes.'

'They are at the warehouse,' Josiah told her. He rose to his feet and went to the door. 'I have opened my office down there. I have taken on a clerk. He will keep the books for me. It is more convenient so.'

He did not dare face her. He opened the door and slipped away from her before he could see her stricken face.

Chapter Twenty-six

The drive to the Hot Well was not a great success. The day had clouded over and under the dark bellies of storm clouds the little colonnade of shops and the Pump Room did not look pretty and inviting, but seemed overwhelmed by the lowering cliffs above. The tide was out, the river oozed between greasy banks of brown mud and the sweet sickly smell of sewage lingered. Every day that the sun grew hotter increased the stench. The wind ruffling the low-tide river was heavy with it.

The Pump Room was built on an imposing scale but it had the inescapable appearance of a warehouse. Frances, looking at the blank wall fronting the river, and the windows set square in the three-storey-high stonework without any relief or decoration, thought that in every corner the city of Bristol was dominated by trade. Even this most important building had an uneven roof, odd-numbered chimneys, and faced the river as blankly and as plainly as a tide mill for grinding corn.

At the back of the Pump Room, at the free pump which dispensed the spa water without charge, there was a collection of sickly paupers. When they saw the carriage they came forward with their hands out, begging for pennies. Josiah waved them away and the hired coachman gestured with his whip. One of them, a young woman, raised her face blotched livid with a skin disease. Frances shrank back into the carriage.

'Aye, they're off-putting,' Josiah conceded. 'Get back, you!' he shouted. 'You're upsetting my wife.'

They stepped back but Frances heard a muffled curse as

she hurried out of the road and into the assembly room. The place was busy. Josiah looked around, visibly counting the number of customers while Frances swallowed a glass of the water. She was hoping that it would quiet the fluttering in her chest which had pained her ever since the quarrel with Mehuru in the morning. Josiah noted the white faces of the invalids with consumption, and heard the dry racking coughs of those with chest complaints. There were fashionable people visiting for the day and taking tea, or expensive hot-house strawberries with cream, but there were not enough.

'Can we make it more fashionable?' he asked. 'What would you do?'

Frances thought. 'I would rent consulting rooms cheaply to good doctors,' she said. 'They will bring the patients in. And perhaps build a bath house, with beautiful mosaics, and plants, and furniture, like a winter garden.'

Josiah nodded. 'The bath house,' he said. 'What would it be like?'

Frances considered. 'What about large windows and a terrace overlooking the river? And build it like a hot house, like the hot house at Whiteleaze. Oh! I forgot you have never seen it. But it is a fine large room and very light. Very well-heated with many plants. It is a pleasant place to sit in winter. And when the fruit comes into season it is like sitting in a garden. We could call it the Bristol Winter Garden! So that the Hot Well was popular all the year round.'

'That's it!' Josiah exclaimed. 'Frances, you are a genius! Do you know who should design it for us? Who is the finest architect?'

'We need someone who designs follies and grottoes,' she said. 'Something charming and romantic and out of the ordinary.'

Josiah shook his head. 'I don't mix with such people. There's a grotto at Goldney House, in Clifton, I know. But I've heard it is very strange. Full of shells and pagan statues, and a fountain.'

324

'That's the very thing,' Frances said decidedly. 'A fountain and classical statues. We want a Gothic bath house. Lord Scott will know the best man to design it.'

'Gothic!' Josiah exclaimed. 'Will it not look very strange?'

'A little strange.' Frances smiled at his uneasy face. 'But it has to be a little strange to draw people from Bath. Bath is such an established place, everyone knows of it, everyone goes there. We need to create something very fanciful, something that will draw people who love a novelty.'

'You know best,' Josiah said firmly, reassuring himself. 'Will you write to his lordship and ask him?'

'Yes,' Frances agreed. 'I was writing to him this morning, I have not yet sealed and posted it. I was telling him that Sir Charles Fairley wishes to buy my uncle's manor. He will come to us to sign the papers and he wishes us to hold his capital for his house and deal with his land agent.'

Josiah grimaced. 'Will it not take a lot of letter writing and bother?' he asked.

'Josiah!' Frances exclaimed. 'We are to hold his capital! We can invest it as we wish! I should have thought that it was worth a good deal of letter writing and bother!'

'I have always done my business face to face,' he excused himself. 'I hate writing letters.'

'It is very little effort,' Frances said. 'I can do it, and my uncle advises on investments for Sir Charles. All I have to do is to keep a note and render him an account.'

'Will you do it? Or ask Sarah?'

'I can do it,' Frances said easily. 'Sarah prefers ships.'

'She should have been a captain,' Josiah agreed. 'Did you hear her at lunch today? She cannot tolerate the thought of spending money on anything which does not float.'

'She has your interests at heart,' Frances said pacifically. 'And it has been a big change for her, moving house, and my arrival.'

Josiah nodded, and glanced once more around the room.

'Does it get busier later on?' he asked the woman serving the water. 'What is the trade like in winter?'

'On a weekday in winter it is like the death house,' she said cheerfully. 'Sometimes no-one is here at all, and sometimes the only visitors are the incurables. Very gloomy, sir. If you want a jolly place you had better go to Bath.'

'Why, I thank you,' Josiah snapped, instantly irritated. 'We were going anyway.' He offered his arm to Frances and swept her from the room. 'As soon as we purchase the lease that woman is sacked,' he said. 'Telling paying customers that the place is like a death house!'

The skies outside were darker than ever. As they got into the carriage there was a low warning rumble of thunder and a few drops of rain started to fall. The horses were restless. 'Here!' Josiah said to the coachman. 'Put the hood up, please.'

The man called to a lad and ordered him to hold the horses. He got down from the driving box and came to the back of the carriage to try to lift the folding roof, which was made of canvas, folded back on wooden hoops. It should have unfolded easily from both the back and front of the carriage and stretched over the seats to lock together in the middle. But the joints were rusted and would not shift. The coachman pulled at them. The rain started to fall more heavily. Frances seated herself in the carriage and pulled a rug over her knees.

A cold wind blew down the gorge. The tide was on the turn and little waves slapped against the mud, the wind whipping them into white-crested ripples. The thunder was blown in with the incoming tide; there was a loud roar immediately overhead and the rain fell harder and faster. Frances shrank back into the carriage and tried to wrap the rug tighter around her knees. She was wearing only a light coat and a silk gown underneath. Her bonnet flapped dangerously in the wind.

'My wife is getting soaked!' Josiah exclaimed. 'Can you not get the hood up?'

'I am sorry, sir, it is stuck,' the man apologised. 'I am trying.' His words were drowned out by a tremendous thunderclap.

Frances screamed as the whole world went brilliantly white for a moment and then black.

Josiah leaped down from the carriage and pulled at the other side, trying to free the rusty catches. The horses moved uneasily, and Frances called, 'Hold the horses, Josiah! They will bolt!'

There was a sudden scud of bitterly cold rain. 'This is hopeless!' Josiah shouted. 'Get down, Frances, and we will wait for it to pass.'

'I'm so wet,' she cried. 'Let us just drive home as quick as we can.'

'Drive then!' Josiah shouted at the coachman. 'But I shall not pay for this hire!'

The coachman swung himself on to the box and let the frightened horses go forward. They sprang into a trot and he had to steady them. The speed of the coach whipped rain into Frances's face, tumbled her hair, blew her bonnet. She had the driving rug clutched around her legs but it was quickly soaked through. Rain collected on the brim of her bonnet and then poured down her neck. She was shivering and chilled.

The rain pelted down on them. There was no shelter at all. The rug around Frances's legs was sodden in moments and she could feel the damp seeping through her skirt and through the thin soles of her shoes.

By the time they drew up outside the house she was wet through to the skin and her teeth were chattering from the cold. Martha, who had been on the watch for them, threw open the door and Mehuru came running down the steps, opened the carriage door and pulled the folding steps out so that Frances could step down and he could rush her into the warmth of the house.

Elizabeth swept her upstairs and within moments Frances was stripped of her wet clothes, wrapped in warm blankets and seated by the fire. But still she shivered and the colour was drained from her face and her lips were pale.

'You cold, Mrs Cole?' Elizabeth asked, looking anxiously at her. 'You sick?'

'Just chilled,' Frances said, trying to smile and hold her chattering teeth still. 'Fetch me some hot tea. I am quite well.'

Elizabeth nodded and went from the room. Mehuru was lingering outside. 'Is she all right?' he asked in Yoruban. 'Can I go in and see her? Is she all right?'

Elizabeth shook her head. 'You cannot go in, she is undressed. She says she is well. She does not look well to me. You are the healer, what can you see?'

Mehuru hesitated. It had been so long since he had used his priestly gifts, they were like a tool he had mislaid. He had watched Frances as a lover, not as a healer. He paused for a moment and brought her face into his imagination, noted the heavy sweep of dark hair and the shadows which were always there under her eyes, the transparent skin and the frequent rosy blushes. He sensed a pain in his chest which he knew was her pain, a permanent squirm of discomfort like a murmur in the heart. He felt a tightness across the lungs, and thought of Frances's continual gesture of putting her hand to her throat when she was breathless. 'She is a white woman,' he said, trying to reassure himself, discounting his insight. 'They all look sick to me.'

Josiah treated himself to a bowl of steaming punch and called Kbara to light a fire in his study. As he warmed the seat of his dressing gown there was a tap at the door and Sarah came in.

'I heard that you and Frances were caught in the storm,' she said. 'The slave Elizabeth thinks we should send for Dr Hadley for Frances. Should you see him, Brother?'

He noted her controlled tone. 'No, I am well. What's amiss with Frances?'

Sarah did not hide her lack of concern. 'She's always ill with something.'

'What do you want, Sarah?' he asked.

She took a deep breath and faced him. 'I want sight of the books,' she said. 'The ships' accounts. I have done them all my life, Brother. Even if you have a clerk he will still need to be overseen. Let me check his work for you. Let me see the ships' books.'

Josiah turned his back to her to warm his hands at the fire. He could not let her see them. *Rose* had gone out uninsured for the middle passage and Sarah would spot the discrepancy at once. Sarah had no idea of the household debts, nor the interest Josiah was paying on his borrowings. He could not face her distress if she saw the full figures.

'Certainly,' he said. 'I will bring them home for you to see. At the moment the clerk is studying them, to make sure he does things your way.'

'I could teach him . . .' Sarah volunteered hastily.

'In a week or two,' Josiah interrupted. 'You shall see him and go through the books with him.'

'It is not just the work,' Sarah said hesitantly. 'Though it is hard for me to do nothing, to do worse than nothing, when I have been so busy for all my life.'

Josiah glanced at her over his shoulder. Her mouth was working, she was biting back rare tears.

'I do not feel at home here,' she said pitifully. 'It is not what I am used to.'

'You cannot miss the noise and the stink of the quayside, Sarah!'

She nodded. 'Even the smell of the dock at low tide,' she confessed. 'I have nothing to do here. And I am of no use to you. Frances runs the house, and you talk to her about your schemes.'

He almost turned and held out his arms to her, he almost showed his deep abiding love for her, the sister who had mothered him through a harsh loveless childhood. But the habits of coldness were too strong for them both. He gave an awkward shrug and cleared his throat. He could think of nothing to say.

She stood for a few moments, waiting to see if he would reply. Then when he said nothing she turned and went to the door. 'I shall send for the doctor if you insist,' she said unpleasantly. 'I imagine Frances will want to linger in bed for weeks.'

Chapter Twenty-seven

Frances was seriously ill after her soaking at the Hot Well and Mehuru could not see her for several days. He had to hand over the coal scuttle for her bedroom fire at the door to Elizabeth or to one of the other women, and the hot water for her washbasin was taken from him by Martha, Mary or Elizabeth. One of the women carried her meals up to her on a tray, and Elizabeth was ordered to sleep at the foot of her bed on a little truckle bed in case she was ill in the night.

With Josiah absorbed in his plans for the Hot Well and Frances sick, the slaves were freer than they had ever been. In the afternoons the women would take the children to play in the gardens of the square. No-one complained, people soon became used to seeing little John, and eight-year-old Susan and Matthew on the grass beneath the young trees playing the tiny intricate children's games of Africa which Elizabeth taught them.

They became a new kind of family, an invention all of their own. An African family which mostly spoke English, a black family clothed in cotton and heavy serge, a community with two men but headed unquestionably by the women. And – less comfortably – a family that snatched at a little space and a little time, and could be torn apart and sold away from each other at any moment.

They never forgot that they were slaves and that their happiness and security depended completely on the slender thread of their owner's whim. In the evening, when they sat around the kitchen table, the boys and girls painstakingly reading, or the girls sewing while the boys played jacks, the adults would talk softly about what they could do to secure their freedom, how they could gain their liberty and stay together.

Dr Hadley came and said that Frances was suffering from an inflammation of the lungs brought on by the chill. He prescribed rest and warmth. Mehuru waited outside the house and held the horse to create an opportunity to speak to him.

'She's not desperately ill,' Hadley said cheerfully. 'But she's not strong. She's one of these delicate highly strung women. She cannot bear much anxiety and anger, and there are weak hearts in her family. Her mother died when her heart failed and Mrs Cole has that pale, dark-eyed look. She needs a calm life. She should be living in the country. She has delicate lungs and the air here is poison.'

'Would she be well in the country?' Mehuru asked. He had a sudden vision of Frances seated at her leisure on the terrace of a little farmhouse in the hot reliable sunshine of his home. He imagined a parasol of silk shading her from the sun, and her skin flushed with heat and health.

'She'd be better,' Hadley said. 'Will we see you on Tuesday night? We are hoping for news of the Abolition debate. Wilberforce will speak on Monday night to the house. Caesar has promised to send us a messenger.'

'I would not miss it for anything,' Mehuru declared. He glanced at the windows of the house. 'But I had better go now.'

Hadley pressed a coin into his hand. Mehuru instantly recoiled. 'I don't want this!'

'For holding my horse,' Hadley said patiently. 'I would give it to anyone who held my horse for me.'

Pride and necessity fought across Mehuru's face. 'Very well,' he agreed unwillingly. 'I thank you.'

Stuart gave him a quick boyish grin. 'Well, I thank you for taking it. I thought you were about to throw it back at me.'

Mehuru smiled reluctantly. 'I am not used to being in

service,' he said. 'I do not wish to become used to it, either.'

'Have you had a chance to read those pamphlets?' Dr Hadley asked, climbing into the driving seat.

Mehuru released the horse and stood back. 'I have read them. And I am reading them aloud to my friends. We talk in the kitchen at night.'

'Excellent,' Hadley said. 'The more who understand the better! These are times of great change and you and I can play our part.'

Mehuru nodded. 'I am a radical,' he observed, experimenting with a new word.

Stuart shot a nervous look up and down the street. 'Well, for pity's sake keep it to yourself,' he warned. 'Or you will be a dead radical and I will be blacklisted among the Bristol merchants.'

Mehuru grinned. 'Being black is not such a bad thing.'

'And when you start punning in English you have learned too much,' Stuart said. He waved his whip. 'Good day!'

Scott House.

9th May 1789

Dear Niece,

I Enclose the lease for Sir Charles's Signature. It is a handsome Property and I have sold it to him at a Fair price. You will note that I have Not sold him the Mineral rights to the land. He did not Ask for these and I would rather they Remained in my Keeping. You will Oblige Me if you do not draw his attention to this slight Omission.

In reply to Josiah's question about the Agitation for the Abolition of the Slave Trade, I am assured that Wilberforce has only Pitt's support and Few others. But Outside the House there is a Rising mood of Radicalism in the Country which can only Dismay all men of True patriotism.

As I Understand it – and this News is for you and Josiah Alone – the plan is to Affect to go along with Wilberforce and to Adjourn the debate, For ever. I am assured that No Slave Trader need fear for his Income during the life of this Parliament. Liverpool, Bristol, and the London merchants are Pouring money into the pockets of their Placemen to Stall the Debate and there can be No Doubt that the Abolitionists are A Small minority in the Commons. In the House of Lords of course, There are None, and Never Will be. Every Lord and most Gentlemen have Some part of their Fortune invested in slavery, be it Sugar, Rum, Cotton, or Tobacco – or Even, Shipping, Canals, and House Building – all of Which Depend on General Prosperity.

There is a Powerful Unity among the working Men and the Free Negroes in London. They see their Cause as One and the Same. Our Interest, as Employers of the One and Owners of the Other, must be to Separate them. If we can Persuade white working Men that Negroes are an Inferior Animal then we will Sever this Inconvenient unity. For the meantime – do not Fear. Negroes and Working men will always have one thing in common: they Lack All power. They have neither Money, nor the Ear of the country, nor a Vote to change their Masters. We are Secure.

I have a very Pretty investment in Mind at the moment and if your Holdings for Sir Charles could Advance one thousand pounds I could buy him a share. Let me know by Return of post. It is a proposed Colliery in Kent.

Family news is that Lady Scott is expecting Another child, and she is Confident that this time she will bear me an Heir. You can imagine how Dearly I hope that she is right. She will Remain in her Lodgings at the Sea until Autumn and then I shall Expect her to stay Quietly at Whiteleaze until my Son is born.

As to your question about your Acquaintance who finds herself attracted to A Nobleman. I will speak frankly to You, my dear. I do not like these mixed marriages between the Ranks of Society. A Lady cannot be Satisfied with a man who is in every way, except Financial, her Inferior. She is bound to meet a man of her own Rank whose company she Prefers. However she has Married into a class which does not tolerate Freedom in these matters and an Indiscretion would be fatal. A Lady has to put Aside her own Inclinations and remain Faithful to her husband. Any other

Choice is Disaster for her and for her Family. Her Dishonour
Shames all – Family and friends. I heartily Pity the woman who
finds herself in this Plight but there is no way Open to her. She has
made her Choice and she has to endure it. Please make this Clear
to Your Friend. She has No Choice. She must Forget the Gentleman
she loves and follow her Duty and her Marriage Vows. She has
No other Choice.

I am Very Very sorry my dear.

I look forward to receiving your Speedy Reply about the Business
matters. I remain your Loving uncle,

Scott.

Frances slipped the letter into the drawer of the little writing table which was balanced on the covers of her bed. She felt too exhausted to reply at once and his advice confirmed what she already knew. She had allowed herself to dream, for a moment only, that he might have written telling her that if a person is lucky enough to find a love that transforms the world around them, then nothing should stand in her way. She smiled wearily. Her uncle was hardly likely to advise her to defy the conventions, and her own life had taught her nothing but caution and fear.

All day Tuesday Mehuru haunted Josiah's study, hoping for news of the Abolition debate. Josiah also was restless. For half of the morning he waited for news from London, and then he could bear it no longer and went out to prowl around the quayside.

All along the quays there were knots of men discussing the situation. All sorts of rumours were starting: Wilberforce had been shouted down and left the House of Commons in tears. No! Not at all! Wilberforce had been acclaimed and had wept with joy. The Trade was to be banned outright, as of tomorrow. Josiah and the other men, buoyed up by hope and then flung into despair, spent an uneasy and unhappy day.

They collected in the evening in the coffee house. Stephen Waring was there.

'Cole!' he called pleasantly. 'Come and have a bowl of punch with me! I am awaiting my messenger from London with the news of the debate.'

Josiah wound his way through the gossiping men to the top table. 'I shall be glad to take a glass,' he admitted. 'This is an anxious day.'

'I am confident,' Stephen said easily. He squeezed an extra lemon into the bowl of punch, tasted it, and poured Josiah a glass.

'Yes, but you have investments all over the country,' Josiah growled irritably. 'I have three ships at sea even as I speak. What happens to men like me if they abolish overnight?'

Stephen Waring gave Josiah a long slow smile. 'They abolish!' he snorted contemptuously. 'Do cats abolish cream? Do pigs abolish the trough? The government will never abolish slavery until they cease making money from it. They are milk-maids and Africa is their cow. Slavery will flourish until it ceases to make money, Josiah. You know that.'

Josiah was warmed by the punch, and by Stephen's arrogant certainty. 'You sound very sure indeed.'

'Take another glass,' Stephen said genially. 'Business brings risk, Josiah. Who should know better than you and I? And tell me, are you determined to have the Hot Well?'

Josiah accepted the glass and took another fortifying gulp. He was diverted to his plans for the Hot Well, his fears slid away. Outside over the Redclift and Bristol quays the sun was slowly going down. Coming up the channel on the evening tide was a Bristol slaver, her decks burnished gold, her rigging like threads of brass. Seagulls whirled away from her masts like flying pennants, crying and crying. The wind blew to port the smell of death and despair. It had been an average voyage: four hundred men, women and children stacked on shelves for six months while loading and then a three-month voyage of terror, sickness, and torment. Some had gone mad, some had killed themselves, many had died of disease. Eighty had died on the voyage and been dropped overboard as carelessly as garbage from the galley. Nearly all of them sold at a profit in Jamaica would be dead within four years.

'That's a grand sight,' Josiah said, catching a glimpse of the ship from the windows of the coffee house, and thinking fondly of *Rose* and *Lily* and *Daisy*, loading off Africa.

'Beautiful,' Stephen Waring agreed.

Mehuru slipped out of the back door at nine o'clock. With Frances ill in her room, Josiah waiting for news from London at the quayside, and Sarah reading sermons in the parlour he would not be missed. He ran through the darkening streets to the coffee house and arrived there as Stuart Hadley's phaeton drew up outside.

'Any news?' Mehuru demanded.

'None yet,' Stuart said. He looked grave and excited, like a man who cannot believe that his battle has been won. 'Caesar promised to send word as soon as he knew which way the debate is going. He will not fail us.'

They went in together, ordered ale, and sat in the corner. Edgar Long drifted over to join them, and a couple of other men. Another freed black man came over to meet Mehuru. He was a Zulu, from the far south of Africa. To their mutual amusement they found their easiest shared language was English.

'I am getting a white tongue,' Mehuru remarked with distaste. 'Soon I will forget everything I ever knew.'

The atmosphere was edgy and nervous. Edgar Long had some predictions as to the way that the MPs would vote. He was certain that the Abolition of the Trade would be handsomely and rapidly passed. 'And then the banning of slavery altogether,' he said hungrily.

The evening dragged on. At midnight, many men muttered that they had to be at work in less than six hours, and left. Stuart, Edgar and Mehuru clung on. 'Caesar said he would

send me news as soon as he could see which way it was going,'
Stuart said. 'Surely there cannot be a difficulty. Everyone
knows where they stand. There has been discussion enough,
God knows.'

'Unless the Trade has bought more men than we knew,'
Edgar suggested.

'It cannot be,' Stuart protested. 'It cannot possibly fail.'

At two in the morning a travel-stained man came into the
coffee house and glanced around. 'Over here!' Stuart shouted.
The man came to their table and they pulled him down into
a seat. Other men gathered around, waiting.

'What news?'

'Nothing,' he said bitterly.

'What?'

'There is no news worth the bringing,' he said savagely.
'I waited till the debate was adjourned, I slept for six hours,
and then I rode down to tell you, as I promised to do.
I have ridden all day to bring you the news – there is no
news.'

'Here,' Mehuru said hastily and pushed a mug of ale
towards the man.

He drained it and set it down on the table. 'Wilberforce
started speaking in the afternoon,' he told them. 'He was
simple and clear. He said that they were all guilty, himself as
well, and that they should put the matter right.'

There was a murmur from the listening men. 'He had
twelve resolutions to end the Trade,' the messenger said. 'And
he was ready to put it to the vote.'

'And?' Stuart demanded, anguished.

'And nothing,' the man said.

'Then what?' Stuart shouted with impatience.

'Nothing,' the man said stubbornly. 'They refused to put
it to the vote and half a dozen of them leaped up to speak.
They never debate after midnight – you can be sure that
they'll none of them lose sleep for the likes of him . . .'
He jerked his thumb at Mehuru's scowling face. 'All of the

338

placemen of the Trade were there in their fine coats and gold watches. All waiting to speak. They're going to drag it on, they're going to drag it out.'

'It will be adjourned?'

'They chattered on like fat starlings till eleven o'clock and then they adjourned it for ten days.'

'They will vote then?'

'You may think that,' the man replied scathingly. 'But I wager that they chatter and chatter until the cause is lost and Wilberforce defeated, and this country as far from freedom and justice as ever, as it ever will be.'

Stuart slumped into his chair, put his head in his hands and groaned.

The men exchanged shocked looks. Mehuru felt sick.

'We fight on,' Stuart said, muffled. 'But I am going to bed now.' He looked up. 'I thank you for bringing us the news, however bad. Shall you stay the night at my house?'

'I'd be grateful,' the man said. 'I am as tired as a dog.'

'So what happens now?' Mehuru demanded.

Stuart gave him a crooked smile. 'We fight on. Next week, ten days' time, next month, next year. Shall I give you a lift to your door?'

'I'll walk,' Mehuru said miserably. 'I'm in no hurry to get back there.'

'See you next Monday,' Stuart said. 'We'll have more news then.'

Mehuru nodded and stepped out into the darkness of the May night.

In the next week Frances grew no better. The inflammation of the lungs brought on by the chill she had caught at the Hot Well had left her feeling weak and tired, and she seemed unable to throw off her fatigue. She had been convalescing for a fortnight in her room. For the first week she had seen no-one but the maids and the doctor. Now she was a little better and Josiah would sometimes sit with her after dinner, and he had agreed that Mehuru could come into her bedroom for reading lessons in the afternoon.

Frances wore her prettiest cap for his lesson, and her white embroidered robe. Elizabeth was ordered to sit in the window and darn table linen, acting as chaperone. Mehuru had a seat at the foot of Frances's bed and now and then she would lean forward and point to a passage in his book which he should read, and under cover of the book Mehuru could touch her finger with his.

It was not much of a courtship, but for Frances it was restful. She liked having Mehuru near at hand without his sudden unpredictable flashes of temper. She loved him being close to her.

Mehuru found the intimacy deeply disturbing. When his finger brushed against her hand he could hardly stop himself from seizing it and kissing her palm. When she leaned forward she was close enough for him to smell the light lavender scent of her linen. When she said, 'Catalogue, that word is catalogue, it means a list of things', he watched her lips and listened to the cadences of her voice and hardly heard the meaning of her words at all.

The afternoon was hazy with unfulfilled desire. Even Elizabeth, stitching slowly in the windowseat, was affected by the atmosphere. She rested her hands in her lap and gazed out of the window at the square where the trees were in full green leaf and the birds were criss-crossing the sky with their beaks full of food for nestlings.

Frances leaned back against her pillows and listened to Mehuru reading. She had set him a passage from the *London Magazine* about the prevalence of circulating libraries. Mehuru read fluently and easily, stumbling only once or twice over unknown words.

'How ever have you learned so quickly?' she interrupted him.

He looked up and their eyes met for long wordless moments. They were drenched in desire for each other, there

340

was nothing to say. Elizabeth, daydreaming in the window-seat, was blind to their silent communication.

'I like different languages,' Mehuru explained slowly, the words forming and shaping in his mind while he watched Frances's face, scanning her dark eyes and her soft mouth. He thought she looked quite different from the woman he had seen in the cellar of the warehouse all those months ago. She was alive now in a way she had never been before. Her pulse was more rapid, her skin as clear and light as a girl's. He thought that she had been half-dead when he first met her, and that his desire for her, and her passion for him, had brought her back, back from the very brink of coldness and a death-in-life where all these English women seemed to live.

'You have learned much quicker than the others,' Frances observed.

She was fascinated at the way his eyes could smile at her while his lips spoke of ordinary things. It was a most delicious sensual game, this speaking and listening while all the time his eyes were eating her up, his desire for her showing in every line of his body. His glance over the top of his book was a caress, when his gaze lingered on the neck of her night-gown she could almost feel his touch.

'I speak four African languages, and a little Portuguese,' Mehuru said. 'Until I came to England I thought that all white men spoke Portuguese. English is not very different from Portuguese. Some of the words are the same, as you must know.'

'I don't speak Portuguese,' Frances confessed. 'Just French, and a little Italian.'

'You are very ignorant then,' Mehuru said with provocative impertinence.

Frances reached forwards to slap his hand and only just checked herself in time.

The flirtation in his voice could not be hidden. Elizabeth in the windowseat suddenly turned her attention to the room

341

and looked in surprise at them. Frances blushed scarlet.

'What do you think of the demands for the vote?' Mehuru asked, diplomatically changing the subject.

'I think that it is wrong,' Frances said seriously, repeating her family's received wisdom. 'It cannot be right for people who have no investment in the society to want to run it. The only people who should have power in a country are the people who own the land, they have a genuine interest.'

'In my country no-one owns land at all,' Mehuru said.

'How can that be?'

He smiled at her surprised face. 'Because there is so much land. More than you could imagine. More than all the families could claim. You could ride or walk for days and days and never see anyone. If you want a field for your own, you mark it out, and plough it and water it, and it can be called yours. We are rich in a way you could not imagine, you in this little country where everyone has to own everything for fear that someone else takes it.'

Frances was tired, she closed her eyes. 'Tell me about it,' she murmured. 'Tell me all about it.'

'The capital city is a great walled town, much bigger than Bristol,' Mehuru said. 'It is called Oyo – and the Alafin lives in the palace at the heart of the city. He is like a king, except he takes advice from the people, and acts on their wishes. He is confirmed in his place every year. It is his task to bring their wishes all together, to make an agreement. I was a diviner, I served the Ifa oracle. My patron's task was to read the oracle for the king and I served him.'

'Oh, can you tell fortunes?' Frances asked, not opening her eyes.

Mehuru looked at her pale face with tenderness. 'I can,' he said. 'I tell fortunes for silly girls like you who want to know who will love them.'

Elizabeth could follow most of the words. She put her hand over her mouth to smother a giggle. Mehuru glanced at her and winked.

342

'And who will love me?' Frances demanded recklessly, her eyes still tight shut.

'I shall,' he breathed.

'And how will we be together?'

'I have to see the palm of your hand.'

Frances blindly stretched out her hand to him and he uncurled her fingers and stroked the soft white skin of her wrist and her palm. 'What does it say?' she whispered.

'It says that we will go together to my home and you shall live in my house,' he said. Frances smiled, and snuggled down in the bed like a child listening to a bedtime story.

'And what else?'

'You shall wear gowns of indigo silk and a deep blue head-dress pinned with gold. You will be my wife and you will bear me many beautiful children.'

Frances gave a scandalised chuckle. 'Hush!'

'You will grow well in the sunshine and the hot winds from the plains,' he promised. 'You will like the countryside. The trees on the plains are so broad and strong, their shade is sweet. When the wind is high in the palm trees they rattle and roar, like a rainstorm. When it is calm you can hear a hundred, a thousand birds singing. The rivers are deep and very green, they carry the reflection of the forest so clearly that it is like two forests – one above the water growing to the sky, one below the water growing down. I shall take you to swim in the river where the sand is white and clear and when you lie in the water the little fish will swim around you and nibble at your white skin. There are white and pink lilies which float on the water like little boats, and their roots are sweet and good to eat.

'I shall take you into the forests and you can eat all sorts of sweet fruits that are just growing for free, Frances. No-one owns them, you can eat them all, you can eat all day if you want. You will see the monkeys in the treetops, you will hear the roar of the lions at night, you will see the elephants moving in great herds across the plain, and antelope and deer like a sea of tawny brown hides and sharp pretty horns.' His voice fell silent.

'She is asleep,' Elizabeth said softly in their own language. He nodded.

'You are in love with her.' It was a statement, not a question. He nodded again.

'And she loves you?'

'I think so.'

Elizabeth rose from the windowseat and put her hand on his shoulder. 'You poor foolish man,' she said, and there was a world of pity in her voice. 'Mehuru, it was bad for you already. You have made it a hundred times worse.'

Chapter Twenty-eight

House of Lords,
Westminster.

29th May 1789

Dear Josiah,

*Just a Note written in Haste from the House to tell you that We –
the owners, the Masters, the landlords – have Won, as I promised.
The bill for the abolition of Trading in Slaves is Talked to Death.
There will be a committee which can run forever. There will be much
Hand-wringing and Agitation which will change nothing. You can
Ship all of Africa into Slavery if you wish and No-one in England
can prevent you. This is a great Day for men of property. Wilberforce
is Sick with grief, There are some who say his Health cannot stand
the Disappointment. My Regards to Miss Cole and to my niece,*

Scott.

Mehuru read the letter left open on Josiah's desk, his face
grim. He turned to the door and felt himself shrug, philo-
sophically, slavishly – a man who expects little and receives
less. He knew that Stuart would despair and would then
launch into a frenzy of pamphletting, and writing, and secret
agitation. But Mehuru thought that his own anger had been
sapped. You had to be a free man to feel spontaneous anger,
he thought. You had to have power in your own life to feel
rage. When you were a household drudge you thought no
farther than the next floor to wash, the next grate to clean.
When the messenger from London had told Stuart that

Wilberforce had not even reached a vote, Mehuru had known then that the white men would not let him go. They would not throw away their investments, they would not give away their profits. Why should they?

Mehuru heaved the heavy coal scuttle and dumped it on the marble grate. If he wanted his freedom, he thought, he would have to run.

The Merchant Venturers were at their June supper. The cloth had been taken away and the port and rum were being passed around. Josiah was seated in the middle of a long dinner table, taking a little rum and water and smoking a pipe. His fresh aromatic tobacco leaf was passed around for others to sniff.

'Your tobacco, Cole?' someone asked him, and he nodded.

'Can you send me round a hogshead?' the man asked and then dropped his voice as the man at the head of the table tapped the heel of his knife on the wood.

'Shall we get to business?' asked Sir Henry Lord, at the head of the table. 'Before the evening begins in earnest?'

There was a roar of appreciation. Sir Henry nodded at the clerk, who quickly ran through a list of decisions which the Company had to make. All of them went through on the nod. The Bristol merchants moved with one accord, knowing their own interests, and working as a team. When they came to the issue of the Hot Well lease, Stephen Waring spoke up for Josiah's bid.

'May I say, Sir Henry, that I support this bid for the lease by my friend Josiah Cole – a new member of the Company and a merchant of enterprise whose business is well known to us all. He has asked for an assurance that the present rent for the Hot Well lease of nine hundred pounds per annum should remain the same for ten years to enable him to plan his investment.'

Sir Henry peered down the table to where Josiah was

sitting. 'Are you planning new buildings at the site?' he asked.

'I plan a winter garden,' Josiah said. 'A bath house designed on romantic lines with a view over the river and plants. Like a conservatory, Sir Henry.'

'You had best take your profits first,' Sir Henry observed.

'I want to see the Hot Well as the best spa in Britain,' Josiah declared.

Sir Henry nodded like a man prepared to keep his opinion to himself, and said nothing.

'M'friend Cole is prepared to pay two thousand pounds entry to the lease, payable at once, and the rent for the first year at once,' Stephen Waring reminded him.

Mr James, the previous tenant who had resigned from the lease when the Company made their improvements, raised his glass to Josiah in a gesture which could have been seen as a tribute to superior financial acumen. Josiah smiled and bowed his head at him.

'Very well,' Sir Henry said. He looked towards the clerk. 'You have the papers, Browning?'

The clerk produced a lease, and took it to Sir Henry. 'Sign on, then,' Sir Henry said. He scrawled his signature at the foot of the papers and waved them away. The clerk took them down to Josiah with a pen and a standish of ink. Josiah, beaming with triumph, signed his name in his round honest script at the foot of the document and knew that his career as an entrepreneur had truly begun.

'I wish you the best of luck with it, the very best of luck!' Mr James drawled from the other side of the table.

Josiah tried not to look superior.

'You will make a handsome profit from it, I don't doubt,' Mr James went on. 'I should have stayed in longer, I know. But I had to free my capital for other schemes. It should be a little gold mine for you.'

'I hope so,' Josiah said modestly.

'Is it your only investment?'

'My first, not my only, my first on land.'

'I am surprised you are not buying leases and building,' Mr James said. 'I thought everyone was buying building land.'

'I have connections which make the Hot Well particularly attractive,' Josiah said discreetly. 'And I have no knowledge of the building trade.'

'Oh, that does not seem to stop anyone. Half of the men I know are building. It is like a plague and we have all caught it!'

Josiah nodded. 'Timing is everything. Clifton and the Downs is a long-term prospect. The Hot Well is more immediate. It suits my plans.'

'Well, the best of luck,' Mr James said. 'It is a high rent, that, a crippling rent, you know. How will you ever meet it?'

'I shall increase charges, of course,' Josiah said. 'No more family rates, no discounts for local people, no free water given away. And I hope to attract more trade from London. The fashionable crowd, you know. My wife's friends and family.'

The Company settled down into their places again and the chairman went on with other business. They set a new levy on the dock, they set a new rent for the use of the great crane. There was some joke which Josiah did not quite understand about the aldermen of the city, but he smiled and laughed with the others. He had an exhilarating sense of breaking unknown ground. He was mixing at last with the men who controlled everything in Bristol. The jokes, the cliquish references were not yet clear to him, but he felt that he was on the threshold of belonging. In a year, in two, he would be seated farther up the table, he would be party to the private discussions which were now ratified. Josiah had penetrated the Company only to find a further cabal, hidden behind it. Next year, the year after, he would understand all the references, he would be one of the decision makers. For this year he was happy to be one of the new boys who could roar out

'Aye' to decisions he did not fully understand, who could trust his leaders to make the right judgements. Josiah felt he was among friends who would safeguard his interests.

At the other side of town in a dingy coffee house, Mehuru was also attending a meeting. Poorly financed but infinitely more ambitious, he was at a formal meeting of the Bristol Society for Constitutional Information, one of a network of societies committed to reforming the corrupt political structure and bringing in the right to vote for all men. It was Stuart's response to the disappointment of the Wilberforce bill. He was determined to widen their campaign, to bring in the freedom for black men as part of the freedom for white workers. Seated at the head of the table with the door tightly shut and guarded against eavesdroppers, Stuart was chairing a discussion of a motion brought by one of the more radical members: 'This Society should ally itself with our brothers engaged in the struggle for their rights in France, in America, and in the colonies.'

Mehuru was listening carefully, trying to follow the passionate interruptions to the debate. The Society had divided into two broad camps: those that feared that an association with the foreign reformers would invoke a patriotic backlash against them, and those who saw the reform movement as naturally international.

'These are great days,' Dr Hadley summed up. 'These are times for great change. The people taking power in France, the people taking power in America, slaves rising against their masters in every colony – who can doubt that the people will take power in England too? Is the English tyranny of king and church and landlords immune? Can anyone doubt that a hundred years from the last bloodless English revolution we are heading towards another?

'All over the country men are coming together to demand that they be truly represented in Parliament, that their leaders be men of their choice and not some pretty puppets set at their head. In the new industrial towns, even in the quiet market villages, all men of sense are demanding a change and a right to be heard. And in the ports of Britain and in her colonies the black citizens are asking for their rights too. They demand a living wage, they demand their freedom. And they demand the right to return to their homeland. This is a glorious crusade! I am proud to put this matter to the vote. All those in favour say "Aye".'

'Aye,' said Mehuru, along with the other two dozen men in the crowded room. He felt that Stuart was right, that he was at the forefront of a powerful international movement which could not fail. The logic of it was too strong, and its moral power was irresistible. 'Aye,' said Mehuru, from the heart.

Stuart carefully noted the vote in the Society's new ledger and closed the meeting. The men called for drinks, coffee or small ale. Mehuru noticed that all of them were following the self-imposed ban: refusing sugar in their coffee, and rejecting rum. They were all signatories of the petitions to support the banning of the slave trade, they were all refusing to support the plantation trade until slavery was abolished.

'Have you had a chance to read those pamphlets I gave you?' Stuart asked. He took a drink from his pint pot. 'What d'you think now of the Sierra Leone scheme?'

'I think it is a risk,' Mehuru answered. 'The men who planned it seem to have no idea what it is like on that coast. Since the coming of the slavers all order has been destroyed. You have to realise that you are not planting a settlement in a desert, in an empty space; there are people living there now, and they are not people at peace in an ordered nation. The whole coast of Africa and for miles into the interior is in a state of perpetual uproar and warfare. Each bandit is paid and licensed by white men to make war on each other and capture slaves. Every village is like a fort, except for those which are already destroyed and the survivors hiding in the forests and scavenging for food. It is a wild lawless country now, you

350

cannot draw a line on a map and say that inside this line it will be different.'

'They have negotiated treaties . . .'

Mehuru gave a short bitter laugh. 'I was envoy for the kingdom of Yoruba. The mightiest kingdom in Africa. I spoke three of the neighbouring languages and enough Portuguese to make myself understood. On a mission for my king, and with his protection, I was captured, my servant was stolen from me, and I was chucked into a canoe like a sack. I was left naked, I was force fed, I was manacled in the bottom of a ship and left to roll in my own vomit and excrement. If slavers can do that to me, why should they respect a group of poor farmers who have nothing but a piece of paper signed in London, two months' voyage away?'

Stuart Hadley nodded. 'I am sorry to hear you talk like this,' he said. 'I am friend to one of the directors and we urgently need African leaders to live there. Someone like you who could speak many languages would have been ideal. And it worries me if you think it is so risky.'

'Only the ending of the trade in slaves could make it safe,' Mehuru declared.

'And that will come soon,' Stuart promised. 'Next spring in Parliament Wilberforce will speak for it again. Then they *must* agree. And then Sierra Leone would have a future. We could make it a crown colony, give it the protection of the Navy . . .' Stuart broke off as he saw Mehuru's sarcastic smile.

'Oh! I had no idea! We are talking of a new colony for Britain! I thought we were freeing black men to return to their own lands, but we are planning new plantations!'

'I did not mean a colony like a plantation,' Stuart protested. 'And you know that would never be my intention.'

'It is the danger though,' Mehuru said thoughtfully. 'If the European states stop slaving will they also stop seeing Africa as their market? Will they leave us to get our country back into order, to re-establish our own laws?'

351

'Of course there is a strong feeling that Africa should be converted to Christianity and to civilisation.'

There was a little silence. 'They plan to convert Africa to Christianity and civilisation?' Mehuru asked.

Stuart Hadley nodded.

'Then Africa is lost,' Mehuru said simply.

Stephen Waring stood in the doorway of the Custom House, breathing the warm night air. Other members of the Merchant Venturers' Company went past him into the dark gardens, some of them weaving unsteadily from the wines at dinner and the heavy drinking which had followed.

Sir Henry came up behind him and took his arm. 'Walking home?' he enquired.

'Why not?' Stephen replied easily. He tossed his cigar away and whistled for a linkboy to light their way. As they drew away from the others he said, 'A pleasant evening, I thought.'

'Very.'

'I am sorry for that little Josiah Cole,' Sir Henry said suddenly.

'Oh, why so?' Stephen asked. 'He wants his Hot Well and he has bought it.'

'He's paid a high price for it,' Sir Henry said. 'And we both know he will regret it.'

'It's his choice,' Stephen said comfortably. They strolled slowly over the lowered drawbridge. The tide was on the ebb and the river bank was starting to stink. The dark mud and water reflected the boy's moving light.

'Still, he might get his money back,' Sir Henry predicted cheerfully. 'If he can hang on.'

'More importantly, the Venturers have got *their* money back,' Stephen said. 'Anything he pays in rent hereafter represents a profit to us.'

'Where d'you want it invested?' Sir Henry asked. 'Clifton? The Downs?'

'I think we should spend money on the port,' Stephen said.

'We lose trade to Liverpool every day. We must straighten the river and make some deep-water anchorage. It is madness trying to run a commercial port out of a tidal harbour.'

'Oh aye,' Sir Henry agreed lazily. 'But you won't see a profit inside fifty years.'

'Still, it should be done.'

'I'd have thought you would have wanted some investment in Clifton,' Sir Henry teased. 'I heard that you had plans for terraces and assembly rooms and all sorts of grand projects.'

'Did you?'

'But I said that Clifton would never be anything more than a pretty little out-of-the-way place.'

'D'you think so?' Stephen asked interestedly.

'It won't grow until it can be supplied with water,' Sir Henry assured him. 'Limestone. You can't have a town on limestone. It's dry, bone dry. To reach the water you'd have to drill – oh – three hundred feet.'

Stephen nodded. The bobbing light of the linkboy's torch lit his face and then hid it again. 'Would it be that deep?' he asked pensively.

'But *if* you hit water then prices in Clifton would go through the roof,' Sir Henry pointed out.

'Lucky then that we all own land there,' Stephen said simply. 'And that the Company owns the whole manor, Clifton, and Durham Down too.'

'Satisfactory,' Sir Henry said. He paused at his doorway on College Street. 'I like talking to you, Waring. You are always so uninformative.'

Stephen laughed shortly. 'I thought we had understood each other very well,' he said.

By July Frances was well enough to get out of bed but was still easily tired and short of breath. Dr Hadley called once every week and one day detained Josiah for a quiet word as he walked to his waiting phaeton. 'The air does not suit her,' Stuart said. 'It is low-lying here and the river mists are very unhealthy. You can smell the diseases like a fog. Any day now I expect to hear that we have cholera in the old town. Already there is typhoid fever not half a mile from this house. And all the drains from the old town flow into the river which surrounds you. She has a weak heart, she could not survive a major illness.'

Mehuru was holding Stuart's horse, straining to hear.

'I cannot move house,' Josiah exclaimed. 'We have only just bought this one!'

'That is a pity,' Stuart said carefully. 'Could Mrs Cole perhaps go away to the country for a visit once a year, especially now in midsummer?'

'She could go to the Hot Well spa every day,' Josiah offered. 'I have just bought the Hot Well spa, you know, Doctor. She could go there daily.'

'No, that is not what I mean. She needs a more airy situation in summer, and a warmer climate in winter like France, or Italy. She needs warm dry air, especially in winter time.'

Josiah shook his head. 'We have never travelled abroad, I would not know how to manage it.'

Mehuru's face was like stone, his impatience burning inside him.

'It could be managed,' Stuart said earnestly. 'And I do fear for her if she spends the next winter in Bristol. She is delicate, I am afraid, and another serious chill and inflammation like this one could even be fatal.'

Josiah looked shocked. 'Frances might die?'

'She could live for years,' Stuart said quickly. 'But these delicate lungs are very difficult to predict. If it is possible for her to go somewhere warm every winter then she would grow stronger.'

Josiah was badly shaken. 'I will consider it,' he assured Stuart. 'It is just that we have never thought of such a thing. My sister and I have never even taken more than a day's holiday. We have never been away from Bristol. I would not know how to set about it.'

Mehuru fidgeted at the horse's head, unable to stand still for anger.

'Arrangements are easily made,' Stuart said. 'No doubt Mrs Cole would know people who travel abroad. She has many friends and family, does she not?'

'But she would be away from Bristol for such a long time,' Josiah protested. 'I bought this house for her enjoyment and only she knows how it should be run. I thought this house would suit her very well.'

'I am sure it does,' Stuart soothed him. 'But in very hot weather such as these last few weeks it is not salubrious for anyone. And it may be that next winter she will need a little time in the sun. That is all.'

'I will consider it,' Josiah assured him. 'I would spare no expense to keep Frances in the best of health. Whatever a trip abroad would cost I would be prepared to pay. Anything that I can do, shall be done.'

He shook Stuart's hand and turned back into the house.

'Fool,' Mehuru spat through his teeth, released at last. 'What a fool!'

'I pity him,' Stuart said shortly. 'He chose a woman to bring him money and connections and he finds himself obliged to provide things for her which he does not even understand.'

'He runs a shipping company.' Mehuru's voice was an angry mutter where he wanted to roar. 'He has three damned ships going anywhere in the world. He could put her on a ship, couldn't he? He could send her to Africa, couldn't he? Or to the Sugar Islands? Good God, if she were my wife and you told me she needed sunshine I would carry her on my back if there was no other way.'

Stuart smiled wearily at Mehuru's rage. 'Do you love her so much?'

Mehuru checked, looked at Stuart's face for any signs of mockery and saw none. 'Yes,' he said shortly.

Stuart shook his head and climbed up into the high perch

seat of the phaeton. 'Then I am sorry for you,' he said conversationally. 'And for her too.'

Mehuru would not release the horse, but held the rein, forcing Stuart to wait. His expression was sharp, as if with a pain held inside. 'Because she is ill? Is it worse than you told Mr Cole? Do you pity me because she will die?'

Stuart kept his true opinion of Frances's health to himself. 'I pity you because there is nowhere for you,' he answered. 'She cannot leave him, you cannot freely love her. If I were you, my friend, I would rather go to Sierra Leone with all the risks that entails, than fall in love with a married woman, the niece of a peer of the realm, and my owner.'

Mehuru's face lightened, his smile started at his eyes and then his whole face lit up into an irresistible beam. 'When you express it like that,' he said ruefully, 'it does not sound like a very good idea. But Stuart, when I touch her hand, it is more than the whole world to me.'

The two men were silent for a moment.

'Have you any news from France?' Mehuru asked. 'I read in Josiah's newspaper that the Bastille had fallen. How far do you think they will go?'

Stuart was instantly animated. 'Who knows? It is great news for all lovers of liberty. They will be sick with fear in Westminster. People are taking their power all around the world. The future must belong to us.'

'They will free the slaves?'

'Certainly. I imagine they will make their colonies departments of France and we will see black Frenchmen representing white constituencies.'

Mehuru smiled. 'It is like a miracle.'

'And so fast!' Stuart said. 'They will bring the king to realise that he must consult the people. And our king,' he lowered his voice, 'God help him, the poor madman, will become a people's king also. The Trade will end, slavery will be abolished, working men will get the vote. These are great times.'

'There must be a place for me,' Mehuru said determinedly.

'In these times of change. I must have a voice.' He thought for a moment. 'And I must have Frances,' he continued. 'If prisons can be opened then marriages can be ended. If we are to be free we must be free to love as well.'

'She surely could not leave him for you?' Stuart asked. 'It would be her ruin.'

'In an age of miracles?' Mehuru reminded him. 'Why should it not be possible?'

Stuart shrugged. He could not bring himself to tell Mehuru that he thought Frances would not live long enough to see the freeing of English slaves. He could not tell Mehuru that to free a lady such as Frances from her loveless marriage would be a harder task than to free Mehuru from slavery.

'Will you let my horse go now?' Stuart asked. 'If it is all the same to you, I have other patients to visit.'

'I was thinking of my home and how good the sun is there,' Mehuru said absently. 'If I could take Frances there, how well she would be!'

'Look, here's someone calling on you,' Stuart said.

A large travelling carriage with a crest emblazoned on the door was drawing up behind the phaeton. Stuart glanced from it to Mehuru's face and was surprised to see a look of coldness and hatred such as he had never seen before. All at once Mehuru's charm and warmth had frozen into a grimace of absolute distaste.

'Who is it?'

'A man called Sir Charles Fairley,' Mehuru said. His voice was sharp with contempt. 'When he visited before he raped a woman, a Yoruban slave, and when she ate earth he had her bolted into a bridle. She is dead now. He was poxed and he made a baby on her.'

Stuart covertly glanced across at the carriage. The footman was putting down the steps and a black slave got out first to assist Sir Charles.

'A slave owner,' Stuart observed quietly.

'A Sugar Island nabob,' Mehuru said. 'He should be hanged.'

Stuart could not disagree. 'And soon he will come home to retire and buy a borough and stand for Parliament,' he predicted. 'Truly, we have to cleanse England. But next spring ... Mehuru! Next spring!'

Mehuru's face was dark. 'You are hopeful,' he said curtly. 'But I saw how sure you were last time, and your man was talked into silence.'

'This time it will happen. We must keep up the campaign to support it. We are wiser now, we know our enemies. And then your fine friend will find his business is very much changed.'

Mehuru watched Sir Charles swagger past them up the steps to the house and nod to his slave to hammer on the door.

'I wish his business could be ended completely,' Mehuru said. 'And his slaves freed.'

'I too. But we have to move in small stages. First we ban the trade in slaves and that will force them to treat their slaves better. Then slavery is abolished altogether, it will just wither away, Mehuru. Slowly they will pay wages and your brothers will earn their freedom. We will see it. In our lifetime we will see it.'

Mehuru gave him a wry smile. 'You are confident.'

'I am certain! Now let me go, Mehuru, I have work to do.'

Mehuru nodded and stood back from the phaeton. Stuart clicked to his horse and drove off as the black slave preceded his master up the steps to the front door and hammered on the knocker.

Mary answered and Mehuru saw her look of shock when she recognised Sir Charles, before she drew back to allow him and his slave into the house. Mehuru followed them in.

Frances was seated in the morning room embroidering Josiah's waistcoat but when Sir Charles came in she put it aside and held out both her hands. 'Sir Charles! How delightful!' she said. 'And you are so early! The roads must have been very good.'

He kissed both her hands and thought privately that she looked very pale and drawn. 'The roads were filthy with dust,' he told her. 'But at least they were passable. I do not know how I shall tolerate them in wintertime!'

Frances laughed and nodded to Mary. 'Fetch the tea tray, Mary, and tell Miss Cole that Sir Charles is here. Will you have tea, Sir Charles? Or in this hot weather would you like some lemonade? Or shall you have some punch? I remember your preferences!'

'I will take some punch,' he decided.

Frances sat down and gestured to Sir Charles to take a chair but he stood before the window gazing out over the square.

'And how do you like your new home, ma'am?' he asked. 'You are very grand here. Quite a change!'

Frances kept her smile fixed on her face. 'It is a little small after Whiteleaze,' she remarked, as if she had never served dinner and then withdrawn to the fireplace in the same poky parlour over the warehouse. 'But we are very comfortable here.'

'And in the height of fashion,' Sir Charles commented, looking at the corner of the room where two red porcelain dragons glared at each other in a fixed snarl.

'Do you stay in Bristol for long?' Frances asked.

'No, I shall drive on to Lord Bartlet when I have signed my paper with you,' Sir Charles said. 'Miss Honoria is already there. Between you and me, Mrs Cole, I think there may be a match of it between her and Lord Bartlet's son.'

'Not Sir Frederick!' Frances exclaimed, thinking swiftly that Lord Bartlet must be hard-pressed indeed if he had let his son and heir be caught by such a one as Miss Honoria, whatever her fortune.

'No, his second son, Nicholas.'

'Ah, Nicholas,' Frances said. Good for neither church nor army, Nicholas would do very nicely with a Sugar Island heiress. 'He is such a pleasant young man.'

'A good match,' Sir Charles said with satisfaction. 'Nothing is settled, mind, but Lord Bartlet and I have tipped each other the wink.'

Frances smiled politely but inwardly shuddered at the thought of the impoverished old gamester winking his red-veined eye at Sir Charles. Compared with that crude bartering, her own marriage to Josiah seemed a love-match.

'I will not delay you then,' Frances said. 'I have the lease to hand.'

She went to her writing table, took out the lease and spread it before Sir Charles on the parlour table. He seated himself and read through the clauses. He did not notice that he had not bought the mineral rights.

'You sign here,' she said politely.

Sir Charles signed.

'And here are the accounts for your capital laid with us,' she said. 'There is no interest to show yet, for it is paid annually. But you can see what investments I have made on your behalf, and Lord Scott has suggested a colliery in Kent for an investment of one thousand pounds.'

'Excellent, excellent,' Sir Charles beamed. 'His lordship is most kind, and I am very glad to have you take care of my capital. I should not have found my new house without your good offices, Mrs Cole! I am indebted to you!'

Frances smiled. The parlour door opened and Sarah came in followed by Mary with the tea tray and Mehuru carrying the punch bowl on a silver tray which he set down before Sir Charles.

Frances was instantly aware of Mehuru's anger. It was present in the precise way that he placed rum, water, sugar and lemons within Sir Charles's reach. It was present in the way he looked at her with his eyes like a black frost and said, 'Will that be all, Mrs Cole?'

'I say, he speaks well!' Sir Charles exclaimed, swinging around in his chair and inspecting Mehuru as if he were some exotic pet.

'We have made much progress since you were last here,' Sarah said pleasantly. 'My sister has been tireless. They can all speak and understand English now, and the two younger men, and this one can even read.'

'Well, that is remarkable,' Sir Charles said, staring frankly at Mehuru. Mehuru stared back, his face blank and insolent. 'Make him read for me.'

Frances drew a breath. 'He has other duties now. He will read for you another time.'

'A handsome buck,' Sir Charles commented.

'You can go, Cicero,' Frances said quickly.

His bow was an insult.

'I tell you what I shall send you,' Sir Charles exclaimed. 'Little slave collars, very pretty.'

Mehuru checked in the doorway and looked back to meet Frances's anguished glance.

'They're the very thing,' Sir Charles went on. 'Like a dog collar, you know, but finely made. A little chain and on the front a little metal tag, I like silver myself, with the slave's name engraved. They all wear them in London. They look very smart. You shall jot down their names, all of them, and I will send you a set.'

'You are very kind,' Frances said. She could feel her breath becoming shorter in her anxiety that Mehuru would make a scene.

Mehuru wheeled around in the doorway and suddenly strode into the room. Frances started up and her workbox spilled to the floor with a clatter, shedding silks and ribbons and bobbins of cotton. 'Oh, how careless!' she cried. 'How careless of me! How silly I am! Cicero, fetch Martha, or one of the girls. Go at once, please! Go!'

For a moment he hesitated as if he would defy her.

'At once!' Frances insisted, her voice sharp with fear. 'Go and fetch one of the girls at once, please.'

He turned unwillingly and obeyed her, stalking from the room, prickly with anger.

'I do apologise,' Frances said. She could hardly breathe at all. 'So silly of me.'

Miss Cole regarded her with suppressed irritation. 'Shall I pour the tea, Sister?'

'Oh, please do! And Sir Charles, do make your punch and tell us all about London. And the Scott Ball in the winter! Did Miss Honoria enjoy herself?'

The girl Ruth came in to clear up Frances's workbox. As she entered the room and saw Sir Charles she recoiled and her face went a grey sick colour. Frances knew that she was taking tea with a rapist and that she was commanding the people who had witnessed his crime to serve him.

'Hurry up, Ruth,' she ordered. 'Is the punch to your liking, Sir Charles?'

It took all her carefully learned social skills to chatter through Ruth's slow resentful tidying. It took all her charm to divert Sir Charles, and to distract Sarah from Mary's sullenly reluctant service at tea. She heard her voice, a little breathless, but still light and frivolous, and she despised herself for the facade she presented. She longed to tell Sir Charles that she knew him for what he was, that she loathed him, and that she would never forgive him for the abuse of a woman who had been in her charge. But her social self, which always had the upper hand, stirred the tea, passed cakes, and laughed at his jokes, just as she had been trained to do. Just like a little pet dog, she thought miserably, which sits to order, and begs when told, and barks a little, and perhaps has forgotten altogether that it was ever a real dog.

The visit was mercifully short. Sir Charles wanted to be on his way to Lord Bartlet's country seat at Kings Weston.

'My brother will be sorry to have missed you,' Sarah observed.

'I shall have the pleasure of his company another time,' Sir Charles said gallantly. 'This was a business visit, merely.'

Sarah nodded, a little surprised. 'I am glad that Frances can transact your business. I had thought you would want to go over the figures with my brother.'

Sir Charles smiled. 'Mrs Cole is an excellent agent for my little fund. I need no other!'

'As long as you are satisfied,' Sarah said doubtfully.

'I am indeed. My only regret is that I cannot stay to dine, but I hope to be at Lord Bartlet's in time for supper.'

Frances rang the bell and Sir Charles's own slave came with his cloak, hat and cane.

'Will you have a hot brick for your feet in the carriage, Sir Charles?' Sarah asked. 'Despite the season it can get cool at night.'

'I hope my boy has placed one there already,' Sir Charles said. 'Done hot brickee? Sammy?'

The man glanced at him with one weary look. 'Yassuh,' he said.

Frances closed her eyes for a moment to shut out the man's bowed head and empty eyes.

'Here, Sammy has a collar,' Sir Charles said. 'Sammy! Show chain! Show chain!'

The man's hand went to his neck to open the collar of his jacket. Tight around his throat was a silver chain and a plaque. In elegant flowing script it was engraved with the name 'Sammy'. 'Charming, ain't it?' Sir Charles demanded. 'You jot down the names of your slaves and I will send you a set.'

Frances held on to her smile as if it were a mask in a carnival ball. She took a page of paper from her writing desk and wrote down carefully the eleven names, from Cicero to little five-year-old John.

'Charming,' Sir Charles said. 'Eleven now, eh? You have eleven?'

'From an original consignment of twenty,' Sarah said. 'We have had only nine deaths. Seven in transit but only two here. We are pleased.'

Frances's hand trembled and the pen made a blot on the page. She wanted to tell him that the woman he had raped

363

had died. She wanted to accuse him. Instead, she handed him the page of names and looked at his slave, Sammy. The man would not meet her gaze. She did not know that at home in Jamaica he would be beaten for looking at a white woman. It was considered to be impertinent. Under her stare he ducked his head and gazed at his boots. On the delicate skin at the back of his neck and curving up behind his ear Frances could see the puckering of a deep scar from an old misplaced lash.

'I'll bid you goodbye,' Sir Charles said, throwing his cloak around him and bowing over Sarah's hand and then lingering his kiss on Frances's hand with moist lips.

'Safe journey,' Frances said quietly.

They escorted him to the front door and stood on the doorstep in the late afternoon sunshine, waving him farewell as the carriage pulled away.

'Isn't he a *charming* man,' Sarah sighed with pleasure as the carriage rolled out of the square and disappeared.

'Delightful,' Frances replied. Her lips were very stiff on the lie. 'Quite delightful.'

Chapter Twenty-nine

Next morning Sarah woke early and was dressed and out of the house even before Josiah. She called Mehuru to the hall and told him to put on his green livery coat, and attend her for a walk. Mehuru bowed, hiding the curiosity in his face, and followed her at a polite distance as she walked from the square towards the river.

He called the ferry for her and held her parasol as she stepped from the greasy steps into the little boat. The dock was stinking in the heat of midsummer but Sarah did not seem to notice it. Mehuru was first out of the boat on the other side and handed Sarah up the steps to the Redclift quay.

The warehouse door was shut; Josiah's clerk had not yet arrived. Sarah stood with calm patience on the doorstep of her old home. Mehuru waited beside her. She did not speak to him, she never spoke to any of the slaves except to give them orders.

Just as the bells of St Mary Redclift struck eight o'clock Mehuru saw the clerk hurrying down the quayside. At once he sensed Sarah's attention sharpen.

'Good morning,' she said. 'I am Miss Cole. I wish to see the ships' logs and the company accounts. Please let me into the office.'

The man hesitated, glancing at Mehuru. Mehuru's face was impassive.

'I don't know . . .' the clerk began.

'Thank you,' Sarah said magisterially. She took the key from his hand, let herself into the warehouse and walked upstairs to Josiah's office. As she had hoped, the books were in their usual place, on his desk. She nodded over her shoulder at Mehuru. 'You can wait outside,' she told him.

Mehuru and the clerk retreated over the threshold. Sarah shut the door on them and then they heard the key turn firmly in the lock. The clerk looked at Mehuru as if for advice. Mehuru shrugged and waited, as Sarah had ordered him to do.

Inside the room Sarah seated herself at Josiah's desk and drew the company books towards her. She did not like the clerk's handwriting but his work was adequate. She turned to the other page, the debits, and frowned. There was a massive £5400 outstanding to Hibbard and Sons, a small banking house, including £2000 for the lease of the Hot Well and £1000 for the Queens Square house. Josiah had given them a note of hand of £500 to pay for the furniture and fittings. Sarah thought of the red Chinese dragons and put her hand to her mouth. Josiah had borrowed the first year's rent for the Hot Well of £900 as well. He had borrowed £1000 to equip *Rose* and £500 to buy cargo. Sarah's face trembled. There had never been such amounts in the debit column of Cole and Sons in all their years of trading. She did not curse Josiah, she did not feel anger. She felt icy cold and nauseous with fear. It would take a miracle voyage to clear such a debt, and profits were falling, not increasing.

She knew the debt was a long-term loan, negotiated and managed by Josiah. The first payment was not even due until November, when the *Rose* was due, with *Daisy* close behind her; but the books had always been Sarah's work and she resented any entry into the debit column. To see them in a state of permanent debt made her as uncomfortable as other women would be with a dress done up wrongly at the back. And this was no small debt. Greater merchants than Cole and Sons had been ruined for less. The *Rose* alone would not clear it. It would take four, perhaps five, voyages to clear it over at least two years.

They would have to borrow to repair and refurbish *Rose* as

soon as she arrived, and there was no money to hand. They would not be able to take a large share in her next voyage. 'We will be sailing the ship for the benefit of the partners,' Sarah muttered miserably to herself.

Sarah drew *Rose*'s account book towards her and ran her eye down the cargo list. The usual goods were listed for sale to the African slave traders – brass cooking pots and kettles, knives, necklaces of paste polished to sparkle like diamonds, special poor-quality cotton known as negro linen, negro looking glasses, and negro guns. Then Sarah looked at the account again. For a moment she thought Josiah had made a mistake and entered the goods twice for the total cash value was almost double. She checked the amounts of goods against the previous pages. The amounts were almost double too. Josiah had sent the ship out equipped to double the African trade.

Sarah frowned slightly and pulled towards her the account book of the *Lily*, which was their last ship out. No, *Lily* had sailed as usual. It was just *Rose* which Josiah had laden with goods and sent out to trade. Sarah scanned through the other totals for the voyage. The accounts had been made up in Josiah's neat hand, they were easy to read. She had wondered at the time why he had insisted on doing them himself; usually he was very ready to hand over a fistful of cargo manifests to her and let her copy out the totals into the ledger. But this time Josiah had done them, and this time they were different.

She could see nothing untoward elsewhere in the ledger until she came to the cost of insurance. It was unusually low. Sarah's finger traced the row across the page to Josiah's clearly written entry.

4th September 1788

For insurance, the ship Rose and her cargo outbound to Africa, and homebound from West Indies to England. . .

Sarah sat very still, her mind reeling. Josiah had not insured the ship or the cargo for the perilous middle passage, the transport of slaves on the long stormy, sickly, mutinous journey from Africa across the vast dangerous sweep of the Atlantic Ocean to the shelter of the West Indies. He had not insured the precious cargo of slaves on their single dangerous voyage.

She nodded, piecing it all together: Josiah's difficulty in getting insurance; his complaints about the ruling on the ship *Zong* which had made all insurers suspect that slavers simply tipped slaves over the side to claim on their policy; his acceptance of too few partners. Josiah had taken on his new wife and a massive gamble together. He had been so determined to rise in the world, he had been so determined to make a fortune for his family, that he had doubled the number of slaves he was carrying, and he had gone out without insurance. He had not even shared his potential loss among a full complement of partners. He wanted to keep the risk, and the profits, all to himself.

Sarah pinched her lips together, her face looked gaunt and old. She hated risk, she hated expenditure. The lesson of her childhood had been the amassing of a small fortune by steady laborious work. She had watched her father make one little voyage after another, ferrying goods up and down the Severn. It was Josiah's childhood that had been fired by the prospect of great wealth. It had been Josiah's formative moment when their Da brought the French brig the *Marguerite* into port. Ever since then Josiah had loved the grand risk, the great gamble. Sarah, ten years older, scarred by early poverty and always more conservative, preferred the security of steady earnings.

A noise from downstairs distracted her. She took her hand from her mouth. She had been biting her fingernails while reading the account books, and her index finger was nibbled bloody and raw.

'What the devil is going on?' came Josiah's voice on the stairs.

'It's Miss Cole,' the clerk replied. 'And she has locked herself into your office.'

Sarah crossed to the door, turned the key, and opened up. 'Come in, Josiah,' she said.

Josiah was prepared to bluster but one look at her face silenced him. She closed the door on the waiting clerk and took her seat at Josiah's desk once more, leaving him standing, looking like the little brother that she used to smack and scold for naughtiness.

Josiah looked from her face to the account book emblazoned with the name *Rose*.

'Oh,' he said.

'Yes,' Sarah said bleakly. 'You have no insurance for the middle passage.'

'I could not get it, Sarah. Before God, I tried. It was impossible.'

'You have insured the others?'

'Sarah, once I was inside the Merchant Venturers it was easy. We all insure each other, we all take a little of the risk. But *Rose* sailed before I was invited to join. I went all around Bristol. No-one would take me for the middle passage. She was covered from here to Africa, and she is covered for the voyage home.'

Sarah took a little shuddering breath. 'But the risk . . .'

He shrugged. 'What could I do? She had to sail. She was costing me money sitting on the quayside. I thought when she was at sea I might be able to get insurance for her then. But I could not.'

'Have you heard from her captain?' Sarah asked. The longing in her voice was like a woman asking for her lover. 'Is *Rose* safe?'

'I have heard nothing since he was off the coast of Africa, loading. But I would expect to hear nothing until he is in Jamaica. He would only send to me if he happened to meet a Bristol ship homeward bound. Compose yourself, Sarah. It may all be very well with him and we hear nothing until he docks.'

She nodded. 'I know,' she said. 'I know.'

'I am sorry,' Josiah apologised awkwardly. 'The insurers left me no choice.'

'And the trade goods? You are carrying so much?'

Josiah glanced at the door, as if a spy might be hidden outside. 'You will not like this, Sarah, but I had to earn capital quickly.'

She understood him at once. 'Oh God! You are smuggling.'

'One load,' he said. 'One load only. I have ordered them to be packed as tight as they can go and Captain Smedley is under orders to sell them to the Spanish plantations. He will take no notes of credit, he will take only gold or sugar at the best prices. No-one will know and I will make a small fortune.'

'You have spent a small fortune,' she answered bitterly. 'And that is why we are in this strait.'

'This one voyage will pull us clear,' he said. 'When *Rose* comes home in November I shall pay off my debts and we will have cash to spare. It is a gamble, Sarah; but they are familiar odds. Why should we lose a ship now? We have done the voyage a hundred times and never lost a ship yet.' He tapped his hand against the wooden door frame for luck. Josiah was talking confidently but he never forgot to touch wood.

'How much should we make?' Sarah asked. She was reluctantly tempted by the thought of a shipload of gold.

'Say he carries six hundred slaves . . .'

'Six hundred!' Sarah exclaimed. 'But *Rose* has room only for three hundred!'

Josiah gleamed at her. 'I told him to pack tight. He will. Say he carries six hundred and lands four hundred and fifty.'

'A hundred and fifty die during the voyage?'

'Packed so tight they are bound to get sick,' Josiah reasoned. 'And with so many he will have to ration water and food. Maybe it will not be so bad. Anyway, say he lands four hundred and fifty and sells them for fifty pounds each . . .'

370

'Not more?' Sarah demanded.

'Many of them will be only little children ... that is £22500.'

She opened the account book. 'Less £8732 paid in trade goods.'

Josiah beamed. 'A profit of nearly £14000.'

'A fortune,' she said. 'It will clear your debt on the house, and on the Hot Well. It will pull us clear.'

Josiah nodded. 'I owe a thousand on the house, and I borrowed my deposit of two thousand on the Hot Well. I have debts for the furniture and carpets for Queens Square, and I have borrowed to start the season at the Hot Well. I borrowed more than a thousand to equip *Rose*. Altogether I owe more than £5000, call it £6000 with interest. I plan to pay it off, all at once, in November when *Rose* arrives. It is only four months.'

Sarah nodded. 'It all rests on the *Rose* then. If she comes in safe, we will have made a fortune worthy of a nabob. But if she fails . . .'

'It is as near a certainty as you can get in the Trade,' Josiah said. 'I am confident, Sarah. Be confident too. You are a trader's daughter and sister to a Bristol merchant. We have to take risks. And we will show such profits!'

'She is sailing without insurance,' Sarah said heavily. 'In the most dangerous seas in the world, overloaded, and bound for an illegal destination. If we lose her we are ruined, Josiah. Not even the new house is safe. We own nothing outright but our two remaining ships and this warehouse, and we would have to sell the ships.'

Josiah hammered on the wood of the door frame again. 'I know! I know this, Sarah! Why d'you think I am so desperate to see the Hot Well pay? Why d'you think I am here on the quayside every morning, selling and dealing in barrels of other ships' cargoes? Why d'you think I draw on every ounce of credit I can get from the Merchant Venturers? I know how close to the wind I am sailing! No-one knows better than me!

But if I succeed then we are wealthy and established. It is a risk, Sarah! It is the nature of the Trade!'

Her hand was at her mouth again, biting the cuticle around her fingernail. She tasted her own blood.

'Don't, Sarah,' Josiah begged. 'I hoped to spare you this.'

'It is better that I should know,' she said, her voice low. 'I was fearing worse.'

'Well, you know now,' Josiah said.

'You will not deceive me again?'

'You will not stand in my way?'

'Josiah . . .'

'I will be master in my house, I will run Cole and Sons in my own way, Sarah.'

'This is all Frances's fault!' she suddenly burst out. 'If you had not married her you would have been content!'

'I was not content!' Josiah exclaimed. 'I married her because I was not content with the warehouse. I wanted more, and I am getting more. You will not stand against me, Sarah, I will not allow it.'

She turned away and looked out of the window. Below them a rival's ship was safely docked, swarming with sail-makers come to collect the sails for repair, half a dozen sailors crawling over the deck caulking the planks with tar and hemp rope.

'We used to stand together,' she said.

'I know.'

There was a silence. Sarah sighed. 'I will not go against you. So trust me, Josiah. Don't keep things from me. I am not a silly girl. I am not a lady of leisure. I was brought up to this business, I can help you.'

He nodded and came across the room to her. He put his arm around her waist and held her for a brief moment. 'I know,' he repeated. 'I have been miserably lonely with this worry.'

They stood still for a moment, watching the ship, as bereft parents will watch someone else's baby in a cradle.

'I must go,' Josiah said briskly. 'I have a horse waiting.'

'You have hired a horse again?'

Josiah laughed. 'Sarah, I have bought the Hot Well. I have to check on my business! Of course I have hired a horse and as soon as I can find one that suits me I shall buy one! I need to ride out and see that my business is thriving. I would not be doing my work if I were *not* riding out to look at it. Surely you see that!'

She smiled unwillingly at him. 'Yes. It is the expense which worries me.'

'It would cost me more if I did not inspect it,' he said briskly. 'Now let me go.'

She watched him from the window. Mehuru held the horse's head for him as he mounted. It seemed odd to see Josiah setting off for his work on horseback. All his life he had gone no further than the quayside outside their house. Now he looked like a gentleman, in riding boots and with a cape on his shoulders. Sarah thought that if she saw him at a distance she would not recognise him. The little brother she had reared was going far away from her and she did not understand him, nor his business, any more. The figures in the ledgers were no longer small manageable amounts, easily understood, added and subtracted. They were dangerous sums, perilous debts. And Josiah was no longer her little brother who came to her for advice and never sent out a ship without her checking the figures. He was a man prepared to take great risks, to take a massive gamble to win the home he wanted for the wife he had chosen.

Unseen by Josiah, she put up her hand to wave goodbye in a gesture which looked more as if she were calling him back.

Josiah's heart lifted a little as he rode along the riverside to the Hot Well. The tide was coming in and the sunshine sparkled on the water. The woods on either side of the river had lost their lush greenness, the leaves dulling in the heat and glare of the July sun. Josiah felt better for confiding in

373

Sarah. She had been his business advisor for so long that any secret from her made him uneasy. And in reassuring her, he convinced himself.

The Merchant Venturers' expensive avenue of trees were dusty after months of carriages going to and fro beneath their spreading branches. The waves were slapping the river wall of the Pump Room in a pretty irregular sound. An onshore breeze had lifted the constant smoke away from the city, and the sky was blue with fleecy strips of white cloud. Josiah rode down the little avenue with his hand on his hip and felt the novel pleasure of being a proprietor of land. He inspected the building with smug care, he took in the sky above it and the circling birds as if they too were part of his investment and a credit to his acumen.

At the back of the building the tap, which had traditionally dispensed water for free, was being bolted off. The workmen looked up as Josiah rode past and pulled at their caps. Josiah responded with a small jaunty gesture.

He could have hitched his horse to one of the posts outside the Pump Room. There were others there, bearing the traditional Bristol saddle – a two-seater – for a lady to sit behind the groom. Instead Josiah chose to whistle up a loitering urchin and promise him a penny to hold the horse. It was not that the animal was too high-bred or skittish to be left unattended. The stable knew Josiah was not a confident rider and they always sent him a placid slow-moving hack. But Josiah was learning the pleasure of spending money. A penny was a little enough sum, but to Josiah hiring a child to hold a horse when there was a hitching ring for free was an extravagance. It excited him to be extravagant. He foresaw a future when he would become a liberal tipper, a spendthrift in small, enjoyable ways, a man who carried loose change in his pocket and had spent it all on trifles by the end of the day.

He strolled into his Pump Room and looked around. The perennial invalids were in their usual places, drinking water or loitering under the roof of the colonnade, taking their

374

prescribed exercise. Josiah hardly glanced at them. These were not the people whose custom would determine the success of the Well. He needed the fashionable crowd, the London pleasure-seekers, the day-visitors from Bath. They had come here in their hundreds in previous years and Josiah had been at pains to advertise that the spa was under new management and offering advantageous rates for this first season. Surely, with a sky so blue, and an outlook from the large windows of the rooms so beguiling, they would come in their hundreds again?

'Ah, Mr Cole.' The Master of Ceremonies, newly appointed by Josiah but chosen by Frances, came forward and bowed to him. 'Mr Cole, our proprietor! We are all prepared, as you see! All ready for the launch of the new management. I have already received several cards notifying me of the arrival of Ladies of Quality. I think we shall have an enjoyable year! I do indeed! We are starting a little late, a little late in our season to be sure. But people do not go to London till October or November, and I am confident we can charm them from their country houses to here. We have the rest of this month and all of August and September, after all!'

Josiah smiled. He could not help but be uneasy with the man who wore such tightly strapped stays under his clothes that his waistcoat fitted without a wrinkle and his coat was one smooth line from padded shoulders to stiffened hem. 'Good,' he said shortly. 'I see they are shutting off the free tap at the back of the building.'

'Certainly,' the Master confirmed. 'It would be fatal to our atmosphere of elegance to have the back of the building crowded with dirty and sickly people. Besides – how can we charge for water inside the building if we are giving it away free outside?'

'Yes,' Josiah agreed curtly. 'The room looks well. I will take the attendance book and the cash register home with me.'

'Certainly, certainly,' the man said sweetly. 'But I think you will be happy. *I* am content enough with how it is going. We

375

have our poor little invalids here as usual but also a fair number of pleasure-seekers, and it is they who give the spa the air of fashion that it needs.'

'Yes,' Josiah said, rather at a loss.

'There are a few little improvements I would suggest?' the Master of Ceremonies continued archly. 'I would have put them in hand but they *do* cost money and I wanted to speak to the holder of the purse strings. I cannot have you thinking me extravagant, now!'

'What are they?'

The man held up his slender hand and ticked the items off on well-manicured fingers. 'One: the quartet only plays in the summer season and I think it is a shame. In the winter when it is grey outside we so badly want music and light and laughter inside, don't you think, Mr Cole? Don't you agree, sir?'

'Yes,' Josiah said, goaded. 'Keep them on.'

'And I want to hire a little woman, a pretty little woman to stand behind an urn and make tea in the afternoons. You can *order* tea but I want it here, visible, so you can see it, and want it, and have it in a flash. In a flash! D'you see?'

Josiah shook his head at the volubility of the man. 'Do as you think best,' he said. 'But check any expenditure with me of more than ten pounds.'

'Now that is a reasonable way to do business!' the man cried. 'But how silly of me, you are a businessman first and foremost, aren't you, Mr Cole? Now is there anything else I wanted to ask you?' He put his head on one side. His wig released a little puff of scented powder. 'No! Not a single thing! Now, can I tempt you to a glass of your own water?'

Josiah recoiled hastily. 'No, no. No need. The men bring bottles for my wife to drink when they deliver in town. She likes it. I – er – I do not take it. I am in perfect health, thank God.'

The man laid a gloved hand on Josiah's sleeve. A faint but unmistakable scent of geraniums blew sweetly and powerfully into Josiah's rigid face. 'Are you sure I can't tempt you?' he cooed.

'No, no.' Josiah nearly choked in discomfort. 'I have to go! Business, you know, business.'

He got himself out of the room at speed, mounted his horse and threw a penny at the boy. But once he was safely out of reach he turned his head and looked back. He chuckled. He could not help but wonder what his Da – the son of a collier – would have made of the family's meteoric rise, and this new fanciful trade.

Chapter Thirty

'I have been thinking what we can do,' Mehuru said to Frances. She was sitting on the bench in the central garden of Queens Square, with him standing beside her. Frances had just walked around the square, obeying Stuart Hadley's instructions to take light exercise in the open air.

Frances turned to look at him, shading her pale face from the sun with her little parasol. The August day was hot; she was wearing a muslin gown flecked with pink and a pink shawl over her shoulders. Mehuru had to curb his desire to straighten the shawl and wrap her tighter. Ever since Stuart had warned him of her health he found he was desperate to keep her warm, as if she were some rare African plant which would wither and die under the cool damp skies of England.

'We,' she repeated with a little smile. She did not say whether or not she recognised his right to speak of them as a couple.

'Has the doctor spoken to you about your health?'

'No,' she said. 'I am well now.'

Mehuru made a little grimace. 'He thinks that you have weak lungs.'

'Oh, I knew that,' Frances said. 'It was my mother's complaint too.'

'He told Josiah that you should go abroad in wintertime.'

'Josiah never said.'

'Josiah cannot see how it can be done,' Mehuru replied grimly. 'Three ships of his own and he cannot see how you can be sent somewhere warm for the winter.'

Frances twirled her parasol and peeped up at Mehuru from under the fringe. 'Don't be unkind about Josiah,' she reproved him. 'It is not fair to criticise him.'

'Mmm.' Mehuru suppressed his disagreement. 'The point is, the doctor thinks you should be in a better climate than here for the winter months.'

'How do you know all this?' Frances suddenly demanded.

'I was holding the doctor's horse and listening,' Mehuru said without embarrassment. 'Servants always know everything, Frances, you know that.'

'But not about us? They don't know about us?'

'Frances,' Mehuru said patiently. 'I am trying to make plans.'

'My reputation . . .'

'They know nothing about us,' Mehuru lied quickly. 'I want to plan . . .'

'To plan what?'

'The doctor says that you should go away in the winter for your health. This is not a light matter. He means it. He is afraid that your lungs are damaged and the wet and cold weather is bad for you. This house is low-lying, too near the river. And the air of this city is unbreathable!'

Frances nodded more seriously. 'I have never felt well since I came to Bristol.'

'I want you to come away with me.' Mehuru finally took the plunge. 'I want us to go to Italy, or better than that, to France. I think that the political situation in France is perfect for us. I want us to live in France together, as man and wife.'

Frances was stunned. She sat bolt upright and snapped the parasol shut. 'France!' she exclaimed.

'They will have a parliament governed by the will of the people,' Mehuru predicted. 'And negroes from the French colonies will sit side by side with white representatives. They will free the slaves in the colonies and black men and white men will be equal under the new French law. It is the ideal place for us. I will work as a journalist, I will earn a living as a writer.'

She shook her head. The cluster of pink silk flowers on her bonnet quivered as if they were afraid.

'Why not?'

'They cannot free the slaves,' she said disbelievingly. 'They will not.'

'I am assured they will, and France would be the very place for us to live together.'

She shook her head. 'I could not live in France,' she said in a small voice.

'Italy then.'

'I could not live abroad. The only family I have is in England, I could not go abroad.'

'But you never see your family.'

'My family name is important to me.' She looked at him as if she could never explain. 'People know who I am in England. This is where I belong.'

He curbed his impatience. 'Let's walk,' he suggested. He could not bear to stand behind her seat and not be allowed to touch her while she threw away her chance of health and their only chance of happiness. She rose up obediently and they went down the path to the centre of the square; he walked a scant half-pace behind her.

'Very well then,' he said. 'Let us find a house with good healthy air, perhaps near your old home. You liked it there, did you not? At Bath?'

Frances felt her heart speeding and her breath coming short.

'You don't understand. We could not live together, Mehuru, I would be ruined.'

'I understand that Josiah's friends and family would not recognise you,' he said carefully. 'But your own family would surely still care for you?'

She put her hand at the base of her throat, trying to still her panting. 'No,' she said. 'I would be ruined, Mehuru.

They would cut me off. I would never see any of them again.'

'What about your uncle, the one who writes to you, Lord Scott?'

Frances, thinking of his lordship's unequivocal advice about the fatal results of infidelity, gave a shaky laugh. 'Him least of all!' she said. 'If I left Josiah at all it would be the end for me, Mehuru! If I left him for you I would be outlawed by my family. They would never speak of me again.'

He had a growing, painful sense that he was defeated before he had even started. 'Frances,' he said. 'I have lost everything. My house, my family, my country, my work which was the greatest joy of all, and I am beginning again. Why cannot you and I begin again together?'

She shook her head. 'It's not possible, not possible. You do not understand.' She turned away and started to walk, a little quicker, down the westward path towards her house.

'Why not?' he demanded, catching her up.

'We would have no money,' she said. She was breathless from walking too quickly. 'I have nothing except what Josiah gives me, and you have nothing at all. We could not take a house, we could not even rent a room. The only work I can do is governessing, and you cannot earn at all.'

'People would help us,' he argued. 'We could go to London. I already have made friends with some Englishmen, members of a Constitutional Society. These people would be our friends, we could live near them. There is a place in London called Wapping where a friend of mine lives. We could leave Bristol and stay there.'

The look she turned on him was simply incredulous. 'You have been to radical meetings?' She was stunned. 'Mehuru, how could you? How could you even get to them?'

'I crept out. I have been to several.'

She gasped. 'But these are dreadful people! They threaten the whole nation. These are dangerous radical agitators!'

He tried to laugh at her alarm but he felt a growing fear

381

at the gulf which was opening between them. 'You have not met these people, Frances, and I have. They are not dangerous agitators, they are quiet sensible men who wish to see sensible changes made in this country and the ending of the slave trade. Two or three of them are my countrymen and they understand my position.'

She was quite white with horror. 'You have been plotting with runaway slaves?'

'They are not runaway slaves,' he snapped. 'They are free men.'

Frances put her gloved hand to her cheek as she tried to catch her breath. 'Mehuru, this is awful. I had no idea that you were doing this. They are dangerous agitators and they will be arrested and hanged or transported. If they catch you, they will send you to Australia or to the plantations. You must promise me never, never to go again.'

'Or what?'

She did not hear the warning note in his voice, she was too absorbed in her fears for his safety. 'I shall tell Josiah that the doors have to be locked at night. You must not meet with these people.'

'Or you could chain me up,' he suggested bitingly. 'Or have me whipped.'

She suddenly realised what she had said. 'I don't mean that,' she recanted swiftly. 'I meant that you are a foreigner, you do not speak the language, you do not understand the people you are mixing with. I want to protect you.'

'I think I do not need the kind of protection that locks up a grown man and forbids him to choose his friends.' He was toweringly angry. 'I think I do not want a woman who threatens me with imprisonment. And I do not want a woman who desires me but will not acknowledge that she desires me and still plans to spend the rest of her life with her husband.'

He spun on his heel and was walking away from her when Frances, reckless of who might see her, ran after him and

382

caught at the sleeve of his coat. 'Don't!' she cried. She was panting for air. 'Please! Mehuru!'

He stopped when he saw the whiteness of her face and heard her breath coming so short.

'Oh!' he sighed, and turned back to her. 'Sit down, breathe slowly.' He pressed her into a seat. 'Come, Frances, breathe properly. I will not be angry with you. Breathe!'

With his hand on her back she took three shaky breaths and he watched as the colour came back into her face.

'I am very sorry,' she said as soon as she could speak. 'Please don't be angry, Mehuru.'

'It is I who am sorry,' he said. 'I should have remembered your health.' He glanced around at all the windows facing the square, longing to take her into his arms but knowing he did not dare. He waited until her breathing steadied. 'Now,' he said. 'Frances, I must tell you that these are good men and friends of mine. Anything you have heard against the societies is not true.'

She nodded, anxious to avoid a quarrel. 'Perhaps.'

'And they tell me that English women often marry men of my colour,' he continued. 'And they live happily with them.'

She nodded. 'I have heard of that.' She did not tell him that she had heard of it because of an article in a newspaper deploring the tendency of white women to marry freed slaves and accusing them of the grossest immorality.

'These would be our friends,' he said. 'Our neighbours. We would make a new life for the two of us.'

Frances drew a breath and tried to speak calmly. 'Mehuru, I know that you mean well but it could not happen,' she said quietly. 'These are working women, they are not ladies. Wapping is a poor part of London, it is not like Queens Square, it is even worse than the Redclift quay. It is dirty and unhealthy, and all the people there are poor people, labouring men and women. They would despise me, I would hardly understand their speech. I could not possibly live there. I would be miserable living in poverty and so would you.'

He gave her a swift unhappy look and straightened up.

'Josiah might pursue us,' Frances said. 'He could have you arrested as a runaway and then I would be there on my own.' Her voice trembled. 'There is a pit of poverty underneath me. You never saw me before my marriage. I had to work or tumble downward into charity, and I was never very good at my work. I dare not leave Josiah, I dare not leave my family. It is their name and their wealth that feed me and house me and clothe me. Without them I would be ruined.'

Mehuru said nothing. He stood behind her, as a slave should stand, alert for her command but detached from her. He looked over her head, over the bonnet with the small bobbing flowers, and he felt his heart ache for her, and for the unlikely romantic future he had dreamed for them. She turned her head and looked up at him. She looked very small and vulnerable, like a scolded child. Her eyes, as dark as his own, were huge, shadowed with blue bruises from her illness.

'What are we to do then?' he asked tenderly. 'What do you want to do?'

She shook her head. 'I don't know.'

Josiah was on the quayside, watching his rival's ship preparing to set sail, his own berth achingly empty. The sailmakers dragged heavily laden sledges across the cobbles and the runners screamed in protest. When one of the sailmakers saw him, he hesitated and then came over.

'Your bill, Mr Cole,' the sailmaker said. 'From *Lily*, in March. I would appreciate it if you could settle it now.'

Josiah put his hand to his pocket and then checked. 'I am sorry, George,' he said. 'I have left my purse at my house.'

George looked uncomfortable. 'Do you have nothing at your office, Mr Cole?'

'No,' Josiah said. 'I keep no gold here, it is not safe with no-one living here any more. I shall send one of my slaves to your loft this evening to pay what I owe.'

The man made a little bow and shouted to his lad to unload

the sails. Josiah went down the steps to the ferry over to the Bristol side of the river. He sat in the bow and looked back at the ship. She was sailing direct to and from the West Indies. Josiah's neighbour and rival had given up the trade of slaving. Josiah hawked and spat in the filthy water – he knew better. When *Rose* came home in November, when *Daisy* followed her into port with *Lily* not far behind, they would all know that Josiah had been right to cleave to his own trade – the only trade he knew. The ferry nudged against the steps of the quay and Josiah tossed a ha'penny to the lad and stepped ashore, heading for the traders' coffee shop.

Stephen Waring was at the top table taking breakfast when Josiah came in. He raised his head and nodded an invitation. As Josiah came over Stephen regarded him rather grimly, without his usual smile.

Josiah ordered a plate of meat and bread and a pint of porter.

'I have heard some news which I hope you will not take amiss,' Stephen began. He finished the last of his meat and took a piece of bread to wipe around his plate, sopping up the juices of the rare beef and the remains of the mustard.

Josiah cocked an eyebrow at him.

'The Company has been told that you have shut off the tap for free water at the Hot Well.'

Josiah nodded. 'I have.'

'Why is that?'

Josiah smiled. 'I should have thought it would be obvious. I have leased that Hot Well from the Company and it has cost me two thousand pounds deposit and nine hundred pounds a year. I have staff to pay, and I have this very day spent two hundred pounds on an architect's drawing for a winter garden. I am hardly likely to give water away. At your colliery, Waring, do you give away coal to anyone who calls?'

Stephen nodded at the jest but still did not smile. 'I do not have a lease,' he said slowly. 'I own my colliery outright.'

'So?'

'I do not have a lease which says that I am bound to give away my coal to anyone who calls for it.'

Josiah looked a little flustered. His breakfast came but he pushed it to one side. 'You are not telling me that my lease says I have to give away the water?'

'I am afraid that it makes clear that the poor and sick of Bristol have a right to draw water from the Hot Well,' Stephen said smoothly. 'That was the agreement when the spring was first walled in and enclosed in the building. There is a general feeling that you have to abide by it.'

Josiah took a long draught from his drink. 'That is the letter of the lease,' he expostulated. 'But surely no-one seriously expects me to give water away! After all that has been spent on the Well? After all the work we have done to make it more fashionable, to make it more exclusive?'

Waring pushed back his chair from the table and shrugged slightly. 'That is the lease,' he said easily. 'I wanted to warn you – as a friend – that the Company would wish to see the conditions of the lease fulfilled, including this one.'

'But this is preposterous!' Josiah exclaimed, still disbelieving. 'We cannot have the riff-raff of Bristol turning up night and day and queuing at the tap with their kettles and their pots, wanting the water! There is no place for them! There is no provision! They will be in the way of the carriages, they will spit and soil in the gardens! The Company cannot want that!'

Stephen Waring shrugged again. 'You signed the lease, Josiah,' he said. 'It makes it clear that water shall be provided free to the needy poor of Bristol. I think you will have to obey.' He rose from his seat. 'I must go. I am expecting a ship in port any day now. It is a worrying time waiting, isn't it? Where are your ships now?'

'God knows!' Josiah snapped irritably. '*Lily* may be loading off Africa, *Daisy* should be in the middle passage and the *Rose* in the West Indies by now. And I would be a richer man today if I had stayed in shipping. At least with my ships I know my rights. No-one has yet told me that I have to give away half my cargo. I must tell you, Waring, I cannot see my way clear to opening the tap. There is no room for the needy poor at the Hot Well!'

Stephen Waring nodded. 'As you wish, Cole,' he said equably and walked out of the coffee shop. Outside he put his hat on his head and strolled towards the quay. 'I think you will find that you are wrong,' he said thoughtfully to the wheeling gulls in the clear sky. 'I think you will find that the Company knows what it is doing.'

Frances and Sarah rose from the dinner table to leave Josiah alone with his port.

'I wish Lady Scott could have come to the Hot Well,' Josiah said uneasily. 'I was counting on your family to visit, and to tell others.'

Frances raised her eyebrows. 'She is not allowed to travel in her condition,' she said. 'They have been much at the sea this year. My uncle says he will come later. And Lady Scott will certainly come in the spring.'

'But now is the important time,' Josiah insisted. 'This is the middle of our season, we are far busier in summer than in the winter. In the winter people go to London. Summer is the time for the country and the spas. People must come *now*. If they don't come now they may not come for another year.'

'I can ask my cousins,' Frances suggested.

'What good are your cousins to me?' Josiah demanded rudely. 'You can ask your father's parishioners, but if they are not lords and ladies they will not bring in the Quality and they are no good to me.'

Frances flinched at his hectoring tone. 'I am sorry, Josiah,' she said, her voice affected, unnaturally calm. 'I am sure that Lady Scott did not wish to disoblige you.'

'I thought you would bring in the Quality patrons,' Josiah said. 'I was counting on it, Frances.'

'I *have* invited several ladies,' Frances pointed out. She could feel her breath coming short and uncertain. 'And at least two of them have promised they will come and bring their families too.'

'We've put the price of a subscription up so much,' Josiah said. 'It was ten shillings for an entire family, whatever the size, and now it is twenty-six shillings per person for the month.'

'Will that not drive away trade?' Sarah demanded.

Josiah flushed at her tone. 'Not at all. What are shillings to these people? We have to think grandly! I am just concerned for these first few weeks.'

Sarah scrutinised his face. 'We should not be too greedy,' she observed.

'I have to meet the Merchant Venturer rent,' Josiah said. 'I owe a year's rent in advance, I have to pay them. But when *Rose* is docked and I can pay off my creditors for the purchase price of the Hot Well I will be easier. I am known to be credit-worthy and I expect to see a large profit on the *Rose* voyage.'

'The sugar crop is so good at this time of year?' Frances asked.

It was nothing to do with the price of sugar, but Josiah could not tell her about the slaves, double the usual number loaded into the small space, or the Spanish preference for women and children workers who were more obedient and less likely to rebel against the particular cruelty of those plantations. 'Oh. Yes,' he said simply. 'Very good.'

'And what day will the *Rose* arrive?' Frances asked.

'She is not a wagon,' Sarah answered acidly. 'You cannot say what day and what hour.'

'She is due in November,' Josiah said. 'But please God she will come in early and my worries will be over.'

'I am sorry you are worried,' Frances said pleasantly.

Josiah nodded unsmilingly. 'You could reduce your expenses,' he remarked.

Frances glanced swiftly at Sarah. Her sister-in-law was staring at them with avid curiosity. Frances realised that it would not occur to Josiah that such a conversation should take place in private.

'I will certainly do so,' she said with quiet dignity. 'I had no idea that matters were not as prosperous as they seem. If you had told me earlier, Josiah, I would not have ordered my autumn gowns. I shall cancel them.'

Josiah's anxiety warred briefly with his ambition. 'Oh, keep them! Keep them!' he said irritably. 'I can't have it said that my wife goes around in last season's dresses. Keep your gowns, Frances. But save on things that don't show. Underwear or shoes or something.'

Frances flushed scarlet at his indelicacy and went to the door. 'Certainly. I shall be in the morning room if you wish to continue this conversation in private.'

Sarah gave a snort of laughter as Frances closed the door on the two of them. Frances crossed the hall to the morning room, shut the door and leaned back on the white-painted panels with a sigh of relief.

Mehuru was there before her, lighting the fire. Although the September days were bright there was a chill in the air, and so Mehuru always lit a fire when Frances was sitting in a room. The children were to be brought to her at six o'clock; she was teaching them their catechism. Frances's smile was immediate and delighted. 'Oh! Cicero!' she cried.

'Call me by my name.'

'Mehuru,' she said, her voice low and passionate.

He wanted to draw her to him and kiss her, but he heard footsteps in the hall and stayed still. They looked at each other across the room.

'Frances,' he said tenderly. 'Are you well today?'

'I am perfectly well,' she replied. She sat down near the fire and smiled at him. He scanned her face for any trace of pain.

'Truly I am,' she assured him. 'Perfectly.'

He knelt at the fire to put coal on it, and sat back on his heels to look at her.

'I *am* well,' Frances said softly. 'If you wished it . . .' She broke off. He looked carefully at her. She was flushed but smiling, her eyes were bright.

'If I wished what?' he asked, half-guessing what she might say.

'If you wished to come to my room . . .' she whispered so softly that he could hardly hear her.

He was silent for a moment. 'You know I desire you,' he said hesitantly.

She took up some embroidery, as if she wanted to avoid his gaze. He watched the dark sweep of her eyelashes on her cheeks. 'I think so,' she said. 'I thought so . . .'

'But I cannot . . .' He stopped. 'Not here. Not in Josiah's house with him asleep next door. He could wake and come in at any moment.'

She nodded briefly and stole a quick glance at him. 'I was afraid . . .'

'What?'

'That you did not . . .'

'Desire you?'

She looked down at her embroidery and her colour rose again. 'Yes.'

He gave a short laugh. 'Frances, I lie awake every night burning up for you. All these long weeks of your illness I have thought of nothing else but holding you again. I am sleepless for you, I am hungry for you. Sometimes I think I shall go mad for you.'

'Oh,' she breathed.

'I see you are not worried about my lack of sleep,' he said.

She gave a delicious gurgle of laughter. 'I am sorry, I suppose I should be.'

'But I cannot come to you, with him in the room next door,' he said more seriously. 'I should feel a fool. I should feel . . . shamed.'

390

'You did once,' she reminded him in a whisper.

'I don't forget it,' he said. 'I was mad for you, we were both mad that night. But I cannot creep around the house every night like a thief, Frances.'

She nodded. 'I understand how you feel. I am glad that you told me.'

He laid the long poker and tongs either side of the grate and swept up the coal dust. He rose to his feet. 'So what shall we do?' he asked. 'Are we never to be together again? Will you not leave him and come to me? Or set me free so that I can make a place for us to be together?'

At once the joy was wiped from her face. 'I have been thinking,' she said. 'I have been thinking all the time. We will find a way. Somehow we must surely find a way.'

'I will wait,' he said. 'Not forever. But for a little while. Perhaps Wilberforce will win the vote next spring and slavery will be ended. Perhaps I will be freed by law, free to leave here, and you will be forced to choose then.'

She nodded, still grave. 'Perhaps.'

'And how would you vote?' Mehuru asked. 'Your whole fortune depends on the Trade. Josiah's wealth, this house, everything you own. Would you end the Trade if it was your choice?'

Frances looked up. It was a question she had never put to herself. On the one hand was her tenderness for Mehuru and her recognition of the terrible wrong done to him and to the other millions, tens of millions, of Africans. But on the other hand was Frances's determination to cling to gentry status and her deep fear of poverty. Anything which could endanger her prosperity was bound to be her enemy.

She hesitated, and then she did not dare to tell him the truth: that she did not know. That she would not force herself to decide. 'I wish it had never started,' she said, taking the easy way out. 'I wish with all my heart that we had left Africa alone. I wish they had never taken you, nor all the others. I do wish it, Mehuru.'

He nodded, put the coal scuttle carefully in its place, and left the room.

In the kitchen Cook was slicing a pie for the servants' dinner and Mary and Elizabeth were hulling bowls of late rosy Cheddar strawberries for Frances's supper.

'Mehuru,' Mary said hesitantly. 'We have been thinking, Elizabeth and Martha and me . . .'

'Yes?'

'We have been thinking of running away,' she said.

Chapter Thirty-one

The Vessle Rose,
at Sea between Africa and the West Indies.

4th July 1789

Dear Mr Cole,

I Send this to you by a Reliable friend who Hove-to beside us Today to exchange News. He is First mate Stephens, travelling in the Bright Guinea to Bristol and likely to be in port In early September some two months Ahead of us who have yet to make Landfall in the West Indies. I have told him to put this into Your hands and None other and he is a Trustworthy man.

Firstly you will be Happy to hear that we are making good time in the middle passage with Clear skies and favourable winds. I Expect to see the Spanish Islands within a month, please God. According to your Orders in the letter I have shipped mainly Women and children and packed them Tighter than I would have believed Possible. We are carrying nearly Double the usual number and have had a Quieter voyage than I have Ever made, on account of the fact that they have Never mutinied nor threatened to fight but are simply Dying very quiet and Melancholy. I do assure you that I am doing every-thing you might wish to keep them Bright and lively, but to No avail. I have let the Youngest children stay with their Mothers and I have them up on Deck as much as I can, I am keeping them Clean, and the sailors have Not Molested them overmuch. But despite my Best endeavours there is a Great loss of life on the voyage from their Temperament which is the Worst I have ever experienced. We have Nets rigged to prevent them Throwing themselves off but when I tell you that One woman squeezed her Infant through the net and threw him Overboard to Drown him rather than Keep him with us you will understand what a Reckless bunch they are.

Of the Load of five hundred and seventy-three I have lost only ten by them drowning themselves, and in a long voyage with most of them Unchained you will know that Shows my care. One of them managed to Pierce a vein in her Arm by hammering her spoon flat and Stabbing until she was through the skin and I lost near a dozen this way, who Learned the trick and Bled to death during the Nights, and another Twenty whose cuts oozed and turned Black and thus poisoned themselves. Twenty-two of them Starved themselves to death and Vomited up when we got the brace on them and forced Slabber down their throats, and could not be saved, and near a Dozen are being fed by force now. Four made a party to Hang themselves and made their own Rope for the purpose from their clothes. In the haste of Loading, according to your Orders, some were taken on with the Flux and it is spreading to the others. Thirty have already died from the illness, and Four of my crewmen whom I sorely miss. Four babies have died in their Mothers' arms but we do not know Why.

Altogether then we have near five hundred for Sale and we will start preparing them for inspection and auction next Month. Nearly a hundred look poorly, some are Old with drooping breasts and others sick. But we will Bung up the ones with the Flux, and Boot-black those with sores. Trust me – I will be rid of them.

The ones I cannot Clear I will sell in a Scramble, and any I cannot be rid of I will Drown on my way to Jamaica.

I will buy as much Top-grade sugar as I can conveniently obtain and Load and make all Speed home. I hope this meets with your Satisfaction, Sir. For my own Pride I regret the loss of so Many but that was a Risk we ran as you yourself acknowledged at the Time. The profit will no doubt console Us both.

I remain your obdt. servant,

Stephen Smedley
(Capt).

Josiah read the letter from Captain Smedley in the back parlour which Frances had furnished as an office for him. He read it through once again and then he drew a sheet of paper towards him. He estimated that there would be about four hundred and fifty slaves who could pass as fit once Captain Smedley had finished painting their sores and blocking their anuses. They could be sold for a total of about £22000. A scramble – when greedy or poor planters paid an entrance fee at the gangway and were allowed down into the hold to take pot-luck in the dark, grabbing as many slaves as they could and only finding if they had sick or even dying workers when they dragged them out into the daylight – would earn no more than a couple of hundred pounds.

Once *Rose* docked and Josiah shared the profits with his partners he should be left with little more than ten thousand pounds. He nodded. He had over-calculated the amounts as a man always does, speaking grandly to Sarah of profits of £14000. But even this would clear all his debts and leave him with a profit greater than Cole and Sons had ever shown before.

More slaves had died than he would have believed possible and there were more sick and unsellable slaves than Cole and Sons usually carried. Never before had a captain written in a matter-of-fact tone about dumping sick women and children over the side. Josiah shrugged. He would come out of the venture with enough profit to settle all his debts and still show a handsome margin.

He went to the fireplace where coal and kindling were laid. He took a tinderbox to the incriminating letter, carefully lit the corner and sat back on his heels to watch it flame up and then crumple to ash. The letter had taken two months to reach him. He might confidently predict that the sale of slaves had now gone through, and *Rose* was even now on the seas, headed for home, rich with sugar in her hold and bullion locked safe in the captain's cabin. On this leg of the voyage she was insured, over-insured. Josiah's gamble – overloaded slaves smuggled to the Spanish colonies – had paid off.

'Two more months and I am clear,' he said softly to himself. 'Two more months and it will be November and she will be home laden with gold and sugar.'

He went back to his desk and looked at his other letters. One was addressed to him in an unfamiliar hand. He opened it and read, then re-read, the letter.

It was a summons to appear before the Bristol magistrates. He had been summonsed by the Merchant Venturers' Company for failing to comply with the terms of their lease – namely, to provide water from the famous healing spa the Hot Well for the needy poor of Bristol.

For a moment, Josiah was too stunned to take in the meaning, and then he felt himself gripped by a rage so total that he could not see the letter in his hand, nor the desk, nor the window before him overlooking the little backyard where Kbara was slowly sweeping.

'My God,' he said. He was almost awed by the passion which shook him. 'My God.'

He could not think why they should persecute him for the little tap, why they, who had grown rich on the sweat of the Bristol poor and on the blood of the slaves of Africa, should suddenly suffer a crisis of conscience about one little tap. He had heard Stephen Waring's warning but he had never dreamed that the Merchant Venturers' Company – his own club, his own new-found friends – would take action against him.

He rose from his chair, he almost staggered and, clasping the letter to his chest, went to find Frances.

She was seated in the ornate parlour, with some sewing in her hands. She put it down as soon as she saw his face.

'Josiah?'

'Read this,' he said and thrust the letter at her.

He watched her face as she read it through, and read it through again. He saw her grow suddenly wary, as if she had found something to fear.

'What do you make of it?' he asked her. 'Waring warned me but I had no idea they would go so far. Why should they take me to court for such a trifle?'

Frances frowned. 'Did he warn you that they would take you to court?'

'No! I would not have believed it if he had! He told me only that he had heard that the Company wanted the tap open. I had no idea . . .' Josiah trailed off. 'I would have opened it if they had insisted. But why should they insist? Why should they want to spoil the spa with sickly paupers hanging around and collecting water in buckets? Why should they want beggars at the Hot Well?'

Frances shook her head. 'I don't know. It makes no sense. I thought their whole idea was that it should be elegant and exclusive.' She thought for a moment. 'When is the hearing?'

'Next week.'

'Can you open the tap before then? Prevent this case getting to court?'

'I should think so. It is only bolted off. But I don't see why I *should*! Why should anyone ask it of me?'

'Do you have a lawyer, Josiah?'

He shook his head miserably. 'I have never needed one before,' he said. 'All my dealings, all my father's dealings, were done on a handshake. You can ask anyone; when I give my word that is as good as a bond. I have never used a lawyer. I have always thought them more trouble and expense than they were worth.'

'I think we need a lawyer now,' Frances decided. 'There is something happening here and we need a friend who can tell us what is going on.' She opened the summons again. 'Who is the presiding magistrate? Mr John Shore?'

'That is Stephen Waring's brother-in-law,' Josiah said. 'And his partner.'

Frances's face was grave. 'I think we need a lawyer.'

* * *

397

The lawyer's advice was simple. Even Josiah conceded that he had given value for money. The tap was to be opened at pre-arranged times every day and only then could the needy of Bristol disturb the gentility of the spa by queuing for their water. There was no fine to pay, and aside from the lawyer's fee there were no costs incurred. Josiah went before the magistrate, John Shore, who nodded pleasantly to him from the bench, while Josiah explained that there had been an oversight and that all was remedied now. It turned out to be a simple little matter.

Josiah would have kept it from Sarah if he could, but the week after the court hearing she read of it in the newspaper. A journalist made a great to-do over it, writing as if a moral victory had been won over the grasping new tenant of the Hot Well. It appeared as if the Merchant Venturers had stood firm for the rights of the poor and defended their health. The Merchant Venturers had protected the defenceless paupers' right to the miracle of the spa water. The Merchant Venturers had saved the Hot Well for the people of Bristol. Someone had given the journalist a great deal of information and none of it reflected very well on Josiah. Someone had gone to a deal of trouble to show Josiah as a newly rich, grasping landlord who had tried to ride rough-shod over the rights of the common people. The water from the Hot Well was said to be the saviour of the Bristol paupers – the only water they could safely drink in the whole contaminated, dirty city. It was a miracle water which had cured countless patients of skin ailments, digestive troubles, lung and heart complaints; and now the new landlord, a self-made man, a Trader, would snatch this natural boon from the mouths of the needy.

'It means nothing, Sarah,' Josiah said. She had brought a copy of the newspaper to his office.

'We have never appeared in a newspaper before,' she said, her voice throbbing with suppressed emotion. 'And they are calling you an upstart.'

Josiah flushed. 'It means nothing.'

'You did not tell me,' Sarah reproached him.

'It was not ships' business, I did not want to worry you. I saw a lawyer and took advice. It is a storm in a teacup.'

'We are all out of our depths in these matters. The Merchant Venturers' Company was your new-found friend only last month, and this month they take you to court.'

Josiah nodded. 'They surprised me,' he acknowledged frankly. 'I will take it as a warning shot across my bows, Sarah. Things are not always as they seem.'

'In this town they are never as they seem,' Sarah said.

Josiah smiled. 'You are prejudiced. You are a Welsh girl at heart, Sarah.'

She shook her head. 'I am the daughter of a self-made man,' she said simply. 'I will never trust the gentry.'

Josiah was teased very roundly at the October Company dinner for oppressing the poor and he took it with a small grim smile. No-one saw fit to tell him why the Company should have gone to the length of threatening one of its own members with prosecution, and Josiah did not find himself confident enough to demand an explanation. When the decisions were nodded through he heard to his surprise that Cole and Sons would be excused charges at the lighthouses all the way down the Bristol channel for the next two years.

A smiling nod from Stephen Waring suggested that it was a favour from him. Josiah raised his glass in thanks and hid his confusion. In the roaring bonhomie of the songs and the toasts there was no opportunity to draw Stephen to one side and ask why he was so unexpectedly favoured. When he woke up the next morning with a nauseating headache he merely assumed that the Merchant Venturers had brought the case against him to demonstrate their care for the people of Bristol and had paid him for his embarrassment with an easing of their charges. It seemed a reasonably fair exchange.

The publicity about the re-opening of the tap did not damage the reputation of the Hot Well at all. It made it appear even more exclusive. Another London paper reprinted the story, emphasising the increased elegance of the spa, which certainly led to a couple of extra bookings. Then the story died away and was forgotten.

Only Frances wondered why the Merchant Venturers' Company had taken such pains to appear as heroes and defenders of the common people. She wondered why they had taken the deposit for the lease and a full year's rent from Josiah and then threatened his business in its first season. And she wondered why they had cast Josiah, their new tenant, the newest member of their company, as the villain of the piece.

When she mentioned her worries to Josiah he snapped at her and ordered her to go and look at the Hot Well herself and tell him what he could do to make the spa more profitable. Frances and Sarah drove out together, on a bright sunny day towards the end of October.

The avenue was bare and stark, the broad yellow leaves blown away from the little plane trees. On the far side of the river Rownham Woods glowed with autumn colours, reds, yellows and golds. Frances was wearing one of her new gowns and a pretty fur-lined jacket, but when she saw the saddle horses standing idle outside the Pump Room, and the places for the waiting carriages standing empty, she felt that she should have taken Josiah's angry demand to heart and cancelled all her new outfits.

'It looks quiet,' she remarked uneasily to Sarah.

Sarah said nothing.

The two women dismounted from the carriage and went inside.

'Mrs Cole! Miss Cole!' The Master of Ceremonies surged forward. 'What a pleasure to see you both. You will take a dish of tea, I know!'

Sarah nodded and Frances allowed him to draw them to one of the little tables. A smart maid came forward and gave them tea.

Frances looked around the room. A few invalids were

reclining in seats around the echoing room. The quartet played brightly. The card tables stood empty, new packs of cards still in their wrappings at each corner. A few people walked slowly up and down the room, undertaking their exercise with mournful expressions. It was deeply depressing.

'I did not know you had so little company here,' Frances said.

'Today *is* a little thin,' the man said, as if he had suddenly noticed. 'But in the middle of the week it is often quiet. We don't have the local trade that we used to enjoy. We still have our residents though.'

'Because it is too expensive,' Sarah said abruptly.

'Let us say – too select!' he replied sweetly.

'If it is too select for the Bristol merchants and their families then it is too select to succeed.'

'Sarah!' Frances whispered. To the Master of Ceremonies she said: 'I hope it will improve. Do you think it will improve, Mr Tucker?'

'I am certain,' he said. 'When our new winter garden room is built we will be packed every winter. And in summer we always succeed. These are the worst months for the Hot Well – autumn, and of course winter. You can see it in the records. These are the months when the Quality are in Town. We have to be patient and wait until spring. More tea, Miss Cole?'

'No thank you,' Sarah replied, containing her irritation with some difficulty.

'Perhaps we had better go,' Frances suggested. 'Mr Cole asked us to call and see how things were.'

'Tell him they are well,' Mr Tucker said with breezy confidence. 'A little slow today of course, but busier every day the sun shines. And all of us here, all of this little team are ready and confident for spring.'

'But it is October now,' Sarah hissed through her teeth as they got into the carriage. 'How does the booby think we will manage until spring?'

'Perhaps the *Rose* will come in early,' Frances said. Both

401

women turned and looked towards the mouth of the river. Seagulls wheeled and cried over the empty water.

'She must come in next month,' Sarah said. 'She must come in when she is due. It is not long to wait now. Only four weeks if she is on time. With so much riding on her, she *must* come home on time.'

Chapter Thirty-two

On the first of November Josiah's debt to Hibbard and Sons fell due. He had planned to pay them out of the profit which *Rose* would bring home. But *Rose* had not yet returned. He wrote a brief letter to Hibbard and Sons explaining that his ship was slightly overdue and that he would be obliged if they would extend the life of his loan for another month.

Hibbard and Sons wrote an equally brief note back within the week, saying simply that they did not wish to extend the loan for another month. Josiah would oblige them by clearing his debt of £5400 plus interest at once.

Josiah stared at the letter for a long time in silence. He did not know what he should do next. He opened the front door and looked down the street to the river. His dock was empty, and the tide was coming in. The *Rose* could sail in on this tide, or the next, or the next after that.

He called for Kbara and told him to go round to the stable and hire a horse. Perhaps takings at the Hot Well had increased.

He rode along the river with little pleasure. There were no large boats, the tide was too shallow and uncertain. A single trow, like Josiah's father's first ship, was sailing up the river, moving swiftly on the flowing tide. Josiah had an odd fanciful notion that he would have been a happier man today if he had stuck to a single trow to sail up and down the river carrying little loads, and coming home at night to Sarah.

He hitched his horse to the ring in the wall of the Hot Well and strode into the room. The beautiful long assembly room, newly whitewashed since his purchase, was all but deserted. The string quartet played mechanically without spirit in one corner of the room, the card tables were still empty with new unopened packs of cards laid invitingly on the green baize. A silver urn hissed in the corner with a smartly liveried maid beside it waiting to serve tea. The visitors' book, prominently displayed at the doorway, was empty of any new names.

Only the invalids, sick and pale as ever, were slumped in the chairs around the room. Josiah glared at them as if he wished they would relapse and die rather than linger and give the place its depressing atmosphere of a hospital.

'Where is everyone?' he demanded of the Master of Ceremonies. 'It may be mid-November but the place should be busier than this. I've seen last year's attendance book. It should be better than this. It's not midsummer but there should be people on repairing leases from the London Season. Where is everyone?'

'Most disappointing,' the man replied. 'I too am most disappointed.'

'I am sorry for it,' Josiah said grimly. 'I shall add your disappointment to my other worries. Why is no-one here?'

The man shook his bewigged head. 'I can't say. I don't know.'

'Very well,' Josiah said carefully. 'What is your opinion? Do you have any opinion? Would you venture a guess?'

The man regarded him warily. 'I think it is a number of things,' he offered cautiously. 'A number. Shall we take tea?'

'No. What number of things?'

'Well, the charges,' the man said delicately, looking longingly at the urn and the maid and the diversion of teacups. 'They are rather high now. Higher than Bath, I believe. Perhaps too high, you know, Mr Cole. People don't want to pay them. I think they won't pay them, in fact. No-one from Bristol comes at all now, the spa has a reputation in the town of being too expensive, of being too fashionable.' He simpered slightly. 'Perhaps we have been too successful?'

Josiah nodded. 'And what other things?'

'Well, the atmosphere,' the man went on. He waved his hand exquisitely gloved in white kid at the row of desperately sick people. 'Very dreary. Not quite the place you want to come for amusement.'

'It's a spa!' Josiah exclaimed. 'Of course there are sick people here. You're supposed to come here for your health. That is rather bound to attract ill people.'

'Of course. But it's just that they all seem so very ill indeed, don't they? They are calling Dowry Parade "Death Row", you know.'

'What?'

'Mmm, lowering, isn't it? You can see that it would put people off.'

Josiah clenched his teeth together. 'Anything else?'

'France, I'm afraid.'

Josiah felt his teeth grind. He carefully relaxed his jaw. 'France?'

'A lot of the younger, wilder fashionable set are off to the French spas. They're interested in France this year. The French, you know.'

'What?'

'The French, sir, the Jacobins! You know, *Liberté, Egalité* . . .'

'What the devil has this to do with my Hot Well?' Josiah bellowed. The quartet died into silence. Josiah flushed scarlet with suppressed rage and embarrassment. 'Tell them to play on,' he muttered.

The MC waved an airy hand at them. The quartet bowed to Josiah and started their little rippling tune again.

'What has the fall of the Bastille to do with my Hot Well?' Josiah demanded through his teeth.

'There is a great enthusiasm for liberty and France and so on. They are all rushing off to France this year. We cannot make poor little Bristol appeal at all.'

Josiah sighed. 'I can make no sense of this. Anything else?'

405

The man shrugged. 'I don't know. It is a shame. I *do* think it's a shame.'

'So all we have to do,' Josiah said bitterly, 'is drop our subscription, stop sick people coming here, and put an end to the revolution in France and our worries will be over.'

The Master of Ceremonies looked at him coyly. 'Rather a task, isn't it?' he smiled.

'It's damnable,' Josiah said. He strode from the room. The Master of Ceremonies fluttered behind him.

'But don't be disheartened, I implore you. It's only November. Anything could happen! Once the winter is over – and I so *dread* the winter, don't you? Once the winter is over and the spring comes I am sure anything could happen . . .'

Josiah turned to face him and the man skidded to a standstill, his high-heeled shoes slipping on the polished floor.

'Anything *is* happening!' Josiah cried sharply. 'This place costs me nigh on one thousand pounds a year for the lease alone, and the running costs are near a hundred pounds a week. Anything and everything is happening with the sole exception of this place earning a living.'

'Oh! Money worries! Money worries!' the man exclaimed. 'They are so wearisome, aren't they?'

'How much do I pay you?' Josiah demanded unpleasantly.

'Why, by the Season, you pay me eighty guineas a Season, Mr Cole.'

'At least I can save that!' Josiah said. 'You are fired.'

'I?' The Master of Ceremonies was genuinely amazed. 'You cannot fire me, sir. You are making a mistake.'

Josiah trudged to his horse, his head down. 'I have fired you,' he said grimly. 'You can pack your bags.'

'I? Pack?'

'Or leave 'em here. But you are out of this place by the end of this week, so help me God! You were hired to bring in the fashionable set. I don't see one of them. So you are fired!'

'Well, I doubt very much that it will help you.' The Master

of Ceremonies teetered to a halt and flung the words after Josiah's back.

Josiah unhitched his horse from the ring and mounted it in surly silence.

'The Hot Well will not pay because you bought it at too high a price!' the Master of Ceremonies called up at him. 'You can blame me but it is your own fault! Blame me all you like! But everyone knows it is your own fault!'

Josiah's face went so black that the man sprang back, half-fearing him, but Josiah dragged the horse's head round and headed away, down the track to the docks where *Rose* with her cargo of gold and sugar was due this month and soon would surely arrive.

He did not go home, though it was nearly dinner time. He returned the horse to the stable and walked, rather uncomfortable in his riding boots, down to the quayside. The lad in the ferryboat was moored on the far side but at Josiah's shout he rowed over.

'Been riding, Mr Cole?' he asked.

Josiah scowled at him and made no reply.

The lad rowed in silence, slightly surprised. Josiah's good nature was well-known on the quayside. But the rumour that he was over-extended had been growing lately. The boy took his ha'penny in silence and pulled his cap as Josiah went up the slimy steps to his quay.

The familiar noise and bustle comforted him. The porters' sledges screeched on the greasy cobbles, the men swearing and cursing as they pulled heavy loads. The quay next to Cole and Sons was again busy with a ship newly in from the West Indies. As Josiah watched they ran a gangplank up to her and the captain came down and greeted the owner. Josiah hung back until they had spoken and the owner gone on board to see for himself the full sweet-smelling hold, then he called to the captain.

'Holloa! Captain Smythe?'

The man turned. 'Oh! Mr Cole, is it?'

'Good crossing?'

'Moderate.'

'How long did it take you?'

'Eight and a half weeks from quayside to quayside.'

'You will have seen my ship, *Rose*?'

'*Rose*? No, I have not seen her.'

Josiah tried to smile but he knew his face was strained. 'Come now, you must have done. I had a letter from her writ in July. She was just off the Sugar Islands then. She will have bought sugar and set sail for England. Surely you will have passed her in the channel. I cannot think why she is not ahead of you.'

The man shook his head gravely. 'I have not seen her, Mr Cole. Not sailing home, nor in the West Indies. No-one spoke of her either. I hope she has not gone astray.'

Josiah laughed mirthlessly. 'Not *Rose*! She is the luckiest ship that ever was and she is commanded by Captain Smedley. If he does not know the way home then no man at sea knows it! She will be home within the sennight, I am certain.'

'Indeed I hope so,' the captain said. 'And we had some black storms. I could have passed within inches of her and not seen her on some of the nights.'

'Exactly!' Josiah exclaimed. 'No. I shall not worry. She will be home any day now.'

The owner came out of the hold, his face bright. 'There's no better sight in the world, is there, Cole?' he demanded. 'A full hold and the smell of fresh sugar!'

Josiah found a weak smile. 'No,' he said with difficulty.

'Here is Mr Cole asking me after his ship *Rose*,' the captain said indiscreetly.

'Is she late?'

'No!' Josiah replied quickly. 'She's just due. I just thought that they might have passed her.'

'Well, I daresay it does not matter to you now,' the owner said jealously. 'With your other interests. Your fine house, and your membership of the Venturers, and your Hot Well. I daresay *Rose* late or early matters very little.'

Josiah's smile was ghastly. 'Very little.'

He went into his warehouse to avoid their stares and up into his old parlour. It was empty and dusty. Only the pieces of furniture which were too shabby to move had been left. He found his father's old broken-seated chair and dragged it to the parlour window.

He sat, looking out over the quay, over the dock, downriver. The tide was going out and the new ship at the quayside would have to be unloaded tomorrow. They were loosening her ropes to let her drop down on the ebbing water to settle on the mud. She would not split her sides, even with her heavy cargo, she was built 'Bristol fashion', strong enough to withstand the stress of the tidal port which dumped all the ships on to their keels in the mud twice a day.

There was no point looking for *Rose*. She would not come into port against the tide. He would have to wait until tomorrow for her now. For a moment Josiah imagined her, riding easily in the water with her cargo of sugar stowed evenly in the hold, moored for the night safely in the Kingsroad anchorage with her lanterns lit fore and aft. He sat still, his eyes on the swiftly draining water, picturing his ship so passionately that it was almost as if he could call her into life.

'*Rose*,' he said.

When Josiah arrived home at five o'clock, late for his dinner, he was irritated to see a travelling coach emblazoned with the Scott arms waiting outside his door. In the morning room Lord Scott was sitting with Frances and Sarah. Josiah came in reluctantly.

'Why, Cole!' Lord Scott exclaimed. 'We thought you had gone down with one of your ships.'

Josiah flinched at the image of a sinking ship. 'I was working,' he said irritably.

Frances glanced at his riding breeches and boots. 'You have been to the Hot Well! Is everything as it should be?'

'No,' Josiah answered shortly.

There was an embarrassed silence. Frances gave her breathless society laugh. 'I am sorry to hear it,' she said. 'You must tell us about it over dinner. Shall I ask them to delay dinner while you change your clothes, Mr Cole?'

'No,' Josiah said stubbornly. 'I can dine like this.'

A shadow crossed Frances's face. 'Whatever you wish,' she said smoothly.

'You are kind to keep me in countenance,' Lord Scott smiled. 'Here I am in my travelling clothes but my niece insisted I stay for dinner. I only called for tea on my way to Whiteleaze.' Lord Scott's travelling clothes were an immaculate suit of light grey cloth with a matching light grey cloak. He looked as if he had never seen a dusty road in his life.

Josiah nodded curtly. 'I hope you will come back to visit the Hot Well and bring your wife.'

Lord Scott shot a quick look at Frances as if to see how he should respond to such a brusque invitation. 'Well, of course we shall come,' he said smoothly. 'As soon as Lady Scott is strong enough to go visiting again. And sorry I am to hear that it is not going well for you there. But these are early days, surely. And it is a new line of business for you.'

'What is wrong, Josiah?' Sarah cut through the light patter of conventional pleasantry.

He looked directly at her. 'Hibbard and Sons are pressing me, the Hot Well is losing money and I am still waiting for *Rose*.'

She nodded, her eyes never leaving his face. 'Early days yet,' she said bravely. 'We've had many a ship come in later than this and bring us nothing but good news.'

Her calmness was like a sheet anchor in a storm. His face cleared a little. 'Yes,' he said. 'You are right.'

There was a short silence.

'I have brought you a gift,' Lord Scott announced, bridging

410

an awkward moment. 'Not of my own choosing, I am sorry to say. I am a messenger for Sir Charles Fairley. He ordered some slave collars for you after his last visit here and had them delivered to me. They are in the hall. Would you like to see them?'

'Of course,' Frances said. She reached out and rang the bell. Mary came and Lord Scott asked her to tell his coachman to bring in the boxes.

'What are these things?' Josiah asked as the coachman carried in eleven narrow boxes and put them on the table at Lord Scott's elbow.

'Slave collars,' Lord Scott replied pleasantly. 'They are very much in fashion in London for slaves. Sir Charles has ordered you a most pretty set, each one engraved with your slaves' names.'

He opened the first box and held one up. It was a light decorative silver chain, carrying a label at the front, also of silver. Engraved on the label was the name 'Julius'.

'Which are you?' Lord Scott asked Mary.

'Mary,' she answered, unsmiling.

He opened a couple of the boxes. 'Ah yes! Here it is.' He turned the black woman around as if she were a doll and fastened the chain around her neck. 'You get a blacksmith to forge the final link,' he told Frances. 'So they are fixed on. They are of ornamental value only, symbolic, if you like. If a slave runs off and wants to be free he can break the chain if he tries hard enough. It is a fancy, merely.'

'Very pretty,' Sarah said. 'Mary, fetch the others. They can all have them on.'

Frances put her hand out to stop her, but could think of no excuse. The other slaves came into the room one by one. Mehuru came in with the little boy John and glanced across at Frances. She met his eyes with a look of veiled warning.

Sarah had taken a few of the boxes and Lord Scott had the others. Without explaining to the slaves what they were doing, they ordered them to stand still and then fastened the chains around their necks and sent them back to the kitchen. Mehuru was the last of the line, left alone in the room with the white people. When Lord Scott held out the chain, Mehuru recoiled. 'I will not have that thing on me.'

Lord Scott hesitated. 'I do not think you have a choice,' he said with a little smile. 'Come here.'

Mehuru took another step backwards. 'I will not have that on me,' he repeated.

'Cicero . . .' Frances said quietly.

He threw her a look which demanded her support. 'It is not my name,' he said desperately.

Lord Scott turned the label around. 'Cicero,' he read. 'It is your name. It is. See the "C"? That means Cicero.'

'I can read,' Mehuru exclaimed. 'My name is not Cicero. My name is Mehuru. I am an envoy of the Yoruba Federation. I will not be labelled like a dog.'

Josiah's temper, which had been on the edge of breaking all day, suddenly snapped. 'You will wear what you are bid!' he shouted, his voice horribly loud in the pretty room. 'You will wear what you are bid and damned well do as you are told!'

With a bound he launched himself across the room and pounded his fist into Mehuru's face, thumping him in the eye. Frances screamed and leaped to her feet. Mehuru, stepping back from Josiah's onslaught, stumbled against a table and fell. In a moment Josiah was on him, forcing him to the ground, pummelling his face and his shoulders. The coachman, at a swift nod from Lord Scott, grabbed Josiah from behind, pinning his arms and dragging him off.

'Josiah! Josiah!' Lord Scott said swiftly. 'Not here. Not before ladies!'

The coachman released him and Josiah felt for the back of a chair to haul himself to his feet, pulling at his neckcloth. The coachman had fallen on Mehuru as soon as Josiah was off him and turned him face down on the floor, twisting his arms behind his back. Mehuru did not struggle; he lay still, his face forced into the carpet.

'Please . . .' Frances said. She was ashen, her hand at her throat, she was gasping for air, 'Please . . .'

'Sit down, Frances, and calm yourself,' Lord Scott said, glancing towards her. The habits of her childhood obedience were very strong. She sank into a seat but did not take her eyes from Mehuru.

'Put it on him.' Lord Scott handed the chain and label to the coachman. 'I advise you to be still,' he said quietly to Mehuru. 'Or you will be taken and beaten.'

Mehuru gave no sign of hearing. He lay completely still. Even when they put the chain around his neck, and fastened it, and crushed the soft metal clasp together so that it could not be undone, he did not move.

'Let him up,' Lord Scott ordered the coachman. The man released Mehuru but stepped quickly back, ready to knock him down at the least sign of disobedience.

Mehuru climbed slowly to his feet. His eye was badly bruised and was swelling fast, the eyelid closing. Frances gave a little cry, hastily suppressed, and turned her face away from him. He looked towards her and his mouth twisted at being shamed before her. Lord Scott thought he had never seen a man brought so low.

'You had better go to your room and wash your face,' he suggested gently.

Mehuru gave him one burning look and stalked from the room. His slave collar caught the light as he turned. The lettering said clearly: 'Cicero'.

Josiah raised his head. 'Lock him in,' he said shortly.

Lord Scott hesitated. 'Is that necessary?' he asked. 'You were not cruel. He surely would not go running to a magistrate with a complaint of cruelty. And this is Bristol after all, no-one would listen to a slave.'

'I don't want him running anywhere,' Josiah retorted crudely. 'Order your man to lock him into his room for the night and bring me the key.'

'Very well.' Lord Scott nodded at his man who bowed and

quietly followed Mehuru. 'You are perhaps right to take care.'

'That is a hundred and ten guineas of bloodstock walking round,' Josiah said sullenly. 'I don't want it walking into the Avon and drowning itself for despair.'

Dinner was late and served with sulky unwillingness. Kbara and the boys had tucked their slave collars under their high neckcloths; but the lower necklines of the women's dresses meant they could not conceal them. Their chains glinted in the candlelight as they moved around the table, each one labelled like a decanter of drink. Frances thought that at last they were clearly marked for all to see, a Bristol commodity, as much goods of the city as sherry or port wine.

Josiah drank heavily at dinner and ate little. Lord Scott, seated on Frances's right and opposite Sarah, kept up an easy flow of talk. He had news of Frances's cousins, and of the health of Lady Scott, banished to Whiteleaze for her lying-in. And he had news of London and the gossip from the City and from Parliament.

'The Abolition debate is rather subdued at the moment,' he reported. 'But there is no doubt that it will rise up again next year. They cannot succeed, not while the gentry is against them, but they can stir up a lot of bad feeling.'

'It will never come to anything,' Sarah said firmly. 'Mr Wilberforce knows nothing of what he is talking about. He should turn his attention to the conditions in the northern cotton mills, that is nearer to his home! But no, he is one of these meddling minds who has to see things at a distance. Why, he has even been party to the setting up of a school for farm labourers' children near Cheddar. There have been many complaints from farmers that they cannot get the children to work as they should, they are forever running off to Mr Wilberforce's school. I should like to see how he would like it if we meddled in his business and started trying to pass laws to ban it.'

'No,' Lord Scott said, smiling at Sarah's indignation. 'I do

414

not think he would like it at all. But surely we cannot hope to avoid Abolition forever. Your company might do well to perhaps consider another venture.'

'I do consider it,' Josiah said grimly. 'I consider my land-based venture every day, and every day it costs me more.' There was a brief embarrassed silence. Lord Scott glanced across at Frances.

'I was sorry to hear that you were unwell, Frances,' he said. 'Are you quite recovered? Bristol suited you so well. I was so pleased when you wrote to me that you were feeling so strong and so happy.'

Frances started, she had not been following the conversation at all. 'I am quite well,' she replied. She was desperate to know if Mehuru was badly hurt, and she was still shocked at the explosion of violence in her own parlour. She could not look at Josiah. Brought up in a vicarage and shielded from the reality of life both by her status and her sex, she was frightened by the least sign of violence. Josiah's anger, erupting in her own morning room, was enough to make him a monster in her eyes.

At the end of the meal when the ladies withdrew, Frances whispered to her uncle that she felt unwell and that she would bid him farewell. He rose from his seat, drew her to him and kissed her on the forehead. 'I am sorry to see you thus,' he said and the phrase took in the whole evening: Frances's sick pallor, and Josiah's despairing rage.

'Such a thing has never happened before . . .'

'I will call again,' he soothed her. 'As soon as Lady Scott has been brought to bed. And you must come and stay with us.' He turned to Sarah and Josiah. 'And you too, Miss Cole, and Josiah. Lady Scott would be delighted to have your company.'

Sarah looked frankly disbelieving, and Josiah hardly heard the invitation. He was slumped in his chair, staring at his glass. Lord Scott's quick assessing gaze passed over him.

'Goodnight,' Frances said, and slipped from the room.

Chapter Thirty-three

As soon as the family had gone to bed the slaves had unlocked Mehuru's door with Cook's spare set of keys and brought him down to the kitchen. He sat, with the children at his feet, in the fireside chair. The women slaves were seated on the kitchen bench, facing him in a solemn row. Kbara sat at the kitchen table. Cook, her feet on the fender, was seated in the opposite chair and clasped her hands in her lap, controlling her sense of outrage. In the flickering light from the fire the slave collars on the women's necks gleamed.

'It isn't right,' Cook said softly. 'I want no part in it. I won't order you. I won't work for them any more if they treat you so. There are many kitchens where I would be welcome. I don't have to stay here and be a party to this.' She rose to her feet and stirred the coals with a poker through the door of the range. 'It isn't right,' she repeated.

Mehuru nodded. He was reminded for a moment of the lengthy counsels of the villages at home. To an outsider it might look as if no-one was capable of any decision, to an outsider it might look as if the men were sitting around idly, chattering. But what was happening was the difficult stages of discussion, working through to a hard-won consensus. What was primitive, Mehuru thought, was the notion of government as a state of permanent warfare – first one side having the upper hand and then the other. The English justice system was no better – a battle between two opposing points of view. The African way was slower and harder but it worked on the belief that agreement was possible, that men and women could come together and find a course to suit them all. It was neither victory nor defeat.

Kbara was in favour of them taking all that they could carry and running away this very night. But the women, especially Elizabeth, were afraid of what might happen. The newspapers were full of advertisements for runaway slaves and the rewards offered would tempt anyone.

'But don't you see,' Mehuru argued, 'that the rewards show that slaves are hidden by English people. The owners have to offer a high reward to make English people betray the runaway slaves. The rewards should make us more confident, not less. We could not stay in Bristol, of course. We would have to go to London and there are thousands of people of our colour living there.'

'Maybe,' Mary said slowly. 'But they would offer a high reward for all of us, and if we stay together, as we want, we would be easy to find. Besides, what could we do?'

'Mehuru and I could work,' Kbara said.

'Doing what?'

'On the quayside, there are lots of black men working at the port.'

'And we could work as house servants,' Martha suggested. 'Laundry, or waiting tables, or housework. We've been trained well enough. Elizabeth could be a parlourmaid or even a lady's maid. I could try out as a cook.'

'Could we get the boys apprenticed to a trade?' Elizabeth asked. 'They need proper work. I don't want them working down at the docks. It is rough and it is dangerous, and besides, anyone who wants a slave can just come by and thieve them away from us.'

Mehuru's face was hard. 'They can't get an apprenticeship in London. The Lord Mayor himself has ordered that no black boys can be trained for work. They passed a special law to ban black boys from being trained.' He gave a bitter little smile. 'They must think us very skilful, if the white men have to be protected against our apprentices.'

417

'And what about the girls?' Elizabeth pressed. 'The girls need work too. I don't want them growing up with nothing to do but dirty work. Little Susan is as bright as any child I've ever known. She should be sent to school, if we were at home . . .' She broke off. At home a bright girl could find herself a training, she could work in the palace and rise as high as her skills took her. 'It seems a long way away now,' Elizabeth said sadly.

'What about going home?' Kbara asked. 'What about this Sierra Leone? We could go to London and take a ship to Sierra Leone. It's not Yoruba, it's not my people, but at least we're in the right place. At least we're in Africa. And we could maybe travel overland, back to our homes.'

Mehuru shook his head. 'We can't travel home. The trading routes have been destroyed, there are no caravans we could join. There are no villages we could visit. Inland from the coast for miles and miles the country has been wrecked. The people are enslaved or in hiding, the fields are growing weeds. No-one travels down the rivers unless they are hunting for slaves. The country is unsafe.

'And I doubt very much that this Sierra Leone is safe either. I've seen the pamphlets, I read them to you all, but I also heard from a man at the Constitution Society. He says that it is not a proper colony at all but just somewhere for England to dump unwanted freed slaves. They got volunteers for the first settlement by refusing black beggars their dole unless they signed on and went. When the ships were blown ashore at Plymouth the captains battened down the hatches and wouldn't let the black people go ashore. They had to eat the rations they had for the trip while they were waiting, so they were hungry on the voyage. They would not let them have stoves or candles. What does that remind you of? A long sea journey with not enough to eat and cold all the time? What does it remind you of, Kbara?'

'But if Africa is at the end of it? Africa and freedom?'

'What if at the end of it there is a couple of farms, a stockade

418

fence, and the whole of the country from north and south making war to take slaves, selling slaves at a profit? How long do you think we would last? And these little children would be taken by slavers again. Do you think they would survive that journey twice?'

Kbara was silent for a moment. 'So what shall we do?' he demanded. 'What shall we do? We have to do something now, while Josiah is away from the house all day and Sarah is too worried about the business to watch us. And we will not bear these collars. This is our chance, Mehuru.'

'I know,' Mehuru said gently. 'You are right. Our chance is now and we should take it. I don't think we can go back to Africa and I don't think we should stay in Bristol. But there are other cities and towns. There are places where we could get work, perhaps send the children to school, teach them trades. Stuart Hadley would help us get away, he would advise us where to go.

'I cannot stay here.' He touched his shirt where the silver collar rubbed against the skin of his neck. It was smooth and well-made but he flinched as though it scratched him with every move he made. 'I cannot bear it,' he said.

'We stay together,' Mary decided. 'I want to stay with you, all of you.'

Elizabeth dropped her hand on Mary's. 'You are like my sister. I could not bear to be without you.'

'I will ask Stuart to advise us,' Mehuru said. 'I will creep out and find him tomorrow.'

Josiah wakened in the morning with a thick head and a foul taste in his mouth. He washed quickly and dressed without care. He brushed past Kbara in the hall and his silent sulky step to one side reminded Josiah that Mehuru was still locked away.

He turned, ran up the stairs and tapped on Frances's bedroom door. She was awake but still in her bed. When she saw him she shrank back against her pillows and her hand went to her throat. She was afraid of him. She remembered the sullen rage of his drinking through dinner, and the sudden explosion of violence when he had pummelled Mehuru to the ground. Frances flinched at the sight of him and underneath her fear was resentment.

Josiah did not even notice. He was too anxious about his business – too absorbed in the disaster which was building every day. He had forgotten the slow growth of confidence and ease between them, he had forgotten the pleasure of making Frances smile. He had forgotten the ease and sense of plenty in the luxurious house and the slowly blooming beauty of his expensively bought wife. All he could see now was the mounting weight of his debts and the steady tick-tick of accruing interest. All he saw when he looked at Frances, pale and defensive in her bed, was another expense.

'The slaves are supposed to be in your keeping,' he said brusquely. 'See that Cicero is fit to be released this morning, and have him ready for sale. If I can speak with Stephen Waring I shall close the sale today. And the little boy. I will sell the others as soon as they can be advertised. We are desperate for money and I am sick of having the house cluttered up with their idle bodies.' He tossed the key to Mehuru's room on the bed where it fell with a weighty clink.

'He cannot be sold,' Frances protested. Her voice was a little thread against Josiah's angry gruffness.

'Why the devil not?'

He had never sworn in her presence before. Frances flinched. 'I . . . He is promised to my Uncle Scott,' she lied quickly. 'You can sell Julius to Mr Waring. He will not know the one from the other but my Uncle Scott specifically asked for Cicero.'

'He's a fool then,' Josiah snapped. 'After the man's behaviour he should be shipped out to the plantations.'

'You would not . . .'

'Only because it would not pay,' Josiah said spitefully. 'If I could sell him for hounds' meat at a profit I would do so.

420

Now get up, madam, and set the house to rights. You are idling here while everything is going wrong. The slaves are your charge and they are running wild, God knows how much they cost me. God knows how much you all cost me.'

He stamped from her bedroom, leaving the door carelessly ajar. Frances stayed very still in her bed, frozen with fear, until she heard his feet thunder down the stairs and across the hall, and the front door slam.

It was a brisk November morning in the square. A gardener was sweeping the fallen leaves into large damp piles. Josiah did not look up at the pale sky nor enjoy the fresh cold air on his face. He could smell the tang of the incoming tide as it washed the flotsam and garbage back into the heart of the city. This tide should bring in *Rose*, he thought, and strode down to the quayside to scan the splashing water for his ship. He looked along the length of his quay in all its neat lonely emptiness. He looked downriver to where the gorge started to rear up. There was no ocean-weary ship being towed inland. There was no sign of her. There was still no sign of her.

In the house in Queens Square Frances dressed quickly and then climbed the stairs to Mehuru's room, the key in her hand. She tapped on his door.

'Yes?' he answered in Yoruban.

'It is me,' Frances said. 'I have the key.'

She fitted it in the lock and opened the door. Mehuru had washed and shaved and changed his linen. He looked elegant and impassive. His eye was bruised, a dark shadow against the darkness of his skin. 'I am sorry,' Frances said inadequately.

'Will you take my collar off?'

She looked down at his feet. 'I don't dare,' she admitted shortly. 'I don't dare go against him.'

'I will run away,' he warned. 'I will run and you will never see me again.'

She stole a quick glance at his face and then looked away

421

again. 'Indeed I think you should go,' she said, her voice very low. 'He wants to sell you, he said he would close the sale today. I have delayed him with a lie and so he will sell Julius instead. I cannot keep you safe, Mehuru. I cannot keep any of you safe. I am sorry, I am so sorry.'

'We will go tonight,' he said.

She nodded without looking at him. 'Very well.'

'We will never come back.'

They stood, a foot apart, neither touching nor looking at each other.

'I know I will never see you again,' she whispered. 'I wish you God speed.'

'Won't you come with me?' he asked. 'Take the chance now, Frances. Now while there is nothing to stay here for. Josiah is in trouble, Sarah openly dislikes you. Come away with me, we will find somewhere to live, we will find somewhere that we can be together.'

She shrugged her shoulders, a small unhappy gesture of defeat. 'I cannot,' she said. 'I dare not. I have no money and I cannot work. I am ill, Mehuru. You would not get very far with a sick woman. And I have no courage.' She looked up at him honestly. 'I have no courage at all. I saw him strike you last night and I did nothing but jump to my feet and say, "Josiah!" and then I poured him his tea. I am ashamed.'

He shrugged. 'There was little you could do,' he said tightly. 'And I have had worse beatings.'

'But I did nothing,' she persisted. 'Nothing to save you, nothing to save Died of Shame. I lack courage, Mehuru. When I was a girl I was full of spirit, but I have been made into the very essence of an English lady – all I can do is watch and wring my hands, and pour the tea.'

'You could run away from it all,' he suggested. 'Run away to be the wife of an African, be an African woman.'

'I dare not.'

There was a noise of a door opening below them. 'Frances?' Sarah called, her voice sharp.

The colour rushed into Frances's face as she turned to go at once, instantly obedient. Mehuru put his black hand on the white sleeve of her gown.

'Hire a carriage,' he said quickly and insistently. 'Let us drive out together this afternoon, for the last time, Frances. Let us be together this afternoon for we will never see each other again.'

She kept her head turned away, she could not bear to look at him, she did not dare to risk looking into his intent face and seeing the longing in his eyes.

'Yes,' she whispered and went downstairs.

Josiah went for his breakfast to the quayside coffee house. The door was swinging open and shut as busy men pushed in and out. The cold draughts billowed in and the sweet smell of rum, tobacco smoke and sugar billowed out. There was a small silence as the traders saw Josiah – a pause no longer than a heartbeat – but Josiah heard it. It was the silence of the herd when they notice an animal mortally sick. They were ready to turn on him and drive him out. They were ready to eat him alive. Their own survival was a stronger force than any friendship or loyalty. The word was out that Josiah was over-extended and that *Rose* was two weeks overdue.

A man rose from a table in his path and put a hand on his sleeve. 'Josiah,' he said pleasantly. 'A word with you.'

Josiah was on his way to the top table, to the Merchant Venturers' table. He hesitated, scowling at the man from under his brows. 'Yes?'

'A little bill overdue, a trifle,' the man said. 'From fitting out *Lily* when she was last in port.'

Josiah nodded. 'An oversight,' he said gruffly. 'I'll see to it. Send it in again, it must have been mislaid.'

'I *have* sent it in,' the man said. 'Twice. I would trouble you for the money now. It is thirty guineas.'

Josiah twitched his sleeve from the man's grasp. 'D'you

think I settle my bills at my breakfast?' he demanded. 'Come to my warehouse at noon and I will pay you then.'

'I knew you when you paid your bills at breakfast, and when you touted for business at dinner,' the man replied angrily. 'And I have been to your warehouse twice yesterday and once today and there was no-one there to give me satisfaction. If it's no trouble to you, Josiah, I'll take my thirty guineas now.'

'Oh, for God's sake!' Josiah exclaimed. He plunged his hand into the big pocket of his cape and drew out a leather purse, which he tossed at the man. 'Take that, and if it is not enough I will settle up with you later, it is all I have on me. Unless you would like the buttons off my coat? They are solid brass.'

The man stood his ground. 'I am sorry if I offend you, Josiah, but it has been a long time. I cannot give you more credit. I dare not take the risk.'

'I do not trade on credit!' Josiah exclaimed, goaded beyond endurance. 'I am not a bad risk.'

The man said nothing. The whole coffee shop was silent, listening to the exchange. Josiah glared around and the men, who had been staring, at once turned to each other and chattered noisily or applied themselves to their breakfast plates. They all recognised the anger of a man cornered, whose luck is running out.

'I bid you good day,' Josiah muttered and strode to the top table.

The man turned and rejoined his friends. Under cover of the table he tipped the contents of Josiah's purse out into his hand. There was £23. 10s. 8d. He counted it quickly, returned it to the purse and tucked it in his pocket.

'It's not the full amount,' he said quietly to his neighbour. 'But I think it's the most I'm going to get.'

'He owes me for some stores,' the man replied uneasily. 'I had not thought to press my bill.' He glanced up at the top table. 'And there's nothing to be had from him now. You've picked the bones clean this morning, Tobias.'

The man nodded. 'Catch him another morning. It's the

only way you will get your bills met, I believe. There will be no more credit for Cole and Sons from my business. Take my word for it: he's going down.'

Chapter Thirty-four

Frances changed into her driving gown and waited at her bedroom window for the hired carriage to come round to the door. When she heard the rattle of the wheels and the ring of the horses' metal-shod hooves in the street she ran downstairs. Sarah was in the hall. 'You hired the carriage?' she demanded, outraged.

'I wanted to drive out,' Frances said.

'We cannot afford your extravagance,' Sarah said bitterly. 'Do you know how much we owe the stable already?'

'I won't do it again.' Frances pulled on her gloves and would not meet Sarah's accusing stare. 'Just this time, Sarah.'

'This time, and then another time, and then another. We cannot afford it,' Sarah maintained. 'Do you not understand? We have no money to pay for such luxuries. We cannot afford it. You must send it back.'

Mehuru came into the hall and opened the front door for Frances.

'Wait!' Sarah snapped at him.

'I have to go!' Frances breathed and slipped out of the door and down the steps before Sarah could catch her.

Mehuru bowed to Sarah and swiftly followed Frances to the carriage and handed her into the driving seat.

'Sit beside me,' Frances said breathlessly. Mehuru nodded to the lad from the stables to let the horses go, and swung himself up beside her. 'You must fold your arms and sit very straight,' she said. He gave a wry smile and did as he was bid. Frances flicked the reins to make the horses go forward.

When they were clear of the square she relaxed a little. 'I thought she would stop me.' She gave a quavery little laugh. 'I thought she would lock me in my room rather than see me spend money.'

'They are getting desperate,' Mehuru observed.

'I would have insisted, however angry she was.' Frances flicked out her whip and feathered it neatly back. 'Shall we drive up to the Downs?' she asked.

'Anywhere,' he said. 'Let's drive to Africa.'

She caught her breath on a little sound halfway between a laugh and a sob. 'You know I wish I could,' she said.

He nodded. 'This is our last time together, Frances. I will not ask and you need not refuse. Let us just be together for this afternoon. At least we have these hours, and the sun is warm, and you are well, and I am going to be free.'

'Perhaps we can be happy just for this afternoon,' she said doubtfully.

'Yes we can.'

She steadied the horses over the little bridge and then let them walk up the steep hill of Park Street. Even in the short time since they had last ridden out more building work had started and foundations were outlined where new houses would rise.

The workmen were stripped down to their breeches and torn ragged shirts in the cold November sunshine. Mehuru looked at their skinny muscled backs and weary faces. 'It is a cruel country,' he said. 'I have yet to see a working man or woman who looks properly fed and rested.'

Frances did not turn her eyes from the road between the jogging ears of the offside horse.

'Do you not see?' he asked.

'There is much hardship,' she conceded but still she did not look round.

'I am talking about these men,' Mehuru prompted her again. 'These, working here, digging this trench.'

Still she did not look round.

'Will you not look at them?' he demanded.

She glanced at him and he could see her face was pink with embarrassment. 'They are half-naked, Mehuru!' she said with quiet indignation. 'I cannot stare at them!'

He gave a shout of laughter. 'Oh, Frances!' he exclaimed. 'If I live here until I am an old man I will never understand. You are a married woman, you see Josiah, don't you? You saw me.'

Frances caught her breath. The memory of Mehuru in her bedroom with the moonlight cascading down the darkness of his body was too vivid.

'Why cannot you look at some poor working man in his breeches?'

'Because I am a lady,' Frances snapped, goaded to reply. 'There are things I should not see. There are things I should not discuss – even with you.'

'I wish I could hold you,' he said softly. 'And kiss this nonsense from you.'

At once her face softened. 'I wish it too,' she whispered.

He smiled at her profile. 'Sometimes I think you are two women, not one,' he said. 'The stiff cold lady with her strict manners and rules, and sometimes you are my love, my little love, and as natural and easy as an African woman.'

She nodded. 'I have been brought up to be an English lady, I think it is too late to change now.'

'I don't think so,' he muttered stubbornly under his breath. But she just shook her head and would not say any more.

At the top of Park Street, the buildings petered out into rough yards and the road became a mud track through the fields. Frances took the left-hand fork for Clifton, skirting the round mound of Brandon Hill. High up on the hillside washerwomen were spreading out their linen to dry on the grass.

Frances clicked to the horses and they went forward at a brisk trot.

'These are good horses,' she said approvingly. 'Josiah

promised to buy me a pair and a carriage of my own when the Trade mends . . . if the Trade mends.'

'Why did you ever marry him?' Mehuru demanded.

Frances was silent for a moment. 'I don't know if I can explain it to you,' she said. She slowed the horses and pulled them over to let a wagon pass by which was carrying glass bottles carefully packed in straw. Ahead of them they could see the pretty hills and valleys of the approach to Clifton. On their left was the boggy ground of Rownham Meads. Migrant birds crossed and recrossed the sky, searching for homes for the long cold winter ahead. Higher above them the seagulls soared and circled, their white wings gleaming like silver in the bright sunshine. In the pools of standing water and the marshy mud a tall grey heron was fishing.

'What you must realise is that there was nothing for me,' Frances began. 'Absolutely nothing. I had no money, I did not even have a home. My home had been the rectory and then the new rector and his family moved in. I did not want to be a poor relation living on charity in Scott House.'

She paused and glanced at Mehuru, who was listening carefully and trying to make sense of what she was saying. In his country a girl without money or a husband would still be an honoured member of a family. They would naturally take her in and she would help with the work of the family and eat with them, and play with the children. The idea of a person being redundant was impossible to his way of thinking.

'Was there nowhere that you could go?' he asked.

Frances shook her head. 'I took employment,' she said. 'As a governess.'

'Like a servant?'

Frances made a little grimace. 'In some ways worse. The pay is very poor but you dare not complain. The children can treat you as they wish, they can be cruel –' She broke off. 'I had not known how cruel children could be,' she said. 'I could not make them mind me and their mother laughed at me.

429

Every morning I used to wake up and dread the day ahead. I was unhappy every moment of the day.' She paused. 'I am not exaggerating. Every single moment of the day.' Mehuru was silent. The horses walked briskly along the track away from the river up the hill towards Clifton, where they could hear the rumble of wagons and the sound of chisels on stone.

'Josiah advertised for a governess. I applied for the post and met him. He did not tell me what the work was, but said he would write to me. Then, when he wrote proposing marriage, it was as if my prayers had been answered. In return for being his wife I am fed, I am clothed, and when I get old I will *still* be fed and clothed and live in a fine house. I would do anything rather than go back to governessing again, Mehuru. It was worse than slavery –' She stopped. 'I am sorry, that is a foolish thing to say to you; but it was a little like slavery in some ways. I was not free to do as I wished. I could not come and go as I wished. And they were free to get rid of me whenever they wanted.'

'You are not free now,' Mehuru pointed out.

'But neither is Josiah,' she replied. 'We are both bound by our agreement. He has to keep me, whatever else happens.'

They drove in silence for a little while, the horses straining in their collars to climb the hill away from the river. They were driving along the edge of the rising gorge to the heights of Clifton. To their left, and far below, hidden by the over-hang of the cliff, was the riverside and Josiah's colonnade of shops and the Hot Well. A pretty track, too steep for anything but the most nimble of the Bristol saddle horses, zig-zagged in sharp hairpin bends down the cliffside to the Hot Well at its foot. The few healthy clients of the Hot Well would some-times climb up to Clifton to enjoy the view and walk in the woods.

Before them was a handsome street, built as a terrace, in pretty uniformity but stepped irregularly to match the mount-ing ground. They started along a terrace marked 'Granby Place' which deteriorated at the far end to a pile of builder's

430

stones and an earth track. Frances laughed and pulled up the horses. 'We should have brought a guide,' she said. 'I have got us hopelessly lost.'

They looked to their right. There were thick woodlands tumbling down the hills to the track, cleared here and there by the lime burners, whose stone kilns could sometimes be seen among the thinning foliage of the trees. Above them there was a large attractive stone building and a high scaffolding of some kind of winding gear.

'That can't be a mine,' Frances said. 'There are surely no collieries here in Clifton?'

'Do you want to walk up and see?' Mehuru asked. 'Someone can hold the horses.'

'Why not?' Frances replied. Mehuru whistled at an urchin who had been sitting on a wall observing them and the lad came forward to hold the reins.

Mehuru got down from the box, helped Frances to the ground and took her arm. They strolled together up the grassy track to the new building. In a sea of dust and dirt workmen were drilling a hole with the winding gear screeching above their heads. To the right of them other men were setting square-cut stones on the foundations of what would be a grand and imposing building.

'Ask them what building this will be,' Frances said. 'It looks big enough for a town hall.'

Mehuru went over to speak to one of the men who had a paper plan pinned to a board. The man looked back at Frances, pulled off his cap and came over.

'Good day, madam,' he said. 'The darkie said you were asking about the building.'

'Yes.'

He held the plan before her. It showed the outline of a large square building subdivided into small rooms at one end with a large assembly room or ballroom at the other. Over the top of the plan in handsome script was the legend: 'The New Hot Well: Pump Room and Bath Houses.'

Frances read it, and then read it again. 'What is this?' she demanded.

'The new Hot Well,' the man replied.

'What d'you mean?'

'It is a new Hot Well, madam. A new spa. Here we are drilling down for the hot water, and here will be the spa building. You can see it here, on the plan. It will be a handsome assembly room, and here you see bath rooms for immersion in the hot water. There will be houses built on each side as well and they will be supplied with hot water from the spa. Hot running water! Think of it!'

Frances put her hand to her throat which felt as if it were closing tight. 'I don't understand. There must be some mistake!'

'I hope not!' The man's broad face grinned. 'For we have drilled down nearly two hundred feet and we will hit the spring soon.'

'But what spring is it?' Frances demanded. 'You must be near the Hot Well, at the foot of this cliff.'

'We are straight above it, madam,' the foreman said. 'It is directly below us. That is why we know that we will hit a hot water spring. The old Hot Well is sited on it. We will tap the Hot Well spring.'

Frances recoiled and staggered. At once Mehuru's arm was around her waist, but she did not even feel his touch. 'Who knows of this?' she asked, her voice sharp. 'Who gave permission? Whose land is this? How can you just drill here without permission?'

The man was offended. 'You'll have to take all that up with the landlord. I am just ordered to supervise the men. I am sorry if I have given you offence, madam. You did ask.' He bowed and turned to walk away from her.

Frances tore herself from Mehuru's support and ran after him. 'But who is the landlord?' She snatched at his arm to detain him. 'You must stop your men working! They have no right to do this! My husband will hear of it!'

He pulled himself free and glanced at Mehuru, hoping he would take her away. Frances's face was white and agonised, and the man feared a scene. 'I suppose a man can do what he wants on his own land, madam,' he said defensively. 'I have to do my work, I have my orders; you must forgive me.' He walked away from her, holding his plans.

'It is not possible!' Frances screamed. Again she ran after him and caught his hand. 'You *will* tell me who has ordered this! Who is the owner? You *must* tell me! My husband is an important man. He is a member of the Merchant Venturers. He will stop them!'

'Why, it is owned by the Merchant Venturers of Bristol!' he shouted impatiently. He pulled himself from her grasp and turned away. 'It is their project, sub-let by them to Mr Stephen Waring and Mr James of the old Hot Well,' he threw over his shoulder. 'You must speak to them if you have a complaint, madam, it is nothing to do with me.'

Frances stumbled back to the carriage, staggering blindly on the uneven ground and Mehuru had to lift her back on the driving box.

'What is the matter? What is it?' he demanded.

'Get me home,' she gasped.

Mehuru drove while Frances clung on to the box seat, her hat askew, her face white.

'What is it? Are you ill, Frances?'

She gave a little moan. 'I want Josiah.'

'What the devil is wrong?' he nearly shouted at her. He flicked the horses and let them rattle down the hill.

'I think we are ruined,' she said through numb lips. 'I want Josiah.' And she would say nothing more.

'Tell me,' he said. 'Tell me what the matter is. I don't understand.'

She looked at him but she did not see him, he was irrelevant to her. 'I want Josiah,' she whispered. 'Take me home.'

He set his jaw and drove as fast as he dared on the rough track. He saw Frances was clinging to the rail on the carriage, and was badly jolted, but he did not pull up the horses, and she did not ask him to drive slower. He glanced sideways at her once, and saw that her face was set and agonised. They rumbled down the hill of Park Street and she clung to the rail and looked straight ahead. A carriage coming up the other way paused, and Mrs Waring waved to her. Frances went by, unseeing, her face ugly and blank.

'Get me home,' she said as he pulled the horses up to let another carriage come across the bridge. 'I want Josiah.'

As soon as they were at the door, she clambered down, not waiting for him to come round and lift her for that precious little moment of intimacy. She had forgotten that this was their last time together. Everything was pushed aside by her need to see Josiah. She jumped down from the carriage step, lifted the hem of her driving gown and raced to the front door, her little kid boots pounding up the steps. She snatched the knocker and hammered it until she heard someone coming.

Kbara hurried to let her in. She pushed past him without explanation and whirled down the hall to Josiah's study. She flung open the door without knocking as Josiah turned in surprise from company ledgers.

'Why, Frances!'

'Do you know of a new Hot Well?' she demanded, the words tumbling over each other. 'Do you know of a new Hot Well in Clifton?'

'What?' he asked. He took in her white face and her dishevelled appearance. 'Frances, what is the matter? Sit down, let me ring for Elizabeth. You look ill.'

She nearly screamed at him. 'Josiah! For God's sake answer me! Do you know that there is a new Hot Well being built in Clifton?'

Her meaning slowly sank in. 'A new Hot Well?' he asked. 'A new Hot Well? In Clifton? That is not possible. There is no spring in Clifton. It is on limestone. It is dry.'

She dropped into a chair and wrenched at the ribbons on

her bonnet, and stripped off her gloves. 'I drove up to Clifton,' she recounted, her voice low. It struck Josiah she was like a woman who has seen a fatal accident, who has to set the scene, who has to describe the surroundings.

'I saw a new building and beside it some winding gear. I was curious so I walked towards it.'

'Yes,' he said. He could feel himself growing cold, as if the sun were not streaming in through the window, as if there were not a good cheerful fire in the grate. 'Yes. Go on.'

'Mehuru spoke to the foreman and he brought me the plans of the building,' she went on. 'It is to be an assembly room, a big ballroom and promenading room, and bath houses. They are drilling down through the cliff above our Hot Well. They are going to take the water from our spring. Do you hear me? They are taking the water from our Hot Well. They are even planning to pump the water to new houses to be built in Clifton. It will be a great spa resort, with a terrace of houses each with their own hot mineral baths.' She licked her dry lips and swallowed down the lump in her throat. 'He showed me the plan,' she said helplessly. 'And the foundations are dug and the walls going up.'

'This is not possible,' Josiah said weakly. 'There must be some dreadful mistake. I shall go up there at once. D'you still have the carriage out? Cicero shall drive me up there at once. It is not possible, Frances. You must have made a mistake.'

She shook her head. 'I saw the winding gear. I saw the winding gear where they are drilling. The foreman told me they have gone down two hundred feet, but they know they will find hot water, because they are drilling down to the Hot Well.'

Josiah refused to believe it. 'It cannot be. How could such a thing happen without the permission of the Corporation? Without the consent of the Merchant Venturers? It must be a mistake.'

'It *has* the consent of the Merchant Venturers!' Frances

cried out with sudden passion. 'Don't you see! Don't you see, Josiah? It is their land! They are the landlords. That is why they are buying land in Clifton! Why they own the freehold for Clifton and all the Downs up to the very cliff edge! They own everything! And they are developing Clifton as a new spa. They have cheated you, Josiah. They have cheated you of everything and now you own a spa with no water, and you have signed a ten-year lease!'

He stared at her open-mouthed. 'Who said this?' he cried angrily. 'This is a calumny! They are my friends. It is a mistake!'

'Who advised you to buy into the Hot Well and gave you sight of the account books and sponsored you at the Merchant Venturers' dinner?' Frances hissed at him, her teeth bared. Her hair was falling down, her face was ashen and bony.

Josiah hated her at that moment. 'Waring,' he answered. 'My friend Stephen Waring.'

She sunk back in the chair as if he had knifed her in the heart. 'He is the landlord of the new Hot Well.' She could hardly speak through her cold lips. She could hardly breathe. 'Him and Mr James, the old tenant of the Hot Well. They have sold you a pup, Josiah. They have taken your money and now they will take your spring water too.'

Josiah staggered and felt behind him for his chair. His knees buckled and he dropped into it. 'It is not possible,' he whispered, his face grey. 'I have borrowed and borrowed against the profits I thought to make. I paid two thousand pounds for the purchase alone. And I have to find near a thousand pounds a year for ten years for the lease, and the interest on the borrowing and the wages and the furnishings.'

Frances moved her head restlessly, her eyes closed.

Josiah looked at his desk, put his hand on the papers before him, stroked the page of his ship's accounts. 'I am ruined,' he said disbelievingly. 'They took me in and ruined me.'

Frances put her hand to her throat, pulling at her collar, gasping for breath. Her face was even whiter than before.

'Josiah,' she gasped. She could hardly catch her breath to say his name.

'I am ruined,' he said again. 'They have ruined me.'

'Josiah . . .' she began and then she gave a sharp cry of pain.

Mehuru, who had been loitering in the hall, could not stop himself. He burst into the room in time to see Frances pitch forward out of her chair. He caught her up but her head had hit the fender and she was bleeding from her temple. Her lips were blue, she was not breathing.

'Fetch the doctor!' Mehuru shouted. 'Fetch Stuart Hadley!' He gathered her to him, trying to warm her. Her neck lolled as limp as a broken doll. Not knowing what to do, Mehuru rocked her, holding her tight. 'Frances!' he cried urgently. 'Frances!'

She was not breathing. Mehuru sprung to his feet.

'I am ruined,' Josiah repeated quietly. He had not moved from his desk.

Mehuru threw a quick contemptuous look at him and then ran for the hall. 'Kbara!' he yelled.

Kbara came running up from the kitchen. 'Take a horse from the carriage shafts and ride and find Stuart Hadley the doctor!' Mehuru commanded. 'Tell him Frances is ill, she is like a dead woman. Go at once!'

Kbara nodded and dashed out of the front door.

Mehuru turned with Frances still in his arms and strode towards the stairs. Sarah Cole appeared in the parlour door. 'What on earth is happening?' she demanded.

'Fetch the women,' Mehuru threw over his shoulder. 'Frances is ill.'

Sarah looked incredulously at him, carrying Frances in his arms and then ran up the stairs behind him. 'Put her down!' she ordered. 'At once.'

Mehuru strode up the stairs without even hearing her. He kicked open the door to Frances's bedroom and laid her gently down on the bed. He took the high neat-buttoned neck of

437

her driving gown and ripped it open, sending buttons spinning across the room.

'How dare you!' Sarah exclaimed.

He caught Frances up and shook her gently. 'Breathe!' he urged her, passionately low-voiced in his own language. 'Breathe! What is there to stop breathing for? Breathe, you little fool!'

Sarah recoiled from his passion. Elizabeth dodged around her and came into the room with a tumbler of brandy in one hand and a bottle of water in the other. She dashed the water in Frances's blue face and then Mehuru held Frances's limp shoulders while Elizabeth dribbled brandy into her mouth.

Frances choked then struggled against their hold and sat up whooping and gasping for air.

Mehuru nodded and ripped her dress further, pulling the wet cloth away from her skin. Elizabeth snatched up a warm comforter from the foot of the bed and Mehuru put it around Frances's naked shoulders and held her tight.

'Don't try to speak,' he said urgently. 'Stuart will be here in a moment. Just breathe, Frances. Breathe!'

The dreadful blue was fading from her lips though her skin was still waxy white.

'Get a warming pan,' Mehuru directed Elizabeth. 'She is too cold.'

Elizabeth pushed past Sarah in the doorway and shouted down the stairs in a string of incomprehensible Yoruban. There was an answering shout from the kitchen, and one of the boys came running upstairs with a tinder box. He dodged under Sarah's elbow and knelt to light the fire. Elizabeth came back into the room and started to remove Frances's skirt.

'Cicero, leave the room,' Sarah demanded, coming forward, trying to reclaim some order.

He gave her a look which threw her back on her heels, and raised Frances as if she were a little girl. He picked up a pair of scissors from her dressing table and cut the laces of her stays. Elizabeth pulled the skirt away and turned back the covers of the bed. Mehuru lifted Frances, wrapped in the comforter and wearing only her shift, into the bed as Martha came into the room, pushed around Sarah's back to thrust the warming pan under the covers at the foot of the bed and take the chill off the sheets.

The fire blazed into life as the kindling caught and then the little pieces of coal. Frances opened her eyes and managed a weak smile at Mehuru. He caught her hand and crushed it to his mouth. 'Little fool,' he said. 'Lie still. And don't speak.'

She closed her eyes again. 'I hurt,' she whispered in a small voice. She put her hand between the swell of her breasts. 'In here,' she said. 'My heart.'

'Shall I open the window?' Elizabeth asked Mehuru.

He glanced at Frances's pinched face. 'No,' he said, fearful of the cold English air. 'Let us keep her warm until Stuart comes.'

He turned around. 'Now go,' he said to the boy. 'Martha – out.' He was suddenly aware of Sarah, standing like a stone in the middle of the room, taking in everything, his easy air of command, the instinctive obedience of the others, and his loving intimacy with Frances. He did not hesitate for a moment. 'Please leave, Miss Cole,' he said. 'Frances needs to rest.'

'What *do* you think you are doing?' she demanded and her voice was like a blade.

He stepped forward and swept her, physically swept her from the room. 'I said, she needs to rest,' he repeated as soon as the door was shut behind them both, and Frances could not hear. 'Her health is the most important thing. You can speak with me later.'

'I shall have you whipped,' she promised. 'What do you think . . .'

'Your brother is sick too,' he interrupted her. 'You should go to him.'

She checked, half-disbelieving, half-alarmed, but he turned from her and went back into Frances's bedroom. 'I have noted this,' she said threateningly to the closing door. 'My brother shall know of this!' She stood irresolute for a moment but then her anxiety for Josiah overcame her and she ran down the stairs to his room.

He was sitting at his desk, flicking the pages of the big account book forward, and then flicking them back again. Something in that careless, almost childlike movement arrested Sarah on the threshold.

'Josiah?'

When he turned to look at her the years had fallen away from his face and he had the open innocent gaze of a child. 'They have gulled me, Sarah,' he said. His voice was small, like a little boy shocked by some hurt. 'They took me in and played me along and they have gulled me for all of our money.'

She could feel herself chilled all through. 'How so?' she asked very steadily. 'How so, Josiah? What have they done to you?'

'They sold me the Hot Well and a ten-year lease, nine thousand pounds over ten years and two thousand pounds down,' Josiah said.

Sarah closed her eyes, briefly repelled by the large capital sums. 'But you saw the books, it will pay,' she said. 'We knew this, we knew we could manage it. When the *Rose* comes in . . .'

Josiah nodded. 'It looked like safe investment. And I borrowed money to buy it.'

'But it *is* a good investment,' Sarah repeated. 'You saw the books. It will run at a profit. You would not take a risk. Not with those sums!'

Josiah cleared his throat. 'It would have done,' he said. 'And I was out daily to inspect the business. You know how often I have been down there, Sarah. You know I hired an architect to draw up plans, I was not careless. I was not careless with our business.'

Sarah nodded. 'I know, Brother. I know.'

'Then they sued me, to make me keep the tap open,' he

440

continued softly. 'I could not think why they did that . . . but now it seems . . . it seems to me . . .' He broke off. 'If I complain of them there will be no-one on my side. The people of the city, the Corporation, the Company . . . everyone thinks that I am in the wrong. The Merchant Venturers have the interests of the city at heart and I am – what did they call me? – an upstart.'

Sarah nodded silently.

'They have destroyed my reputation,' Josiah went on in a thin little voice. 'No-one will defend me now. They made me look like a mountebank. No-one will speak up for me now.'

'But the Hot Well will still earn money . . .' Sarah started.

'I did not think to look up,' Josiah said inconsequently. 'On the cliff top high above my Hot Well . . .'

'Why?' Sarah prompted urgently. 'Why should you have looked up?'

'Because they are drilling down,' he said simply. His face was ghastly. 'They are drilling down into my spring. They are building a new assembly rooms, new bath houses, they are piping the water away from my spa. And they are calling it the new Hot Well. They have not even chosen another name. They are advertising to everyone that my Hot Well is the old one. Soon it will be dry. They are calling theirs the new Hot Well.'

Sarah hissed like a snake through her gritted teeth. 'The new Hot Well? Are you sure?'

He nodded. 'Frances has seen the building. The foreman showed her the plans.'

Sarah strode over to the window and gazed out into the backyard, seeing nothing. She turned back to him. 'Can we do nothing?' she demanded. 'Have you looked at your lease? Do you not own the rights to the water? Surely one cannot buy a spa without buying the water?'

He shook his head, still numb with shock. 'I bought the buildings, and the furnishings,' he said. 'I did not know. I did not think. I was too foolish to foresee this. I did not think to

441

buy the water. I am a trader, I sail my ships on the sea – I do not buy the sea. Water is always there.'

'Who has done this?' Sarah cried passionately. 'Who has done this to you? Who owns the new buildings?'

He could not meet her eyes. 'Stephen Waring,' he answered dully. 'He will have done well from us, first and last. He has plucked me like a little pigeon.'

She did not reproach him. Her shoulders went back as if to strain against a weight. 'We still have the ships,' she said. 'We still have the ships and we still have the slaves, and the warehouse. We are not ruined yet, Brother.'

He riffled lightly through the pages of the account book. 'We will have to see,' he said idly. 'But I do not know what will be left when all the debts on this are paid. If I shut down the Hot Well and sack all the staff and sell the furnishings . . . I do not know, Sarah. I used to know to a penny, didn't I? When you kept the books and the Trade was good. But I have such interest charges to meet, and they will not defer payment . . . I have quite lost track, Sarah.'

He rose on unsteady legs. 'I think I'll go now.' He looked at her vaguely. '*Rose* could come in any day, you know. Come in full of gold and smelling of rum. I like to be on the quayside when my ship comes in. She is late already, perhaps she will come in today. On the next tide. Or the tide after that.'

Sarah put a hand out to stop him, but he went past her quietly, as if he had not seen her, as if he did not know she was there. He took up his hat from the table in the hall. He did not wear a coat, he went out like a labouring man in his shirtsleeves into the grey twilight and the sharp evening air.

'When *Rose* comes in, we will be laughing about this,' he said uncertainly. 'We will be rich.'

Only when he was gone, and the front door shut behind him, did Sarah sink into the chair, gaze blankly at the empty hearth, and let herself wonder if they were ruined indeed.

Chapter Thirty-five

Sarah heard the hammering on the front door but she did not turn her head. The noise of it came from a long way away. She heard Stuart Hadley's pleasant voice; but she did not go out to greet him. She let Elizabeth show him upstairs.

He went into Frances's bedroom and sent Mehuru outside while he examined her. She had regained a little colour but she was hunched with pain. The cut on her forehead had dried and a small bluish bruise was spreading over her temple.

She answered his questions in a strained little voice, hardly able to catch her breath, and she could not move readily for the pain. He thought that her weak heart had taken a seizure from the shock, and her damaged lungs were in spasm also. He gave her a large dose of laudanum and watched the colour slowly come back into her cheeks as the drug worked its way into her body.

Stuart Hadley had never before seen her without her tightly laced stays. For the first time he was able to see the outlines of her body, only half-hidden by the sheet and blankets. He asked her permission and pressed gently on the round of her belly. It was solid and hard. For a moment he feared a growth of some sort and then a smile came to his face.

'How long have you been with child?'

The look she gave him was shocked. 'Child?' she repeated in her thin rasping voice.

'I think so,' he said. He pressed her belly again. The firmness was unmistakable. 'Yes.'

Her face gave her away, the burning flush of colour rising

from her neck to her forehead. She closed her eyes and turned her head on the pillow away from his gaze. 'Oh my God,' she murmured softly.

'Did you not realise?'

Numbly she shook her head. 'I have not been unwell for these past six months,' she said. 'But I thought . . . I thought . . . I have never been regular . . .'

He nodded. Few ladies of her class understood about conception. Virgins on marriage, they were rarely told either by mothers or husbands about pregnancy or childbirth. Even if they lived in the country they were shielded from the cycle of birth and death of farm animals, and Frances had seen the countryside only through the rectory windows. She was not the first lady he had attended who had been advanced in a pregnancy and not known.

'I had been so ill,' she said. 'With that cold. I thought that it had just stopped. And I am not grown much fatter.'

'There is no doubt that you are with child,' he said. He cleared his throat. 'Forgive me, Mrs Cole. This must be a shock.' He hardly knew how to ask the question, but opted for blunt honesty. 'I suppose you are certain that the child is Mr Cole's?'

She opened her eyes at that, and then turned her head away from him to the wall. He was afraid that she was mortally offended. But when she spoke her voice was level and clear. 'There *is* a doubt,' she said steadily, gazing resolutely at the wall. 'Mr Cole is . . .' She broke off, partly through embarrassment and partly because she simply did not know the words. 'I think it unlikely that Mr Cole would make a child,' she explained very softly.

There was a long silence. Stuart took a seat on the side of her bed without permission and took her thin hand in his. She was cold, despite the fire. He did not know if she could tolerate this shock to an already vulnerable system. 'Do not be afraid,' he encouraged her. 'We will find a way to manage this. Do not be afraid, Mrs Cole.'

She said nothing.

'Mehuru is a friend of mine,' he said quietly. 'I honour and respect him. He is a gentleman.' He smiled inwardly at hearing himself repeat the cant of their class. 'A gentleman,' he said firmly.

She shot a quick look at him. 'Is it you who has taken him to radical clubs?' she demanded bitterly. 'Who persuaded him that he must be free?'

Stuart bit back an angry reply. This woman was a patient, he must care for her. 'What I wanted to say,' he went on, his voice very low, 'is that a child of his, even with a white-skinned mother, would be dark-skinned, would be noticeably dark.'

She looked at him so blankly he thought that perhaps she did not understand, that the seizure of her heart had damaged her comprehension. He feared for a moment that he was making the most enormous and foolish mistake. He had assumed that Mehuru and Frances were lovers. He was assuming that the baby was Mehuru's child.

'Any baby of his will show its parentage,' he said carefully. 'Any baby of his would be dark-skinned.'

'Black like him?'

'They call them mulattos in the Sugar Islands,' he told her. 'They are brown-skinned, very beautiful babies, enchanting children.'

She blinked. She remembered, it seemed a lifetime away, Miss Honoria telling her that they always preferred mulattos in the house as servants. She remembered Honoria's easy gliding over unpalatable facts: 'Papa likes to mix the stock'.

She opened her mouth, her face blank as stone, and laughed, a high shrieking laugh. Stuart recoiled, but she did not stop, she laughed and laughed as if nothing would stop her.

'Enough,' Stuart ordered and his voice cut through her screaming laughter.

She looked wide-eyed at him. 'What shall I do?' she asked simply. 'I shall be ruined.'

445

'Do you know when it is due?'

'Yes,' she said quietly. 'It was conceived in May.' Her face softened as she thought of the daffodils in her bed, and the darkness of the May night.

'It will be born in January then,' he said.

'It might die,' she said coldly, but her hand crept down to her belly and she spread her palm over where the little head was lying.

'Do you want it to die?'

Her face quivered into life and her colour rose. 'No,' she replied with sudden surprising conviction. 'It is a love-child. It is my child. It is Mehuru's child. I want it to live. Oh!' She gave a small gasp of desire. 'Oh! I want it to live very much!'

'Then we must be very careful with your health,' Stuart said. 'Avoid all excitement and disturbance, and rest as much as you can. For yourself, and also for your baby.'

She nodded. 'But if my heart is too weak . . .'

'You *must* rest,' he insisted. 'We may get you safely through this, and your little baby too.'

She was silent for a moment, and then she turned to him and faced him honestly. 'I don't care for myself,' she said quietly. 'I have not been very lucky, you see, Mr Hadley. Not in my girlhood, and not in my marriage, and not even in my love for Mehuru. Oh! It was not his fault! But the gulf between us was so great that I don't think we could ever have bridged it. And I have not been good to him.' She paused, thinking. 'So if I am ill, and if you ever have to choose . . . you will save the baby, won't you?'

Stuart grimaced. 'I hope never to make that choice.'

'But if I am dying, and you can save the baby, you will do that – won't you?'

'If it is your wish,' he said slowly.

'It is,' she said. 'Mehuru's baby. Think what a precious child that will be.'

'Could you sleep now?' he asked.

446

'Yes,' she said. 'The laudanum has made me drowsy.'

He held her hand. 'I will stay with you until you sleep,' he said gently.

She opened her eyes for a moment. 'Don't tell Mehuru.'

He hesitated. 'You want to tell him yourself?'

Her eyelids were drooping. 'He has to be free to go,' she whispered so softly that he could hardly hear her. 'He has to be free. I have to set him free.' She glanced at him for a moment, in jealousy. 'You want him free,' she said.

'Yes, I do.'

'And you will advise him where he could go, where they can all go so that Josiah cannot find them and enslave them again?'

'I will.'

'Then he must be free to leave now,' she said simply. 'He cannot stay with me.'

When her eyelids fluttered shut the doctor sat with her a little while, looking at her white face. The bedroom door opened quietly and Mehuru stood there.

'You can come in,' Stuart said quietly. 'She is sleeping.'

Mehuru came in as light-footed as a cat. He checked when he saw Frances, the slight rise and fall of her breasts as she breathed slowly and painfully, the waxy white colour of her face.

'She will need someone to watch her,' Stuart told him. 'Night and day. Her heart is very weak. She needs to be kept quiet. She must have nothing to trouble her at all.'

Mehuru remained silent, his eyes never leaving her face.

'She will need someone to watch over her. I can find a nurse for the first few days, but they are not reliable women. Will Miss Cole care for her?'

'I will watch her,' Mehuru decided.

'You cannot . . .'

Mehuru shook his head. 'It is my right,' he said with gentle dignity. 'I will watch her sleep, and be here when she wakes.'

*   *   *

Josiah did not come home that night, nor did he return the next day. Sarah, walking alone down to the old warehouse on the quay in the wintry dawn, with a shawl over her head like a trader's daughter, found that he had spent the night in their old home, and was sitting in his old office, looking out over the dock, waiting for *Rose*.

In the following week he did not come home to the expensive house in Queens Square at all. He chose to stay in his little warehouse, sleeping on a pallet on the floor wrapped in his cloak at night and sitting in his old place at the window overlooking his empty quay from the first grey light of the morning. He spent his day bargaining and dealing in tiny, pitiful amounts of cash on the quayside; while the bigger debts in the account books at Queens Square grew fat like maggots in the dark of the ledgers, and the letters from Hibbard and Sons warning that they would prosecute for non-payment collected, unopened, on his desk.

He chose to dine in the coffee shop, sitting once again far from the top table. He might have claimed his place and been still tolerated. There were a few men who might have greeted him with sympathy; but Josiah did not try. He no longer wanted to be with them. He sat, neither with his new friends, nor with his old, but at a little table on his own, near the window where he could see his dock and the entrance to the harbour every time he lifted his eyes. He never stopped looking for *Rose* and whenever he saw the shape of a travel-weary brig silhouetted against the sparkle of the incoming water he would rise a little in his seat, drop his napkin on the floor, and start forward. But it was never the *Rose*. Despite Josiah's faith in her, in the short grey days of November she never came.

In the silent house in Queens Square Frances lay all day in her room, with the curtains open, looking out at the squares of sky in the panes of her window. The thick glass made little ripples and whorls of the grey. She tried to get up once or twice but she was so breathless and her colour became so

448

white that Stuart Hadley insisted that she lie in her bed, or at the most on a day bed in her room.

The weather was against her. The bright autumn days had slipped away under a blanket of fog. When Elizabeth opened the windows on Frances's insistence, the yellow smog crept into the room like the coils of a thick snake. The rich dirty stink of the river filtered up the backs of the houses and penetrated even the front windows of the square. Elizabeth closed the windows, and burned scented candles, trying to cleanse the air. Nothing could rid the city of its choking fumes and every draught which came into the room was icy and as dirty as stale smoke from a burning midden.

Sarah sat with her in the afternoons but the women were no company for each other. Frances lay quite still, her colour waxy and her breath short. Her thickening body was concealed completely by the drapes of her robe and the sheets and blankets on the bed. She had no desire to confide in Sarah, nor in anyone else; and Sarah had nothing to say to her. She had never wanted a sister-in-law; she had tolerated her for the sake of the business and because Josiah was determined to have her. Now that Frances lay sick and silent in her bed Sarah could see no use for her at all. Frances's connections with the aristocratic families had not brought visitors for the Hot Well spa, and anyway, the water was cooling and dying away to a hopeless trickle. The new Hot Well in Clifton had tapped into the spring and already they were pumping out gallons every day to the bright fashionable houses high on the cliff above. The only visitors to the old Hot Well were those too poor or too weak to move anywhere else. In Josiah's absence and without the ebullient Master of Ceremonies the business was slipping from bad to worse. Every day the spa took less and less money, and still the wages and the lease had to be paid. Only the paupers still came, on their set days. The new Hot Well was too inaccessible for them, too far from the city, and besides, the Merchant Venturers had made sure that there was no agreement to provide them with a free tap in Clifton.

Sarah brought plain darning with her when she came to sit in Frances's room and stitched irritably, small neat angry stitches, while Frances lay, her eyes half-closed, enduring the soft insistent sound of Sarah's breathing and the puncturing noise of her needle through linen, sensing her scorn.

Frances hardly spoke to Mehuru although he made a point of serving her. He would allow no-one else to carry the jug of hot water to her room in the morning or bring her dinner tray to her room in the afternoon. He would put the tray beside her bed and ask her how she felt and if she were better. But she would not speak to him, she turned her face to the wall and would not reply. She would not tell him about the child. She remembered too clearly her desperate need to see Josiah and her panic-stricken flight for her home. She had showed him, in that moment, where her loyalty lay: with her husband. She felt that she had betrayed him and she was ashamed.

And she was steeling herself for his disappearance. He had said that he would go and she had warned him that she could not protect him in the house in Queens Square. She did not want to hold him back. She did not want his child, their child, to hold him back. She had made up her mind to keep the baby a secret from him, so that he would be free to leave.

'Are you better today, Frances?' Mehuru asked softly, setting her dinner tray on the table at her bedside.

'Yes, thank you,' she said quietly. But when he left, Elizabeth, coming to straighten the sheets, found that Frances's pillow was wet with tears.

'Now what's the matter?' she would ask kindly. 'What's he said to you to make you cry so?'

But Frances would only shake her head and say nothing.

Elizabeth stopped Mehuru on the stairs as she carried Frances's dinner tray down to the kitchen. 'She cries when she sees you,' she said accusingly. 'What have you done to her?'

Mehuru spread his hands. 'I? I've done nothing! I've told her that I love her, and I asked her to come away with me. But ever since that day when she found that they were building the new Hot Well she has not spoken to me. She's Josiah's wife, not mine. She's telling me that in the cruellest way.'

'Well, it's breaking her heart, whatever she's doing,' Elizabeth observed.

'What can I do?' Mehuru demanded. 'I can't be her pet, Elizabeth. I am hers till death, but if she turns her face away when I speak to her, what can I do?'

'You could ask her, instead of standing on your pride,' Elizabeth said sharply. 'You could ask her what is wrong, instead of assuming you know everything. Everything! Or you could use the eyes in your head. You have the Sight! I should think you could see what ails her.' She stamped down the stairs away from him, cursing the stupidity of men as she went through the door to the kitchen. Mehuru scowled at her disappearing back, and then followed her. The others were seated around the kitchen table at their dinner. Mehuru took his place at the head of the table and bowed his head and took a brief moment to thank the Earth for the richness of her goods, and for the breath to eat them.

Kbara nodded to him when he raised his head. 'We have been thinking,' he said in the liquid warm accents of their home. 'We have been thinking we should go soon. We have delayed for Frances's illness, but we dare not wait much longer.'

Mehuru took a piece of bread and broke it. One of the girls set a bowl of soup before him. He nodded. 'I have spoken to Stuart and he knows where you should go,' he said. 'He will give you money for the journey and he has friends who will greet you. Of course, now is the time for you to go.'

'For us to go,' Kbara interrupted quickly. 'We do not want to be parted.'

451

'We are a family now,' Mary said. 'We cannot go and leave you behind, Mehuru.'

He shook his head. 'I am sorry. But I cannot leave Frances like this.'

There was an instant murmur of dissent. 'You must come,' Martha insisted, and the others nodded. 'We have agreed that we should all stay together. You *must* want to be with us, Mehuru.'

'I love her,' he said simply. 'And she is very sick, she could die. I can't leave her to die alone with that sister of hers. Who will hold her with love? Who will wash her face and body when she is cold? You must see that I cannot go until I know what she wants.'

'But she will not speak to you,' Elizabeth argued. 'You say yourself she loves her husband and not you.'

Mehuru shook his head. 'It does not matter. It is not easy for us to love each other. It never could be easy. It does not matter that she will not speak to me, nor that she is his wife. What matters is that in spite of all these things – all these things which have stood like walls between us – she has loved me and I love her still. I will not leave her until I have said goodbye.'

'What if she gets better and sells you?' Kbara demanded unkindly. 'She has already agreed a price for you and for John. What if she sells you and John tomorrow? They need the money. They are in debt.'

Mehuru nodded. 'You must go. For the safety of little John, and for all of your sakes. I will wait until she sends me away. When she tells me to leave I will come and find you. I love you. I love the children as if they were my own, and I love you, my brother, and you, my sisters. But I love Frances as if she were my wife. I cannot run away from her. When she sends me away I will come and find you. But I will not leave her until she herself tells me to go.'

'What if we get separated and can never find each other again?' Mary asked.

'I have to take that risk,' Mehuru replied. 'But Stuart knows a safe place for us all. You can go now, and I will follow you later. We have been through too much, we have survived this far. Surely we will find somewhere to live, and some way of living together!'

Kbara looked unhappy. 'I had thought you would come with us. I thought you would put your own people first.'

'I am torn two ways,' Mehuru admitted. 'You are my people. But look at Frances, she is almost certain to die. How can I leave her?'

'And I'll stay too,' Elizabeth said suddenly.

Mary turned on her in amazement. 'You as well?'

Elizabeth made a small gesture to Mary, under cover of the table. 'I have work to do here,' she said with simple dignity. She faced the disapproving faces of the two men. 'You would not understand. There is work for me here, woman's work. I have to stay and see Frances through to the end of her illness.'

'I don't think . . .' Mehuru started.

'I know,' Elizabeth said with finality.

Both of the men looked defeated by her certainty. Mehuru was reminded of the small village councils at home where the men might talk all day but if one of the senior women came in and said that a thing *must* be done, then that was the end of the discussion.

'I should be glad for Frances's sake,' he said. 'I am not allowed to nurse her, and Miss Cole is cold and hard.'

'I shall care for her until she dies,' Elizabeth declared. 'And the moment she is dead and washed and ready for their burial I shall come after you.' She nodded round the table. 'And I will bring Mehuru with me. They will not catch us and keep us just because we stay now.'

'Very well then,' Kbara said. He looked at Mehuru, who in the old days would have known with his priest's Sight how long a sick woman might live. 'It will not be very long, I don't think? The doctor said it will not be long. You must be able to see?'

'I don't know,' Mehuru said, deliberately choosing blindness rather than foreseeing Frances's death. 'How should I know? I don't know.'

Chapter Thirty-six

Josiah sat in his old chair, at his old desk, in the window of his office overlooking the quay. He had forgotten the house in Queens Square that he had struggled so hard to win and that had cost him so much to buy. He had forgotten his Hot Well, and his ambitions and his plans. He sat at his desk as if the years had never been, as if at any moment Sarah, or even his father, might call him to eat his dinner in the parlour next door.

At a casual glance it looked as if he were working. He had the ledgers of all his ships spread before him and he was carefully going down the profits column, adding them up, and then adding one to another. On another piece of paper he had a note of the debts he had to service, and every now and then he would transfer the total from his profits and subtract it from the money he owed. It was a nonsensical task: a piece of fairytale arithmetic. Every time he did it, the amount of the debt was hardly diminished at all. Josiah was looking at ruin, and he was too shocked to see it.

Only the sale of his ships themselves, his warehouse, and his lease of the quay would settle his debts. Over and over again Josiah added up the value of the tobacco in his bond, the value of the rum in his cellar and the sugar in his store. Again and again he subtracted it from the debt on the *Rose*, on the Hot Well lease and on his house in Queens Square, and saw that thousands and thousands of pounds were still owing.

The room was cold, the rain pattered against the grimy windows making tracks in the greasy dirt on the unwashed panes. The windows rattled when the wind blew up the gorge and the draughts whistled around Josiah's bowed head as he puzzled over the arithmetic of loss. He was not conscious of the cold on his bare head. He could see nothing but the dazzling whiteness of the page and feel the paper smooth under his hands. However he added it, however he subtracted it and then added it again, he could not make it come right. Whatever he did with the figures they came out at a loss.

Only *Rose* could save him if she came home soon, smelling sweetly of sugar, potent with rum and filled with bullion. Only *Rose* could save him if she came home in time, before the next payment on the Hot Well spa fell due, if she came home before Hibbard and Sons closed his loan and demanded the overpriced house at Queens Square, or the failed Hot Well spa and all his ships against his debt. If she did not come soon then Josiah would have to hand over his house, and come back to the little quay and the warehouse which Josiah's father had been proud to call his home and which Josiah had left with such pride just ten short months ago.

Frances woke from light sleep with a sensation akin to someone tugging at her sleeve. Or was it a noise that had woken her? She rested, halfway between waking and sleeping, wondering what it was – a noise in the street outside perhaps, or someone calling her name.

Then she felt it again. A small distinct movement, a squirm, a touch, a caress. Inside her belly her baby had moved and she, lying quietly in sleep, had felt it. It was the strangest feeling in the world and as distinctive as a child's call for his mother. She put her hand on her swelling belly and felt the child kick out. He was alive, and strong. She had been sensing him move and felt that she had learned to love him, this little exuberant swimming kicking being.

'Not long now,' she whispered.

There was a gentle knock on her door. She turned her head and said, 'Come in!', thinking it was Elizabeth.

But it was not Elizabeth who came quietly in the door but Mehuru, and his face was grave.

Frances snatched the bedcovers higher, shielding the round shape of her belly.

'May I come in?' he asked humbly. He paused at the threshold of the room, awaiting her permission.

'Yes,' Frances said. She could not meet his eyes. She felt as if she had betrayed him on the very day which was to be their last together, which was to be a day of farewell, filled with love; and then all she had thought of was Josiah, and the wreck of his fortune. 'Of course you can come in,' she said quietly. 'What is it?'

'There is a difficulty,' he began.

For a moment she thought that Stuart had broken her confidence and told him about the pregnancy. Stuart was sworn to secrecy and besides, there was his professional oath, but still he was Mehuru's friend and he might think that a man had a right to know that a woman was carrying his child. Unconsciously she put her hand to shield her belly; beneath her touch she could feel her baby kick again.

'What difficulty?'

Mehuru's mind was on how to tell her that the slaves had gone without precipitating one of her breathless attacks. But some wisdom, some old awareness in the back of his mind, noted the gesture she made. In Africa he would have read her at once. But Mehuru was becoming more and more of an Englishman. He concentrated on the topic in hand, and made himself blind to other impressions.

'Do you have some medicine the doctor left you?'

She gestured quickly to her bedside table where her laudanum bottle stood. 'But I don't need it,' she said, though she could feel her heart pound warningly. 'What difficulty? Is it Josiah? Is he ill?'

'No, your husband is well, as far as I know. Please do not be distressed.'

'Tell me quickly.'

457

'It is your slaves,' he said softly. 'All except Elizabeth. They have run away, Frances. They are all gone.'

For a moment she did not understand. She looked at him as if his words were meaningless. 'Gone?'

'They went last night,' he explained. 'After Cook locked up. Cook knows nothing about it. They must not blame her.'

'But you knew,' she said.

He nodded. 'I knew.'

There was a little silence. Frances raised herself up in bed. 'And yet you did not go too?'

He came further into the room. 'I decided to stay.'

'Do you know where they are?'

'On a farm, in a place called Yorkshire. We hope that we can farm the land.' His sudden smile broke up the gravity of his face. 'I am sure nothing will grow in this cold soil! But two are Fulani and they can rear cattle. I think we can make a life for ourselves.'

'You are going to join them?'

'It is up to you.' He paused for a moment, carefully measuring what he might say to her. 'I have not changed, Frances. I told you that day that I loved you, and I love you still. I know that you are ill and I know that Josiah is ruined, and that everything here is now different. But if you will come with me, we can go to Yorkshire together. Or I will stay with you. Or you can send me away. You have only to tell me what it is that you wish.'

He stepped forward and took her hand. Something in the way that her other hand rested below her ribs tugged at a memory in his mind. He paused, looking at her, and then saw for the first time the lovely curve of her swelling belly under the concealing drapery of her robe and the coverings of the bed.

'You are pregnant,' he said.

She looked as if she might deny it, but then she nodded.

'Josiah's child.' His mouth had a bitter twist. 'You are risking your life for Josiah's child.'

Frances nodded again, not trusting herself to lie to him in words.

He turned from her pale strained face and went to the window and looked out over the square. The trees were leafless now, their bright colours stripped away and the grey colour of the grass reminded Mehuru of home, at the end of the dry season. 'I still wish that we could go to Africa,' he said, half to himself.

'You go,' Frances whispered softly. She could not bring herself to send him away, she could only give him permission, and tell him nothing that would bind him to her. He had been ready to run and she had seen him humiliated too many times before her. She felt she owed him his freedom, even though he was the father of her child – especially since he was the father of her child.

He shook his head. 'It makes no difference,' he said finally. 'It makes no difference to how I feel for you – whether you are carrying Josiah's child or not. You are ill, and your husband is never at home. I love you and I have promised myself that I will stay with you until you tell me to leave.'

'I never asked you for a promise,' she interrupted. 'I will not keep you here.'

'I promised myself,' he replied. 'You are the first woman I have ever loved in my life, Frances, and I know now that it was a mistake for me. There is too much that separates us. Our colour is less important than everything else.' His gesture took in their politics, their culture, their expectations, and their sense of what was important. 'But it does not matter. None of it matters now with you so ill, and your life ruined. I love you and I will stay with you until you tell me to go.'

'And if I say go?'

'Then I will join my people.'

'And if I say stay?'

'Then I stay.'

She looked across the room at him and into his open tender face. She thought that she should let him go, let him run while he could and make a new life with his people. She did not doubt that they would make a success of their farm. They were all dogged survivors, and they were in touch with the reality of the earth and with their own tenderness in a way that she and Josiah and Sarah had never been. They would court and marry and bear children, and the children would grow up as English men and women, only knowing Africa as a deep memory, hidden in their souls.

She put a hand out to him. 'I will not ask you to stay,' she said stubbornly. 'I think it would be safer for you to go. Josiah could still sell you and I could not save you and . . .' She broke off. 'I am ill,' she told him honestly. 'I am fatally ill, Mehuru. I saw my mother die like this. There is nothing to stay for.'

He crossed the room and took her hand. She was as small-boned as the skeleton of a little bird. The flesh had wasted from her hand in the short time of her illness; he could feel the light bones of her wrist. He turned her hand palm upwards and gently pressed a kiss into it.

'I will stay for as long as you need me,' he promised.

They both knew that it would not be very long.

Frances did not see Sarah until she came to her room before dinner in the afternoon. The two women now lived almost separate lives. Sarah still dined downstairs in solitary state in the ornate dining room. Frances had her meal on a tray in her bedroom. Neither woman ate very much. Josiah never came home at all. Sarah did not disturb him. She had a faint hope, a trace of wishful optimism, that Josiah's struggles with his debts would suddenly come right and he would swagger home again with his hat set jauntily on his head and another scheme in his hand to right them all. She knew it was not likely, but she could not keep herself from hoping.

In the meantime she could not bear to see his demented concentration. The third night he had not come home for dinner she had walked down to the quayside to fetch him.

She had seen the light burning at his window and looked up. She had seen him hunched over his desk, she had seen him move the papers from one pile to another and then shuffle them and move them back again. For half an hour Sarah had waited on the quayside, trying to find the courage to go to Josiah and bid him come home. But the habits of coldness and distance were too strong for her to break. In the end she had left him to his pointless vigil over debts, and gone back alone.

Sarah blamed Frances completely and entirely for their ruin. She could not speak to her except with the coldest courtesy. She saw Frances grow weaker and she could find no pity for her at all. Stuart Hadley advised her that Frances's heart was fatally weak and vulnerable to shock; and Sarah merely nodded and said, 'We are none of us as strong as we appear,' as if the news meant nothing to her.

Stuart had said, 'Perhaps I did not make myself clear. Another shock could kill her.'

Sarah had merely looked at him and said: 'She was always weakly.' She spoke as if Frances were a bale of shoddy cotton, sold as good, and indeed she felt as if the Scotts had joined with the rest of the world in gulling her and Josiah, in selling them substandard goods and trapping them into ruin.

The only time she could bring herself to see Frances was for a once-a-day ritual before dinner when she came to her sister-in-law's room and enquired glacially if Frances felt any better.

'No better,' Frances replied. 'But I have had some very bad news today.'

Sarah raised an eyebrow. She did not sit down. She paused at the foot of Frances's bed, ready to leave as soon as the courtesies had been paid.

'The slaves have gone,' Frances said baldly.

'What?'

'Run away,' Frances said.

'But I saw Cicero just now!'

461

'He and Elizabeth are the only ones left.'

Sarah moved away from the bed and sank into the pretty blue chair at the fireside. 'I don't understand,' she said.

'They went last night,' Frances reported. 'Cicero told me this morning.'

'Why did you not tell me then?' Sarah demanded. 'We could have informed the magistrates . . .'

'I daresay they had it well planned,' Frances said dryly.

'Have they stolen our goods?'

'I don't know.'

'Why did you not tell me at once?'

Frances looked at her wearily. 'It did not seem to matter much,' she said coldly. 'Not now.'

The gulf of their loss opened up before them. Sarah's protests were stilled. Soon, she thought, they would have neither home nor business. If they had made as much as fifteen hundred pounds on the slaves it would only have gone to pay creditors.

'They were your dowry,' she said sullenly. 'And much good they have done us.'

Frances nodded at the implied criticism. 'It has not been a success,' she observed. 'Not the slaves, not the business, and not the marriage. When did you last see Josiah?'

'Last night. He is living down on the quay. He did not see me, I saw him through the window.'

'Is he ill?'

'He is trying to save his business,' Sarah said loyally. 'He is working all day and all night.' She would not tell Frances that he was working as a madman works, little detailed actions which change nothing.

Frances nodded. 'Will you tell him about the slaves?'

Sarah shook her head. 'I will advertise for them. And if we cannot get them back I will tell him then. There is no point in running towards bad news. Josiah has enough to worry him.'

She rose from the chair as if she were achingly weary. 'That

Cicero and Elizabeth,' she said. 'Do they know where the others are gone? Will they help us fetch them back?'

'They do not know, but even if they did they would not tell us.'

'If they know we could make them tell us. We could have them whipped.'

Frances sighed with impatience. 'All of them have run away except these two. Is this how we reward loyalty? With a beating?'

'Why did they stay?'

Frances looked away from Sarah. 'I don't know,' she said. 'But I am glad that they did. We cannot afford to pay anyone to do the work, I suppose.'

Sarah shook her head. 'There is no cash for the housekeeping books. All the tradesmen are giving us credit but soon they will know that there is no money to pay them. I do not know if anything is left from the profits of the *Lily*. I have avoided asking Josiah, but I will have to find out soon. I think it has all gone into this house, and into the Hot Well. I think it has all gone and there is nothing left at all.'

Chapter Thirty-seven

There was a loud hammering on the door knocker at seven o'clock on a cold December morning, hard with white frost. Mehuru, carrying hot water to the bedrooms on the first floor, put down the heavy jugs and went to the front door.

A round-faced man in brown serge, followed by two others, stepped into the house and put his hand on Mehuru's arm.

'Bailiffs,' he said abruptly. 'Is your master at home? Savee? Big boss? Savee?'

Mehuru jerked his arm away. 'Mr Cole is at the warehouse.'

The big man blinked in surprise at the perfectly spoken English. 'Here, we'll have you straight away,' he said, tightening his grip.

'What's this?' Cook asked, surging up the passageway from the kitchen.

'Bailiffs,' the man said shortly. 'Come to distrain goods to the value of more than two thousand pounds.'

Cook squared up to him. 'And what d'you think you're doing with him?' she demanded, plucking Mehuru's sleeve away.

'He's goods,' the man said. 'And worth a lot, I should think.'

'He's free,' Cook lied instantly. 'He's a free man, a servant.'

'We'll see about that,' the bailiff replied. 'I've got authority to seize household goods here.'

'You wait there,' Cook ordered. She nodded Mehuru to go upstairs. 'Wake Miss Cole and tell her,' she said.

Mehuru nodded and went up to Sarah's bedroom. He tapped lightly on the door. At Sarah's sharp command he opened the door and spoke from the threshold.

'A man is here called Bailiffs.'

He heard an abrupt exclamation from inside the room and the noise of Sarah getting hastily out of bed and throwing a shawl around her shoulders. She peered around the door at him. 'Bailiffs?' she asked.

'Yes,' he confirmed.

Her face was more pinched and angry than ever. 'Go out of the back door,' she hissed. 'Run to the warehouse. Find Mr Cole. Tell him to come home at once. Tell him he must come at once and bring everything he has, all the money he has to hand, all the notes of credit, a note of what we still hold in bond.'

Mehuru nodded.

'Go without them seeing you,' Sarah cautioned. 'And be quick.'

Mehuru went quietly downstairs. In the hall Cook was blocking the way. Another man with a handcart had arrived, and a pony and cart behind him. Mehuru slipped like a shadow down the hall and out through the back door into the yard.

He ran down to the dockside and whistled for the ferryboat to take him across.

'Ha'penny,' the lad said.

'Mr Cole will pay on the way back,' Mehuru promised. He still had no money in his pockets.

The lad nodded. 'He better had.'

The prow of the little boat nosed against the green slimy steps. Mehuru jumped ashore, clearing the tidemark of garbage and filth and ran up the steps to the Cole warehouse. He hammered on the front door and shouted until the window above opened and Josiah stuck his head out.

'Oh, it's you,' he said. 'What's the matter?'

'Bailiffs,' Mehuru told him. 'Miss Cole said to come home at once. She said to bring everything you have, all the money and all the notes of credit, and a note of what you have in bond.'

Josiah laughed shortly, a cold mirthless sound, staring down at Mehuru below him. 'I'll come,' he said. 'But I've nothing to bring. Nothing. D'you hear?'

Mehuru waited. There was a bitter wind blowing up the gorge and a cold frost on the quayside. The garbage in the dock was rimmed with white. The door before him opened and Josiah came out. He was wearing an old suit of homespun brown and his linen was dirty. His stock was badly tied and his jacket pulled on carelessly with one pocket flap tucked in. The two men went side by side to the ferry, the immaculately dressed black man in livery and his shabby master.

'Do you have a penny for the boy?' Mehuru asked.

Josiah bared his stained teeth. 'It's about all I do have,' he said. 'And I suppose I have to pay for you too, good money to bring me bad news. You should have run around the long way and not cost me your fare.'

The boat edged against the steps on the Bristol side of the river. Mehuru got out first and gave Josiah his hand. The older man moved as if he were stiff and tired, but at the entrance to Queens Square, as he took in the waiting carts and the bailiff's men, his pace grew swifter.

'What's this?' he cried as soon as he was at his front door. 'What authority?'

The bailiff turned to him. 'Are you Josiah Cole?'

'Who wants to know?' Josiah demanded with pointless cunning.

'Bailiffs. I have a warrant here for the distraint of goods.'

Josiah looked indoors to the shadowy hall. Sarah, coming downstairs in her plainest gown, nodded at him. Brother and sister's eyes met. Neither of them smiled but there was a grim recognition of mutual need and a promise of mutual support. Mehuru thought of the warriors of Oyo who sing that only those who fear nothing, not even the hornbill who feasts on the eyes of dead men, can march with them. The taut readiness for disaster was there in Sarah and Josiah. Upstairs, Frances still slept.

'How much?' Josiah said evenly. He thought he might part

466

with some of the more extravagant pieces of porcelain and keep the basic goods.

The bailiff looked at his list. 'It's £2300. 17s.,' he said.

Josiah staggered as if he had been knifed in the belly. Sarah came swiftly forwards and drew him into the hall, half-supporting him with her arm around his back.

'Show me,' Josiah said. 'Who has done this?'

The bailiff handed over the warrant with the bills and signatories attached. Josiah read them with minute attention, as if he hoped to spot an error of a few pence. His lips moved as he scanned the words but Mehuru could tell that he was not seeing them at all. He was turning the pages, one after another, but his eyes were sightless.

'Let me see.' Sarah's voice was gentle. She took the papers from Josiah's hand and looked from one bill to another. They were the bills for the wallhangings, for the carpets, for the curtains, for the pictures. The plasterer, who had repaired the broken beak of one of Josiah's beloved ornamental plaster-work ho-ho birds, the carpenter for a new step on the stair. The chimney sweep who had cleaned all the chimneys before they had moved in, the coal merchant for the last delivery. Not a bill had been settled since they had moved into Josiah's great house. While Sarah had been balancing the housekeeping books for butcher and baker, Josiah had been letting the costs of the house double and re-double, with one eye on the Hot Well and the other on his ships.

The second set of papers were the bills for the Hot Well: wages, new furnishings, running costs. Sarah turned page after page as the bailiff looked at her, his stolid face carefully impassive.

There was a third set of papers from the chandlers, the sailmakers and the ropewalk, unpaid since *Lily* had sailed, still owing from *Daisy*'s sailing nearly a year ago.

'You will have to give us a few days to settle these,' she said.

The bailiff shook his head. 'I am sorry, Missis,' he said.

'My orders are to take goods to the value for sale. They are to be taken today.'

'I don't believe we have goods to the value of two thousand pounds,' Sarah said, her voice sharp and unemotional. 'Much of the furniture belongs to my sister-in-law.'

'Married to Mr Cole?'

'Of course.'

'Her goods are his, then,' he said. 'If they're married.'

'Even so,' Sarah maintained, 'we do not have goods to the value of these bills.'

The bailiff nodded. 'Then I have to ask you to vacate the premises, Missis. I have instructions to claim the property itself. You can take your personal clothes and belongings.'

'Go back to the warehouse?' Josiah was suddenly roused from his daydream. 'Back to the warehouse? But we've only just come from there!'

Sarah turned to him. 'It doesn't matter, Josiah,' she said urgently. 'We can go back for now, while we get this sorted out. The house will not be sold for weeks. *Rose* could come in any day and then we will settle our debts. We can go back for now.'

'No!' Josiah yelled. He suddenly plunged towards the bailiff, his hands snatching for his throat. The bailiff side-stepped him easily and his man, waiting behind, seized Josiah and wrestled him away. The man with the handcart raced up the steps and the three of them bent Josiah's arms behind his back and held him. 'No!' Josiah yelled again.

Mehuru hesitated, then he heard Frances's bedroom door open. At once he turned for the stairs and ran up to her. He saw a glimpse of her pale face and her tumbling dark hair.

'Not so fast, you!' the bailiff called. He took three swift steps up the stairs behind Mehuru and flung his arms around him. 'Here! Sam! Help me with this!'

Mehuru twisted in his grip. 'Let me go,' he said steadily. 'I must go to Mrs Cole . . . she is ill . . .'

'You're goods,' the man said with sudden abrupt viciousness.

'And I'm distraining you along with everything else.'

The second man raced up the stairs towards them. Frances from above could see Mehuru's danger. 'Mehuru!' she screamed. 'Run! Run!'

At the sound of her voice Mehuru kicked out and threw the bailiff backwards against the banister. There was a splintering sound and the banister creaked outwards, away from the stairs. He stumbled against the other man and Mehuru punched him straight-fingered into his round belly. The man slumped down, whooping and gasping for breath, knocking the other man off balance. Mehuru tore out of his grip and raced up the stairs to Frances.

She was clinging to the door frame. 'What is happening? Who are those men?'

Mehuru swept her off her feet and carried her back into her bedroom, kicking the door shut behind them. 'It is nothing, nothing. Be calm, Frances!'

She struggled out of his arms and stood unsteadily before him. 'Mehuru! Tell me! What do they want?'

He could feel her rapid pulse thudding in her fingers.

'Please,' he said. 'Please, Frances, be still. They have come for money. That's all. They want money.'

'Bailiffs?'

He nodded. 'That is what they said.'

Her face was wax-white. 'We will lose the house. We will lose everything.'

There was a loud bang on the door and then it was thrown open. The bailiff stepped into the room. 'Beg pardon,' he said heavily. 'But I'm distraining him for sale.'

Frances staggered. 'He is sold,' she improvised swiftly. Her face was ashen. 'You cannot have him, he is the property of Mr Waring.'

The man hesitated. 'Mr Waring?'

Frances held her hand to her heart. She could feel its erratic pounding. 'Ask him!' she said. 'And he will be angry if you touch his servant.'

The bailiff recoiled. 'Leave my room,' Frances said. 'How dare you come in here?'

He was impressed by her frosty air of command. 'Beg pardon, ma'am. Just trying to do my job, and he struck me.'

'Mr Waring will compensate you,' Frances assured him. 'You must complain to him.'

He nodded and left. They were silent as they heard his heavy tread going down the stairs.

Frances gave a little gasp. Her face was ashen. 'You must run,' she whispered breathlessly. 'Get out of the back door, Mehuru. And take Elizabeth.'

'I won't leave you,' he said stubbornly. 'He won't touch me. He thinks I am Mr Waring's slave.'

'That won't save you. Mr Waring could come and claim you. You must go.'

He caught her in his arms. 'I promised that I would stay with you.'

'Look at me!' she cried in sudden passion. 'I am dying, Mehuru! And you have a life before you! Go! I want to know you are free!' She gathered her strength and pushed him away from her, thrust him to the door. But as she did so, her face suddenly changed and went into a spasm of pain. She doubled up. 'Oh God, Mehuru! The baby is coming! The baby!'

He scooped her up and laid her on the bed. She screamed a sharp cry of pain and then gasped for breath.

Mehuru recklessly flung open the door and shouted for Elizabeth. She came running down the stairs. 'The baby is coming,' he said. 'Go to her, I will fetch Stuart. Lock the bedroom door and let no-one in but me.'

He glanced down to the hall. The bailiffs had given up on him for the time being, they were arguing with Josiah. Brother and sister were blocking the doorway, shoulder to shoulder and insisting on seeing one bill after another, haggling as if a reduction of a few pounds would make all the difference. Mehuru thought that the two worlds of the house had split off from each other completely. Downstairs Sarah and Josiah still struggled for money, upstairs the slaves and Frances struggled to bring life into the house, and to cheat death.

Mehuru went quietly down the hall, slipped out of the back door and then took to his heels towards Stuart's house.

He was lucky, he saw the doctor's phaeton waiting outside the Merchant Venturer almshouses at the back of the square. 'Stuart!' he shouted to the squat white-painted facade intersected with black beams, and was rewarded by the sight of his face at a small leaded upstairs window.

'It's Frances! The baby is coming!'

Stuart made a grimace at Mehuru's crashing lack of discretion, vanished from the window and then appeared at the little door.

'She's in pain! Come!'

Stuart swung into the driving seat and Mehuru leaped for the footman's hold behind the carriage.

'Did something bring it on?' Stuart shouted over his shoulder.

'Bailiffs in the house,' Mehuru said. 'A fight. They tried to catch me.'

Stuart scowled.

'You knew of the baby,' Mehuru accused.

'I am her doctor.'

'You did not tell me.'

'Why should I have told you?' Stuart hedged. He steered the horse carefully around the square and pulled it up well clear of the bailiffs' cart.

'Because I was caring for her,' Mehuru said. 'I needed to know. She needs my protection with Josiah away all the time. You should have told me.'

'And who do you think is the father?' Stuart asked conversationally. He reached into the phaeton and pulled out his bag.

'Come on! Hurry!' Mehuru was dancing on the pavement with impatience. He had forgotten all about the bailiffs.

471

Stuart gave him a brief quizzical look and let himself be rushed towards the house. Inside the hall they could hear Josiah and Sarah conducting the bailiffs from room to room.

'That is porcelain, it is worth a hundred pounds,' Josiah was saying in the morning room. 'And that is an heirloom, you can see the crest, the Scott crest.'

Mehuru led the way up the stairs, taking the steps three at a time, Stuart behind him. At Frances's door he suddenly checked, listening to the low moaning noise from inside.

'The father?' he suddenly demanded, at last registering Stuart's look and his question. 'The father of her child?'

Stuart put him carefully to one side and tapped on the door. 'I will call you when she can see you,' he promised. 'But, Mehuru, don't expect too much. She is not strong.'

'Let me see her now.'

'In a moment.' The door opened and Stuart went in, firmly closing it behind him. Mehuru collapsed on the stairs outside and listened.

He could hear Frances gasping for breath when the pains crushed her. He heard Sarah draw Josiah out into the hall leaving the bailiffs in the morning room, pricing the furniture.

'Let it go, Josiah,' she begged urgently. 'Let it go!'

'The heirlooms . . .' Josiah said. 'And the dragons.'

Sarah grasped the lapels of his jacket. 'Josiah, listen to me,' she said. 'We have a chance, we have a good chance.'

Josiah looked at her with his old keen attention. 'How?'

'They can have it,' she said recklessly. 'The house, the furniture, the Hot Well spa, everything. They can even have a ship! They can even have two! We can deal! Don't you see? We can deal on the debts.'

'We lose the house?' Josiah asked.

'Let it go!' Sarah repeated. 'As long as we have the quay and the warehouse, and one ship. That's all we need, Josiah! We can start again. The warehouse and the quay and one ship!'

472

'Frances cannot live there,' Josiah said suddenly.

'Frances can go too. Along with the other luxuries.'

'She is my wife . . .' Josiah protested weakly.

'We are not suited for marriage, you and I,' she ruled. 'You have forgotten how our mother died. She died alone while Da was out trading on the trow. He said then that business and love do not mix. D'you remember?'

Josiah shook his head.

'He did,' Sarah said convincingly. 'And we chose the Trade. We chose the cruellest business that ever has been. That ever will be. You cannot make your money as we have made ours and still be tender-hearted, Josiah. Your wife is sick and dying upstairs. Down here we can bargain with the bailiffs and take our kitchenware to the warehouse and start again. Tell me what it is you wish.'

Josiah hesitated for only a moment. 'If *Rose* comes in tomorrow . . .'

'Then we are rich. If she never comes in at all then there is still *Daisy* and *Lily*. One of them will come in, and both of them could come in at a profit.'

He nodded. 'Pack up the kitchenware and everything you think we can get away with,' he said softly. 'I will get the best price I can for these things. Those dragons should be worth something. I always said they were the thing.'

'And her furniture,' Sarah said. 'Sell her furniture. She cost us enough from first to last. She can pay now.'

Mehuru sat at the top of the stairs listening half to them, half to the painful hard gasps of breath from Frances's room. As he sat he gathered his old skills around him. He sat quite still, focusing his mind to give her ease. He closed his eyes. The noise of Josiah going protestingly from room to room downstairs faded away like the chatter of parrots. All he could hear was the rasp of Frances's breath and then slowly, slowly, she grew quieter.

Mehuru felt himself drawing her pain from her, and watched it flow through his own body, the griping pain at the heart, the hot rasp of breath in the labouring lungs, and the powerful, unimaginable vice-like grip of childbirth. He opened his body like a cave, like a cavern, and let the pain flow through him like a fast deep river, scarcely touching the sides. His conscious mind heard Frances's sharp breathing ease as the pain left her, and he held the river of pain close to him, to keep her safe.

The bedroom door opened and Stuart looked out, his face drawn. 'You had better come in,' he said. 'I am losing her.'

Mehuru straightened up and went slowly into the room. Frances was lying back on the fine linen pillow, her face as white as her sheet and her hair stuck with sweat to her forehead and neck.

When she saw him she managed a little half-smile. 'Mehuru,' she said, and the way she spoke his name sounded like 'water'.

He knelt beside her bed and gathered her gently into his arms, cradling her head on his shoulder, holding her close. She closed her eyes and clung to him, one hand around his shoulders and the other reaching up to touch his throat. 'Oh God, Mehuru. I have been a fool.'

'We both have been fools,' he said. He could feel a deep slow pain in his own chest which he thought was probably heartbreak.

'I've been such a fool,' she said, snatching a little gasp of air. 'All the time I was trying...' she lost her breath and stuttered as she tried to inhale '...t...t...trying to keep a position...'

He nodded. 'I know.'

'To be a lady!' She gave another little gasp. 'At such cost!'

He held her very close, willing the pain to pass. 'I know,' he said softly. 'I understood from the very beginning.'

'All your pain... and the wreck of Africa...' He rocked her gently, letting her speak, letting her finally speak honestly to him from her heart. 'And you... and I... Such a waste, Mehuru!'

He laid her back on her bed and buried his dark head into the warm curve of her neck. She put her arms around him and held him close. 'I love you,' she said quietly.

He pulled back and looked at her face. The twisted frantic look had gone and she was smiling slightly. Mehuru looked into her eyes. He had watched men and women die and he knew that nothing could keep Frances now. 'I never said so before,' she whispered. 'But I loved you from the moment I first saw you.'

'Stay,' he begged urgently. 'Stay with me, Frances.'

She smiled almost lazily. 'Look in my writing box. Later. Hold me now.'

'Stay . . .' He was speaking like a man and not an obalawa.

'Maybe one day,' she said very softly. 'Maybe one day there will be a world where a man and woman like us might love each other, d'you think?'

'Stay now . . .'

She suddenly lunged forward, her eyes black with the grip of sudden pain, and she cried out, once. He caught her to save her from falling, calling her name. When her body went limp and he laid her back on her pillows, she was gone.

Stuart dragged him from her bedside and pushed him to the window. 'Don't look,' he said forcibly. 'Look out of the window.'

Mehuru stumbled to the window and leaned his head against the cold pane of glass and looked without seeing at the frost under the trees and the white incised blades of grass.

Then Stuart said, 'And here we are!' and Mehuru heard a strange little noise, a cry, a tiny breath, and then another cry.

He turned to see Elizabeth wrapping a tiny thing, smaller than a doll, in soft white cloth, and dabbing at its head.

'See?' she smiled, though her eyes were still running with tears. 'Your son, Mehuru. You have a son.'

Hardly knowing what he was doing, he put out his hands and she gently put the little bundle into his arms. The baby looked up at him. It had black black eyes, as dark as Frances's, as dark as his own. Its little face was a rich colour like rum and milk, like the colour of the palms of Mehuru's tender hands. Mehuru staggered for a moment, as the truth finally hit him. The child's smooth skin was a rich brown colour, a mixture of Frances and himself. It was not Josiah's child, it had never been Josiah's child. It was his own son.

'My son,' he said incredulously. 'My son.'

The baby looked at him with his wise dark eyes as if he could understand everything, everything that was in the world. He opened his little mouth and yawned, a complete thorough yawn, as precise as a kitten.

'Hello, my son,' Mehuru said in English, and then in Yoruban: *'Baa woo ne o moo me.'*

The baby's eyes widened as he solemnly considered his father, and then his little face constricted. He squeezed his eyes shut and began to cry.

'He will be hungry,' Elizabeth said. 'Give him to me.'

'Can you feed him?' Mehuru asked.

The look she gave him was rich with love. 'I have been waiting and preparing for him for months,' she said. 'Frances knew. She knew I would care for him.'

Stuart turned from the bed. 'I am sorry, Mehuru. I could not save her. I will send a woman to lay her out.'

'I will do it,' he said instantly. 'I have stayed here, all this time, to do it as it should be done. She is an African woman now. She is the wife of a Yoruban, she is the mother of my child.'

Stuart nodded. 'I will wait for you in the kitchen. I will take Elizabeth there, with the baby, and make sure they are safe. We should go from here, as soon as you are ready. You can join the others now.'

Mehuru nodded. He held the door for them and watched Elizabeth take his son downstairs. She was holding him close,

476

tucked into the curve of her neck, and all he could see was the crown of the little black head. His son had inherited his hair; it was as tight and as curly as the fleece of a little black lamb.

Mehuru shut the door on them. Downstairs he could hear the bailiff's men taking furniture out to the cart, he could hear Josiah's baffled arguing and Sarah's sharp complaints. He heard it all as if it came from many miles away.

He straightened Frances in her bed and took the blood-stained sheets away. He poured the warm water from the jug into the ewer and sponged her body, her face, her arms, and her thin white fingers. He combed her hair and he braided it close to her head in the manner of his people. She looked very beautiful with her hair in African braids, he thought. They showed the fine structure of her face, and she no longer looked weary. She no longer looked as if she were warring with herself. She looked at peace, she looked as if she finally had understood that there was no need to hunger and struggle.

He went to her chest of clothes and drew out a blue gown, blue the colour of coolness, of *itutu*: composure. Carefully he put it on her, drawing it around her, and holding her close as he fastened it. Into the pockets of the gown he slipped the things that she should take with her when they put her in the earth: her comb, a teaspoon from her breakfast tray, a pinch of salt. He opened her sewing basket and took out her little silver embroidery scissors. He cut one of the tight black curls of hair from his head and tucked it under her handkerchief. He closed her eyes and kissed her, her cool eyelids, her lips, and the still-warm hollow at her collarbone. Then he drew the white counterpane over her.

At the doorway he hesitated. She had told him to look in her writing box. He took it to the windowseat and opened it. Laid neatly on the top was a single sheet of paper. At the foot was Frances's seal and name and two other signatures: Stuart Hadley, and Mary Allen, the cook. It read:

477

This is the Last Will and Testament of Me, Frances Jane Scott Cole, signed this 29th day of November 1789 before Stuart Hadley and Mary Allen.

To my Sister-in-law Sarah Cole I do Bequeath all my Dresses and Gowns and Jewellery. To my Dear husband Josiah I bequeath all my Furniture and Heirlooms.

I Direct their attention to my Work as Agent for Sir Charles Fairley. They will see that the Agency is now of a size that it could be registered as a Bank and I do bequeath to my Sister-in-law and to my Husband Jointly all my Interest in these Matters, and Recommend to them that They develop this Bank as their Business, Abandoning the Slave Trade.

For my Own Slaves I hereby Grant them their Complete and Absolute Freedom: Julius, Mary, Martha, Elizabeth, John, Susan, Ruth, Naomi, Matthew, and Mark are hereby all Freed. The man Mehuru, once known as Cicero, is also Completely and Absolutely Free.

I send them my Dearest Blessing and the hope that they may make a Home in England and Find it in their hearts to Forgive me – and all English people – for the Very great wrong that we have done to Them and to their Country. It has taken me a Long Long time to realise what we did to you, I am sorry, I am Sorry. Perhaps one day we can learn to live together in Love and Respect?

Author's Note

I have never before written an author's note for one of my books, believing that the mingling in a novel of history and fiction should be seamless. But this book is about a topic so important to me that I wanted to emphasise some of the historical facts.

Josiah, Sarah, and all the individuals of this book are fictional, but they work and struggle as eighteenth-century Bristol merchants did. Their plan to introduce slaves directly to Britain is unusual, but not unique. Their historical background, the statistics of the Trade, is as accurate as I can make it. The picture of Mehuru's homeland in the civilised and complex kingdom of Yoruba is also accurate. The grotesque character of Sir Charles Fairley is no worse than Thomas Thistlewood of Jamaica, who kept an explicit sexual diary of his rapes of slaves. The bridle which is strapped on Died of Shame was in common use on the West Indian plantations.

It is also true that in the eighteenth century there was a substantial number of black people living in England. London alone had a population of about fifteen thousand. The black population in England diminished after the end of slavery in the eighteenth century until the recruitment of cheap labour from the Empire in the nineteenth and twentieth centuries. The earlier black men and women married white partners and their children appeared as white within a few generations. It is one of the delights of history that a racist supporter of the BNP today may well have a black great-great-great-great-grandfather.

The history of these most courageous people – taken against their will from established and stable countries and enslaved in conditions of barbarism – can be read in a number of accessible books. I particularly enjoyed James Walvin's *Black Ivory*, HarperCollins, 1992. For the long and honourable history of black Britons, I recommend Peter Freyer, *The History of Black People in Britain*, Pluto Press, 1984. His story starts with a black legionary on Hadrian's Wall and grows more and more fascinating. But the last word should be with the African peoples themselves, in an anthology edited by Paul Edwards and David Dabydeen, *Black Writers in Britain 1760–1890*, Edinburgh University Press, 1991.

Philippa Gregory
Bristol, 1994